The Rappahannock Line

Martin Hicks

authorHOUSE®

AuthorHouse™
1663 Liberty Drive
Bloomington, IN 47403
www.authorhouse.com
Phone: 1-800-839-8640

First published by AuthorHouse 2/11/2011

ISBN: 978-1-4567-7336-6 (sc)

Printed in the United States of America

This book is printed on acid-free paper.

For Amanda

Contents

Prologue   ix

Chapter 1 Between a Rock and a Hard Place   1

Chapter 2 First Bloodshed   24

Chapter 3 Slaughter on the Grandest Scale   61

Chapter 4 Light in the Darkness   118

Chapter 5 The Face of the Enemy   142

Chapter 6 The Return of the Fallen   158

Chapter 7 Mission of Mercy   203

Chapter 8 A Matter of Railroads   225

Chapter 9 The Scum of the Earth   244

Chapter 10 Snow and Shortage   289

Chapter 11 The Song Bird   312

Chapter 12 The Spotsylvania Wilderness   335

Chapter 13 Against All the Odds   358

Chapter 14 Salem Church   398

Epilogue   420

Prologue

Winter was stretching its cold hand over the landscape of middle Virginia as the men of the Ogeechee Volunteer Rifles established their camps in the lee of the range of low ridges and hills, whose eastern slopes stretched gently down towards the Rappahannock River. The trees, which had so recently clothed those slopes with lush green, now stretched their bare branches towards surly grey skies and the fields lay stripped or, at best, covered in yellow-brown grass, already scarred earlier in the month by that first blanket of snow. But, as was seemingly typical of central Virginia winters, that initial blast of cold weather had passed. It had been replaced at first by storms of wind and rain, which, together with the snow melt, had turned the ground to expanses of mud, only for this too to be supplanted in its turn by dry cold, carried on the harsh north westerly winds that blew down the river valley. It was time, the newly-arrived troops told each other, for an end to this damned foolishness of winter season campaigning. A halt should be called in the fighting, in order for men to devote their remaining energies to surviving the impending winter. But, regardless of this near universal desire among the soldiers, there was little sign of this happening, or that the generals and their political masters, were in any way sympathetic to the idea.

This nearest stretch of the Rappahannock flowed almost due south, having turned, just upstream, from a meandering west to east course, to begin the final leg of its journey to the salt waters of Chesapeake Bay. Here was the limit of the river's navigable reaches, which was, by all accounts, what had put the town of Fredericksburg there, just south of the bend and downstream from a stretch of islands, shoals and rapids, in the first place. Fredericksburg was as far upriver as one could sail, even in a shallow-drafted ship, before the depth of water, the rocks and shoals and the width of the river became insufficient for anything other than lighter craft and muscle power.

The town had seen its beginnings here over a hundred years ago, so the men on the ridges now knew, and the place certainly had a look of genteel, Virginian antiquity about it. Buildings, of stone, brick and wood, formed a succession of orderly rectangular blocks, flanking streets which stretched along the western bank of the river, with the tallest spires, of the two main churches and the courthouse, together with the more solid but somewhat shorter tower on the Presbyterian Church rising as landmarks above the other rooftops.

But for all of its apparent character and its tranquillity, it was clear to any who now looked upon it, that Fredericksburg had gotten itself caught in a trap, or maybe that was an over severe statement of the situation, since Fredericksburg itself had done little to bring about its present predicament. Its misfortune was simply to be situated here, in this part of middle Virginia, on this stretch of the river. The, "trap," was to do with the war, coming in a few months to the end of its second full year. The war had set and was now in the process of closing the trap, for it was the war that had brought the armies into existence. Those armies, had spent the previous year ranging across the landscape of Virginia, even spilling their destruction briefly northward into Maryland as they strained, by manoeuvre and counter-manoeuvre, to gain an advantage over each other. Now, in the final days of autumn, their advance units, with their endless processions of men, wagons and guns, had come in numbers to these lower reaches of the Rappahannock River and therefore to Fredericksburg.

Here, on the ridges and hills to the west of the town, as November ended its third week, six brigades of Confederate infantry had assembled, under the command of Major Generals Robert Ransom and LaFayette McLaws. They had arrived in the last of the Wednesday's daylight, after a miserable, three day march, having been dispatched by General Robert E. Lee, from their previous camps to the northwest near Culpeper Courthouse. The soldiers had endured the muddy morasses of roads, in the rain and buffeting winds of a late autumn storm. They had forded freezing creeks and the fast-flowing upper reaches of the Rappahannock and Rapidan Rivers before tramping the final miles on the Orange Turnpike and Plank Roads to reach the Rappahannock valley and occupy these low heights behind the town.

None of these newly-arrived defenders were Virginians. Almost to a man they hailed from states further to the south, from North and South Carolina, from Georgia and from Mississippi and their presence here, was the latest twist of the great strategic minuet. The eleven thousand of them were now spreading along the river's western bank, to forestall the current thrust southwards by the United States Army of the Potomac. Their arrival here, confronted the threatening union hosts, who now occupied the eastern side of the Rappahannock, imposing a pause on their further advance. Each side now occupied its own bank of the river, with the southerners stationing themselves on that vital high ground, attempting to delude their adversaries as to their actual numbers and maybe stall them on that far side of the river till further Confederate reinforcements could arrive.

The men had immediately begun setting up positions on those low hills, from which their sentinels were able to look out over what was, for the most part, a gentle descent of the ground, stretching on from the foot of the hills down to the buildings of the old town, and on across the river to the far bank, where the enemy forces lay. Their arrival on those hills was carrying the great strategic game a further step, since the Yankee Army would now be forced into an opposed crossing of the river. The prospect of such a clash was thus acting as a magnet for further elements of both armies, attracting each side to progressively gather its forces here to secure or oppose that river crossing. So the simple truth for Fredericksburg was that, while many soldiers had gathered here already, there was now an inevitability that many more were on their way and would be arriving soon.

Those Yankees on the eastern bank were already there in considerable strength, for, from the southern positions on this side, white-tented expanses of their camps were in clear view. Detachments of them could be seen moving to and fro on that far side, while their artillerymen busied themselves in setting up their guns in steadily multiplying emplacements on the commanding high ground over there, known as Stafford Heights. That high ground on the eastern bank lay closer to the river than the hills on this side did, so, regardless of their superior numbers and calibres, the Yankee cannon already dominated the town and from those positions, their silent, ugly muzzles conveyed an implicit threat of destruction. They already vastly outnumbered the Confederate force on this side, in men as well as in guns, but surely, the southerners speculated, if they had been in any real hurry to negotiate the river, they would have gotten themselves over before any appreciable number of Lee's soldiers had arrived to oppose them. But they had dallied, making no move to cross, and now, the balance of the infantry and artillery units of James Longstreet's First Corps of the Army of Northern Virginia, nearly forty thousand in number, were well on their way. When they arrived, the enemy would find that the task of crossing over the Rappahannock River had gotten considerably harder, with a large scale fight guaranteed for when they tried it. So this was the substance of Fredericksburg's, "trap," for the town now lay between these two steadily gathering armies, helpless and impotent, while, all around it, the preparations went on for a further chapter of the great continental bloodletting.

LaFayette McLaws' division was now home to the Ogeechee Volunteer Rifles, a regiment recruited from Savannah and its surrounding counties in eastern Georgia. Its men now faced their first winter in Virginia, experiencing, with the others of Brigadier General Tom Cobb's brigade, conditions unfamiliar to them in the warmer climate that they hailed from further south. They had served in Virginia since the springtime and were now far removed from the raw recruits who had enlisted the year before. Although a majority of the soldiers in its ranks were native Georgians, the Rifles, or, "Blues," as many of them still called themselves in memory of their original uniforms, also counted significant numbers of immigrants in some of its companies. Men whose ancestry traced back to a number of European countries, as well as a sprinkling of volunteers from other states, including some transplanted Yankees, also served in the regiment.

Daniel Ryan, from County Kerry in Ireland, was one of

these immigrants, serving with his comrades in Company B in defence of his adopted state and country and now, nearing the completion of his second year of military service, he was a seasoned and experienced soldier. The orders, drills and rituals of military life, in camp and on the march, had become second nature to him. He had seen action also and, on several occasions, had experienced the shocking ordeal of full blown battles, now knowing these for what they were. These grim and obscene episodes of savagery and destruction were far removed from the gallant and triumphant vindication of manhood that the orators and politicians back home had promised and the boys, who had rushed to enlist in such numbers back then, had imagined. Such innocence was now a thing of the distant past to the still-serving soldiers. In the camps now, especially in the wake of the brutal campaign in Maryland in the autumn, the first mutterings of, "rich man's war, poor man's fight," were being heard and desertion, in some of the army's regiments at least, was beginning to drain significant numbers of men from the ranks. Daniel, in common with most of those around him, soldiered on, if no longer for the naïve notions of 1861, with a persisting sense of stubborn resolve to see the struggle through to victory. He and his comrades had few remaining illusions as to how that victory would be won and the cost in blood and life that it would demand, especially since all the efforts of the previous two years had not secured the quick success that had originally been expected. Instead, the enemy had proved to be capable and stubborn soldiers, this too being at odds with the contemptuous opinions of them harboured in the south at the onset of the war. So now men had been forced to acknowledge that, so far as this struggle was concerned, they were in it all for a longer haul.

In appearance also, they were very different now from when they had enlisted almost two years previously. Hard exertion, irregular rations and the toll of various illnesses had swept away most of their weaker brethren and toughened those who remained into lean and sinewy specimens, with little in the way of fat to be found now on their frames. They had accumulated a steely endurance against hunger, heat, cold and were inured to the other more subtle hardships of military service. Thus, with the comrades of his mess, a relatively uncommon mixture of Irish and native Georgians, Ryan attended to his duties and followed his orders, sharing the hardships, the privations and the tedium, along with the friendships, and the humour as the southern army attempted to win by dogged persistence what had not been secured by their initial valour and elan.

In their mess group, in addition to Daniel himself there was Mick Daley, Irish also, intensely loyal to his friends, but chronically belligerent, given to complaint and quick to react to any kind of insult.

Association with Mick could be repeatedly exasperating, but it was seldom dull. The native Americans of the mess were an equally varied group. There was Joseph Thompson, a Georgia farmer and now a sergeant. Thompson was a significant presence, in the company as well as the mess, being big, bluff and competent, with a commanding voice and a full farmer's measure of shrewdness and sense. Otis Ballard was stockier and hailed from Bulloch County. He was a practical though sarcastic soldier, who allowed few to escape his scathing wit. Saul Phillips was a tall and loose-limbed Eden Station boy. He too was amiable, sensible and reliable, though a chronic rumour spreader. These five shared duties, food and free time together, having forged a deep bond of loyalty and interdependence that bound them in their group and presented a united front to outsiders.

Detached now were a further three of the company, previously of their own mess, their separation due to a rancorous dispute, which had originally arisen at the end of the previous summer. Group loyalty had been strained and fractured back then by the refusal of these three, in common with many others of the army, to cross the Potomac River with their comrades, after the victory at Second Manassas, and continue the campaign in Maryland. Many friendships had faltered or foundered as a result of that episode, and even after the retreat from Maryland, the rift in their group, as in some others, had not been healed. Thompson reckoned that, with stubborn cusses like Mick Daley and Edwin Jones on either side of their divide, nothing was likely to be resolved soon and thus far his view had been borne out by events. For the meantime at least, Jones, together with John Fitzpatrick and Isaac Kane, still messed separately from the others, with little sign of anything in the way of conciliatory moves from those on either side.

Having established initial camp south west of Fredericksburg, in the woods beyond Howison Hill, the men of the, "Blues," in company with the rest of their division, now set about building more lasting shelters, turning the camp into a place where, for off-duty time at least, a modicum of comfort could be had. Most of their periods of duty were spent on the hills behind the town, with their thin blankets, in lieu of overcoats, around their shoulders for the winds here were keen at this time of year. The lack of warm overcoats was just one of the shortages, which were endemic in the Army of Northern Virginia. Some uniform replacements had been procured, by various means during their six week autumn sojourn in the lower Shenandoah Valley, but many of the troops were still suffered severely from the cold and rain through lack of suitable clothing and a range of other necessities.

The worst deficiency among the enlisted men was in shoes. Almost a fifth of Company B were barefooted, covering their feet with scraps of canvas, carpet or cloth, or, in extremis, with nothing at all, while a further proportion of them made what they could of crude moccasins or sandals, manufactured in the Shenandoah camps during the autumn. Blankets were substituted for overcoats, though only some possessed even these, and fewer still had those waterproof, "gum," or oilskin, blankets, mostly plundered from the Yankees, which could keep one dry, when used as a cape or poncho, or serve as a tent half in all but the worst weather. Enlisted men's uniforms in general, save for those who had obtained replacement garments in the autumn, were shabby, worn, and much repaired, with a fashion still in vogue of affixing flamboyantly, coloured or patterned patches, shaped like hearts or cherubs or worse, to garment holes, indicating that the wearers could, at least to some extent, still poke fun at themselves and their near destitution.

Food supplies too, after the comparative plenty of the autumn in the fertile Valley, had gone back to their customary irregularity and inadequacy. The Confederate commissary, reliable only in the most favourable circumstances, struggled to keep pace with even relatively modest movements by the army and the current redeployment to the Rappahannock, over roads that alternated between ice expanses and quagmires, had now exposed its shortcomings once more. Rations were issued every few days at best and in proportions of what was available rather than bearing any resemblance to the regulation issue. But, notwithstanding all of their trials and tribulations, the weapons of Cobb's soldiers, in common with those of the rest of the army, were still bright, polished and greased by men, who, a long time since, had mastered exactly how to use them to best effect. If it was indeed the intention of General Ambrose Burnside, the new Yankee commander across the river there, to bring his boys over to this side of the Rappahannock in order to resume their advance upon the city of Richmond, then, for all of their numbers, equipment and guns, with these men in their path, the task those Yankees faced would be daunting, to say the least.

This latest route to the southern capital was already a hazardous one and, if the current rumours were reliable, it would become steadily moreso. For even as Longstreet's soldiers and guns continued to arrive, Stonewall Jackson's Second Army Corps, almost as strong as Longstreet's, was said to be getting ready to march from the Shenandoah to the Rappahannock, a development which men reckoned would make these hill positions along the river near to impregnable. As the days passed, not only was General Robert E. Lee steadily assembling his entire army here to dispute the enemy advance, but those who had already reached the Rappahannock valley were hard at work, fortifying the commanding high ground. So Fredericksburg lay there, wedged along its western river bank between the hills and the water, the silhouettes of its buildings emerging in their familiar pattern each dawn, but, to its misfortune, now the focal point of this relentless build up of military force.

Chapter 1 Between a Rock and a Hard Place

The late November days stretched on, steadily contracting the daylight to that narrow span of hours on either side of noon as full winter drew ever nearer, while the military activity continued along the banks of the Rappahannock River. Marse Robert himself was now regularly to be seen on the heights behind the town, riding among the gaggle of generals and their staff officers, who came around to inspect the positions along the line of hills. Work was well under way on those hilltops, providing the artillery with protective redoubts for their cannon and improving the roads between the camps and the hill positions, while more and more of Lee's divisions arrived to occupy the various sections of this river line that he had now elected to defend.

The last of the earlier snow had gone, but the varying weather mixture, of cold, bright days followed by dull damp ones, remained the biggest trial for the needy soldiers, while the still growing presence of the enemy across the river was a continuing threat. Until the balance of the Army of Northern Virginia arrived there was a possibility that the

Yankees on the far bank might use their superior numbers to seize a foothold on the Fredericksburg side, but many concluded that this risk had already passed. If the enemy had been willing to risk a fording, rather than wait for a bridging of the river then a lodgement could have been made in those middle days of November before appreciable numbers of Confederate troops were here to oppose it. No, was the informed view, the Yankees would wait for their pontoons and that would give time enough for the southerners to prepare for the coming fight.

As always in the army, a host of rumours and stories went daily around the camps, telling of all kinds of things: of gathering numbers being readied for imminent enemy crossings of the river, of parleying between the generals of either side, of threats to bombard the town and of ultimatums for evacuating its people. The men speculated on them all, as they spent their duty periods on the hills and their off-duty time in the expanding camps to the west. There was scepticism towards many such stories. There were no tangible signs of an imminent enemy advance and surely nobody, not even the Yankees, would bombard a whole town of people or turn them out of their homes at this time of the year. So, while the generals planned and the men laboured and speculated, ever more reinforcements arrived, but still the enemy across the river made no move.

The Saturday was harsh and cold again, with a renewed threat of snow on a gusting wind under the lowering leaden sky. The barefooted men of the companies were, in such conditions, excused their routine duty spells being permitted to remain in their camps in the woods behind the lines. Daniel Ryan and the others of his mess were back there this morning, off duty also and working on improving those shelters. Throughout the morning, camp talk had

2

largely been on the subject of the exchange of letters over the previous day or two, which was supposed to have followed that barbarous Yankee threat to bombard the town. This talk had barely concluded when the latest news on the same subject arrived and it was Mick Daley, as close to incredulous as Daniel Ryan had seen him, who brought it to the camp.

"They're movin' out," he told them.

"Who's movin' out," Thompson wanted to know?

"Them in town," was the answer.

"Movin' out, where," Ballard quizzed?

"Away, somewhere, outa there, before the Yankees open up on the place."

"But there ain't no army down there now," Phillips snapped. "The old man pulled 'em all out."

"It ain't the army, it's the local folks," Daley blurted out, "every damned last one o' them. We can't protect the town from the Yankee artillery, so the mayor's advised 'em to leave and they're packin' up to go." Around the camp, others had stopped work and gathered around to listen and comment. Maybe they were not for taking such news at face value right away, but it was certainly enough to halt work on shelters and other chores, at least till the whole thing was talked about some more.

"They won't do that," Philipps said. "We ain't occupied the town and it ain't fortified or nothin'. Even the Yankees won't do that......, would they?"

"Surely not in the middle o' winter anyway," Daniel Ryan added lamely.

"The hell they won't," Ballard growled. "They shelled the place a piece last week, afore we even got here."

"Where'd ya hear all this," Thompson wanted to know?

"The word's goin' around over on the hill," Daley replied. "They say the general advised the city council men that he

3

couldn't stop the Yankees shellin' the town, or protect the folks there if they started doin' it, so they'd be best leavin' the place." From the groups of men who had gathered to listen, Fitzpatrick's voice came.

"But the town…," he spluttered. "It's women and little kids down there. The only men in the place are old or sick. Why've they got to go shellin' it?"

"The Yankees want the town," Thompson said. "There ain't no reason fer them bein' over there, 'less'n it's to come across the water. This is their new road to Richmond and they don't want no trouble gittin' over the river or movin' on through the place."

"When's this all supposed to be happenin'," Ballard interjected?

"They reckon it could be today," Daley said.

The hill sides became steadily more crowded as the day drew on, with men having arrived from the camps, in addition to the duty watch, to occupy vantage points along the line and, though there was little to be seen as yet, the signs of activity from Fredericksburg could certainly be heard. Distant voices, including anguished female tones and the various tell-tale sounds of vehicle traffic, clattering wheels and whinnying or snorting animals, came from down there in the streets, carrying in fragments up to the men on the hills some three quarters of a mile away.

Three of the roads that left the town led inland, away from the river. From the docks quarter, south of the Richmond, Fredericksburg and Potomac Railroad and near the southern edge of town, Frederick Street stretched initially to the west, running parallel to the rail tracks, before crossing them and curving away to the south west. Nearer the centre of town, Hanover Street and, two blocks to the north of it, William Street emerged also, coming almost due west, to cross the canal spillway, which also served as a millrace, by means of wooden bridges, before approaching McLaws' and Ransom's positions on the hills. The former then sent a branch, known as the, "Telegraph Road," to the south along the eastern foot of Marye's Hill by a sunken dip, which then turned south west and led off inland around the southern slope of adjoining Willis Hill. The main thoroughfare of both roads passed on through a further dip between the northern shoulder of Marye's and Cemetery Hills, before heading off to the west. Thus, if anybody was leaving Fredericksburg to move away from the enemy guns, then, save for those who could obtain scarce space on a train, it would be on one of these roads that they would almost certainly travel.

Already all three thoroughfares were busy with military vehicles, some of them ambulances, which went rumbling down into town, to assist, some were saying, with the coming evacuation, though few vehicles were yet leaving the place. Among the watching Confederates there was a general murmur of subdued talk and much of what was being said was bitter and vengeful. To some at least it was as though this latest development underscored, after all of the blood and effort of the past year, the inability of the southern army to protect Virginia's people from the northern invaders. But there were also those who still wanted to doubt what they had heard. Even the Yankees, they still said, surely wouldn't shell a town of defenceless women and children. They wouldn't turn the whole town into a battlefield. They wouldn't see them all turned out, surely?

The talk still ebbed and flowed as the time passed. Afternoon came and, gradually, before the watching eyes of the men on the hillsides, the evacuation commenced. Movements down on those streets and roads increased with growing numbers of people, old men, women and children, visible as they moved among the built-up blocks. They gathered steadily onto those main exit roads, starting to make their way up towards the bottleneck at the overspill bridges where they were within easy sight of the watchers on the hillsides. At first it was not a convoy or a cavalcade, but these initial, more isolated groups, were soon followed by more, who slowly gathered into steadier processions as they made their way out of town. Some were carried on the military wagons that had gone down earlier, while others of them came on civilian carts and buggies, drawn by a variety of plodding, worn down, draught animals. Many more walked, pushing handcarts, barrows or even children's baby cars, with almost all of them, children included, carrying bundles of possessions in their hands or on their backs. Some women carried infants, in their arms or even on their backs, while others led toddlers or small children.

Along the hills most of the talk had died as the soldiers watched the evacuation take shape before their eyes. The slopes and crests were now lined with men, grim-faced and angry at this latest persecution of their people. Over at the foot of the hills, nearer the roads, some of the troops left the forward positions, moving down to meet the refugees, taking baggage from them and assisting them up the hill, but watching it all, Daniel Ryan thought such help seemed superficial. It seemed in ways to emphasise the failure of the southern army to protect these people who, through its weakness, in the face of the colossal Yankee menace opposite, had just lost their homes.

The brigade commander Tom Cobb, newly promoted to Brigadier General, had also come to witness the event. He appeared with his staff, making their way along the forward slope of the hill in front of where groups of artillerymen had been setting up their cannon in dug earth emplacements. The brigadier stopped and his officers did likewise, gathering in a group as they watched the refugees. Daniel Ryan saw

Cobb's face flush steadily as he took the scene in, watching intently, like everyone else on the hillside, while the parallel processions of people moved out along the three roads. Cobb, though a Georgian, was said to have kin in town, so all of this was therefore more personal for him. He went on watching as the stream of refugees continued until, after a further time, with the pathetic procession showing little sign of easing, he turned to look along the lines of his men who stretched across the slope in front of the wrecked Willis buildings into the grounds of the elegantly pillared "Brompton," house, which crowned the far end of the hill. He paced along for a short distance in front of the soldiers, to call out at last to those of them who were within earshot, his movement and his voice breaking the men's concentration upon the scenes on the roads in front of them.

"See it boys," he yelled. All along the hillside a row of pale faces, not many of which were unadorned by beards of one kind or another, turned to look at him.

"Look at it," Cobb called, "see it and remember it and, if there is ever a time when you are not sure about what you are fighting for, then remember this day." He paced on a further few steps as he pointed an accusing finger at the straggling groups of old people, women and children, while his men altered their gaze again to look where he indicated, back out along the lines of the civilians as the general continued.

"This," he yelled, "is what you are fighting against."

There was a mutter of talk along the lines at his words as still they looked. It was not that the men were in any doubt as to what they felt about the sights that were unfolding before their eyes, but somehow the general's words had summed it up. Invasion of the southern states was what they had enlisted to prevent, but here in this Virginia river valley, they could only watch, for there was nothing that they could do to prevent this. The powerful Yankee guns, on the far side of the river, commanded the town and the whole of the nearside bank, for the Confederate army did not have the ordnance, either in numbers or in size, to compete with them. That was another good reason for the southern positions being back from the town itself, quite apart from the more easily defended higher ground being back here, they were also spared from the full menace of that overwhelming enemy artillery. No, there was nothing they could do about this. They were compelled to tolerate it and await the time when retribution might be gained. Their turn would come, some of the men muttered. It would come.

As a flurry of sleety rain blew across the ground, flapping the clothing of the soldiers and of the families out on those roads, they could only stand and watch the ordeal of these miserable people, forced from their homes, at the onset of winter. The enemy invaders saw them as rebels and showed them no pity, while their defenders watched, powerless to prevent any part of it. There was nothing that could be done, Daniel Ryan found the thought sticking in his mind, as he pulled his woollen and gum blankets closer around his shoulders against the shower. They could not prevent the invaders causing this today, but if those Yankees over there did decide to come on across to this side of the river, then they would pay, they would be made to pay.

The people from the town were arriving at the army positions in numbers now, crowding up on the half- frozen mud of the roads. Some of them moved steadily on through the lines and on up the hill, while others came on more slowly, stopping to rest and adjust or change hands with burdens. Many of their heads were swathed in scarves and some had blankets around them like shawls against the bitter cold. Their faces looked out, some already white and pinched, notwithstanding their makeshift protections as they divided at the foot of the main hill to follow the Plank or Telegraph roads, away from the homes that might be ruins in a matter of days, or even hours. On many of those faces there was an expression of something like disbelief or shock. It was easy to understand, Daniel Ryan thought. A week or two ago, this place had little to do with the war. Sure enough, troops of both sides had passed through the town, and some of them had tarried, occupying the place for days or even weeks before moving on in the deadly ritual of manoeuvring that had run its course all across Virginia this year. When their own division had arrived here this week, after the appearance of the Yankees on the higher ground across the river there, the town had hosted only a nominal garrison of troops under a colonel. These people had never expected this war to come looking for them like this, but it had come, and now they were at the centre of where the two assembling armies had set themselves up, to glower at each other across the dark river. They were caught in the grip of this confrontation as the Yankees lunged yet again to the south, to head deeper into Virginia and on towards Richmond. It was stark and it was simple. The residents of Fredericksburg, had the misfortune to have their town where the roads and railroad led and where the river could be crossed. They were therefore an obstruction, in the way of this great enemy juggernaut's advance, something that had to be either removed or destroyed, so the conclusion was simple also. The people would be removed and the town would be destroyed, unless of course they waited around and, in that case, they too could be destroyed in an eruption of raw military force and their destruction would be a mere detail of this latest invasion. Virginia's brief, eight week reprieve from the presence of the Union army, secured at such cost in the summer at the bloody, second battle of Manassas, and further extended by the march into Maryland, was now, emphatically ended.

The weather stayed cold as November ended and the evacuated inhabitants of Fredericksburg sought shelter inland. Some had left the town on the few, overcrowded trains, heading for destinations further south. Others, who had moved out on the roads, headed for the homes of family or friends, while still more sought lodgings of sorts in the hamlets, farms and churches of Spotsylvania County and in Orange and Culpeper Counties beyond. The army, facing a steadily worsening supply problem of its own, did what it could, but what could be done was sorely limited. Renewed shortages in its own food supply, as well as the perennial army weakness in transporting what there was to any place else, hampered attempts to assist the refugees from town. It therefore fell, to the citizens of the County initially, but gradually to those of the whole of central Virginia, already foraged extensively by the armies over the previous year, to do what was possible to sustain those refugees. These delved into their now meagre reserves, giving food, clothing, bedding and shelter to the displaced townspeople, while, back on the hills, the army's gaze was returned to the enemy across the river.

The Yankees were now assembled over there, with their guns along Stafford Heights and their army, so the watching Confederates heard, gathered and poised, but for what? It all suggested that a fight was definitely on the way, but no sign of its arrival was yet to be seen across the river, where the enemy gave few signs of any preparations to cross. Maybe, the men speculated, the Yankees would move up or down river, seeking a less hazardous place to make their attempt, or maybe they had at last concluded that enough was enough for the season and decided against further campaigning, so winter quarters would be the result. Some rumours in the Southern camps said the enemy crossing was delayed by the absence of pontoon bridging that would get their men over with dry feet. It seemed strange, to many of the amateur strategists on the Confederate side, that they would try to build bridges across a river whose far bank was occupied by the enemy, but, if not at Fredericksburg, where else would they cross? Downstream the Rappahannock gradually widened as it approached Chesapeake Bay. Upstream, beyond the bend and the rapids, the river narrowed, but then came its junction with the Rapidan River, which would give the enemy two rivers to negotiate if they went too far that way. Maybe they would go upstream or maybe down, but they had shown little sign of doing either so far, though at least the town of Fredericksburg had been spared bombardment. Dispatches had been exchanged and officers had conferred under flags of truce until it was finally agreed, so the enlisted men heard, that, at least for the time being, the Yankees would not shell the town provided the Confederate army did not occupy and fortify it and the Confederates would not occupy the town provided the Yankees did not attempt to cross the river there. It all seemed pretty convoluted to the ordinary soldiers, since the truce depended on an army, that had assembled here to force a crossing of the river not attempting to cross, but at least it meant a respite of some kind though the threat remained.

The uneasy truce dragged on into December, with the weather remaining cold. A few of the evacuated families took the risk of returning to their homes, straggling back into the town, preferring to live under the threat of the enemy cannon than face the hardships of homelessness inland. On either side of them, the two armies still glowered across the Rappahannock from their respective riverbanks, each deploying its numbers and improving its positions while everyone awaited General Burnside's pleasure. He, more than anyone else on either side, had the fate of Fredericksburg in his hands. As for everyone else, be they civilian or soldier, it was a simple matter of waiting for him to make up his mind and for something to happen.

As December came in, Stonewall Jackson's Second Corps men began arriving, in fulfillment of those camp rumours, having marched from their camps around Winchester in the Shenandoah Valley. They had dallied there somewhat longer than, "Old Pete's," troops in an attempt to delay the advance of the Yankee host, by menacing its flank, but now they too were assembling here, to extend downriver the lines that faced the now huge numbers of the enemy. This river valley was exerting a kind of magnetic force, attracting these hosts of soldiers and guns, with all of the threat of approaching further bloodshed that such a gathering implied. There were rumoured to be a hundred and twenty thousand Yankees on or near that eastern bank now, with something approaching eighty thousand Confederate troops along, or soon to arrive on the heights on the western side of the river, ample, as everyone well knew, for a considerable killing.

As the first week of December progressed, the weather turned again, with rock hard ground and icy winds giving way to overcast days of rain and mud. On the fifth day of the new month, a Friday, a cold and dismal rain pelted down all through the day, with strong winds adding their chill to the dispiriting mix of weather. The roads were once again turned into muddy quagmires and the barefooted men were again excused duty and allowed to remain in camp. As evening came it grew colder and the rain turned to a wet, feathery sleet that attached its cloying flakes to the clothing of the duty men, soaking them steadily. By the time that darkness had come that sleet was falling as large flakes of snow, which quickly covered the ground with a layer of slush. Throughout the night it fell, weighing down the branches of trees and obscuring the paths, roads and fields in its steadily deepening blanket of white. Men huddled in their shelters around flickering fires, blown this way and that by the strongly gusting wind, with only sentinels remaining on duty. These, on the major's orders, were relieved every two hours to be allowed to stumble their way through the blinding storm back to their camps to gather in their turn around their fires and begin thawing out their chilled limbs and their numbed hands and feet.

The Saturday morning dawned to reveal a thick covering of snow, blanketing the land to a depth of several inches, keeping the barefooted men in camp again and causing still more commissary difficulty. The snow bound roads were now so much more hazardous that such traffic as was able to move on them at all, could do so only at a laborious crawl. The railroad up from Richmond was badly affected, with no trains running till the places where the snow had blocked the line could be cleared enough for the service to tentatively resume on a reduced timetable. No rations came around that day and only a small ration of flour arrived in the camps of Company B on the Sunday. This was distributed in the afternoon for cooking as the respective messes saw best. Ryan and Ballard took charge of that, supplying each of the five in the mess with a couple of flour and water pancakes, with some chopped up wild onions folded in, to taste the mix.

The persisting Yankee threat along the lower Rappahannock, had frustrated any hope the southern troops had previously entertained of wintering in the Shenandoah, where supplies were more readily available. Instead the Army of Northern Virginia had been compelled to match the continuing manoeuvres of the union host, as initially George McClellan, and then his successor Ambrose Burnside, had pushed their formations ever further through northern

Virginia. Men still clung to the long established convention that armies, tied to horse drawn transportation over largely dirt roads, could hardly move during these coldest months. Surely even now, some of them pronounced, the Yankees over there, seeing that their passage of the Rappahannock was blocked, would figure that enough was enough and call a halt, to see to the setting up of their own winter quarters over there, freeing up the southerners to do the same on this side. Maybe not, said others, since the traded or captured Yankee papers were still full of how the administration in Washington was on their new general's back, exhorting him to move on and push his advance to Richmond. He would move, these men asserted. The northern press and those politicians would nag him till he moved, whether he went downriver or upriver to cross over he would do it and there would, as a result, be no winter quarters till the thing was attempted. Some men consoled themselves with talk of taking their frustration and anger out on the enemy when, and if, they came across the river, maybe even securing plunder from the Yankees to make good some of their own shortages, but such talk added nothing in the way of comfort to their current Spartan existence and the uneasy stand off along the river continued as the shortest days of the year drew steadily closer.

But as the second week of the month commenced the weather grew slowly milder and the snows gradually melted. Minor avalanches slipped and cascaded from building roofs and tree branches, while brown grass tussocks began to emerge from the receding white covering on the ground. Before long, bare patches of dull, brown earth or expanses of dead grass began to appear and the ugly slush on the roads turned to wide puddles of equally ugly mud as the days regained a suggestion of warmth and the snow continued its steady retreat. Word went around of some further shuffling of infantry and guns taking place up and down the riverside, to forestall any Union attempt at a crossing to outflank the Confederate positions, but most of that shuffling was seemingly being done by the cavalry and by some of Jackson's men. Longstreet's Corps largely stayed put, save for an extension of the line, to their left a little, to cover the stretch of the river that lay upstream past its bend to the north west of Fredericksburg.

The men of the rank and file, like their superiors in the army high command, while discussing the Yankee intentions at length, were stuck with a wait and see approach. The weather, since the initial snow thaw, now changed again, bringing frosty nights, which gave way to almost unseasonally warm days when the low winter sun took a tentative hold, slowly clearing the mists, which gathered in the river valley overnight, and softening the hard icy ground into mud, only for it to chill or freeze hard again as the sun sank and the cold of night re-asserted its grip. The fields had largely re-emerged from their carpet of white, with only corners and crevices in the ditches and the lee of walls now retaining a white remnant of hardened snow, though the dirt roads and tracks remained muddy slides, handicapping the essential traffic that sustained the army. There was still no sign of a crossing, either here around the town, or elsewhere on the river, rather, from their respective positions on the higher ground on either side of the Rappahannock, the two armies continued to observe each other, seemingly passive in the meantime but now so close to each other that a fight of some sort was becoming almost inevitable.

This theory gathered substance on the Tuesday after the snow fall, for that was the day when Thompson told them about the pontoon boats.

"Sure 'nough," he had said. "Yankees are bringin' pontoon boats in on wagons. Our artillery boys up on the top reckon they've seen 'em over there and that means they're aimin' t' cross over, right here under our damn noses." His listeners were skeptical.

"They won't do that," Daley exclaimed, "ain't nowhere to form over here and we'll be able to shift men into town to shoot 'em to hell while they're crossin' over. They won't do that." Others, like Ballard were more matter of fact.

"If they ain't crossin' here why, tarry round here 'tall," he said?

"It's a bluff," Daley countered. "They want us to think they'll cross over here when they're goin' to shift on to some place else, down to Port Royal or somewhere upriver maybe. Nobody'd be stupid enough to cross over and attack us here." Thompson was unconvinced.

"Bluff or no, the general's aimin' to git some of our boys back into town to watch the river and the Yankees. So he ain't takin' it fer granted that nobody'll us attack here. Fact that they're still over there means that they want to git across and if they do, I reckon we'll be hearin' from them. Sooner or later they'll be comin' over."

"When that happens, the folks that are back in town'll find that this war'll get even worse for them than it has so far," Daniel Ryan commented. Ballard snorted at that.

"Ever since the Yankees decided that this was the way to Richmond, that there town's bin stuck between a rock and a hard place," he said

On the following day, the Wednesday, came more news, but this time it was of a very different kind, coming from within their own regiment. It was Ballard who was the first of their mess to hear of it. A corporal, John Ellis of Company H, was under close arrest on some kind of a serious charge. The off-duty men passed the story quickly through the camps, furiously speculating, especially as to what the offence could be. Ellis was known as an experienced and reliable soldier, who was no stranger to the customs and rituals, as well as the regulations, of military life. It was therefore surprising news to hear of such a man in such a predicament. Evening came and with it there was further news, which set the camps to talking even more, for it was no minor matter that saw the corporal under guard, far from it, for he was apparently guilty of attacking an officer. The rumours of the Yankee pontoons were again put aside as the men sought out more details of this closer to home event. Thompson was quizzed on his return from duty and he was able to give further news of what had taken place.

"It wuz over the boys who had no shoes," he told them. "Ellis had told his barefooted boys that they didn't have to do outpost duty over on the hill with the snow and all, but their new lieutenant came by and told 'em the snow wuz near gone and he ordered the barefooted boys out on duty with the others. When he heard from them that they were excused goin' down there, he told 'em he was puttin' John Ellis on report for takin' it on himself to excuse them duty in the first place. He sent fer Ellis and yelled him out in front o' the other men and Ellis got mad and gave him some good answers back. All o' that made the officer worse and it all ended up with Ellis under arrest fer insubordination, but as they were takin' him away, the lieutenant said somethin' about Ellis's family that led to John hangin' one on his nose that laid him on his back in the mud and movin' on t' do him some more damage afore the others could stop him. So now he's facin' charges that could see him hanged or shot."

"Who's the lieutenant," Philipps asked?

"That new one, Gilby," Thompson replied.

"Which one's he," Daley wanted to know?

"He's the real dandified one," Ballard told him.

Daniel glanced around the group as he took in the news, seeing other faces that showed clear astonishment. This was the kind of thing that always seemed to happen in other regiments or other brigades instead of in their own. Punishments happened more in Jackson's divisions, mainly because Stonewall was such a stern disciplinarian. Old Pete certainly wasn't lax, but, by comparison, Old Jack could be downright ferocious, court-martialling his men, and some of his officers also, with a vindictive and relentless resolve. Nothing like this had happened in the regiment before. Sure there had been punishments among the Ogeechee Volunteers, like there were in any regiment, but these had been for more routine breaches of regulations. There had been men paraded through the camps for theft and suchlike and one had even been tied to a post all night for some more serious kind of insubordination. But, in a volunteer unit, where most officers had originally been elected by their men, more severe punishments were not common. Things tended to get sorted out and beyond that scattering of offences, which had taken place and been specifically punished, it had been the normal run of extra duties or fatigues, which often meant digging or filling in company latrines. Even boys who had taken days away from the march to forage around the column had often either had this ignored, if they were back for evening muster, or had gotten extra duty if they were not. No, this latest was something new and altogether different.

The mess fell silent briefly and Daniel Ryan pondered the news. He knew next to nothing about this Lieutenant Gilby, other than that he was a newcomer who had arrived at the camp near Winchester as a replacement during the autumn, that and the fact that he was, "quality," coming from a rich and privileged, "planter," background. He was still ruminating over this when Ballard broke the short pause in talk.

"Reckon that John better git to sayin' his prayers 'n' tell the good lord he'll be along shortly." The others looked at him.

"If it's the same Gilby's that I'm thinkin' on then they're some kind o' kin o' Preston's," he added. Thompson nodded.

"That's 'em," he grunted. "Preston's wife's sister's kin." Daniel Ryan sniffed.

"Just John's damned luck," he said. Philipps however was still sceptical.

"They surely won't shoot him," he said. "They need every man, 'specially if there's as many Yankees over there as the papers are sayin'. They'll punish him but they won't shoot him." Thompson shook his head emphatically.

"Reckon there's nothin' puts a skeer on officers more than the idea that their own men might turn on 'em. They call it maintainin' discipline, but it's more of a warnin'. If the officers here hold out fer it, he'll be shot and Preston'll likely hold out fer it," he added grimly, "'specially seein' as how it's about kin, cuz blood's thicker 'n' water."

"John Ellis ain't the first," Ballard added, "not by a long way, and he surely won't be the last. There's bin plenty o' men shot or hung afore."

"But that's mostly been in Old Jack's units," Daley said, "on account o' him bein' all god fearin' and religious and hard on the sinners and all." Thompson shook his head again.

"Fer what it's worth," he said, "Barnard Jeffers reckons John ain't got much of a chance. With Preston as well as Gilby lined up against him, he's as good as dead."

The day had begun with intense speculation along the

line as to how, when and where the Yankees would cross the river, but the men of the Ogeechee Volunteers had thought progressively less about this, engrossed as they now were with the news of their own comrade. Throughout the day rumour had followed rumour, that Ellis would be hanged or shot the next day, then another, that lots would be drawn throughout the regiment to shoot him, that Captain Wallis of Company H, had gone over Preston's head and appealed to the general for Ellis' life and that Ellis himself had pleaded to be allowed to die facing the enemy. The camps had picked over all these stories, but there had been no word from the officers, with even the more communicative Boyce resisting attempts to get him to speak on the matter. The man appeared to be doomed to a sudden brutal death at the hands of his own comrades, but nobody in any kind of authority was prepared to confirm it, deny it or even talk about it.

But while the men spent most of their time discussing the predicament of John Ellis, further stories of the Yankee preparations were circulating around the camps. Yankee officers had been seen at different locations along the riverside, surveying the approaches and banks as though preparing for a crossing. As if that was not clear enough, the pickets along the river, while engaged in the customary banter with their Yankee counterparts, had learned that the Yankees had been served with three days rations and a full issue of ammunition, a clear sign of imminent campaigning. These things had been enough to prompt elements of William Barksdale's brigade of Mississippi troops, from their own division, to be sent back into the town to observe the enemy along the river. Barksdale's deployment was being supported along the riverside by others of their own brigade and some Florida troops from Dick Anderson's division, who were next along the line to the north, while John Hood's Texas troops picketed the river below the town. An air of expectation began to divert some of the attention in the camps back across the river, where the enemy seemed at last to be stirring. At evening assembly, orders were circulated demanding vigilance and the men were informed that two cannon shots were to be the signal that alerted the army at the first signs of an enemy crossing of the river. All of it seeming to emphasise the imminence of the threat, but the essembly ended without a word being said about John Ellis.

Night came and the talk in the camps of the Yankees had faded as the off-duty men settled themselves around their fires, with those who had them wrapped in their blankets. But, even if talk on that subject was at an end meantime, what remained, like a niggling discomfort, on the minds of many of the men was the fate of their Company H comrade. It was too bad to have a thing like this, but though rumour had the corporal's fate cut and dried, there had still been nothing official. The whole thing simply hung there, predictable, so most thought, since that was the way that the army worked, but as yet unresolved, waiting for some kind of decision up in the higher echelons, at brigade, division or even corps level, as to what would actually take place.

Daniel Ryan's section had returned in the darkness from their duty in the forward positions along the hill to settle in their shelter in the clear cold night. The structure was draughty in the chilly wind, which had risen as darkness came. There was a clear need for more insulating around its walls and, better still, the building of a proper chimney, but it was still better than what many of the other men had. Daniel lay rolled in his woollen blanket in the blackness between Ballard and Philipps, with the warmth of the guttering fire at the entrance helping keep the bitter cold at bay. Daniel was tired, but his overactive mind kept him from anything but occasional dozes. There was too much to think about between the Yankees and the seeming imminence of their crossing over the river to bring on the next fight as well as the unconfirmed fate of John Ellis and fragments of each of these repeatedly swirled around in his mind.

As morning approached the camp was blanketed again in the descended fog, with the stacked muskets and rows of crude log huts and canvas shelters that made up the company area softened into indistinctness. But even as that fog drifted in, from somewhere out on the line a cannon shot boomed out followed, after a pause of a few seconds, by another. The echoes and reverberations of that second shot had hardly stilled, before the shelters in the camp were stirring, as clusters of mist-wreathed figures scrambled from their blankets and out of their shelters. Musket stacks disappeared in seconds as men assembled into their ranks, fumbling their way into equipment belts as they looked towards the hills and the town, both hidden by the darkness and the swirling fog. Sergeants arrived to take charge of their sections and, within minutes, regardless of its own internal preoccupations, the Ogeechee Volunteer Rifles was ready for whatever the colonel or the generals wanted of it.

It was still impossible to see anything towards the town as they crossed Hazel Run Creek and ascended the slope to file around the shoulder of Willis Hill, with their feet crunching on the frozen, rutted surface of the road. The fog eddied around them on the cold air, chilling their noses, fingers, legs and feet, the latter two soaked from wading the creek. At the head of each company, torches were carried to light the way and guide those behind them but, as they followed on in their files, men looked around them, peering into the darkness and the fog, as though expecting something to emerge, and on seeing nothing, glancing around at each other. Those two cannon shots meant the enemy was advancing and there was only one way the enemy could advance and that was across the river. Maybe their bridges had arrived at last, or perhaps they were taking advantage of the weather to cross under cover of the fog, as well as the darkness? But, where had the crossing been made? Were they already over the river? The questions buzzed around the ranks, as, from the direction of the town, firing could now be heard, as a distant upsurge of musketry came to their ears, but the musketry was soon joined by the loud thuds of the first artillery salvoes of the morning. The talk diminished, with few further comments being made, but one thing was now sure. After all of the waiting, the talk and the speculation, the Yankees were coming over and any thought of them feinting here and crossing elsewhere was now dismissed. They were advancing at last and were doing it right here, at Fredericksburg. The distant firing gradually died down until comparative peace reigned once more along the river. Talk resumed again among the marching files as the men acknowledged that all of the uncertainty was at an end, for the enemy crossing over to this side would surely bring on the long-awaited fight here on the river line.

Chapter 2 First Bloodshed

Summoned by those cannon shots, and hearing the continued rattle of musketry as they came, the various regiments of the brigade were deployed in succession, along the hillside in the darkness, forming in the rear of the guns of the Washington Artillery to await developments there. Out in front there was nothing to be seen and, as the files deployed into ranks, down towards the town, silence again reigned. They waited in their places for morning, as the grey fog cloud swirled around them, puzzling over the meaning of the comparative peace, while comments and theories muttered their way along the lines.

"Reckon they gave it up, huh?"

"It's a goddam false alarm."

Maybe they warn't shootin' at nothin' much."

"Somethin' out on the water maybe spooked 'em."

"Maybe we'll git back to our blankets fer a while." Listening to it all, Daniel Ryan reckoned that, since Barksdale's Mississippians had never struck him as spookable in most situations, the fond hope of a return to their blankets, voiced by one of the autumn's conscripts, was maybe the unlikeliest prospect of them all.

As the daylight slowly came the fog gradually lightened into a whiter more luminous blanket, but its impenetrability remained with even the cannon, up in front of where they stood, still largely invisible. Then, from the direction of the town and the river, there came a renewed outbreak of musketry, its crackling chorus resounding flatly through the fog. The firing grew and persisted while the men on the hills fidgeted still more in their ranks, as they listened intently to its growing volume. Then the cannon came again, adding their deep thumping discharges to the higher pitched rattle, prompting more comments from the waiting men, but up here, with the fog obscuring everything, there was no way of telling for certain what was going on and therefore nothing to do but wait, watch and wonder.

They remained there, near the brow of Willis Hill, balancing their muskets, avoiding the freezing cold metal parts, by steadying the weapons with their knees and elbows while breathing on fingers, swinging arms and stamping feet for warmth. The barefooted men, in their places today with the rest, suffered additionally and the smoky breath of all of them rose in clouds to mingle with the fog. Still unable to see anything the boys awaited orders or news, while down in the town, invisible in the persisting white curtain, the shooting continued. With full daylight now here the musketry gradually subsided, and, as the minutes passed, there came hints of that brighter, yellower light, slanting through the fog from the east as the sun rose over the river valley out ahead of where they waited. The white fog cloud slowly began to eddy and thin and, as the waiting soldiers looked along their lines, more and more men were now to be seen emerging from the gloom on either side with the cannon up ahead now in full view.

The gloom around them thinned steadily, wisping away to slowly bare the hill crests and reveal another bright blue sky above them. Long lines of soldiers waited on either side and out in front stood the wet, menacing cannon, with their crews in position around them, poised, grasping their rammers or hand spikes, as they waited in their dug earth emplacements. The white bank out in front slowly started to retreat down the slope into the river valley, as the shooting there receded again. The pale sun now shone on the high ground, beginning to prise the chill from the air and the earth, with a hint of warming, renewing the recent daily pattern of thawing and softening the hard ground into a top layer of soft, wet mud.

The light continued to grow, until the last wisps of mist on the hill crest drifted away. Below the summit, the fog still smothered the slope that reached down towards the town and river, as, after only a brief interlude, the shooting there began to swell into life again. The crackling discharges of musketry rose again in volume, seeming to reverberate and echo through the remaining fog. Then the cannon came again, thudding along the Rappahannock in greater numbers than before, signalling that, whatever was happening along the waterfront, matters down there were now getting a little hotter.

Still the long ranks on the hills waited until, at length, orders came along, but far from any advance or preparation for battle, the word was for watch on watch off, with the off-duty and bare-footed men ordered to stand down. A rippling movement travelled along the lines as these men stepped away from their places, moving to form fresh lines to the rear of those who remained. More orders came now, shouted initially by officers before being relayed along by the NCOs, and at that the ranks wheeled into files and began the march to the rear. Around the southern flank of Willis Hill the returning men descended to rejoin the still frozen road and make their way south west, back into the valley of Hazel Run and on inland towards their camps. Behind them, in the now dispersing fog, the gunfire, both musketry and artillery, continued, but their own withdrawal, and that of other units along the line, seemed to indicate that if the Yankees were indeed trying at last to force a passage of the Rappahannock, they were certainly making slow work of it.

Back in camp their dismissal had been delayed while Rodger had fussed about vigilance, readiness and doing one's duty but, with the Yankees dallying in crossing over, minds were now returned to other matters, though there was still no word in his orders about the subject on most of the men's minds. The company had thereafter been dismissed to breakfast, on whatever morsels of Tuesday's ration that remained to them. As the men resumed gossiping and speculating, their talk alternated between the fight down at the river and the question of John Ellis' fate. But, with still no official word, and the Yankees now advancing, it seemed that Ellis' punishment might well be deferred until some later and more convenient time.

The sparse scraps of breakfast had been quickly eaten, while the shooting from the town persisted. The gunfire did not tell of a continuous fight, though a proportion of the cannon fire went steadily on, but this was joined only at intervals by ebbing and flowing outbreaks of musketry, which crackled faintly up from the now more distant river. Rumours continued to sweep the camps, that the Yankees were laying their pontoon bridges at last and what was more they had started some of them straight across from Fredericksburg. This news digested and no drills or fatigues being called, the men sat around their fires, waiting for more word of some kind about the enemy movements.

The off duty half of the regiment had gone back before noon for their next watch, to spend the middle hours of the day on station near the artillery emplacements, with groups of them being sent periodically up to relieve the forward picket, deployed on the eastern slope of the hill, looking down towards the town. Parts of Fredericksburg were still obscured by a drifting cloud, but no longer was it fog, for that had long since dispersed and this cloud was of battle smoke. The familiar spires as well as other rooftops, chimney gables and walls, especially those of the taller buildings, drifted in and out of sight, as the telltale cloud of blue-white musket smoke, rose up from the buildings along the river, to mix with the angrier, billows from the cannon along the Rappahannock. These clouds drifted slowly downriver, mingling in turn with rising plumes of darker shades, which came from an increasing number of fires that now burned among the buildings along the riverside part of the town.

"Artillery boys reckon this here's only field batteries," Philipps muttered, to any around him who were of a mind to listen. "Heavier pieces over the river thar ain't opened up yet." It was true. These were not the larger Yankee weapons. Regardless of what artillerymen said, the infantrymen could tell that for themselves by the sounds that the guns made. These, although loud and deep, were not the colossal crashes of the Yankees' twenty pound Parrotts or their big Dahlgrens, the latter shaped like strange, menacing bottles lying on their sides, which almost seemed to convulse the earth when they fired. Daniel Ryan let his eyes rove along the river line and the town. If this was only the lighter artillery pieces of the enemy, what fate awaited the place if the bigger enemy guns finally did begin to fire? He shook his head at the thought, hoping that all of the civilians had gotten clear of what had now come to pass.

They had watched and listened through the middle of the day, as the firing continued, to again subside after a time into an uneasy calm. It was some time after noon, when a single cannon boomed out, from the heights across the river, to be immediately followed by the much deeper crashing discharges of others, signalling that those heavier enemy batteries were now, as feared, opening up on Fredericksburg. Along from them the artillerymen had jerked themselves from their mundane duties and relaxations, to gather in their earth emplacements at the forward edge of the hill crest, watching intently as a steady succession of heavy shells descended on the buildings out in front of them. Some of the gunners had immediately gone to work, plotting the discharges and the fall of shot, trying to spot the placing of these heavier guns, a difficult enough job in the clouds of gun smoke that choked the river valley. They called out their observations to officers who noted some of it in notebooks while, down in the town, the fury of the bombardment steadily grew. The blast of the cannon echoed along the river, and, between the reports of the guns and the exploding of their huge shells, those on the hill could hear a range of other sounds, the shattering of glass, the splintering of wood and the collapsing of brick or stone walls as the bombardment increasingly took effect. Buildings down in the town steadily began to show their visible damage from the shelling as they emerged from the drifting clouds of smoke and dust. Large rents were now to be seen in some roofs and walls and occasionally sections of these collapsed in further debris and dust adding to the scene of chaos in the town, before their images vanished once more, engulfed in further billows of smoke.

The fires steadily increased in number and in size, until flames seemed to be flickering all over Fredericksburg, with several of the fires growing and spreading into larger conflagrations. In the almost windless air dark banks of smoke slowly rose from the many burning buildings, ascending steadily and gathering into colossal columns that reached for hundreds of feet almost vertically into the sky before some higher up draught of breeze gradually spread them away to the south and east, merging and joining them together into one great pall that, as time passed, covered the sky far above the town and drifted away only slowly on the faint eddies of those higher up airs. The men on the hill watched the destruction, seeing also, down on the roads, a further scattering of fleeing civilians. These must be people who had resisted the Yankee threats of last month, along with those other few who had left back then, but had subsequently returned to their homes when the earlier menace of bombardment had not materialised. They were going now however, hurrying away out of the beleaguered town once more, again carrying or pushing whatever scant belongings they had been able to assemble. Once more for Daniel Ryan, there was, in watching this, the same mix of feelings, of anger, of helplessness and frustration at the inability of their own army to prevent or protect.

Their relief arrived in the afternoon and their section pulled away, some taking final looks down towards the stricken town before starting for the rear. As they came level with the first of the artillery positions, the gunners were gathered around the front of their gun emplacements, still watching the destruction and calling out their observations to each other. The shouts and comments attracted Daley's attention, and typically, he called out to them.

"Why in the hell ain't you shootin' back and makin' them pay?" A couple of the artillerymen turned in response to the shout.

"Orders," one man called and he took a few steps towards them. "It ain't that simple," he went on, "none o' our pieces'll hurt the Yankee batteries much. If we started shootin', even at maximum elevation, we'd barely reach some o' them, but the Yankees would mark our batteries down and then pulverize 'em with their long range guns. We got almost nothin' to match their bigger Parrott's and Columbiads and we got orders to save our fire for when their infantry come on." Daley grunted, as the man finished, but still looked unconvinced as he moved away to rejoin the others of the detail.

They moved on across the summit of the hill to reach their own positions to the rear of the cannon and resume their gaze to the east, unable to see the town itself now, but able to witness its fate, through the great dark pall of smoke that rose and drifted in the clear winter sky. They continued to watch until, eventually, the Yankee artillery fire faded and finally ceased. But, even as the town still burned, the musketry began again, with the dirty bank of blue-white smoke rising until it became visible above the forward brow of the hill, mingling with those darker brown plumes from the town's burning buildings and drift on upwards. Two of the artillerymen approached, carrying a mixture of buckets and canteens. One of them looked around at the waiting men and spoke as he reached them.

"Looks like our infantry down there are givin' the Yankees plenty to think about. Who are those boys?"

"Them's one of our brigades," Ballard told them. "That's Barksdale's Mississippi boys down there."

The artilleryman nodded at the words.

"Makes sense," he said. "Those boys are good. I knew some Mississippi fellers in N'Orleans 'fore the war. They l'arned their shootin' out huntin' in the marshes along the big river. They could shoot a dime out o' a damn squirrel's eye."

"Reckon I wouldn't want to be no Yankee goin' across to where them boys are," his companion said.

Even as he spoke, the thunder of cannon was renewed across the river as the artillery bombardment re-commenced.

This time it was still heavier, with even more enemy guns involved. The town's ordeal continued as more shells went plunging down, out of sight now but clearly audible by their descending scream or detonation, pulverising still more buildings in crashing collapses of walls and gables with renewed splintering of wood and glass. Some of the watchers on the hills moved forward towards the crest again and gazed anew at this further slow destruction of Fredericksburg. The town lay suffering amid its fires, as the shells rained down and that great pall of smoke still hung in the air above it before drifting away across the river, thinning and dispersing only slowly as it did so.

But, as the artillery fire slackened once more, the musketry began again, repeating the pattern of what had happened throughout the day when the shelling had lapsed. Each time the cannon had ceased to fire the musketry in the town had re-commenced and now that higher-pitched, crackling roar was swelling once more, showing that Barksdale's boys were still down there, sticking to their work and certainly not for giving up. The afternoon was starting to wane towards evening and still the firing continued, with musketry and cannon fire alternating as before and gun smoke drifting in dirty off-white clouds, which mingled with the smoke from the many fires. A story came speeding along the hilltop positions, where off-duty men still dallied, that the Yankees were sending detachments across the river in pontoon boats and the fight would soon be on in the streets of the town. The men reacted to this news, with a wave of talk and movement along the ranks as those out in front were recalled, but the time continued to pass and there was no word of any reinforcements being sent down to support the Mississippians.

Far from being advanced into Fredericksburg, orders came along the line for the men of the regiment to return to their camps. They moved back, as further ranks of infantry arrived to occupy their positions then formed their column of march and headed down the reverse slope of the hill once more, descending onto the Telegraph Road, while still the thunder of battle continued behind them. They made their way along the now muddy road to find, on reaching the camp, that there had been a rations "issue," of flour and nothing more, so the meal consisted of further flour pancakes, washed down by cold water, and little else. Over the bulk of Howison Hill the pall of smoke from Fredericksburg still rose and drifted, visible for miles around, until, as night came closer, the Yankee gunfire finally ceased. Assembly was called and the ranks were formed. Rodger was there, pacing nervously around as the men answered the roll call in their turns. Finally, with the muster complete, he stepped forward to speak.

"The regiment has been ordered to return to the forward positions on the Telegraph Road," he called, "to take up station there in readiness for an enemy advance. Duty watches tonight will proceed, according to the rosters, in our new positions." A tiny ripple of anticipation ran along the ranks as the captain paused before continuing.

"Tomorrow, we will stand to our positions at first light. If there is no further move by the enemy, the company will then assemble, with the rest of the regiment, to witness punishment." A noise, something that resembled a subdued sigh, ran along the ranks as the men heard those final words. Sidelong glances were exchanged as the captain turned to Jeffers and nodded to him to form the men for the march back to the hills. They had known, or almost known, for the best part of two days, but now it was official. "Punishment," could mean little else but that tomorrow morning, after standing to their positions for duty at first light, the Ogeechee Volunteers would watch while one of their comrades was killed by his own. Daniel Ryan felt a knot forming in his stomach. It came even though he was not directly involved and would have to do nothing but witness the sordid event. Battle was now imminent and the tensions of that were already evident around the camp. There would, in all likelihood, be plenty of killing to come with the Yankees seemingly now over the river. Those Yankees were the enemy and he would shoot them as required, as he had done before. He would live with that, he thought, but killing your own, or being forced to watch while others did it, was something else entirely.

The light of the short, winter day had faded almost completely as Company B assembled again into a column of files in their camps, to make their way in the gathering gloom back out, along the now established tracks, onto the muddy Telegraph Road. Around Daniel Ryan there was little in the way of talk, not even much speculation as to the state of affairs in the town. There seemed instead to be more absorbing things to think about and, in the absence of rumour, banter or bravado, the main sounds were the familiar, rhythmic clink of metal equipment and the sloshing trample of feet in the already hardening mud. Although the middle part of the day had been mild, for December, the coming of night had brought a return of the harsher cold and the men's feet now crunched anew on mud which had begun to freeze once more. As on the previous day, a cold wind had risen at dusk and this flapped at men's clothing and chilled their inadequately clothed limbs as they tramped steadily on.

Their way wound between the hills before angling down from the higher ground and crossing the bed of an unfinished railroad, to skirt along the bank of Hazel Run for a stretch before wading the creek and curving away from it, this time to follow the road around the southern base of the hill, upon which they had spent much of the day. Up there to their left the cannon still waited, but almost nothing was now to be seen in the darkness. Down to their right, firing still came from the direction of the town, but now it was spasmodic clusters of musket shots with the cannon at last silent. They turned to the left at the intersection where Frederick Street went on down towards the town. The column filed along the road that followed the eastern base of the hill, tramping on past the Hall house, from the windows of which faint, yellow gleams of light cast pale fingers of illumination across the hardening dirt of the road and onto the dead grass of the lower hillside. On they went, north now, towards where Hanover Street lay in the darkness, following the line of a stone wall, which stretched along the right side of the road, visible in the light of a rising moon.

They passed a second building, one they knew as the home of the old lady Stephens, from where more subdued gleams of light issued. The files moved on along a further, downward stretch of the road before halt commands came along, relayed by the sergeants. The column came to an untidy standstill for the men to be faced to their right and deployed towards the town and the river. They spaced out along the line of the stone wall, which stood a shade higher than a man's waist, and settled there, pushing their muskets across the top stones while they crouched to gaze out towards the town. Above their heads was a crystal clear winter sky, showing its full array of diamond stars and the moon, now well above the eastern horizon was large and clear. A scattering of pickets clambered across the stones of the wall and moved away, quickly disappearing into the darkness, as they headed down towards where the distant lights of many fires still flickered, illuminating sections of the town with a lurid orange glow.

After a time, from out in front, there came distant shouts and the men gripped their weapons, but there was no command to load. Shadowy figures were emerging from the darkness, making their way up from the town and coming from the left. Some of them could be glimpsed clambering over a fence barrier out in front of the wall as the men craned their necks to see.

"It's Barksdale's boys!" The word went ranging along the line like a flame.

"It's the Mississippi boys."

"They've bin welcomin' the Yankees over." More of the dark figures were in view now drawing closer to arrive in front of the wall, looming above the men who lined it, as they began stepping across, while the word came, relayed by the, "Blues'" NCOs, to open ranks. Along the wall Mississippians scrambled wearily down onto the road, pushing their way through the waiting men on the other side. Calls from the Georgia men rang out as they passed.

"Good shootin' down in town boys huh?"

"Had a good killin' down there." A few of the arriving men answered with their own versions of humour or sarcasm, but many only grunted, while still more said nothing, likely too wearied, Daniel Ryan reckoned, to engage in much in the way of banter. Behind on the road the Mississippi soldiers were formed into ranks as their officers and NCOs took charge, while still more of their number arrived at the wall to make their way across and join their comrades. Eventually, when all were in place, orders rang out and the column stepped away, while those at the wall returned their gaze to the front.

Down there among the buildings towards the river, some of them thrown into stark relief by the light of the fires that still burned, fleeting signs of the arriving enemy could now be seen. They were visible in brief glimpses, moving shapes that crossed intersections, silhouetted there momentarily in the pulsing glow of the flames, which reflected from swaying musket barrels, while the sounds of their coming carried clearly up to the watching men at the wall. A muttering rumble now came of tramping feet and trundling wheels on the muddy streets, mixed with shouts of command. The town of Fredericksburg now had new occupiers. The Yankees were over and they were over in numbers.

The men of the Ogeechee Volunteer Rifles waited in their places at the wall, looking out intently, seeing and hearing the coming of their enemy. If the traded Yankee papers were to be believed, this was the largest host ever assembled on this continent and, as he saw and heard, Daniel Ryan could not help thinking of this as the approach of a mighty giant, which, having destroyed this much of what lay in its path, now moved on to wreak further destruction. This great enemy host, re-provisioned and reinforced since that last great struggle up in Maryland, was closing on them again, steadily and inexorably, looking to continue its advance ever deeper into Virginia and tomorrow might well see them coming on to give battle again. Men along the wall still watched, with some of them making disparaging comments or cracks, but to others, there was something unnerving and menacing about these noises that went on and on, seeming to emphasise the Yankee preponderance in everything needed to wage war. It was an unintentional demonstration of strength and power that spoke of the enemy's determination to prevail. They were here now, having surmounted the river barrier, and the latest trial of strength could now not be long postponed.

After a time a duty watch was detailed to remain at the wall while the others withdrew to gather wood, kindle fires and catch some kind of rest, but hardly were the fires alight and the men settling to the job of warming what remained of their rations, when artillery shells began to arrive from across the river to explode on the hillside behind them. Orders came along to extinguish the flames, so that the position might not be punished with such ease by the enemy. Deprived of these markers, the cannon soon ceased firing, while deprived of their source of heat and comfort, the off-duty men huddled into blankets and collected into groups for warmth. After a while the duty details were changed, with more men heading out to relieve the pickets, while those on watch at the wall were replaced. Those relieved headed across the road to settle with the others, taking their turn of gnawing on cold rations and huddling with their companions for warmth. As the night wore on, the wakened and still shivering men lay in their groups, listening to the pervasive and continuing sounds of the gathering enemy that came from the town and the river, till, chilled as they were, some kind of sleep finally took most of them.

The approach of morning brought the same curtain of fog to the Rappahannock valley as on the previous days. The off duty men of Company B were roused, while it was still dark, to assemble once more in the white obscuring blanket. They collected weapons and deployed along the wall again, pushing in beside those already there, to face towards the town, with the front rank forward at the stones while the rear rank stood behind them on the road. Behind these were the sergeants and officers, the former eyeing their squads with practiced, critical eyes while the latter paced along, with comparative unconcern, behind their company lines. Preston passed, in conversation with the major, Henry Randolph, while along the wall, men strained their ears to hear what they could of their talk.

"If they are still crossing over in numbers," they heard

Randolph say, "then I think it unlikely that they will advance today, so we have some time to look to our position here."

"And we will use it" Preston answered. "We did not think that we would have to make our fight here, but now it seems that we were wrong." The major's reply was lost as the two officers passed along, while the ranks of men waited with the fog drifting in wreathes around them.

Daniel looked out into the whiteness. Was this it? After all of the talk about manoeuvring and crossings elsewhere, it seemed to have come down to this, a straightforward push across the river here at the town, followed by a straightforward advance on the hill and ridge line beyond. Well that was fine with him. Sitting here and waiting behind the cover of a wall was easier than marching around on the frozen roads. But then the other thoughts came back to him, of what was about to take place somewhere up there over the ridge crest towards the camp, and of the man who would not live to see anything of what happened with the Yankees. He still felt an element of disbelief about it, as though there was something unreal about the whole thing. He only slightly knew Ellis and had barely seen this newcomer Gilby, but he knew well enough the ways of the army. Orders had been given and now, within the next hour if all remained quiet down here, they would be carried out. Before a drop of enemy blood was spilled on this ground, some of their own would be shed on it.

Daylight was coming now though the fog remained thick, as still the men waited at the wall and watched, and thought. The light grew and still there was no sign of movement from the town. Then the colour of the fog began to alter, indicating that the sun was rising. The ranks at the wall gave little reaction, standing in their places, they simply waited and stared into the whiteness out in front. There was no sign of the enemy in the town, save for a faint, persisting rumble of wheels, perhaps on the distant pontoon bridges or maybe closer in the town itself. The ground out in front remained clear, but now it was possible to see a little farther down the gentle slope where a wooden, board fence had swum vaguely into view, revealed by the start of the slow retreat of the white cloud towards the river. Word had come from the pickets out in front that, while more Yankees had crossed over during the night, there was, so far, no sign of them massing for any advance. There would be no reprieve, however temporary for John Ellis for, as more of the field out in front became visible in the thinning fog, the men were called to form files. Companies of the Twenty Fourth Georgia were arriving, moving along the road as they extended to their left to cover the positions, while the

Ogeechee Volunteers stepped away from the wall, mingling briefly with the newcomers as they went.

"Shootin' one o' yer own's a goddam miserable excuse fer a relief," one man said as he moved up to take his place at the wall.

"Ain't our idea," Ballard grated, "took our betters to think that up."

"Be better shootin' them then," the man drawled as he laid his musket across the top stones.

They formed their marching files and moved away on the order, initially retracing their route of the previous evening, following the Telegraph Road, but only briefly, before moving off onto a smaller track and filing at last into a claustrophobic little meadow, to be placed, as they arrived, in ranks along one side. The remaining companies entered the field in their turn, being positioned around the meadow. The eight of them now made up three sides of a square on the hillside, which, being now above the fog line, was bathed, as it had been yesterday, in winter sunshine, though the remains of the white cloud still hung along the line of the river below. This place had clearly been used over the preceding days by wagons, for the tracks of the vehicles and the hoof prints of their animals were embedded in the ground, flattening much of the browned, dead grass to mud, with further deposits of animal mess lying around, all of which had frozen and thawed alternately over the preceding few days since last week's snow had begun to melt. There was, however, still a tiny margin of dirty white snow, wedged in an irregular remnant along the base of the north facing wall at the farther end where the lower winter sunlight did not fall.

Daniel Ryan looked slowly around, seeing the companies in position in their respective places in the little enclosed area. Built into the field boundary wall, at the open end of the three-sided formation, was a higher section, which formed the rear wall of a small, seemingly derelict building, whose front faced out onto the track beyond. It was, Daniel thought, an altogether depressing scene and a sordid place for a man to end his days. Close to that higher section of the wall a post had been planted into the ground and a hole had been dug between post and wall, the grave, at least temporarily, of the man about to die. Coming here and seeing these things had brought the reality of what was about to happen into sharp focus for him, and likely for other men also, since the mood around the meadow as they waited there was sullen or even angry. It was here, it was time and there was now no putting it off, or dismissing it from one's mind. He had watched intently as the final companies had followed into the field, looking carefully for the new man, Gilby, who was at the centre of this episode. Ballard, standing on his left, had nudged him as Company H had arrived and Daniel had recognised the new lieutenant immediately by the cut and quality of his clothing.

Way back at the start of the war, many southern units

had gone off to fight in colourful, even gaudy uniforms, ideal for parading in, or for impressing the ladies at home, but less suited to campaigning in the field. Some regiments, with wealthy planters, or sons of the, "quality," families, in their ranks as enlisted men, had arrived in camps with trunks full of spare clothing, camp furniture, silver cutlery, ornate meal services and engraved decanters and wine glasses, all carried and maintained by servants and attendants. Near to two years of hard duty had swept away these things and anything else that could not be carried on the army's many marches. These same planters' sons now soldiered, like everyone else, in worn and much-repaired uniforms. They crawled with lice, ate their meagre meals off tin plates and, like their, "lowlier," comrades, now had scarce a spare shirt or pair of socks to their name.

Officers still tried to maintain a degree of regulation, uniform dress, though, depending on their means, with varying degrees of success. With this arriving youth however, it was clear that none of the army's current shortages applied to him. He made a resplendent picture of military elegance, particularly when compared with those around him. His tunic was cut from fine cloth of cadet grey, tailored to a perfect fit, with its blue collar and cuffs to denote the infantry. Brass buttons lined those cuffs, with Austrian knots embroidered in gold braid on his sleeves and the gold bar of his rank marked either side of his collar. His grey trousers were likewise finely made and sported a blue stripe down each outside seam. His kepi cap was embroidered with a strip of gilt around its base and he wore white leather gloves. At the left side of his polished, leather belt hung a sword, its hilt engraved heavily, while on his right was a gleaming pistol holster.

But it was the man's manner as much as his dress that struck Daniel Ryan. He was young, very much so, but on his slightly swarthy face was a faint smile, as though he knew that the eyes of the regiment would be on him today and he would play to it. He strode along in his place, his polished boots, muddy only at the feet, with that same air of confident ownership that reminded Daniel of landowners and gentry, back in Ireland as well as here in America. He continued to watch as the youth took his place to the left of the company and he heard Ballard mutter beside him.

"He surely ain't lettin' any o' this upset him none." Daniel grunted in acknowledgement.

"He looks like he's enjoyin' it," he said quietly.

The brief conversation was cut short by the arrival of the execution detail. Eight men, preceded by an officer, whom Daniel recognised as Parker, the other Company H lieutenant, entered the field, with a sergeant following. The detail paced up to the pole and wheeled into line to face it, grounding their muskets on the order. There was a brief delay before a further formation arrived, with the company First Sergeant in charge, behind him the rangy, sandy-bearded figure of John Ellis, accompanied by Jedediah Poulson the regimental chaplain walked in the midst of a group of four further men. The corporal, now deprived of his uniform tunic, wore a tattered light blue shirt and ragged brown pants, as, flanked by his escorts on either side, he paced past the waiting execution detail, to halt at the pole. Ellis was shepherded into place there by the two sergeants and his hands were tied behind it. Lieutenant Parker stepped up to him with a handkerchief in his hand, but Ellis shook his head, upon which the officer withdrew to one side, followed by the chaplain. Major Randolph stepped forward and unfolded a paper.

"You, John Ellis, have been found guilty of the crime of attacking a superior officer and have been sentenced to death by shooting, in accordance with army regulations. General

Longstreet has approved the order for your execution. Do you have anything to say before the punishment is carried out?" Ellis looked at him stonily.

"I only got one thing to say," he said. "You boys there," he looked past the major at the rank that faced him. "Aim good, and if ya got a spare shot ya know where to put it." Over to the side, Daniel Ryan saw Preston redden at the words, but he said nothing in reply. Randolph nodded formally and stepped back to return to his place beside the colonel.

"Duty Officer," he called, "proceed with the punishment." Parker stepped forward and called out in turn to the sergeant in charge.

"Carry on Sergeant Cantrell!"

"Yessah!" The sergeant turned to the detail.

"Detail! Tenshun!" The men came up to order pulling their weapons straight as they drew their feet together.

"Shoulder arms!" The long muskets were brought up to rest at an angle on the owner's shoulder.

"Port your arms!" The weapons were brought around till they rested across the front of each man.

"Cast about Cap!" The musket hammers were pulled to the half-cock position and fingers scrambled in pouches for the little copper thimble shapes, which were placed over the musket nipples, upon which the hammers were lowered. Cantrell turned to face Parker.

"Detail ready as ordered, sah," he called. Parker nodded, but said nothing in reply. He turned to the detail and Daniel saw his throat convulse as he swallowed deeply.

"Detail......, make ready!" he called. The muskets went from across the chests of the men in the firing squad to point out across the few yards between them and where Ellis stood, tied to the post. There was a series of faint double clicks, as the hammers were cocked, before the next order came.

"Aim!" The barrels came up and steadied as the weapons were presented and in the brief delay, Daniel saw one or two of them waver slightly. Over in his place, he noticed that Lieutenant Gilby still wore the same half-smile as before.

"Fire!" Parker almost screamed the word, which was followed instantaneously by the crash of the muskets and the billow of bluish-white smoke, which engulfed the men of the detail and drifted slowly across the field, obscuring briefly the ranks on that side as it thinned and dispersed. As it cleared, Daniel looked at the pole where Ellis now hung, with his bound hands keeping him from sinking to the ground. There was a mess of blood on his shirt, and on his face. Surely none of them had gone for a head shot, Daniel thought to himself as he watched the blood run from his nose and trickle off onto the ground below.

"Detail!" It was Parker's voice again, with something of a quaver in its tone. "Recover arms!" The muskets came back to their position across the chests of the men. Ellis did not move as the lieutenant stepped over and pulled gently at his shoulder, satisfying himself that he was dead. He straightened up and looked towards where Preston and Randolph stood.

"The punishment has been carried out sir," he called.

"Thank you Lieutenant," Randolph replied. "Carry on!"

"Shoulder arms!" The weapons were moved to be rested again on the owner's shoulder sloping there at an angle.

"Carry on Sergeant Cantrell!"

"Sah!" Daniel continued to look at the dead man as the detail who had killed him withdrew. He then shifted his gaze across to where the young lieutenant still stood, resplendent in his tailored uniform and gleaming boots.

This was the man who, if the word around the camp was to be believed, had been the cause of all of this. The thin smile had never left Gilby's face and he stood there now looking at Ellis, as he hung in his contorted pose from the post. Daniel Ryan felt a surge of resentful loathing run through him as his gaze ranged from the dead man to the smirking officer, before a further movement caught his eye, as two of the men who had escorted Ellis to his fate moved up to where he hung. One of them carried a knife and with it he cut the cord securing the dead man's hands behind the pole and at last his body slipped down to lie in the mud and turned dirt around its base.

"Rest in peace, John," Daniel Ryan said inwardly, acknowledging, even as the words came to his mind, that lying in the mud and dirt however demeaning the sight might seem to the onlookers, meant nothing whatever to John Ellis now.

From up along the ridge to the north, cannon suddenly commenced to fire and the eyes of almost every man turned to look in the direction of the gunfire, which seemed to Daniel to re-assert the call of the real killing event which awaited them all. Around the meadow, the companies were quickly called to order by their officers and NCOs, to be marched in succession past where the corpse lay on their way towards the field entrance. Daniel felt a churning feeling in his stomach as he passed the blood-soaked figure. Having witnessed the grim ritual, it left him feeling a mixture of pity and anger. Pity he felt for Ellis, for the man had died for no real reason except that he had fallen foul of this new officer. Sympathy he also felt, in a measure at least, for the men who had had to kill him. It was a miserable and distasteful job and one he hoped that he would never have to face himself.

He felt anger also towards the unfeeling system of

military, "justice," that had ordered it all, and, even on a day when battle might already be commencing, found no shred of clemency for a good fighting man. But the particular focus of his anger was the slim, elegant figure, who now paced across the field with Company H in his polished boots and immaculate uniform, to inspect his victim with the same faint smile, that had sustained him throughout the whole episode, still stitched to his features.

"Guess I was wrong then," Ballard said to nobody in particular. Several heads turned to look at him.

"Wrong," Daley returned, "wrong about what?" Ballard shook his head slowly, then nodded towards Gilby.

"I always thought an asshole was supposed to stick out the bottom end of a shirt," he said. Nobody said anything, though several of those around him grunted.

As the leading company left the meadow a mounted captain clattered up the track, his horse's hooves sounding in their rhythmic, splashing thud on the half-melted dirt. He reined in at the entrance, to the meadow, wheeling his horse hurriedly, spattering the nearest men with mud, as he made to address Preston, who stood there at the edge of the field with Randolph, as though taking the salute of his passing soldiers. The mounted officer saluted and spoke.

"General Cobb's compliments colonel," he called, managing the hurried respect on his still-turning horse. "If you have finished killing your man, he would be grateful to see your battalion returned to the brigade position without delay."

"You may tell the Brigadier that we are already on our way," was Preston's terse response. The captain saluted again, wheeled his horse and spurred immediately away as, behind him, a mutter swept along the files of those who had heard.

"Don't sound like Cobb had much time fer this," Phillips muttered beside Daniel Ryan.

"He's big on discipline," Ryan answered, "but that doesn't mean he wants good men shot."

"They must have trouble down there," Ballard added, as their own file reached the lane, "if they can't even let us enjoy a good shootin' without hollerin' out fer us."

"It's a wonder he never brought the brigade up to watch the show here," Daley said. "Or maybe there ain't any votes in a shootin'." Thompson heard the remark and spoke up.

"Boyce said that the general declined to attend with the brigade on account of the Yankees comin' across the river. Maybe he reckons the war comes afore things like this," he said.

"Likely that's why we bin sent fer without gettin' no breakfast." Daley grunted.

"They ain't gonna attack here," Philipps growled. "Even the Yankees ain't that stupid."

"They could wear themselves out if they do come up this way," Daniel replied.

"They're down there now anyways," Thompson said softly, "and that don't give 'em too many choices. Either they come on ahead, or they skedaddle back over the river and their general knows better'n anybody what the folks back in Washington'll make o' that." There was no argument or comment from anybody about the truth of his words.

The battalion had marched promptly down to the base of the hill and had made their way along the road to deploy again, resuming their places at the wall. All along the way, men were at work, digging the hard ground at the side of the road nearest the wall. The fog though thinning, still shrouded the town as, with few tools, the men attempted to break up the hard-packed, unyielding earth with bayonets, before shovelling away what they could with tin plates, bare hands or even cups. The "Blues," were returned to their previous position, while the men of the Twenty Fourth Regiment moved away towards the Hanover Street end of the road. Stacking their arms they set quickly to work, to soon discover for themselves the nature of the task. It was slog, for little tangible result. Below the first few inches where the ground had begun to thaw into mud, the earth remained frozen and rock hard, causing bayonets and plates to bend in the ground, as complaints rose.

"Godawful waste of a man's time and spit," Daley complained. "Do they think we're goin' to have a real fight here or somethin'?"

"What else," Ballard grunted? "Yankees're over, so there ain't no place to manoeuvre round here with the river at their backs and the hills in front. The Ol' Man must think they'll come straight on now, or mubbee that's what he wants 'em to do." Daniel nodded to himself as Ballard spoke. That was the sensible explanation. This wall, being between three and four feet high along its length, was not quite high enough to serve as a real rampart, but, by digging a trench on this side, the shelter it gave would be increased. In addition, the officers had ordered their men to dump the dug earth over the wall and this would further obscure it from view on that side, making it less of a target for enemy artillery.

After a time, Randolph came along the line with Rodger and Jeffers, the latter calling men from the digging to assemble. The officers moved on and Jeffers eyed the group, which now included Daniel Ryan and the others of his mess.

"You lucky boys," Jeffers growled. "You lucky, lucky boys. Seems the general wants to give you a break from diggin' so's you kin go out front and pull down them thar fences and sech that could give the Yankees cover if they come on up this way, so git movin' and git to it while the fog gives ya some cover." He nodded to Thompson.

"Yore detail," he drawled. Thompson nodded in acknowledgement and turned to them.

"Git goin'," he snapped. Daniel turned and pushed through the labouring men till he reached the wall, clambering up onto its stones he stepped down onto the layer of shovelled earth, noticing immediately how low it was on that side. Why the road they had just left was sunk into the base of the hill with only the top few stones of the wall visible on this side so banked up was the slope of the field in front. He let his gaze continue on down the gentle, undulating slope towards the fog-shrouded canal overspill that ran diagonally across the ground maybe a quarter of a mile away, beyond which lay the still hidden buildings of the town. In front, past the garden fences of the houses along the road and part of the way down the gentle slope, lay an uneven area of grass, surrounded by a wooden boarded fence that stood maybe four or five feet high. Daniel turned as Thompson called and saw him gesture towards the closer garden fence.

"That first, then we'll move on down and git the other one." They paced down the slightly sloping ground of the garden to reach the remains of a board fence, much of which had already been pulled out for last night's abortive fires. They immediately began to attack the remnants, pulling at the surviving board fragments and levering the remaining posts over. Within minutes, the fence had disappeared. Thompson then waved them on and they moved off down the gentle slope towards the enclosure fence, a more substantial structure of posts to which three broad boards were securely nailed.

"Take it away," Thompson grunted and the men got to work again, prising and splintering the planks away, pulling at the posts till they could be wrenched free and heaving them on down the slope to litter the ground there. Along the line of the fence, further details, from other companies, laboured on their own parts of the fences and soon the entire barrier was no more. As the fog thinned, they could now make out, down past the farther fence of the enclosure where they stood, the line of the partly screened overspill gully. Spaced along its length were the vague, hunched shapes of their own skirmishers now beginning to emerge from the white gloom, while, over to the left towards Hanover Street, other men were also in view at the overspill bridge there, levering and pulling at its planks. Nothing, it seemed, was being overlooked in preparing this ground for whatever was coming.

Philipps had moved a pace or two beyond the others of the detail on the slope, as he manhandled a section of planking clear and he suddenly stopped working to listen, before gesturing to the others to pause their levering and hauling. Beyond that spillway gully the nearest buildings of Fredericksburg had emerged from the dispersing fog, and the noises they now began to hear came from down there in the town itself. Those distant, continuing sounds of Yankee troops and vehicles crossing on the pontoons, and traversing the streets of the town, that they had heard over the previous hours, were now being obscured by other noises. There were voices of many men shouting and yelling to each other, now coming clearly to them, mingling with peals of raucous laughter. Mixed with all of that there were more sounds, of breaking glass and smashing wood, and now even the distant, discordant sound of someone thumping the keys of a piano. The whole incongruous medley of noises were carrying in a weird chorus up the gentle half-mile slope from Fredericksburg itself, as distant cannon fire came from downstream, briefly drowning out the sounds from the town.

All along the dismantled fence the soldiers had stopped and were looking down the slope as the winter sun finally lit up the town, shining on its wet roofs and revealing drifting tendrils of smoke, that still rose from the ruins of yesterday's bombardment, to eddy away along the riverside on an occasional breath of breeze. Other things could now be seen down there among the buildings, at street intersections and gap sites. Yankee soldiers, in their light blue winter overcoats, were there in numbers, many of them passing along the streets in formation. But others too could be glimpsed roaming in groups around other parts of the town and it quickly became clear to the watching southerners that, having suffered yesterday's bombardment from the Yankee guns, a further episode of destruction was beginning in Fredericksburg today. The noises they could clearly hear and these sights of the growing, gathering numbers of roaming northern soldiers, were clear evidence that the old town was now being looted and ransacked by its invaders. Up at the dismantled fence, the watching men were quickly chivvied back to their task by sergeants, but, as they worked, they continued to hear and see the plundering proceed. Before their eyes, the place was being pilfered and wrecked by its Yankee occupants and, the whole southern army, up here on its ridge line, as it had been during the shelling of yesterday, was powerless to stop them.

The enclosure fence was by now a mess of dismantled posts and planks, most of them tossed down the slope to litter the ground beyond. Some of the boys, having finished their own task of destruction, returned to watching the events in town till they were whistled to by Thompson, who had just acknowledged a shout from the main position in the sunken road. He waved the men at the wrecked fence

52

line back up the slope, dallying himself until the others had started away. Some retrieved sections of the fence boards and posts, likely in the hope of being allowed to burn them, as they started away, and carried them on up towards the wall. On the way back up the gentle climb Daniel's eyes worked along the foot of the hill for a sight of the road and the wall. Why, it was hard to make out where it was at all. His mind went back to how the arriving Mississippians had seemed to tower over the men on the road behind the wall, when they had passed through last night. From where he now approached, he could just make out, as he got closer, the heads and shoulders of the officers, who paced along the line of the road. Daniel caught a sight of Cobb, as the brigadier passed on his way, followed by a couple of his staff and, when one looked carefully, there were further, occasional glimpses of the bobbing heads of some of the men as they continued working behind the stones. But, as for the position itself, it was pretty near impossible to see it at all from the Fredericksburg side, unless you knew exactly where to look.

They reached the original dismantled fence, with the garden beyond, deviating towards it to pause there among the trampled furrows, foraging for anything that remained in the way of vegetables. It had already been gone through, but Ballard and Philipps came upon a couple of battered beetroots, from which they brushed the dirt as they moved the last few yards to the wall.

"That'll test yore cookin'," Philipps muttered and the others smirked at each other.

"Ain't nothin' much to do with beets other'n roast 'em," Ballard said. "Ain't no point in tryin' to cook 'em any other way."

"You're the expert then," Daniel told him, "so you can see to cookin' them."

The digging went on in the rock hard earth behind the wall, with the men, some of whom had discarded their tunics, now sweating in the unseasonally warm sun. Gradually a trench, upwards of a foot in depth, was dug, which stretched away along the length of the road and men now tramped the earth at the bottom to level and firm it. Having seen the work completed, the officers left a duty watch along the wall itself while the balance of the men were stood down to prepare and eat such food as they had. Fires were permitted in the daylight and once the retrieved fence sections were well alight in a crackling blaze, the two beetroots were baked, portioned and eaten, but for the five of the mess there was nothing else, beyond a drink from their canteens. The "meal" concluded, Daniel crossed the road to look out from the wall towards the town and the river with the whole scene now bathed in the bright sunlight of a surprisingly mild afternoon.

From where he stood, the edge of the town lay perhaps a little less than half a mile away while over to his left Hanover Street, and the slightly more distant William Street, led down the slope from the Confederate line and on into Fredericksburg itself. Buildings were dotted along these roads for some of their length and these would doubtless obstruct the field of fire of that left portion of the southern line, which faced them. Out ahead however, the field was relatively clear, save for one brick house, square and substantial, that lay to the left front of their own position. Otherwise, the wrecked garden fences and that rectangular enclosure down the hill, the further fence of which still stood, were the main features, together with the three houses spaced along the road, which bordered or interrupted the wall itself.

Further down the slope from the surviving enclosure fence was that mill race, the overspill of the town canal, built to power the local mills and bypass the shoals and rapids on the river. Its gully, concealing the waterway itself, stretched diagonally across their front, though some scrubby bushes and trees stood in places along its margin marking its line. Down there, along that overflow, the Confederate pickets were still positioned to watch the Yankees in the town. Over to their right, Frederick Street stretched down from its junction with the sunken Telegraph Road, approaching the town in company with the railroad line, which curved in from the south, to run into town parallel with the street, though the cutting for an additional unfinished branch line stretched from the main track up towards the right flank of the southern positions along the road. Down there, at the edge of town, were more buildings, and a further enclosed space adjoined the street. This led on to a walled brickyard, which was situated on this side of the spillway near Frederick Street. It was not particularly open ground and the field of fire from the wall, if the Yankees did choose to come on, was not clear, but, as he looked out across it, the prospect of advancing up that slope still struck Daniel Ryan as an intimidating one.

Beyond all of these features lay the bulk of the town, with its fires still smouldering and trails of smoke still rising almost vertically into the air, while its destroyed and damaged buildings stood out, like livid scars of its ordeal of the previous day. Along its streets the ransacking and plundering continued, with sounds of it all carrying clearly up to the southern line on the mild air. Daniel let his eyes sweep across the vista again. It was a damned shame that this sedate, old place was now little more than an expanse of ruins, with its people dispossessed and fugitive. It was the reality of this war, plain and ugly, but it was also the visible evidence of why he stood here, a soldier. He had enlisted, first and foremost, to protect his own home and state and that duty of defence had been extended to the southern states as a whole. Yet, in spite of all of their efforts of the summer and autumn, here were the invaders again, spreading their trail of destruction ever wider. Daniel Ryan clenched his jaw as his anger gripped him, while the sounds of the wrecking and plundering came plainly to his ears. If those thieving, destroying Yankees would just venture up that sloping ground, he thought, as they now seemed almost inclined to do, by the living god they would be made to pay for these last two day's work.

The afternoon slowly passed, punctuated by artillery exchanges along the line of the hills, while along the road the work of preparation went on. But, between these upsurges, the noises from town were still heard, continuing on into the evening, as Fredericksburg suffered this further chapter of violence and destruction. As the daylight waned, a ration of bacon and cornflour was delivered and issued. Details of men from each mess had made their way along to the end of the road in the charge of a sergeant, to form lines at the wagons and await their turn. With Mrs Stephens' well almost played out, water details had gone on to the creek beyond with their collections of canteens. The rations issue completed and canteens eventually returned, the fires from earlier had been banked up with what remained of the fence rails, for the ration to be quickly cooked and ravenously eaten, though Daniel, mistrusting how long it might be till the next issue, hoarded most of one of his corn dough pancakes in his haversack for later.

As full darkness came, mindful of the enemy guns, the fires had been extinguished and the off duty men had turned in to rest. But the mayhem of the day had not ceased with the coming of night. Down in the town the sounds of destruction, though fewer now, still mingled with those of the arriving formations. Noises, of breaking glass and wood still came to the ears of the watching, listening men, along with what sounded like drunken shouts and laughter, much of which had gone on for most of the day. Fires now burned on some of the street intersections, fed by whatever had been hauled from the workshops and homes of Fredericksburg. They cast their flickering yellow glows around the surrounding buildings and walls, illuminating snatches of what still went on in the streets. God knew there could be little left to destroy now in the looted and wrecked town, but, by what could still be seen in the glow of those fires, whoever was down there attending to the job was being pretty persistent and thorough in completing it.

As the night began to pass, the noises from Fredericksburg finally died down, as though the vandals and thieves down there had at last exhausted their desire to ransack and destroy. Daniel Ryan noted the subsiding of the plundering as he stood his duty watch at the wall. With the town now thoroughly wrecked, it seemed that there was nothing much left for tomorrow but battle. The Yankees had come to this river and this town in order to force a crossing and move on south. There was no other reason for their being here for Fredericksburg itself was of no military value, so they would likely come on tomorrow and his stomach had steadily continued to tense and tighten at the thought. They would come on because, as Thompson had said, there was nothing much else to do, unless retreating back across the river, and admitting that the whole thing was a mistake and a failure, was an option open to their new commander. No, he thought, those politicians and newspapers in Washington would never permit that. They had been pushing and cajoling at Burnside, with their headlines and articles, for the previous month. It was, "On to Richmond," again, no matter what, so tomorrow they would come on and the next bloody clash between the two armies would be the result.

In common with many of those around him, Daniel Ryan slept little that night. Few seemed to sleep much when a fight was expected and here, especially with the bitter cold to help in keeping the shivering men awake, it was no exception. Once again the off-duty men had not been returned to the camps beyond the hills, but had stayed behind the positions along the sunken Telegraph Road after taking their watches. Daniel Ryan had returned from picket duty along the overspill gully down towards the town with the others of his detail, feeling exposed and vulnerable, with the near to full moon high and luminous white in the sky above them. They then took a turn at huddling together in groups, along the base of the hill, on the far side of the road and tried to rest. With no fires, the cold seemed to settle around a man, penetrating into his heart and soul, even when he lay among his comrades, still fully clothed and additionally cocooned in whatever was available in the way of woollen or waterproof blankets. All along the line, men were kept awake by the cold and also by the continuing noises from the town down that brief half mile towards the river.

As on the preceding night, and all through the intervening day, they could hear the tramping feet and the thud of animals' hooves ringing on the now hardened and frozen mud of the streets. The remaining fires of Fredericksburg had burned down to a few places, where pulsing, lurid glows marked the remains of those that still smouldered. Any of a mind to watch from the Confederate line, could still make out shadowy images of movement, where columns of men and convoys of wagons and guns crossed the street intersections where some of the flickering flames still cast their now diminishing light.

Daniel looked around the moonlit road a number of

times during the night, seeing the duty men crouched along the wall, illuminated by the haloed moon, hearing muted snatches of their conversation and the occasional scrape of a weapon on the stones of the wall above the fading chorus of noises from down towards the river. He saw too that others around him were awake, looking out towards the wall and beyond, each of them with their own thoughts as they looked and listened to the final stages of the ordeal that the old river city had suffered.

Fredericksburg, with its genteel streets and antique buildings, had reminded Daniel Ryan of Williamsburg, that other old town, down on the peninsula that had been abandoned to the Yankees last year. Now, as back then, the fate of these vulnerable Virginia places that stood in the way of the invader had made an impression on the men of the company, and, even with best part of a year of active soldiering up here, there were still some who were not completely hardened or inured to the grim and brutal sides of this war, which they were repeatedly made witness to for these people were not combatants but the weak and the sick. God knows, Daniel thought, if a man ever got to the point that sights like these failed to move him then he had gotten just about as bad as the damned Yankees were.

Still growing in him was the tension of coming battle, the trepidation that came as the fighting drew close. The quicker heartbeat, that solid knot in the stomach, a tightness in the throat, that repeated swallowing could not ease, the beginning of a tremble in the limbs, an inability to relax or rest, the impulse to testiness with comrades. They had all re-appeared. He wished it was over, for this waiting period, when a man knew that the fight was imminent was the worst, worse even than battle itself. Once the fight started, a kind of hectic energy came and this seemed to get many men through the actual event. But all around him now in the darkness, the story was only of waiting, and of vainly trying to rest, until, as the moon sank behind the hill above the road, and rest had still not come, Daniel Ryan's section was called for their next turn of duty at the wall.

Chapter 3 Slaughter on the Grandest Scale

The off-duty men were again roused before dawn by the NCOs moving along the road as the fog hung around them in a thick blanket. The newly awakened, having collected their muskets from their stacks, were ushered across to the wall, by Jacob Morsby, the Regimental Sergeant Major, for the men already on duty there to be moved back and sent along in sections to the end of the road, where, according to Morsby, the ammunition wagons now waited. They stood in line to receive their supply of cartridges and caps in turn, which, once issued, were jammed into pouches and pockets. The men took sixty rounds, rather than the usual forty, that were taken when a march was pending, reasoning that the extra weight and bulk was not an issue, since they would likely be shooting these cartridges off well before they were going any place else.

The issue complete, they were headed back to their positions along the wall to form into two sparse ranks, allowing the remaining sections to move off to the wagons, on Morsbys' command. Feet scraped on the hard ground as the ranks moved away. They returned shortly after, still distributing their cartridges in pouches or pockets and then moving across to take their places in the now frozen mud of the trench, to form the front rank at the wall. The rear rank men, who had been on watch, were again stood down briefly to toilet and then eat whatever rations remained to them.

Daniel Ryan placed his musket in a stack and moved away to the far side of the busy road, looking to find a place against the hillside across from the wall. He stepped up the bank a few steps before unbuttoning his pants flap, feeling the cold intrude as he relieved himself. He hurriedly fastened the flap once more as he moved back down the slope and sat down, leaning against the bank, with its covering of dead, brittle grass, as he pulled the brown paper wrapped cartridge bundles from his pockets, tore the paper away and arranged the cylindrical cartridges in his pouch in vertical order. Forty you could fit into these pouches. Some units carried larger ones, most of them captured from the Yankees, which were supposed to take sixty rounds, but the weight and unwieldiness became a problem with that many. Daniel settled his forty into the pouch and fastened it. He then distributed the extra two packs in the side pockets of his tunic before pulling his haversack around to retrieve the remains of last night's ration issue. Fog was continuing to drift and weave around him as he pushed the now hard pancake into his mouth, pulling at it with his teeth to chew the fragment briefly into some sort of pliability, before pushing more of the food in. He had no particular desire to eat, with his stomach churning as it was, but Jeffers always reckoned a man fought better with food in his belly and there was no telling when the next chance would come. He dutifully worked on with his chewing and swallowing, pausing only to stuff the final portion of the hardened dough mixture into his mouth before pulling his metal canteen around, to unscrew the cap and take a draught of the freezing water, that numbed his tongue and rasped its chill along his throat as he swallowed it down. He grimaced before screwing the cap back onto the canteen and scrambling to his feet. He then took a further few seconds to stretch his arms out to full extension before he moved back out onto the road, still chewing, to retrieve his weapon and rejoin the men at the wall. The returning men thickened up the ranks there, but only briefly, as the other sections of men moved away on the order to take their brief relief time.

At last all had returned to their places and the sergeants occupied themselves for a few further moments shuffling their men this way and that, with a sequence of curt instructions and growls, to even out the line. Daniel Ryan's section eventually found themselves on the downward slope in the road, a little way north of old Miss Stephens' white-painted board house that broke the line of the wall, at the crest of the gentle ascent, but, for now at least, the building was only a vague shape in the misty gloom of the thickening fog. Some men had again brought blankets with them, and as the company stood in a double rank, those with this luxury wrapped them around their shoulders gripping the corners around their fingers as they held their freezing cold weapons. Other men rubbed their hands up and down barrels and stocks to warm both as they looked out into the white gloom towards where the still invisible slope and the town beyond it lay. Out in front there was little sign of life and no word had yet come back from the picket line of any enemy activity.

The fog remained thick here at the foot of the hill, drifting around in wreathes and strands, so that a man standing in his place could see clearly only a half dozen soldiers on either side of him, beyond which the shapes of men and weapons grew indistinct and grey before vanishing altogether from sight. Behind them the officers paced along the road, a foot or two higher than where the men stood nearer to the wall in their trench, with space on the far side for others to pass, before the hill began to sweep upward from that side of the road. There were murmurs of conversation along the line, occasionally shooshed by sergeants, but out in front towards the town, the noises were beginning to grow. The shuffling of feet, the rumbling of wheels the renewed clop of animals hooves, the clink of metal equipment and occasional shouted orders, growing steadily in volume and intensity, signs of a gathering of the huge host of the enemy were now coming to them clearly through the fog.

"Must be a hell of a lot o' them right enough," Daley muttered from his place beside Daniel.

"Maybe they're marchin' back and fore to put a skeer on us like ole, "Jeb," did up at Manassas," Philipps mused.

"Mubbee they've figured out what a shit awful hole they've gotten themselves into and they're off to wreck someplace else," Ballard rejoined, "but I ain't countin' much on that," he added. He turned as Jeffers figure loomed out of the fog.

"Maybe you ain't heard," the First Sergeant growled, "but we got officers 'n' generals around here to work all o' that out.That means that we brainless, unthinkin' soldiers in the line git saved the effort and the worry of figurin' out what the enemy are goin' to do, so all we got to do is stand here, stay awake, listen fer orders and keep a good, goddam look out." He rasped the final words at them as he moved on, disappearing into the fog, while those behind him at the wall returned meantime to their looking and listening, while, down in the town, the noises of ever more feet, hooves and wheels continued to tell their own story of what was coming.

Full daylight, in the form of that ghostly whiteness in

the fog, was here now and the noises from town went on without a pause. There was no sign of an advance, or of anything else from out in front and still no word back from the line of pickets, who remained at their stations down at the spillway, beyond that remaining board fence. Out from the wall the fog moved and wisped on faint eddies or draughts in the air, while the waiting men still stamped their feet and rubbed their hands to warm them, as readiness grew into boredom and once again, for some, hunger rather than battle, began to occupy their minds.

The morning began to pass and as it did, the fog started to thin on their own front, slowly revealing the now familiar features of the ground beyond where they waited. First the vague, whitewashed shape of the Stephens house, flanked by its few straggly trees, slowly gathered form, while out to the left, on the Twenty Fourth Regiment's front, the smaller Innis House emerged also from the gloom. The remaining stumps of the garden fence posts were revealed out in front of the wall and then the beginnings of the gentle downhill slope were visible, revealing the dismantled litter of the nearer enclosure fence.

The first posts of its still intact side fences had begun to emerge, stretching away down the slope to the swale, when the artillery fire began. It was distant, coming from downstream and it began with isolated discharges, but these were quickly followed by a more general cannonade. Faces and heads inclined, turning downstream to the right, towards the firing as they always did, even though nothing could possibly be seen in the slowly shifting curtain of whiteness. There was still no word from their own picket line down the slope, but now the mutters of conversation were at an end as everyone waited in readiness, with gazes alternating between their own front and further south, where that gunfire had swelled still more, the discharges coming in flat, echoing salvoes through the white drifting cloud.

After a time, the distant artillery was joined by musketry. Crackling picket fire rang out, which soon grew into louder volleys, higher-pitched, like showers of stones, some said, flung at a barn roof. On it went, swelling and pulsing, as whatever was happening down there grew in its intensity. Along the wall, as the minutes dragged on, the tension began to ease somewhat and some men started to ruminate on what it all might mean.

"Old Jack's stirred a hornet's nest down thar,"

"Looks like them Yankees made up their mind at last."

"Maybe they're tryin' to flank us down there."

"Don't know what everybody's shootin' at in this here fog." The talk ranged along, with some men taking part to make a show of their unconcern.

Daniel however, could feel the renewed tension in himself, now that the fighting along the line had begun, and, looking to either side, he could see the familiar signs of it in others also, a difference in the manner and bearing of men. Some swallowed, or licked their lips or fidgeted with equipment belts or ammunition pouches. It was most noticeable among the newer men, especially the conscripted replacements from the fall, who had not seen this before. They were quiet and nervous, jerking their heads to look around them at every movement and remark. But Daniel noticed that some of the older hands were silent also, watching the events and behaviour around them as they waited for their own ordeal to commence. He ran his eyes along the line again, all too aware that much of the bravado that he had seen and heard, from various men, was exactly that, a concealing by others of their own apprehension of what was to come.

Some men withdrew, falling silent, or even morose,

while a few, who had paper and pencil, took to letter writing, scribbling brief notes on whatever surface they could find to lean on. Still more redoubled their efforts with the witty comments and quips. He could see and hear it all taking place around him, as he had on those previous days of battle. So far he was managing to keep his own breathing regular and unhurried, and his heart, though quickened, had not yet fallen into that fearful, pounding grip of battle, but once one knew that it was coming, the day was very different.

Everyone hoped they would survive and most firmly believed that they would. The bullet or the shell fragment would always take someone else, but the old hands had seen men die and they knew the randomness of it. It was inescapable fact that, by the time that hardly visible ascending sun had gone down beyond the hills behind them, some of those who stood here now would be dead, or, perhaps worse still, under the surgeons' knife and saw, for those older hands at least were well aware that there were worse things than death. Conversely there were other men, like Abe White, who, before every battle so far, had beseeched this or that comrade to take charge of a little, drawstring bag of embroidered leather, with his personal effects, for returning to his family, due to his absolute certainty of imminently approaching death.

"I know it," was his favoured saying, "I feel it in my guts." Nobody knew exactly what was inside the bag, but down at Richmond, in the battles of the summer, different men had gravely taken charge of it for him and others still had done it at Manassas and Sharpsburg, only to have to return the thing to Abe, when he had inconsiderately survived each fight without so much as a scratch. By now, Daniel reckoned, he must be running out of comrades in his mess to look after his things when the fights came around.

More time passed, and the fog receded further, clearing

from the hillside behind them to reveal its yellows and browns, illuminated in winter sunshine all the way up to the summit and along to the big Brompton house up to the left. The view down the slope towards the town was clearing also, though only slowly, with the nearest streets of Fredericksburg having now emerged from the gloom, as the white cloud retreated once again towards the river. Downstream the noise of battle went on without pause, a mixture of artillery and small arms that spoke of a pretty major engagement, but, along the wall, with no signs of enemy activity and no word from the picket line, one watch of the men was again stood down.

Daniel crossed the road with the others, stacking his musket and moving on to the grass beyond, he peered around for signs of the earlier toileting on the slowly thawing, frosty clumps, before selecting a place to sit himself down on the bank, leaning back on the grass and immediately feeling the cold and the damp of the ground working through his tunic and his pants. Still his heart thumped at its faster rate and his mind raced with a confusion of thoughts. Downstream, Jackson's men were already locked in combat and the enemy were there in front of their own positions also. They could still hear snatches of them moving around with all of the familiar marching and moving sounds, more shouted orders and now there even came the sound of distant bands playing lively airs. They were down there, little more than half a mile away in the town, yet still they did not come. With the two armies this close it must mean a fight, the thing was surely settled and, that being true, it could only be a matter of time.

Still they waited, as the day grew warmer, and, the watches having changed again, the newly off-duty men moved across to settle and lounge on the far side of the road, with their muskets stacked in front of them, while the duty watch arranged themselves at the wall, standing once more in the trench that they had dug, with such difficulty, yesterday. Behind them in the higher middle part of the road, officers still paced along, pausing to peer towards the town, whose buildings and wreckage had now almost all emerged from the clearing fog. Overhead, the day was fair, with a clear blue sky, where only a few fluffy white clouds floated and the bright sunlight spread its unfamiliar warmth across the fields and ridges. Cobb passed along again, pausing to speak with Preston and Randolph, before turning to the men on the other side of the road.

"Be ready men," he called, "our time will likely be here soon." His words prompted a succession of shouted responses from the men.

"We're ready and waitin' ginral."

"Don't'cha worry none about us."

"Let 'em come on up."

"We'll whip 'em fer ye if they come up here." The general's wide face creased into a smile at the comments.

"I never doubted it boys," he called, as he moved on up towards where the Eighteenth Regiment stood on the next section of the road.

"Maybe they won't come," Daley said. "I surely wouldn't want to come up that rise."

"They ain't spent blood gettin' all them men across into town for nothin'," Philipps told him. Hardly had he spoken when there came a shout from along the wall.

"Man comin' in!" The officers ceased their pacing to look out again, while the waiting men tensed, with some of those, "stood down," on the far side of the road, standing up to look.

The man turned out to be Silas Norton, of their own, "Squirrel Hunters," group, and he jogged the last few yards, beyond the edge of the Stephens' garden, to step onto the top stones of the wall and pause there, while the duty men pushed to open a gap for him upon which he dropped down to the road beyond. Jeffers was there and he pointed him on towards where Preston, Randolph and the adjutant had arrived, together with Rodger and a couple of the other captains. Daniel Ryan and the others of his mess watched from their places on the hillside, as Norton, coming around to approach on the colonel's left side, gave a quick salute on reaching the group of officers.

"Sergeant Dellin's says to tell y'all that the Yankees are formin' down near the railroad like they're intendin' comin' on up. Looks like a division at least," he added, between recovering breaths, though his words had been loud enough for everyone near the group of officers to hear. Preston nodded and turned to those around him.

"Pass the word to the Brigadier," he rapped, "and call the off-duty men." There were hurried salutes and the company officers hurried away, calling as they went for their First Sergeants. Orders rang out and those lounging at the foot of the hill on the far side of the road sprang into activity. Musket stacks disappeared as if by magic and the men moved across to rejoin the ranks along the wall, gaping down the slope from the higher section in the middle of the road as they went, before stepping down into the trench, which now made it an almost ideal height as a parapet on which to rest their muskets.

Daniel Ryan crouched in the front rank between Daley and Philipps. Looking along he saw that John Fitzpatrick, now stood in the front rank beyond Philipps and as Daniel looked he caught Fitzpatrick's eye. They looked at each other for a second or two and Daniel nodded, seeing Fitzpatrick do the same.

"Stay in one piece John," Daniel said, seeing Fitzpatrick flush slightly.

"You too, Daniel," he replied, before returning his gaze to the front once more. Daniel did likewise, straightening up to steal a quick look down the gentle slope. It had been a small exchange, he reflected to himself, but at least he had communicated with John, whom he had once counted as his closest friend, until those events of the autumn had fractured their mess. Now, at least, if the worst came, they had not parted in an atmosphere of enmity. His reflections were interrupted as the word came along the line.

"Load, but do not prime," and the process of selecting a cartridge, biting open the paper wrapping and pouring the contents into the musket barrel began.

Some men bit the powder end of a cartridge, holding the bullet itself between their fingers as they poured the grainy, black powder down the barrel, dropping the bullet in after it. Those who loaded this way were often distinguished by heavier smears of black powder around their lips. Most reckoned that it was too easy to spill the powder measure doing it that way and, since there was a paper flap at the other end, these tended to bite the cartridge open there, gripping the bullet in their teeth and spitting it into the muzzle when the powder had been poured. Daniel Ryan was one of the latter and he felt the ridges of the cold lead bullet with his teeth and tongue as he balanced the paper cartridge to pour the powder. With the bullet inserted, the remaining paper was stuffed in after it as a wad before ramrods were withdrawn from their channel below the musket barrel and a succession of metallic clangs and clatters sounded along the line as the men rammed their loads home. Then the ramrods were returned, being pressed into place with the little finger of the right hand and, save for the priming, the weapons were ready.

Higher up behind them, Confederate artillery on the hill opened up with a thunderous roar, making Daniel Ryan jump as he returned his ramrod. The smoke from the guns drifted over the slope, moving across from left to right, where the shells had flown, trailing the wispy, smoke of their smouldering fuses as they swept through the sunlit air with a noise like tearing paper. Daniel pushed up to take a further look over the wall. Through the drifting smoke he could see the ground in front, down past the dismantled garden fence and on past the partly dismantled enclosure beyond, but there was not a sign of the enemy yet. Beside him on his other side, Daley straightened up to look in his turn.

"They must be in the gully," he shouted. Daniel looked at him.

"Down at the spillway," he added, "that ditch that drains the canal." Daniel nodded, illogically rankled at Daley's assumption that he didn't know what or where the gully was, but he dismissed these thoughts from his mind as a further salvo of shells passed over. He glanced across at Daley, who crouched beside him, leaning forward, with his front knee against the stones of the wall and his rear foot in the trench. He was tense, like everyone was tense, anticipating what was to come, but there was a look in his eye that Daniel had seen before. Was it just anticipation? Daniel let his eyes rest on his friend as he waited, crouched against the cold, damp stones of the wall. Mick was different. He had saved Daniel's life up in Maryland in a skirmish with local militia, but Daniel had seen that look in his face and had found the same thought flitting across his mind now that he had back then, for it seemed to him that Mick Daley might well enjoy killing. A thing that others did reluctantly, as part of the requirements of duty, was more than that to some men and Daley seemed to be one of them. Battle, with all of the brutality that it entailed, seemed to excite him. He seemed, by his manner, to become almost a different person and the thought and the sight of it, even in the moments when battle was about to be joined, was somehow unsettling.

All around them the artillery fire went on, with Yankee guns from somewhere, maybe across the river, returning fire and sending their projectiles arcing up towards the hill crest. Daniel put the dark thoughts about Daley to the back of his mind and, on an impulse, he pushed up for another lingering look, focussing his gaze down towards where the shells from the southern guns were bursting over the canal race, where the Yankee infantry must be, preparing for their advance. He ducked down again, but hardly had he settled himself when, from around them, came the shouts.

"There they come!"

"They're a formin' down thar!"

"They're comin'!"

All around them men pushed up for a look, ignoring the shouts of their sergeants. Daniel was among them, and sure enough, through the drifting smoke, he could now see the enemy, some of them at least, moving across from the remains of the bridge on Hanover Street to the north, to deploy over the ground in front of them, while more approached from the southern side, emerging from the cover of the canal gully, with long lines of their light blue winter overcoats now visible. It seemed to be a brigade, with four distinct regiments. Above the ranks the swaying rows of polished musket barrels and bayonets caught the rays of the sun and glinted and gleamed in dazzling flashes of light. Over those gleaming weapons the flags flew, with just enough of a light breeze to idly flap and partially spread them.

In front of these assembling formations, there now came a strong formation of skirmishers. These pushed forward, pausing to fire at the brown figures of the Confederate picket line, some of whom still delayed their own withdrawal to shoot at the advancing enemy, with the puffs of off-white gun smoke from their musket discharges drifting away slowly in the diffident breeze. As Daniel Ryan looked, the bombardment from the hill behind the road intensified, sending more salvoes of shells down to burst above and among the ranks of men, who had now begun their advance up the slope. He glimpsed a group of the distant blue figures engulfed by one shell burst before he ducked down again. He had seen at first hand the punishment inflicted on long rows of men by the showers of metal from exploding shells and he shuddered involuntarily as he recalled it. Daley too was watching the advance and he delayed longer before crouching again behind the wall. He looked along into Daniel's face.

"The gunners are rippin' into them good," he said. Daniel nodded.

"Less for us to fight," he said grimly. He pulled again at his ammunition pouch, hauling it round from where it customarily sat on his right hip on its leather strap, until it was almost in front of his body, before opening the fastening catch on the smaller cap pouch which sat on his belt to the right of the buckle. Now he was as ready as he could be. His heart rate was already surging and he could feel the beat of it thumping in his chest. His limbs trembled with that familiar weak feeling that he knew from previous fights. Beads of sweat were forming to run and drip down his face and he could feel the wetness of it beneath his tunic on his shirt, as he waited with the rest of the men close against the wall. Around them the returning pickets suddenly appeared, scrambling across the top stones and pushing their way through the waiting ranks to the roadway.

"They're thicker'n blowflies on a hogshit down there," one man intoned breathlessly as he scrambled past. Above their heads, the shells continued to soar and tear and, crouching where they were, they could hear the flat explosions down towards the town as missile after missile reached its target.

But it was in between the thundering discharges from the artillery on the hill behind them that Daniel Ryan heard the other sound. With the gunfire increasing all around, it came to him only in snatches, but it was the familiarity of it that attracted him to listen more intently. It was one of the sounds of his childhood that now sounded along the line from where the Twenty Fourth Georgia Regiment stood, for it was the sound of the "Carrickfergus." That song, traditional to Ireland in the gaelic, but sung in English more recently, that spoke with such lyrical sadness of the hardship loss and exile that were so intertwined through his native land's culture, was as familiar to Daniel Ryan as his mother's milk. His mind went back as he heard the words, recalling the memory of his father and uncles, raising their voices in that melody at long past family gatherings, while their children had sat and listened. Around him the song was moving steadily along the line as other Irish voices took up the refrain and, hearing it, Daniel Ryan did likewise, joining in as the notes and lyrics gained further strength and the melody rose in volume.

"..........But the sea is wide and I cannot cross over and neither have I the wings to fly

Wish I could find me a handsome boatman to ferry me home to my love and die."

Daniel looked around him as the words coursed on. Beside him, he could hear Daley roaring out the lines, with, it had to be said, a greater measure of enthusiasm than melody, but, on his other side, Fitzpatrick too was singing, joining in this moment when so many of the men of this brigade had chosen to touch and remember their roots.

"For in Kilkenny, it is reported, the marble stones are

as black as ink…." Around them, Thompson and Ballard and Phillips, and beyond them, Kane also, were exchanging curious looks with others of the native Americans at this manifestation of Celtic peculiarity. Daley saw those looks and paused his discordant bellowing long enough to shout to those around him.

"Servin' with you southerners is all very fine, but blood's blood."

Around them, the artillery continued to pound the approaching enemy as the singing resounded along the wall. Daniel saw Boyce, standing behind them on the road with something of a smile on his face, while Rodger, standing along from him a few yards, looked, by his contrasting expression, as though he nursed some kind of combination of disapproval and worry about this development.

"………I'm drunk today and I'm seldom sober, a handsome rover from town to town, but I'm sick now, my days are numbered, come all you young men and lay me down."

As the final lines rang out, the order came relaying along and the infantry were called to prime. Perhaps Daley had been right, Daniel Ryan thought as the song died away. They were southerners by adoption and this defence of the south from these Yankee invaders was their fight, for they had made it so, but blood was indeed blood. The tight pounding continued in his chest as, together with the others around him, he pulled the musket hammer to half-cock, fumbled a cap from his pouch and placed it on the metal nipple, gently easing the hammer down again with his thumb. He straightened up, and immediately swung the loaded weapon to the ready, clenched in his sweating hands, the butt against his hip and the muzzle in the air. He was aware now of the sound of voices out in front, cheering, or more like shouting, coming from the approaching Yankees.

"Hi! Hi! Hi!" men around him were exchanging glances.

"Sounds like they can't wait to git started," Saul Philipps growled. Cobb passed again along the road behind them, followed by a single orderly.

"Wait boys," he called out. "Not Yet!" Along the line men still rose up to take a further look.

"Hell's teeth, they're close," Daley grunted as he crouched down again. Then Ballard gestured along the line and the faces turned to look. It was Cobb again, now waving his hat to attract the attention of the men at the wall.

"Get ready boys," he yelled, "here they come!" The men pushed to their feet, this mass movement followed by a sequence of metallic scrapes and double clicks, as the ramrods or barrel bands pushed across the stones and musket hammers were pulled back to their fully cocked position. Daniel pushed up, getting a fleeting glimpse of a long line of light blue winter coats, darker caps, and pale faces, with gleaming musket barrels and splashes of bright colour from their flags waving above them, as he swung the barrel of the Enfield forward towards the enemy.

"Aim!" The shouts rang along from the sergeants at the signal of the officers and Daniel squinted briefly along the sights.

"Fire!" The wall was engulfed in smoke and noise and Daniel started as the belch of yellow flame, from the closely packed ranks and weapons, surged away from the wall. His musket leapt back on its recoil, punching his upper body backwards as it lunged into his shoulder.

"Clear the wall!" It was Jeffers' voice, bellowing the order as the men moved automatically back, to allow the next rank to step forward into place. The rear rank men pushed past Daniel as he pulled the next paper cartridge from his pouch, tearing the end and the bullet away with his teeth, feeling the cold bullet and the sharp spicy taste of the black powder grains on his lips and tongue. He shook the powder into the barrel, spat the bullet and stuffed the paper after it, immediately reaching for the ramrod as the next volley at the wall crashed out and the stinking smoke engulfed them all once more. Then ram and replace, fumble a fresh cap into place and it was shove up to the wall again to sight through the drifting smoke on the now faltered blue ranks, who had been pushed to a halt at that swale down near the dismantled fence, its edge now marked with a rank of fallen men.

Daniel settled his musket, cocking it as he did so, and squeezed the trigger as he heard the bellow of command. The deafening crash around him made his ears cringe, and the recoiling weapon again thumped into his shoulder, while the smoke stung his eyes and caught in his nose and throat. He pushed back from the wall and reached for another cartridge, coughing furiously as he lifted the paper cylinder up towards his teeth, biting, pouring, spitting and ramming between coughs even as the next volley thundered out from the wall. Then it was up to the stones again, as he hurriedly pressed another cap into place, cocking the musket as he sighted briefly into the drifting smoke.

His rank had blasted their sixth volley into the now dense smoke bank, which shrouded the ground in front of the wall and they had pushed away from the wall again when, as they frantically began to reload, more shouts came along the line.

"Load to the ready! Load and go to the ready!" Thompson took up the shout. There was something about Joe's shout, Daniel thought briefly, not just loud, though it certainly was that, but it had some kind of a penetrating quality that made it carry above almost any other shout or sound, even in the most deafening of battle clamours. He found himself almost grinning ruefully as he rammed home the minie ball and paper wad and replaced the ramrod in its channel. He selected a cap from the pouch and kept it in his hand, having pulled the hammer to half cock and flicked the spent copper thimble away. He stepped forward with Philipps coming up on his right side and Daley on his left. He was panting and his heart was pounding against his ribs, seeming almost to constrict his breathing, so heavily was it thumping in his chest. The sweat continued to trickle down his face onto his collar, and his shirt and trouser legs felt saturated with the collected moisture there, that had now started to feel cold against his skin.

"Look there," Heads turned at the grunted remark from Eli Winder as a murmur passed along the men at the wall. Beyond the town, on the far side of the river, a large yellow balloon was rising slowly into the air with the tiny figures, perched in the basket below it, just visible. The low winter sun glinted, likely on the lens of a telescope, attracting the eyes of the onlookers on the ground. Daniel watched it as it slowly ascended. The Yankees had used these things before. They had seen balloons down on the peninsula, so the sight was no real novelty, but this was the closest he had ever been to the thing and it looked huge at this range, but using the thing in the middle of a battle seemed somehow unsuitable.

"It's the goddam Yankee professor up there to see the killin'," Ballard growled.

"Maybe they want to count their dead," he heard Winder's voice, from a little further along the wall where he stood with Josh and Matthew Hale.

"If they wait awhile and keep sendin' their boys up here, they'll have a hell of a lot more to count," Philipps returned.

Above their heads, they could now hear those curious buzzing sounds of minie balls passing over the wall, mixing with the smack of others hitting the stones. Notwithstanding this, Daniel raised his head and chanced a further look over the top, immediately seeing the grim aptness of the talk in the ranks. Out in front the smoke had thinned and cleared in places and he could see down the slope, beyond the garden fence remains, to where the now-dismantled fairground fence had stood. Down there the ground was littered with fallen men. They lay there, some wriggling or moving, trying to crawl or pull themselves away from this exposed and deadly place, while others twitched or trembled and still more lay sprawled and still. Daniel saw the double shoulder sections of their overcoats move and flap in a brief eddy of breeze. But then, from among them, came stabs of flame and gun smoke, proof that their uninjured comrades were still down there, mostly sheltering in that tiny, rolling swale or dip in the ground beyond where the enclosure fence had stood, with more of them down around the boards of the fence beyond, or maybe sheltering among their own dead. A minie ball smacked into the stone near to his face spraying fragments of dust and rock around and Daniel instinctively dodged down. But just as he lowered his head he glimpsed, through the clearing smoke, down between the fence and the canal gully, fresh moving columns of blue coats, topped by the rows of swaying glinting gun barrels and bayonets with flapping spreading flags above the glinting metal; more men, at least another brigade he thought, formed up and advancing. Another attack was coming.

"There's more of them on the way," he grunted to those around him. Thompson straightened up and looked, staying there for a few seconds before lowering his head again.

"They're jest clear o' the spillway," he said. Behind them Ballard stood in the trench with his musket at the ready.

"Let 'em all come on," he growled. "Sendin' 'em up here's no better'n murder."

"Maybe more like mass suicide," John Fitzpatrick said from where he stood. They all looked along towards him briefly before returning their gaze to their own front. From up on the hill behind them, the fire of the artillery, which had never really ceased, intensified once more, sending the shells tearing over their heads in groups, arcing down towards the town. It was true, Daniel thought, but, be it murder or suicide, the killing up here looked like it was far from finished. They waited for more endless seconds until, along the line, the order came again and the front rank rose up to level their weapons across the wall.

"Fire!" The crashing discharge of the muskets blanketed the wall in its evil-smelling smoke cloud making the ears cringe, then it was back to reload while the second rank stepped up to take aim and fire. The fight was on and the manic tempo of battle was among them as they went through the successive steps of loading and firing with a furious urgency, while out in front, hidden in the billowing smoke, between the artillery and the musketry, they could hear snatches of the screams of dying men.

It was now well past midday and maybe ten or fifteen minutes since the follow-up waves supporting the first attack had been repulsed. Daniel Ryan felt the sweat, whether from excitement, or tension, or fear, or maybe all three, now soaking the inside of the remains of his shirt, while his heart still pounded against his ribs. He sneaked a further look over the wall, letting his eyes run briefly across the ground in front. Out there the Yankees lay, in thicker clumps and groups, where they had been cut down by the artillery, but they were almost in ranks where they had been felled by the searing volleys of musketry from the infantry along the wall.

From the edge of that fold in the ground, and on every few yards closer, the dead and wounded lay thick, but the closest had not managed to advance much further than the remains of that dismantled fence. Farther down the slope, other enemy soldiers, who had survived the blasts of fire, sheltered, loading and firing from the farther perimeter fence or even from behind bundles of wood from the closer, dismantled fence that they had pulled together. There was now a steady sequence of their bullets slapping and chipping at the stones, while others buzzed overhead. Along the wall, southern soldiers were exchanging fire with these men, trying to bring them down or drive them away from their positions.

A scattering of them continued to leak away, the injured and the disillusioned, heading down the slope into the gully where they vanished from sight. Down towards the river they could hear, in between the crashes of cannon and musketry and the cries of the fallen, snatches of a band, or maybe more than one band, playing stirring music for the infantrymen. Ballard took a further turn at straightening up and firing, pausing briefly after his shot to look.

"Looks like there's another mess o' them on the way," he called along the line and Daniel watched the reaction as the men around them again tensed slightly, grasping their muskets, while some straightened up to see for themselves again ignoring the shouts of their sergeants to stay down. Behind them, on the road, the officers paced, but with the volume of fire now being directed at the position, the road was a dangerous place to be. The men, nearer to the wall were pretty safe, crouched in the trench that they had dug, but the road surface was that important foot or two higher than the trench bottom and by walking along there, the officers presented targets to the enemy out in front, not only to those in the swale or hunched behind fragments of the fences, but to still more who had occupied those buildings, which dotted the ground over to the left, leading down towards the edge of town.

Daniel finished his reloading and readied his musket with a new percussion cap. He drew a breath and pushed up to his feet, levelling the musket across the wall as he straightened up, aware, from a movement close by him that Philipps was doing the same. A bullet zipped past him, pulling slightly at his sleeve as he took aim at a movement among the fallen men. He started back briefly, before recovering himself and sighting again, pulling in the tiny trigger slack as he did so, then squeezing more firmly to feel the lurch of the recoil as the musket discharged. He let his eyes sweep across the field again, through the thinning gun smoke, catching glimpses of more ranks of pale blue overcoats down there beyond the ditch. Men were being funnelled off the streets and out onto the ground down there beyond the spillway to gather in crowds around the remains of the bridge. His eyes caught the movements as a few of them jumped down into the ditch as though they disdained to wait under fire for a place on those stringer beams which, thanks to yesterday's work details, were all that was left of the structure.

But nearer, on this side of the canal, just starting to emerge from the gully, came still another rank of men. Daniel ducked back down as several more bullets buzzed past him, indicating that the Yankees, who had gone to ground in the swale or even closer among their dead, were still keeping a pretty fair watch on the wall. He reached for the next cartridge and bit it open.

"Not long now," he said to those around him. "They're comin' up out o' that canal gully again." He started to reload as those around him gripped their weapons and turned to face the wall, bracing themselves for more killing. Along the trench men checked weapons and ammunition, while the few who had been hit were lifted away.

Daniel's eyes strayed on a little way along the road towards the house, where a group of men struggled to lift another prone figure on the far side of the road and now the word was speeding along the ranks like a flame. It was Cobb, for the news was being muttered by successive men. He was down and badly hurt. Men pushed and jostled from their places to look at the party who carried the general along the road, passing behind where some of the reloading had faltered with the news of his wounding. Daniel caught a brief sight of the general's face between two of his helpers. He was sitting up on whatever litter they had brought for him and, though his features were white, his eyes were bright as he called out to his men.

"It's only a wound, boys," he shouted. "It's only my leg. Hold your ground here like brave men and keep up your fire." The litter and its party moved on towards the road intersection as the sergeants took over, chivvying their men, who had stopped to look behind at the general, back to their more urgent business of readying their weapons and awaiting the next advance. The shooting between the swale and the wall was continuing unchecked, with more men taking turns to snipe at the Yankees down there. Winder pushed up and sighted quickly before sending another shot down the hill. He took a quick look along the slope before ducking down again.

"They're on the move agin," he called. "A big brigade comin' this time, six regiments." Along the line came the same order as before.

"Load to the ready!" The men saw to their pouring and ramming and then took the same positions, waiting for the onslaught to begin again.

They delivered the same blistering, initial volley into the

faces of that next formation of Yankees, getting a glimpse of their line buckling and writhing, just as the previous ones had done, as men fell and others staggered around them. Behind them the rear rank stood ready and Daniel pulled back immediately as Ballard pushed past him to the wall. He gripped another cartridge, biting the bullet away and tasting the grains in his mouth as he poured the contents into the hot barrel. In front of him, the next volley roared out, with its cloud of stinking smoke billowing around them all, as he inserted his ramrod and pushed the charge furiously home. Then Ballard was stepping back from the wall and Daniel lurched forward, as he fingered another cap from his pouch and flicked the spent one away with his little finger, pushing the fresh one over the nipple almost in the same movement. Then he was up to the wall and sighting, even as the musket scraped across the top stone. In front there was a brief glimpse through the smoke of the pale blue line, trying to return fire, the remains of their ranks almost engulfed by their fallen. Daniel squeezed the trigger, feeling the recoil jar into his shoulder and smelling the acrid smoke, then it was pull back again as Ballard finished replacing his ramrod and began to move forward once more, fumbling for a cap as he came. Daniel scrambled back, biting already at his next cartridge as he moved away.

On it went through a succession of further volleys by each rank, as, out in front, the Yankees desperately tried to reform and push forward again, but there was no chance of that, caught as they were in those sweeping blasts of canister from the guns on the hills and the flailing volleys of musketry, every twenty seconds, from the wall. Their flags tossed above the smoke cloud, as bearer after bearer was hit. But as quickly as they fell they were borne up again, by the next fool, Daniel Ryan found the thought coming to his mind, men too ready to die. But at last they were going, back into that swale, slowly at first, with some moving back while others paused for long enough to fire a last defiant shot at their tormentors along the roadside. Then beyond the retreating jumble of men, another assembling formation emerged in snatches from the dispersing smoke. Daniel looked at them. There were five regiments forming down there for this attack. He counted the flags, emerging first from the gully, his eye attracted to one in particular, a gently spreading flag above the centre regiment. It was not a Union or dark coloured state, regimental flag, but a green banner that waved in time with the movement of its bearer, together with whatever faint eddies of breeze still wafted across the fields. It spread again and he froze, for emblazoned on its folds was no bald eagle emblem of the United States, but what looked like a golden harp in a wreath. He looked at the banner, ignoring the shots that whizzed past him, simultaneously hearing a succession of shouts rise along the wall.

"Ah Jazuz God almighty," that was Mick Daley's voice to his left that brought his mind back to the present. "It's Meagher's Irish lads they're sendin' up now." Daniel's mind was suddenly in confusion as he turned again to gaze intently at the distant and emerging sight. It was true, that emerald green banner flying down there, was being flanked by lengthening lines of men. The now familiar hedge like sight of bobbing bayonets and musket barrels, which swayed rhythmically with the step of those who carried them, catching the wintry sun and glinting for a few brief seconds, before the heads of those men with their little kepi caps came into view above the line of the gully, then the shoulders and torsos in their light blue overcoats, made to look almost ghostly and mysterious for a few moments in the drifting smoke, as they started up the slope.

Above on the hill the cannon roared out without pause

and he watched the shells plunge down to explode around them tearing big gaps in those newly formed ranks of men. Daniel saw them close the gaps and come ahead, while, above them, that green flag took another idle flap which opened its folds to view and, sure enough, there was the golden harp again, the emblem of Ireland. Ireland was his own birthplace, his home, but could it still be such a thing? He was here now. All these Irish boys in this Georgia brigade were here now, in spite of having, little more than an hour or so ago completed their own assertion of their Irishness through the words of the old song. This was America and all of this was to do with America, not Ireland. But still his mind grappled with this new development, for these approaching men were Irish also. There was a bond, or a link, the same kind of thing as the one that had prompted the singing along the wall here. As Daley had said, blood was blood, they were countrymen and how could a man shoot down his own countrymen?

But, it was not even as simple as that, for as well as being Irish, however transplanted, they were here in this place because they had become Americans and not just Americans, but as southerners they had chosen their side, opting to fight for their adopted states, just as those boys coming steadily closer out there had done. So it was now simply a question of ignoring who they were and doing the job, the same job as they had on those New York boys who, with their white state flag, had come up before these latest damned fools. Out in front parts of that long double rank were, like those before them, being steadily winnowed from their neat lines by the cannon, for up behind them on the hill, the Washington artillery had again speeded up their fire on the field. Daniel watched grimly as the tearing shells smashed successive gaps in the approaching ranks, but all around him he was hearing further mutters of dismay.

Along the wall other voices were exclaiming also, for the flag, flapping weakly in the eddies of breeze, could be seen by all. Nearer to him, he heard John Fitzpatrick's voice.

"What are they doin' here? What are they doin' invadin' other men's country and burnin' and lootin' their towns? What in the hell are these stupid, bog men doin' here?" He thumped his open hand against the top stones of the wall and let out a long hard groan as he looked along at Daniel Ryan.

"They're our own flesh and blood. How can we kill them?" Daniel looked at him and then straightened up once more to look back to where the advancing men came on, as still more shells tore over their heads from the hilltop to burst above and among the approaching lines, even as they came up to the line of the surviving fairground fence. He glanced around seeing where Ballard stood beside Kane and Winder, while beyond them, Thompson and Bayfield crouched, a further step back from the trench on the road, with loaded muskets in their hands, ready to move the rear rank on up, once the first volley had been fired from the wall. Daniel returned his gaze to the slope as the pale blue ranks began to re-appear through the smoke, still closing the gaps being torn in their line as, having negotiated the surviving portions of the fence, they came up towards the swale.

"Get ready!" The order came from William Boyce, who paced behind where Ryan, Daley and Fitzpatrick now stood and looked, as the green and gold banner faltered and almost fell, but was borne up almost immediately, flying still above the men they now had to kill.

"What in the hell are you two waitin' fer?" Bayfield's voice rasped from behind them. Almost instinctively they both straightened up. Daniel looked around seeing the other men of the rear rank waiting with those nearest looking at them intently. Thompson had moved across to stand close beside Ballard.

"Those boys out there," John Fitzpatrick yelled back. "They're Irish just like we are."

"Are ya crazy," Thompson yelled from his place? "It don't matter if they're goddam man-eatin' cannibals from Africa or goddam Chinamen from China, if they're comin' up here in blue they git shot. It's goddam simple! Do it!"

"Jesus, how can we do this," Fitzpatrick groaned at Daniel Ryan?

"Don't think about it," Daniel could feel that lump in his throat and tears forming in his eyes as he yelled at him. "If we don't kill them, they'll kill us."

"Aim" Boyce called the order, to hear it relayed by the sergeants, and around them the forest of muskets were levelled over the wall. Then he looked along with a hint of uncertainty at what was now going on at some places along the road. Muskets had scraped into place along the stones, but not all of the men in the line had levelled their weapons. Daniel turned and presented the Enfield across the wall, but lowered his eyes as he did so, unable to look at what he was about to do.

"Are you f........ insane Daniel," Fitzpatrick shouted. "Anybody can see that they haven't a bloody chance out there no matter what you or I do." From behind them, Ballard's hand reached forward and he pulled at Fitzpatrick's jacket. Daniel turned and he looked at them both.

"Fire!" Around them the deafening crash of the volley came and they were immediately smothered in the choking, eye-smarting cloud of smoke.

"Step back here John," Ballard said, "step back here and jest reload," his voice was even and just audible, even with the noise of the shells and the shouts and orders from all along the line.

"I kin do that," he added, but far from taking this way out of his quandary, Fitzpatrick glared at him.

"Are you sayin' that I can't do my job," he shouted? "You're all nothing but a crowd of ignorant dirt-grubbers." Ballard drew his hand back.

"Have it your way," he said, "but if yo're gonna do yore job then ya better git started." The next rank was now at the wall and Ballard pushed his way there between Fitzpatrick and Daley, even as he, and a few more of the first rank, still hesitated.

Daley glanced across at Daniel Ryan and jerked his thumb towards Fitzpatrick.

"Doesn't surprise me any," he muttered. "He's always been soft on the real business of soldierin'."

"Maybe he still thinks he's human Mick," Daniel Ryan returned. Around them those who had faltered were bundled aside as the commands came again.

"Aim.............. Fire!"

The next volley crashed out around them and the whole space was again shrouded with the powder smoke. The men moved quickly back, to be replaced by the others while they reloaded. But Daniel had not yet fired and even as he moved forward again, and Ballard, Bayfield and Winder pushed past, he felt a surge of hot rage rise in his pounding chest. What were they doing down here? Why were they playing the role of invader? Hadn't they seen enough of tyranny in their own country? He paused there briefly, hearing the clangs behind him as the others twirled ramrods and reached for caps. Daniel Ryan swore and lunged forward to the wall, sighting as he rested his elbow on the top stone. The volley belched across the wall and the Enfield punched back into his shoulder. Then the rank was moving back, fumbling for cartridges as they went and Daniel Ryan went with them, selecting his own next shot. The other rank was pushing forward again, stepping across the trench with muskets reloaded and ready, and as Daniel spat the bullet into his own musket muzzle, the next volley thundered out, enveloping the whole area around the wall with its evil-smelling powder smoke. He finished ramming his charge and replaced the ramrod as he moved forward, hurriedly replacing the cap on his musket nipple and pulling the weapon up to his shoulder, to level it over the large flat stone in front of him and sight briefly. Beside him John Fitzpatrick still stood, a look of utter anguish and desolation on his face and tears streaming down his cheeks. Then there was a movement behind on the road and Boyce was next to him.

"Either shoot or step aside," he bellowed. Fitzpatrick looked at him and then, with his mouth tightly compressed, he turned quickly and rested his musket on the wall with the others of the rank.

"Good man," Boyce called, just as his words were drowned out by the thunder of the volley.

Out in front the mass killing proceeded in all of its intensity. The volleys of musketry crashed out every twenty seconds or so while the artillery, by the whizzing sounds the discharges made in the air as they passed overhead, had changed again to firing canister, which was bringing down whole clusters of the beleaguered Irishmen. Behind the wall, as the frantic loading, firing and exchanging of ranks went on, the men could see little of those out in front. But every few seconds, as the smoke of one volley thinned and before the next one blanketed the area anew, they caught sight of that green flag with its golden harp, tossing and torn by the bullets that tore through its folds, but each time it came back into sight it was a little closer than before and each time it fell, someone out there lifted it again and kept it moving towards the wall. They were still coming. They had not yet been stopped by the hurricane of fire that they faced. Their line had been shredded, but in isolated groups they were still advancing, and from the wall they could catch occasional glimpses of them, out there among their dead and wounded, leaning forward, with hunched shoulders, into the hail of fire as though advancing into a gale of wind, but showing a kind of courage and heart-rending resolve that Daniel Ryan thought was surely a shining credit to any Irishman.

As this notion flashed through his mind, his attention was taken by a difference about their caps, for through the gaps in the smoke cloud, he had seen that they wore little sprigs of green in them. Were they shamrock? He could not tell, but the sight of them brought a further lump to his throat and tears welled anew from his eyes as he sighted and fired, in time with the rest of the rank at the wall, but as he moved back and the smoke drifted, still the remains of those ranks out in front stood, refusing to break and retreat and he felt a further tinge of admiration for the valour of these brave, afflicted men. He set once more to his reloading, hearing the next volley belch out, hoping as he turned again towards the wall that they would have pulled back, but still they had not. It was wasted, utterly futile, and it would only prolong their suffering and bring death to still more of them. Daniel Ryan, saw it all go relentlessly on as he aimed and fired and turned to move away and reload once more, now weeping bitterly and feeling the salty tears course down his cheeks as he did so. Here, on this field in Virginia, a lifetime from his birthplace, he must continue to kill, sending shot after shot into these convulsing, tormented ranks of his own countrymen.

It seemed to go on and on, much longer than the previous attacks had done, and Daniel was almost oblivious to the bullets splintering shards of stone from the wall in front of him, every time he stepped up to fire. The return fire continued to spatter in, from who knew whom, whether it was the decimated ranks of the Irish brigade or others of the enemy who remained out there from previous attacks, hidden on the ground among their own dead and wounded. Finally, the storm of musketry seemed to slacken and as the smoke began to drift and eddy, the scene in front of the wall emerged from the dispersing white gloom. Over onto the slope they looked as the shots continued to pepper the wall and whizz over it. The ranks of bodies lay out there, as they had since the first attack, with many inert and still, while others wriggled and writhed or tried to crawl to the rear, but they lay so much thicker now, with places where dead or dying men lay sprawled on top of others. They were nearer too, now lying less than forty yards from the wall and, on looking more closely, Daniel could see that some of these nearest fallen enemies, in their flapping light blue greatcoats, wore that little sprig of green in their caps that looked so much like shamrock from any distance. He slumped down behind the stones again, while, up behind them on the hill, the guns kept up their fire, which must mean that still more Yankees were on the way up, impossible to see down here in the smoke, but likely visible from up on the hill. Philipps took a turn at looking, staying upright only briefly as the shots continued to pepper the wall.

The sergeants were shouting along, calling their men to load to the ready and around Daniel there came the latest clatter of ramrods. Then the noises at the wall diminished as the men waited, the front rank leaning against the stones, with their muskets almost upright and each man with his back foot in the trench. Above them the shells tore over in salvoes, their fuses glowing orange as they passed. They waited for the order for what seemed an eternity, until Boyce's voice came to them at last, above the din of gunfire and cheering.

"Up men and take aim!" The front rank rose almost as

one and the musket barrels scraped on the top stones as they were levelled. Daniel took a brief aim centring the muzzle button on the groove in the Enfield's rear sight.

"Fire!" The musket lunged back into his tender shoulder as the smoke mushroomed outwards and upwards from the wall. He stepped away, fingering his next cartridge and feeling Daley push back beside him. Daniel caught a glimpse of that grin on his face as he bit the paper of the next cartridge.

They fired six more volleys before the call came along to load to the ready once more. Along the line men sank down to rest against the stones of the wall. Daniel felt the sweat soaking his torso and legs as he looked along the road, seeing the duel with the lurking Yankees in the swale resume. In the distant town, in between the artillery discharges, they could still hear snatches of a band playing "Yankee Doodle," and adding something that was almost comic to the whole tragedy unfolding out in front of them. It was as though these men were dying to music, spilling their blood and draining their lives out here beyond the millrace while others, back there out of range, fingered their cornets and trombones, beat their drums and tapped their feet in time.

Daniel looked round as a flurry of movement came along the line towards them. It was Boyce and Jeffers and they were with another unfamiliar officer, who led a double rank of men along the road behind the wall, pausing every few yards to station still more men behind those already there, congesting the road still further with defenders, as they moved along. The newcomers pushed forward into the trench, forcing the Georgians, who had held the wall thus far, back onto the road behind.

"Who are you boys," he heard Ballard grunt as he moved past the arrivals?

"Forty Sixth North Carolina, Hall's brigade," the

nearest man answered as he stepped into the trench and Daniel moved to let him look out over the wall. All along the road other men were stepping away as still more arrived to push past them and rest their weapons on the top stones. There was almost an enthusiasm in the way some of them moved into position, as though they could hardly wait to get started, in contrast with some of the Georgians, who seemed to step away wearily as still more of the newcomers arrived. Daniel looked around, letting his eyes move along the road. The arrival of these Carolinians was crowding the space along the road at the wall. Various sergeants were pushing and bellowing at their men, trying to organise them into proper ranks. These were now four deep, in the places where the NCOs had managed to form them, but with still more men arriving their task was far from complete. As the men gradually formed, officers moved along, rasping out instructions as to the fire drill that would now be employed. Minute by minute, this deadly place was becoming even more deadly, literally bristling with long musket barrels which glinted and gleamed in the dazzling reflections of the now passing sun. Further shouts now rang out along the wall.

"More comin'!"

"They're formin' down thar again!"

Daniel stretched upwards again to see, through the drifting smoke, the next wave of the enemy moving up from the spillway, again advancing from the Hanover Street side, with their union flags of stars and stripes, and their regimental eagles, spaced out along their long ranks. There were even more of them this time. Daniel counted briefly along the sets of colours he could see. There were nine regiments down there, astride Hanover Street, with those nearest, advancing on a diagonal line towards the upper end of the fairground, gaining a measure of cover from the buildings there, but convulsing nevertheless as the artillery shells tore over to explode among or above them.

"More poor bloody lambs to the slaughter," he muttered, realising as he said the words that, after the previous assault by Meagher's Irishmen, he had begun to lapse into that fatal process of seeing the enemy as people. But they were people, living breathing men, who wrote home to their mothers, wives and sweethearts like anyone else did. Men who had wet feet and blisters on their heels and smarting eyes, like everybody else had, but here they came, pushed into place rather more than the previous formations by their file closers, for they could see clearly what had happened to those who had gone ahead of them. All of this went through Daniel Ryan's mind as this latest formation came on. It could be fatal to think this way, for it reduced a man's resolve to something like jelly. It was one of the first lessons of soldiering, never to see them as people, for it became so much harder to shoot them if you began to think of them in that way. Better not to think but just let the training and drilling take over, loading and firing as automatically as one could, it was much better that way.

He glanced down again. Still the approaching ranks came on, enduring a storm of artillery fire from the hill behind the wall. Great gaps were being torn in their formations as their left regiments came up to the wooden fence that marked the side of the fairground enclosure. As they struggled across what remained of this obstruction, their officers and sergeants pushed them bodily to close the gaps and maintain some kind of cohesion in their ranks. They were still coming on, even as the first volley of musketry from the wall tore through them. A second volley blasted away and then it was the turn of Ryan's rank. They pushed forward muskets held vertically to plant elbows briefly on the stones and take fleeting aim. Then the deafening blast of fire and the violent kick of the recoil before it was back into the road, to begin the reloading again. Daniel Ryan moved back, already biting at his next cartridge, while around him the ranks changed places. He gritted his teeth as he pulled his ramrod clear. They had learned nothing from the slaughter which had taken place so far and so there was nothing to do but go on killing and put any finer instincts as far from one's mind as possible. Still the fire from muskets and cannon tore into them, visible through eddies and drifting gaps in the smoke, but they were going now, in the same ways as previous formations had done, with some men moving back, away into the smoke while others dropped down for the shelter of the swale. The remains of the enemy ranks steadily dissolved until the order to cease firing came along the line and the smoke began to drift away and the ground in front began to clear.

From the swale the musketry began again and the men at the wall ducked down for shelter as bullets began to buzz and ricochet past once more. Along the crouching ranks men were rubbing and polishing at their muskets trying to remove the black powder fouling, which increased the chance of a misfire and made the recoil more violent. Daniel Ryan did likewise, scrubbing at the lock with the sleeve of his tunic. The artillery fire from the hill roared on without pause, suggesting that the respite would not be for long. Ryan rummaged in his pocket for one of the three, blue-wrapped, "cleaner," cartridges that he had gathered there and loaded it carefully, before settling then to await events.

Sure enough, within minutes more shouts came along the wall.

"More comin'!"

"They're comin' up along the railroad."

Daniel pushed himself to his feet and looked down the

slope. This time the Yankees were approaching by the other flank and again there were big brigades on their way, moving up on either side of the rail tracks. Daniel counted ten sets of colours before dropping down behind the shelter of the wall once more.

"Stubborn cusses," he said to the others as he gestured towards the enemy line of approach. Ballard spat.

"It's cartridges now," he said, "same as up at that goddam bridge in Maryland."

The shells continued to fly over in their salvoes with the detonations down on the slope mixing with the discharges from the cannon. Still the men waited behind the stones of the wall, some of them fidgeting as they crouched there, running fingers up and down the wooden stocks of weapons, wiping or scratching at themselves, anticipating the order that would commence the next episode of killing, while the sergeants kept their eyes fixed on the officers, anticipating the call.

Out in front on the field, the Yankees had reached that swale of ground which hid the lower halves of their bodies. But then their legs began to re-appear as they ascended out of the dip and along the wall the men began to move.

"Up boys, up!" It was Bayfield's voice and the front rank pushed to their feet, hearing the Yankee fire from the swale intensify as they rose above the top stones of the wall. A few men fell back as they made ready, brought down by the hail of bullets, but the vast majority were unhurt as they settled their muskets and aimed briefly at the enemy ranks which had just cleared the swale to reach the remains of the fence.

"Fire!" The blast of musketry belched out again from the kicking weapons and the rank moved back past the three waiting formations of men.

The shouts of command were in danger of being lost now

lost now in the ear-splitting crashes of sound and there was little to be seen in the colossal billow of smoke. Along that wall, the flash of bright yellow flame repeatedly stabbed out with its attendant cloud of off-white smoke, thickening the remains from the previous volleys until there was virtually nothing to aim at. In front of Daniel and his comrades there was a wrestling wriggling movement along the wall as the front rank quickly pushed past to the rear, with their places being taken by the next rank, who levelled their muskets even as they still moved to the wall. Out in front dim images of the enemy formation began to appear for an instant or two through the dispersing smoke, but those front ranks of blue seemed to have simply vanished. Then more shouts and the blast of fire from the wall was repeated and now these men moved back and it was the next rank's turn, while the reloading went on behind on the road. Another blasting volley, followed by the momentary confusion as the ranks changed, with still another line levelling their weapons to take brief aim on the struggling enemy. It was back to the first rank again and Daniel pushed forward, sighting into the smoke as he settled the Enfield on the top stone of the wall at the order from Boyce. The smoke was still thick out in front, with only vague light blue shapes visible when the order to fire was bellowed along, the shouted order, like those before it, immediately lost in the torrent of musketry. Daniel felt the recoil of the weapon lurch painfully back into his shoulder and he immediately pushed away from the wall, reaching already for a cartridge, and almost stumbling on the edge of the trench, as the next rank with Kane, Ballard and Jones, their faces grim and tight with tension, pushed past to the wall. On he pushed out onto the middle of the road, biting already at the cartridge paper as he went.

Three times more Daniel Ryan stepped up with his rank to the wall to deliver further sweeping volleys of fire at the writhing mass of blue, which tried to reform just forward of where the remains of the board fence lay just forward of the swale. That fence, already pulled down, was nothing but a few fragmants of broken boards collected by the Yankee survivors as some kind of shelter, with even these now splintered and savaged by bullets. To this side of it was the real killing ground and these men, were no more able to survive there than any of those who had preceded them had been. They too were now breaking, moving back down into the swale or on down behind the splintered, farther fence to crouch or lie there with at least a semblance of cover from the blasts of lead from the wall. The artillery still flailed at them, with some guns sticking to the great shotgun sprays of canister balls, while others had returned to firing shell on the Yankees who streamed away from the swale and the fence remains down the slope towards the spillway ditch beyond. The men at the wall had ceased firing and were called back to re-order their ranks and check weapons and ammunition.

"More of 'em comin up!" The shouts were ringing along the wall again and a succession of heads, particularly among the newcomers, bobbed up to look. A fusillade of shots rang out from the swale and the fence, causing a few of those behind the stones to topple backwards from their places as the heavy bullets caught them with those sickening, squelching thuds. Sergeants moved among their men.

"Git down outa there!"

"Git yore head down afore ya lose it!" Most of them did so, crouching down behind the stones to wait for the word, but a few could not resist the temptation to look, risking the musketry to do so, and they kept their comrades informed as to what was happening down on the slope.

"They're straight ahead this time."

"Whole damn slope's covered with 'em."

Once again, from the hill behind them, the artillery fire swelled, with the salvoes of shells tearing overhead with greater frequency. The bombardment went on, until the calls came along from the officers and NCOs.

"Front rank, on your feet!"

"Ready boys!"

Now, with the more closely packed ranks at the wall, there was hardly room for men to manoeuvre their weapons, but the first discharge of fire resembled a great stabbing barb of yellow flame, wreathed in its shrouding cloud of smoke and deafening in its thunderous noise. Daniel felt his ears buzz and cringe as the next rank moved up, pushing in as the front men withdrew, and within seconds the wall was again shrouded with flame and smoke as the assault on his ears was repeated. The smoke swallowed everything along the wall, catching and irritating throats and eyes and prompting an epidemic of coughing among the men along the line. The fourth volley roared out and now it was back to the Georgians. Daniel Ryan stepped up, with the others of Company B, only to find, as he reached the wall and levelled his musket, there was nothing out in front to aim at. There was only a huge bank of choking, engulfing smoke into which their next crashing volley of shots went, adding its own cloud to the billows out in front. Then away and the next rank was up as Daniel Ryan pushed back while fumbling another cartridge from his pouch, the Carolinians first line were already poised there waiting their next turn. These volleys were now stabbing out at ten second intervals, stupefying in their intensity of sound and fury, making that ground out in front an utter death trap for the advancing blue lines as on the killing went, completely blind now, until the shouts came at last.

"Cease firing!"

"Load to the ready!" The deafening blasts halted and

the smoke slowly began to thin and drift as the men looked down across the wall, to see the extent of the execution, before they again became targets for the surviving Yankees, who lurked out there in the swale and in that red brick house just along to their left.

All along the wall the voices of the men launched into yells and whoops and chatter as the officers bellowed at those around them to move them back into order. Out on the slope an utter tangle of fallen blue shapes littered the ground, from in front of the fence remains back down towards the swale. Some of the recently-arrived Carolina boys were openly jubilant at the apparent ease with which the enemy had been repulsed.

"It's a goddam turkey shoot," one kept shouting to his companions.

"Plenty o' blue-bellied turkeys comin' up fer pluckin'," one of them yelled back. Behind them, the men of Company B squatted down in the road to gain maximum shelter from the wall as the hail of enemy bullets, from the buildings and the swale out in front, swept in with renewed intensity, causing those at the wall to duck down hastily. Behind them, the sun was moving lower in the sky now, but Daniel Ryan felt utterly drenched with sweat. Around him other men behind the wall still occupied themselves by returning the fire of the enemy snipers hidden out in front. Many North Carolinians gleefully took this up, but none of Daniel's mess did so. Their ammunition was low and most of their muskets were fouled from use and their shoulders bruised and tender from the recoiling weapons. Daniel checked his ammunition. He had begun the day, with sixty plus rounds, but his pouch was near to empty now, with just eight shots left. He looked to his musket, the metal parts of which were still searingly hot to touch. The lock and barrel were again thick with the dirty black residue from the gunpowder and, in company with many of those around him, he set to cleaning the weapon. He tried to gather saliva in his mouth to spit on the lock, but his mouth was dry and his throat parched so he had to content himself with trying to rub the black deposit away from the nipple and hammer, with his fingers and his sleeve, before pulling the sharp-pointed pricker from his pouch, to push down through the hole in the nipple, scraping and twisting it to prise the fouling out of it and ready it for further use. He polished hard at the Enfield, succeeding in getting the worst of the residue removed and this done, pulled one of his remaining cartridges from his pouch and reloaded. Out beyond the wall, a lull seemed to have set in, with no word of further enemy approaches along the streets leading up from town and Daniel with the others of his mess crouched along the road, leaning on their upright muskets, getting what respite they could from this pause in the Yankee onslaughts.

The low winter sun was near to setting, moving down closer to the brow of the hill behind them, when the next shout came to warn of a further approach. Daniel chanced a look from where he was, in spite of the bullets which still hummed and buzzed across the wall. He swept his gaze along the whole front before ducking down again. Kane caught his eye and cocked his head inquisitively, while the others around them looked on.

"They comin' back up to start again," he grated?

"There's more of 'em up on the street to the left," Daniel told him, "and there's another crowd workin' their way up on the other flank, but they ain't deployin' out in front yet." Fitzpatrick looked across.

"Reckon they're tryin' to flank us out of here." Ballard was looking on and he spat before commenting.

"Ain't no wall up on the left. The Phillips' Legion boys

got some o' their men up t' where it ends and there's tarheels up beyond that. They were diggin' up there yesterday, but I reckon they'll still be a better target than we are down here." As he finished, speaking, the artillery fire from behind them on the hill speeded up again, while, along the road, the officers began to call their men into ranks. Rodger came along the line calling to them.

"Get ready boys, be ready," he yelled, "but look to your left when the time comes. The Yankees ain't out in front. They're pushing on the flanks this time." Along the road, ramrods clanged on barrels as the men who had spent time exchanging shots with the Yankees out in front reloaded. The musketry from the buildings and the swale out in front, intensified as they readied themselves, the balls giving their peculiar buzzing sound as they whizzed past, with an occasional lurching stagger among the men along the road as one of these enemy bullets found a target.

They waited, tensing themselves, while the guns crashed their shells over their heads and out towards the lines of approach. Daniel looked up, seeing the smoky paths of the shells, trailing through the crystal clear, winter sky overhead, more vividly now as the light began to dim, spotting an occasional orange gleam of a fuse as the shells themselves passed over. They could hear snatches of the deep yelling shouts and cheers of the Yankee infantry, as they approached and then the order came along the line and the first rank of Carolinians rose up to the wall, aiming briefly before the crash of hundreds of muskets deafened the ears and the stink of the dirty powder cloud assailed the eyes and nostrils of everyone once again. Daniel tensed, while, in front of him, the second rank men pushed forward as those of the first rank shoved backwards to reload. His heart was pounding again, thumping hard against his chest at a colossal rate as further beads of sweat formed on his face and began to trickle down, in spite of the chill of the afternoon returning as the sun sank. The second volley crashed out, blanketing the wall and the road with further smoke and noise, and then it was time and Daniel pushed forward, as he heard Boyce's hoarse bellow, elbowing past the men coming back and sliding his musket across the wall. In front of his face, the bullets were buzzing in, slapping against the stones of the wall and sending splinters of stone and dust flying up. He sighted briefly to the left into the smoke and pulled the trigger feeling the kick of the discharge, smelling the smoke and hearing the ear-splitting crash that made his head cringe. Fragments of stone spun into his face as he pulled away and then it was another brief glimpse of Kane and Jones, their faces grimly set as they pushed forward to the wall. Daniel tore at his next cartridge with his teeth, fumbling the open end of the paper over the barrel to tip the black powder inside, while still gripping the conical slug with his lips. The next volley had crashed out and the original rank was pushing forward again all around him, as he spat the bullet into the barrel followed by its paper wad, before pulling at his ramrod, twirling it in his fingers as he manoeuvred it over the barrel muzzle to ram the charge home. Then the fifth volley bellowed out and the smoke cloud engulfed them once again as tangles of men pushed forward or backwards in their turn.

The road was a bedlam of noise, and sweat, and stink, and fear, with more men on this side of the wall now collapsing to the ground from the fire of the enemy who sheltered out in front, who no longer faced return fire with the men at the wall concentrating their efforts on the advancing lines to the left of them beyond the first road. On it went for volley after volley, until, after a time, the enemy seemed to have pulled back whereupon the fire of the men at the wall was diverted to the other flank, by the frantic shouts of the officers and sergeants, to where the unfinished railroad gully ran and where another enemy formation had come forward towards the Telegraph Road. Still the musketry blasted from the wall, flailing into the smoke out in front, until the call finally came to cease firing as the enemy fell back on that flank also. These formations too left a further set of their men behind, sheltering in the railroad bed and adding their fire to that of the other Yankees out in front on the field in the buildings and along the edge of the swale.

The men crouched or sat to gain the best shelter from the wall as Thompson came along behind the lines, stooping as he came to avoid the worst of the enemy fire, shouting to them to check their ammunition and caps. Daniel pushed his fingers into the waterproofed pouch once more, knowing, from his fumbling for the last rounds he had fired, that he was quickly running short. There were three cartridges there. His fingers eased around them in turn and he looked at the others around him.

"Four!" Daley said.

"Five!" Winder grunted. The others muttered their own totals, knowing now that unless there was more sent down, a further attack could overwhelm them.

"It's like back at that damn bridge up north," Ballard growled. "We got pushed off there cuz we ran out."

"We kin hold 'em all day here," Daley called to any around him who would listen. "But they've got to give us bullets. We can't fight 'em without bullets."

"Maybe the Carolina boys got more," Philipps said. "They ain't been here as long as we have."

"Likely," Ballard said, "but it won't be long till, they're out too if the Yankees keep comin'."

Daniel had started work on his musket again and, watching him, some of the others did likewise, scraping and rubbing at the black barrel deposits that made the weapons less effective. He was still rubbing when he found himself being jostled by still more men arriving on the road around him. He pushed to his feet in time to see further files of soldiers in butternut brown, crowding their way along the road, spacing themselves out in yet more ranks behind those who already waited there. On the order, they too crouched to gain the shelter of the wall. Ballard spoke to one.

"And which of the fair southern commonwealths are you boys from," he inquired, with feigned politeness?

"South Carolina boys," the youth answered. "Second Regiment, Joe Kershaw's brigade, come to show you boys how to shoot Yankees."

"We've had a fair lot of practice doin' that already," Daniel told him.

"We're willin' to give you boys a turn at it," Philipps shouted, "'specially since we ain't got hardly anythin' left to shoot at them."

"Stand aside and pay a good heed then," another Carolinian, who sported carpet scraps around his feet, called along. "This here's our favourite thing fer passin' the time." The two of them grinned conspiratorially at each other, apparently highly amused with their wit. The first soldiers reached inside their jackets and pulled out bundles of cartridges, followed by still more.

"They gave us extra bundles to bring down," he said. Others of the newcomers were doing the same thing, passing the paper-wrapped bundles along to the Georgians. Ballard laughed at Daley.

"The generals must'a' heard ya up there, Mick," he drawled.

"They should listen to me more often," Daley retorted. "If they did we'd be in Washington by now." Daniel Ryan took one of the proferred bundles, looked at it and grimaced briefly as he recognised Springfield ammunition.

Springfield muskets were the American cousins of the British made Enfields, that the Ogeechee Volunteers carried, but they were .58 calibre compared to the Enfield's .577. Fouled barrels of either weapon made it increasingly difficult to ram bullets home, but it was well known that the marginally larger barrel of a Springfield, even one fouled from use, could always take the slightly smaller Enfield ball. A newly cleaned and greased Enfield barrel could just take a Springfield Minie ball, but in a fouled Enfield barrel there was no chance of successfully ramming the .58 charge. Some men in other regiments had, over the preceding months, re-equipped themselves with captured or discarded Springfield muskets, which many Yankee units carried, in order to avoid this problem. In Company B however, there had remained a preference for the slightly better balance and for the adjustable sighting slide on the Enfield, which was better for aiming purposes. As a result, all along the line, a confusion of coming and going with cartridge packs was taking place. Men were exchanging Springfield bundles for Enfield ones as far as they could and, encouraged by their officers, they were passing the packages on down if they were unsuitable for the weapon they carried.

This replenishing was still going on when more shouts from further along the wall brought another buzz of activity to the crowded road. Men stretched up, taking their chances with the enemy fire to risk a look.

"They're deployin' again," Kane shouted. "They're down near the gully makin' up their minds what to do." The Carolinian, with the carpet scraps on his feet turned to him.

"I'll tell 'em what to do," he yelled. "Bring them good ol' boots and winter coats on up here Yanks!"

Along the nearest stretch of the wall there was a shout of enthusiasm at his words, even while, all around them, the officers and sergeants laboured anew to form their men so that there were now five crowded and congested ranks lining the Telegraph Road.

The attack, heralded by another hail of artillery fire, came on as the afternoon began to wane and it followed the same sequence of events as those which had gone before it. The enemy were flailed by the artillery all the way up the slope and then set upon by the infantry behind the wall as they emerged from the swale and reached the splintered wooden fence. Here the fallen from the previous attacks lay thick and this helped throw the approaching formations into still more confusion, as the hail of lead and iron tore through them. Along the wall, with five ranks of men taking their turn, the killing efficiency had reached a new intensity, with the changeover of ranks, in the overcrowded space, being the main difficulty that the men now faced. The deep, flaring yellow flashes of the mass musketry discharges were becoming more vivid and dramatic as the daylight waned, spiking out from the wall and illuminating the men who laboured there, in lurid yellow light at less than ten second intervals. Out in front the latest attack, like all of those preceding it, faltered around the swale, with brief images coming through the billowing smoke, of the Yankees, cajoled by their officers and sergeants, attempting to reform and press on. But it was futile to stay out there, let alone press ahead, while that musketry lashed them again and again and the killing ground devoured still more victims, with whole ranks of men being felled by a single volley. Eventually it was enough. The falter became a stall and the stall became a process of dropping among the moving mass of men in the swale, while some edged backward until the edging back became a full retreat. Behind the wall the orders were yelled along and the firing ceased. Men crouched down again into the shelter, while renewing their efforts to clean their muskets as still more brown paper packets of cartridges were passed along the lines and eventually, to his relief, with nothing remaining in his pouch, Daniel Ryan, and the others of Company B around him, fell heir to a sequence of Enfield cartridge bundles.

Daniel crouched across on the far side of the road, working furiously at the lock of his musket, vainly trying to spit on the fouled metal then rubbing at it with his sleeve. Cleaner bullets helped but did not entirely clear the barrel. It really needed a thorough washing and greasing, but there was no chance of that. His shoulder ached from the recoil, even though he had done his best to follow the drill advice, to pull the weapon tightly in to his shoulder when firing, in order to minimise its effects, but the weapons kicked steadily worse as the fouling with powder residue increased and Minie balls became steadily harder to ram down the clogged barrel. He looked around to where other men were urinating into the barrels to dislodge the black residue. It helped up to a point, if you were able to rub the moistened mess away with a cloth pushed through the hole in the ramrod button and then clear the priming hole with the metal prickers. But there was limited time between the attacks, and besides the musket stank abominably when further firing reheated the barrel and whatever remained of the urine? Beside him Daley was busy on the same remedy and seeing this, Daniel resolved to do likewise in spite of the stink. He unbuttoned the flap of his pants, seeing Ballard grin ironically at him as he did so.

"Stink ain't as bad as the kick," he said. Daniel pulled a sour face.

"Only just," he replied, feeling the urine slosh over the hot barrel and onto his fingers as they steadied it.

He cursed and turned to attend more carefully to the

operation and was still engaged in this as the news came along that Rodger was down. The captain had been taken to the rear, so Kane reckoned, hit by a minie ball from one of those many Yankees who still lurked out in front. It was a shoulder wound that the captain had sustained, Kane added, and he should therefore live.

The benign heat of the afternoon had faded, with the sun now down behind the brow of the hill behind them, when the Yankees came on again. This time they came up from the Hanover Street side, using those additional buildings and walls for shelter as they approached, before deploying for their push across the open ground towards the wall. They gathered again around the canal overspill, with many grouping around the remains of the bridge, though others could be glimpsed descending into the gully to wade across. Gradually their ranks formed, with more and more men having crossed the millrace now taking their places. Men behind the wall bobbed up and down, watching the spectacle in the evening light, whose shadows had not yet reached the lower part of the slope. They were able to see it all relatively clearly this time, for, as every man behind the wall had now become aware, the cannon fire from the hill behind them, that had punished every previous attack, had ceased. The fire from the swale and from the buildings out in front continued without pause, but the field with only drifting musket smoke hanging over it, was somehow a different place.

Down at the millrace, the enemy formations had finished their deployment and stepped away. There were four regiments, gathered in the section of ground just south of Hanover Street, but they had begun their advance on a narrow frontage of just two regiments, with the additional two following behind. Daniel Ryan risked the whizzing bullets to take another look, as still the Confederate cannon on the hill remained silent. Other more distant batteries had begun to take the enemy under fire, but the difference was pointed. With no cannon firing from the hill, this formation of Yankees was being allowed to approach with relative ease compared to the others. Along the wall there were shouts of dismay.

"Why don't they lay into 'em?"

"What in the hell's wrong up thar?"

"Where are those goddam guns?"

Daniel Ryan risked a further look to see that still more Yankees were emerging from the millrace gully to begin forming further ranks. What looked like another brigade, of four more regiments, was preparing to support those who had already started their advance. Whatever had gone wrong with the Confederate artillery on the hill was now allowing these Yankees to co-ordinate their attack in a way that no previous formation had done, and anxious shouts continued pulsing along behind the wall. Daniel ducked down again as still more bullets whizzed past or chipped at the stones around him. The leading four regiments had almost reached the farther fairground fence, but here too they were reaping an advantage, for this was no longer an appreciable obstacle, with much of it having been demolished by gunfire, while further sections of it had been pulled down by men from the previous attacks. Daley bobbed up to look, but lowered his head almost immediately as a bullet sprayed dust and chips of stone into his face.

"They're gittin' goddam close," was his only comment.

Behind them Kershaw passed going north, with a cloth tied around a bloodstained arm and two orderlies trying to keep pace among the crowd of men in the road.

"Stand by boys," was his comment as he passed. "Be ready and wait for the order."

Daniel Ryan cocked his musket and raised his head for

a further look. My god those Yankees were close. They had almost reached the swale, but even as his mind registered this thought, his ears were numbed by a colossal crash of artillery fire from behind and above. A ragged cheer rang along the stone wall and in the instant before the whole field was smothered once again in smoke, he saw whole files and groups of the enemy blasted by the canister fire. Men fell, while others around them were flung backwards like rag dolls. Ryan felt his stomach heave at the sight of body pieces flying as the concentrated cannon fire struck the formed ranks at close range. As he made to duck down, he heard the shout of command from Carson.

"Front rank, up boys and ready!" Daniel checked his downward momentum and pushed back up, levelling the musket as he rose above the wall.

"Aim!" the call gave just a second or two to sight along the barrel.

"Fire!" The wall around him seemed to explode as the crowded rank of muskets discharged. The Enfield punched back into his aching shoulder and he was immediately on his way back as more men pushed past him to take the space at the wall. Daniel and the others jostled their way past the waiting ranks, as they rummaged in their pockets or pouches for another cartridge.

Once more the volleys of musketry crashed out from the wall with fearful regularity, competing with the renewed cannon fire to halt the enemy advance, turning it into the same slaughter for the stalled blue formations as before. These men too stood for a brief time, with their flags tossing in the smoke, sometimes visible in glimpses from the Confederate line, trying to return fire on those who were cutting them down in swathes. Then their formations also began to leak men, with some drifting to the rear, while others dropped down among those in the swale, defeated by the deadly combination of close range canister from the southern artillery and the deadly, searing regularity of the musket volleys from the wall.

It was almost dark and nearly half an hour had passed since the previous attack. It was the time when hostilities always ceased, in acknowledgement of the impossibility of managing to manoeuvre bodies of men or conduct any sort of an attack without confusion overtaking the thing and costing further men's lives as a result. Many of those along the middle section of the stone wall, in common with others to either side, permitted themselves the luxury of stepping across the road, allowing pounding pulses to slow, wiping the rivulets of sweat from their powder-blackened faces and easing the shoulders and limbs pounded and bruised by the hours of musket recoils. Suddenly a scream came from the far right, which spread along the road. All around Daniel Ryan men froze for an instant, before lunging back to their posts at the wall. Already, ragged fusilades of renewed musketry were breaking out along that southern portion of the road and the vivid, yellow flashes of the discharges, now startlingly bright in the near darkness, revealed glimpses of still another blue formation out in front, who had approached quietly in the dusk and now seemed closer to the wall than any of the earlier attacks had managed to approach.

"By Jasus," Daley shouted. "They haven't gotten the idea yet have they?" Philipps' reply was lost in the roar of their own volley, and as he fired in the instant before the smoke obscured everything, Daniel caught a glimpse of the ghoulish faces of the enemy and saw the flash of the musketry illuminate brass buttons on the blue overcoats. Behind them Colonel McMillan of the Twenty Fourth Regiment had arrived, limping heavily, but with his sword in his hand. The colonel was bellowing hoarsely between the volley firing, calling the men to steadiness, re-establishing order in their fire drill, after the near surprise that the ranks at the wall had suffered.

"Let's pour it on," he was yelling, "but steady now boys. In your ranks and keep it steady. They won't stand it long." Up on the crest, the cannon had opened up again, but some of their fire was overshooting, whether from the difficulty of marking targets in the darkness and smoke, or through being unable to depress cannon muzzles enough to bear on the head of the column. This attack, Daniel thought grimly, would have to be stopped by the muskets of the exhausted infantry. But, around him, the men had responded to the shouts of the officers and the pushing and cajoling of their sergeants. The ranks were regular now, mixed up, with men of different units in each one to be sure, but fire discipline had quickly re-established itself and the volleys were back to the same regular precision that had met all of the previous attacks.

McMillan was right, they wouldn't stand it for long. Nobody could stand up to that renewed torrent of fire. They would break, they would fall back and then it would be over. This whole sanguine day of killing would be over at last and then there would be the chance to rest. The notions jumbled through Daniel Ryan's mind as he loaded and fired his remaining shots, taking his turn at the wall as before, to discharge the bucking musket into the great smoke cloud, before stepping away again for others to take their turn. Why, those volleys, from the five or six ranks of men in the roadway, were being delivered every few seconds, and was that enemy return fire, spattering the wall and buzzing overhead, slackening at last? He hardly dared to think of it, but it was true. They were going, whether floundering back or dropping down like all of the earlier ones had done, but they were going, while still the fire lashed at them from the roadway without a hint of slackening. Then a shout came from the powerful voice of Joe Kershaw, as he pushed along the roadway, calling on them to cease firing. It was over, Daniel Ryan thought, at last it was over and he was alive.

He stood there still feeling the trembling in his limbs and the pounding of his heart, those things which afflicted him every time, but now it was over and they would begin to pass. Perhaps, with the near surprise of that last attack, there was a further element of fright or fear in him, but now it was done with. He lowered the Enfield, letting the butt thud to the ground as the stock and the burning hot barrel slid through his wet fingers. In contrast to all of those men who now lay out there, with the sound of their cries and screams beginning to be heard in competition with the ragged, fading gunfire, he and those of his mess had survived. They were unhurt, beyond the bruises from loading and firing the brutally kicking muskets for those long hours of daylight. He stepped back breathing heavily, aware of others of the mess and the company around him. Fitzpatrick was there, just recognisable in the almost complete darkness, his face black and streaked with stripes of powder and sweat, and Philipps and Kane and Ballard and the three black men, Winder and Josh, the tall one, and Matthew. They were within yards of where he stood, soiled, dishevelled and haggard, with expressions of strain and weariness on their faces, while their eyes, in the gloom of the now arrived night, seemed more prominent in their expressions and features.

"Goddam long day o' killin'," Ballard grunted. Daniel sensed rather than saw a succession of nods from those around him.

"We musta gotten thousands of 'em," Daley was saying. "That whole slope out there's covered an' there's piles o' them down at the dip." Daniel looked at him, not really wanting to think about how many were dead and dying only yards from where he now leaned on his musket. He turned, lifting the weapon as he did so, and moved away with the others, crouching to keep his head under some sort of cover from the wall. He reached the far side of the road once more and sat down on the bank, presently lying back into the cold, damp grass.

Jeffers was coming along, seeking his own men, trying to separate them from the various other commands, who milled behind the wall. Daniel heard his voice, not catching the words among the jumble of talk all around them, the continued sniping and the increasing screams and cries of the injured from the darkness, though knowing that Jeffers was on his way meant that whatever respite they managed to gain would be brief. But the fight was over, at least for today, and there had never been a day like this in his life before. The simple scale of the slaughter that had taken place out there on that sloping ground, between the wall and the fairground, and on to the spillway beyond, was worse than even Maryland in its intensity. He however had survived it. He was alive and, though bruised, begrimed and exhausted, he was unhurt. He had cheated death again and his thumping heart rate was at last beginning to slacken.

Chapter 4 Light in the Darkness

The cold had returned with the setting of the sun, the same harsh, penetrating cold as on the previous nights, carried on the same north westerly wind, which had freshened at dusk as the last of the Yankees had drawn back from the approaches to the wall over that ground, which was now heaped with their dead. Many of the uninjured ones also lingered out there, among the fallen or crouching in the swale. Perhaps they dared not risk the dash down the slope under the guns of their enemies, or maybe they were under orders to remain, but remain they did. They not only stayed, but kept up a sporadic fire upon any who showed themselves behind the wall, where only a duty watch remained on guard. Now, in the darkness, it quickly became a cat and mouse game of waiting and watching, in the light of the rising moon, for any kind of movement. Men now sought aimed shots, rather than simply laying down a hail of fire, as previously, at a largely unseen enemy through a dense cloud of gun smoke.

The wind gusted and flapped at the blankets that the more fortunate men in the roadway had wrapped around themselves against the cold. It blew at the flames of the little fires that some had kindled with what remained of the fence rails and boards and any other combustible material, sending the flames guttering and darting and whipping gusts of smoke and showers of sparks away down the road across the wall and off towards the unfinished rail cutting into the night. But men had little time to avail themselves of the warmth. Word quickly came along, as before, to extinguish them as they were silhouetting the sentinels at the wall and giving the Yankees out there a target, so soon there were no fires and the men resumed their shivering vigil. In the restored blackness, some opted to run the risks of the sharp-shooting to refill canteens at the wells that served the roadside houses. A few sneaked quietly out, intending to achieve the objective by stealth, while others darted out to reach the cover of the well before the Yankees down at the swale had a chance to draw a bead on them, doing the same when they had gotten their water. Everyone then spent the next while either keeping their heads down or joining in the outburst of firing that followed the scurrying figures back to the shelter of the wall.

Groups of off-duty men were formed into work details, once the darkness was full, for further digging to begin on the trench, widening it so that more of those now stationed along the wall could benefit from the additional shelter it provided. The men worked in relays on into the night, hearing the shots from both sides of the wall and hearing too the other noises, which were far, far worse than gun shots. In the moonlight the scale of the execution could be glimpse down on that shallow slope. From the bottom of the Innis and Stephens gardens on, down past the scraps of splintered wood, that marked where the enclosure fence had been, and on across the swale to the remains of the lower fence, now similarly flayed to pieces by the gunfire. Further still, beyond the trampled fairground, all the way down to the canal gully were more clumps of dead and wounded. By now the field mainly held the more seriously hurt, for any who could move themselves away, or get any sort of help in doing so, had either gone or were going now, back towards town where further fires showed where the enemy still lay, bloodied but in all likelihood far from beaten.

From all across that dreadful slope the noises came, wails, screams, entreaties and groans, rising in a harrowing chorus of sounds that steadily ground on the nerves of the filthy, exhausted men who stood watch, worked or rested along the roadway. They denied sleep to those who sought it and grated on the minds of those who still laboured. Behind the wall were many who were prepared to exult on the extent of the slaughter and the magnitude of their success, but there were others also, less vociferous men, who were troubled by the scale of the killing, even though it had fallen upon their enemies.

In the middle part of the night, Daniel Ryan, together with the others of his mess, was called for a further spell of duty at the wall. They collected their weapons from the stacks and hunching down to make their way across the higher part of the road, they headed for the wall where the men ending their duty watch still crouched. Bryant and Norton were there as was Wesley Corse, the corporal of the guard.

"Don't go lookin' over lessen ya hear somethin'," he told them. "Thar's plenty o' itchy trigger fingers out there still." Daniel grunted in acknowledgement, moving into the space the other two were vacating.

"You boys got it easy," Bryant added. "Thar's only the moon now so ya won't show up the same if ya stick yore head up fer a look." They moved away and Daniel settled into place against the cold stones of the wall. They promptly took up the customary practice of one watching and one resting, but, as on previous battlefields, sleep, beyond fitful dozing, did not come to Daniel Ryan.

From beyond, the wounded cried and moaned still and he and Philipps exchanged glances, though nothing was said of it. Out on the littered ground, the wind pulled continually at the skirts and capes of the coats worn by the dead and wounded, flapping them noisily, adding to the multitude of other sounds that came from the throats of those injured thousands, who now had the bitter cold to add to their other torments. Hours now since dusk, the field remained a frightful jumble of shouts and cries, of screams, groans and moans, of calls and appeals, as the suffering of the fallen stretched on into the night. It did not do, Daniel Ryan repeatedly thought, to think of what lay out there at the source of those cries. The darkness cast a merciful shroud over sights, which would be revealed in the morning, but the sounds on their own were bad enough.

The pervading entreaty was for water. Some groaned or murmured the word between clenched teeth, or in delirium while others called out or implored for it, calling the names of comrades or friends. Common too were simple cries for help or for something to alleviate the agony of wounds, while the darker shouts were for a bullet to bring a final, merciful end to their suffering. The shouts of one wounded man particularly grated on Daniel Ryan.

"C'mon rebs, finish the job on me!"

"Finish me off rebs, don't leave me here half done fer!"

"C'mon, spare me a goddam bullet rebs!" The voice continued to call in the darkness, not the loudest, but bitter and insistent and Daniel found himself almost listening for it as his duty time slowly passed.

Relief, denied to those on the slope, eventually came for the men at the wall and, as others took their places, they moved back to join those who still worked on deepening and extending the trench along the road. It was as well to be working, Daniel thought, for the activity kept the men warm and gave them something to do, rather than vainly trying to get any sort of rest through the harrowing chorus from those thousands of suffering men.

In the darkness more ammunition arrived, packs of cartridges handed along from man to man, with instructions to retain just one pack of ten shots and continue passing the surplus along. This went on for a while until the supply dried up, but it gave Daniel Ryan twelve of the paper cylinders to arrange in his pouch. No percussion caps came along however and the men of the mess pooled what they had, giving each of them just nine.

"Never quite think of everythin' do they," was Daley's comment on it all?

Several times, during the hours of darkness, alarms were raised and the men were summoned back to duty at the wall. Several volleys were fired into the night to dissuade suspected enemy forays, upon which, after a pause to be sure the dissuading had been accomplished, the work and off duty details were stood down again. From above on the hill, occasional cannon shots were fired, whether at any visible or audible target or simply to add to the discouragement nobody knew. Rumours continued to sweep up and down the lines. One story said that Cobb had bled to death from his wound and the general's demise was later confirmed by some of the officers. Another tale was of the capture, since dusk, of a Yankee messenger who bore dispatches, which told of a renewal of the attacks in the morning. As this news spread, the men tensed themselves and set to their work to improve the position with renewed vigour, while the darkness hours stretched on towards dawn. As daylight approached and the fog began to gather once more, orders came for everyone to reform into their companies and deploy along the wall in their separate brigades. Cobb's Georgians, now led by Colonel McMillan, were, with some confusion, consolidated to the right or southern section of the wall between the Hall and Stephens houses, while Kershaw's South Carolinians took over the left or northern section, to beyond the Innis house, towards the junction of Hanover Street, with the Tarheels now holding station beyond them.

There had been shouted orders as the first signs of day had approached, followed by a shuffling of many feet behind those on duty at the wall as the mass of off-duty men moved across the road to form into their successive ranks. The men asembled and still it was freezing. The wind of the earlier part of the night had died away and the fog hung thick and impenetrable, casting its shroud over the ground where the cries of the wounded still rang out in only slightly reduced intensity. Daylight had come, not through any sight of a morning sky, but through that eerie, gradual lightening of the fog to a wet, silver tone. Seeing this wisping whiteness around him as he crouched at the wall, Daniel Ryan rose slowly to look carefully over the stones, stopping when his head was level with the top edge. His limbs felt stiff and sore and his shoulder, punished through the long hours of yesterday's fight by that punching recoil, ached with every movement. He cast his eyes briefly along the front and then crouched again, with his mind registering an image of grey, vague unreality softening and obscuring the prostrate shapes of the many wounded and dead.

"See anythin'," the question came from Matthew Hale who waited in the ranks behind him?

"Only dead men," he answered, as he resumed his crouched position, leaning his shoulder and his left hip against the stones. The outbreaks of musketry had subsided towards dawn with only an occasional shot now ringing out across the field, but the unremitting cries of the injured wore on the nerves, allowing no relief from the knowledge of what lay out there beyond where they waited in their ranks. Daniel still leaned against the stones of the wall as he exchanged a glance with John Fitzpatrick. Truly the aftermath of a battle was almost worse than the killing itself and, if the story of the Yankee messenger was true, there could be more of both to come with this new day.

It had been light for best part of an hour when the yellowing of the mist told of the new winter sunrise. Down on the slope there was no sign of life with only the drifting fog to look at. With daylight full, half of the men were retained along the wall with the others, including the previous duty watch stood down, but hardly had those of Daniel Ryan's mess crossed the road to settle on the trampled grass of the hill, when Jeffers came along, gesturing to them to come. When they had gathered around him the First Sergeant eyed them with his customary expression of disapproval and disdain.

"Cartridges," he said. "Colonel don't want to stay down at next to nothin', so you lucky boys kin shift yore no account asses along there with Sergeant Bayfield here and see to it." He turned to Bayfield. "If ya move their lazy butts, ya kin be back here with the boxes afore the fog lifts and ya become a target for every Yank out there with a gun." Though he spoke to Bayfield, he characteristically made his words loud enough for all of them to hear. Bayfield nodded and waved the group away along the road. Maybe Jeffers was playing fair, giving the places on the ammunition detail to those who had been longest on station along the road, Daniel thought, but there were surely safer places to exercise this morning.

They paced on skirting the ranks of waiting men to the fog shrouded shape of the Hall house, moving beyond, to join a further collection of men, likely engaged in similar errands, to the intersection of the Telegraph Road with Frederick Street, turning right there to follow the road up the short ascent. There were wagons and guns also up ahead there now, on the curve of the Telegraph Road, choking the length of the road before it began its descent into the valley of Hazel Run. They lined the road, protected, to a degree at least, by the shoulder of the hill from the nearest Yankee guns. They were distributing ammunition to troops of one of George Pickett's brigades, so the waiting men told them. They too were South Carolinians and they had been moved up, they said, from positions on the far side of Hazel Run, to enfilade the Yankees who had used the railroad cut for shelter to approach the sunken road. Bayfield reached the first wagon and spoke with the sergeant in charge but got an abrupt rebuttal for his pains.

"We ain't here to supply every damned outfit that can't find its own goddam wagons," he growled in response, "Jenkins brigade only." Bayfield remonstrated with him, and their dispute dragged on, languishing in an apparent stalemate, until a mounted officer approached and, hearing something of the disagreement as he steered his horse through the line of waiting men, he reined the animal in and addressed them.

"Sergeant," he said to Bayfield, "what unit are you from and where are you stationed?"

"Cobb's brigade from the stone wall over yonder sah," Bayfield told him.

"And why would your men over at that wall need more ammunition," the captain asked, in a tone that sounded as though he was humbly seeking information?

"Reckon we shot all that we could git yesterday at the Yankees," was Bayfield's reply, "and what we got last night weren't enough to go around."

"And if the sergeant here," the captain nodded towards the wagon, "were to give you more would your boys run off to Richmond with it, or maybe trade it to the enemy or perhaps you would intend shooting that at the Yankees also?"

"We surely would, if they come on up today like we hear," Bayfield answered, "but it could take us all mornin' to find our own wagons in the fog and this here mess," he gestured towards the jam of vehicles and men.

"So," the officer turned his fidgeting horse so that he was looking directly at the man at the wagon. "How does that sound to you sergeant? Do you have a difficulty with men who want to shoot these here bullets of yours at the Yankees?"

"It ain't that," the sergeant still maintained. "These're Jenkins wagons 'n' I ain't got no orders to issue to no other outfits."

"You have an objection to men shootin' your cartridges at the Yankees," the captain persisted? There was a pause while it was the sergeant's turn to fidget while everyone around the wagon looked on at his discomfiture.

"Guess not," he eventually muttered in a sullen tone.

"Well give them some damn boxes," the captain scolded him, "and let's get on with the damned war. We could have further attacks at any time and I'm not going to wait around here and see our line broken because nobody would give the men down there some ammunition to defend it." He pulled a notebook from his pocket, flicked it open and began to scribble. When he was done he tore the page away and held it out towards the sergeant, who shrugged.

"Lieutenant ain't gonna like it none," he muttered, as he took the paper and turned to Bayfield.

"What kind," he rasped abruptly?

"Enfield," Bayfield told him. The sergeant gestured to

one of the men on the wagon, who immediately began to haul at boxes, while the captain, having seen his intentions under way shook his head and moved his horse away along the road.

"Ya better sign for 'em too," the sergeant told Bayfield, as he passed him the paper. Bayfield turned to his own men who waited nearer the wagons.

"Get started down with 'em," he said, "afore the fog goes and the Yankees down there start usin' us fer target practice." The detail made immediately for the boxes, lifting them away by their wooden handles, and started back down the road.

It was past noon and the fog had long since burned off. The day, like the previous one, had grown almost warm, but still the Yankees did not come. Instead they kept up a desultory fire of musket shots and occasional artillery rounds on the hills and on the positions below them. From the field, the cries of the wounded continued unabated, but they were beyond the help of their comrades, marooned as they were out on that slope between the lines, too near to the wall and the road for any to assist them without a truce. Work went on along the road, with men alternating between watching at the wall, deepening the trench or resting at the bottom of the slope. Most men had spent time during the morning cleaning their muskets, washing away the dark powder residue, though there was nothing in the way of oil or grease to lubricate them. There was also no word of rations. No issue had come since Friday and the men had long since consumed the last of that. As hunger pangs increased, mutters of complaint now spread at the continuing absence of the commissary vehicles.

Daniel Ryan was with the off-duty men of the company,

squatting on the far side of the road, when the mutter came along the line, closely followed by a cluster of shots. Daley was immediately on his feet to head across to the wall.

"Come see this goddam crazy man," he called to them. All along the road, men were crossing to the wall with their muskets in their hands. Daniel reached the rampart and carefully looked over. Across to the left, out beyond the bullet-scarred Innis house, a grey figure was moving. Daniel stared at him, seeing immediately that he carried no weapon, but was instead festooned with water canteens of every type.

"He's one of Kershaw's," Winder said, from in front of where Daniel watched the moving figure, noting the sergeant's stripes on his tunic. From the swale and from the buildings further to the left, Yankees were shooting at the man, who had stopped at a wounded soldier. He knelt beside the soldier, getting cover to some extent at least from the bodies out there and then they saw him raise the prostrate man's head, offering him a canteen to drink from, even as bullets continued to buzz past him and smack into the ground or even into those who lay around him.

"He's riskin' his neck for those Yankees," the shout was repeated incredulously along the wall.

"He's helpin' them."

"He'll get nothin' but a bullet."

"He's crazy!" The comments went along, but not a man moved from the wall, where solid ranks of watching men now stood, ignoring the risk of the enemy sharpshooters.

Out on the field the sergeant had finished giving water to the wounded Yankee, but, before he left him, he pulled the man's haversack around and laid it below his head, like a pillow. There were now further shouts out there from some of the lurking Yankees.

"Hold up Boys!"

"Hold your fire!"

"Don't shoot him!" The musket shots began to fade away as more shouts went along the slope.

Leaving the full canteen on the ground at the man's side and taking the soldier's empty one, the sergeant moved on to another fallen figure, doing the same as before. The firing finally ceased as though men were beginning to understand what this crazy man was doing. Both sides settled to watch disbelievingly as he continued with his self-appointed task, making his way from man to man, offering water and moving the wounded men till they lay in positions that seemed to ease their pain. Daniel saw him arrange what must have been a shattered leg before moving a soldier's overcoat to cover him better. Back at the wall, a range of talk and comment went along. Opinion was mixed, and while the sergeant's single-handed mission to help the enemy wounded attracted the admiration of many, others were critical, reckoning that the Yankees should be left till their own side asked for a truce. Out in front, the working figure remained at his task, oblivious to those who watched or commented. Those at the wall could hear the now empty canteens that he carried clanking and clunking faintly as he moved on to other wounded men.

Presently another murmur went along the line and Daniel looked to see that a second figure had crossed the wall, a Georgian this time, moving across from their own brigade positions and carrying a further supply of bumping canteens. He made for where the sergeant still worked, picking his way among the wounded, to stop beside him and offer the water that he carried. Daniel watched as the two men exchanged full for empty canteens before the Georgian made his way back, moving across the ground towards the Stephens house where the well was situated behind the building, to start the task of refilling the canteens that he had retrieved.

On through the afternoon the two men worked, with one constantly moving back and forward to refill canteens while the other, the sergeant, ministered to the injured Yankees. One by one, men at the wall moved away from their places, their interest in watching having waned, while, over the whole field, the tension of battle had eased. Men on both sides had refrained from firing, while the two grey-brown clad soldiers continued to work, gradually moving across the area in front of the wall. Thompson went along the nearest section of the line.

"Barnard reckons he's from the Second South Carolina regiment," he said.

Daniel looked again at the now more distant figure, hunched over yet another of the enemy. It was crazy. The whole thing was crazy. They had spent yesterday covering that ground with enemy dead and wounded and now he was out there, risking his own life to help them. He shook his head, it didn't do to start worrying about the enemy, he thought. They had their own side to worry about them, but in his heart he knew that, in spite of himself, he felt admiration for what that sergeant and the man who helped him were doing.

The two men finally returned to their own lines late in the afternoon. As the sergeant crossed the wall, a muted cheer rang out from the swale, where the Yankees still lay in numbers, a cheer that was taken up by the southerners along the road. As soldiers they had to kill, Daniel thought, but maybe it was useless to go on hating. People were people, and one could feel hate when they were bombarding and wrecking the town, and in the course of a battle, when it was kill or be killed. But when the heat of battle and anger had gone, it was clear that there were men on both sides who found it hard to sustain any real, individual hatred for those who opposed them. It was, Daniel thought, as though some kind of bond of shared humanity was just too strong, and when he reflected on this notion he found himself thanking god for it if it was true. He stirred himself to look around as he stepped away from the wall. The low sun had disappeared over the hill behind them and, all around, the air had grown cold again.

Darkness had fallen, a clear darkness again in which the stars shone, their tiny pinpricks of light scattered across that seemingly endless carpet of black infinity, making a man feel small and insignificant, a mere speck, when he looked up into this mighty creation of the lord's. The cold had intensified and the men huddled together as before, using what blankets they had for warmth with still no word of any rations. Out on the still-littered ground the only light was again from the rising orb of the moon and the field was now as close to silence as it had been since the battle, with weaker, less incessant groans or mutters now being heard from the remaining wounded.

There had been noises, immediately after darkness had fallen, before the moon had appeared, sounds of movement, the clinking of equipment and the shuffling of feet. The off-duty men had been called and the ranks at the wall had loaded to the ready, peering into the darkness, waiting for a further enemy move. But the sounds had faded and men had begun to speculate that, instead of an attack, it was a pulling back of the men who had spent the whole day and the previous night in the swale out in front. Eventually, the sounds had faded and the off-duty men were stood down once more. A picket detail was dispatched from the wall, to scout the nearer part of the slope, with the "Squirrel

Hunters," prominent among its men, and these promptly vanished into the blackness.

It was around an hour after dusk that the first light began to appear in the sky up to the north, across the river where the left flank of the army rested on the bend. A yellowish glow appeared, a glow that steadily grew until it pulsed and moved, seeming to stretch longer fingers or beams of light up into the darker sky above the river bend. Again the men gathered to watch, standing up in their groups to mutter and guess to each other as to what this could all mean.

"It's Stuart," Thorne shouted. "It's old Jeb, or maybe Old Jack, off up there across the river, burnin' the Yankee supplies 'n' stores agin."

"Don't talk horse shit," Powell retorted. "All o' Old Jack's boys is down south o' here and Stuart's cavalry's out on that far flank too. Ain't nobody goin' off raidin' when the Yankees is all down thar, set to come at us agin." Daniel looked at the growing pulses of light. They were far too big for anything that was burning, he thought, and much more than just a glow of flames in the sky. Why those darts of light were reaching way up now, spreading like a giant fan from that northern horizon and now there were flecks of orange and red in them as they flashed in the heavens.

The lights continued to spread across the sky, gradually extending from the distant horizon until they were almost overhead. The men continued to gaze upwards, many with expressions of total astonishment on their upturned faces.

"What in thunderation is that?"

"What do they mean?" The questions were on many lips, with a mixture of theories attempting to answer them. Somebody suggested a distant electrical storm, but the display was continuous and way larger in scale than any lightning that Daniel Ryan had seen. He had an idea as to what the lights were, having seen episodes of this kind in

Ireland, but this was larger and more brilliant than anything he could remember. Another of the boys in the company reckoned that, with it still being Sunday, these brilliant streams of light must be some kind of divine sign from above. Daniel had little to say in response to the suggestions, so engrossed was he in watching these magnificent barbs of light, whose colours grew more and more vivid, mixing from pale oranges and reds to deep crimson hues, that were now flecked with purples also. They spread their extending strands ever further across the sky until they seemed to take up almost all of it, though with the brightest displays of light always in the north, but other flashes, though less vivid, were now stretching over their heads and on down the river valley.

"I ain't never seen nothin' like that before," Daniel heard Philipps say though it was Fitzpatrick who finally answered him from a little way along the wall.

"I saw things like this when I was a child. My grandma called it, "Saint Patrick's Fire." I've never seen it as bright as this, but I've seen colours and streamers in the sky. It was always winter back then, like it is now and on clear nights, as far as I recall. Back in school Mr Heenan had some big, Latin words, name for it, but I reckon it's the same thing that I saw before." Daniel nodded, half to himself as he listened. Fitzpatrick's words chimed with what he had seen only his mother had called it the, "Northern Lights," but he too had never seen anything as dramatic as this. Those times came back to him now as he continued to look up into the crowded sky, where breathtaking displays of dazzling colour probed almost like pillars across the night, bathing everything below in an eerie half light. All along the line the soldiers watched and wondered and guessed as to what it might be and what it might mean.

For almost an hour the sky exhibited its brilliance,

which seemed to put the pathetic efforts of men and their puny weapons to shame, until slowly the coloured exhibition start to fade, gradually sinking back towards the north, from where it had begun, to eventually disappear. Still the men watched as the display receded, with many of them still unable to offer any recognition or knowledge of what they had just seen. That would be it, Daniel thought. These boys, almost all of whom came from far to the south, would never have seen anything like this before, nor would the others of their families or communities. To any who were unfamiliar with such things, it must all seem like something supernatural and sure enough that was what some of them were now saying. It was a sign to mark their victory of yesterday or maybe an omen of another victory to come tomorrow.

But other men were now less engrossed with what the beautiful patterns in the sky meant, for the harsh pangs of hunger, coupled with the bitter cold, carried on the same north westerly wind, still persisted and now, with the display of light in the sky fading, the attention of the men was returning to their own wants and shortages. Numbers of them had begun quietly absenting themselves from their mess groups, in ones and twos, to head across the wall, seeking boots, blankets, overcoats and food from the Yankee dead. It had been impossible last night with the swale and the buildings occupied by trigger-happy enemy sharpshooters, but now with the live Yankees, save for their wounded, largely withdrawn towards the town, the chance was here to forage in reasonable safety. As the lights had faded from the sky, Daley and Ballard left, heading across the wall to disappear into the comparative darkness. Daniel looked around at the others and saw Philipps gesture to him, the movement being just visible in the light of the moon. They moved away, to lever themselves onto the top stones of the wall, past the duty men who crouched there, and step down onto the heaped earth beyond.

Daniel felt exposed and vulnerable out in the open. The moon, now emerged from some fleecy clouds close to the horizon, cast its subdued light across the field. Moving shapes across the slope told of where others sought their share of the spoils and around them there were muted sounds of activity, as men busied themselves on their foraging and plundering. Occasional grunts and mutters came, as the needy worked upon the dead, pulling shoes first and foremost, but following this acquisition with any other possessions or items of clothing, especially those thick winter coats. Daniel was surprised at the numbers of men who were now moving around out in that space in front of the wall. Why some must have started out even while the lights were at their brightest in the sky, so latecomers like himself and Philipps would have to forage farther down, away from the comparative safety up here between the wall and the swale. They moved on down into the churned up fairground enclosure, with its wrecked fences, down to where the risk of Yankee pickets getting aimed shots at them was far greater.

As they approached the farther wrecked fence of the enclosure, a figure moved in front of them.

"Wouldn't go down much further," a close by voice murmured and they stopped, looking across to where the words had come from. Saul Philipps started to move diagonally towards the ruined fence which lay just in front of them and Daniel followed to where a man crouched behind the remains of a post.

"Yankees're down at the gully," the murmuring tone resumed, "but they'll be able to hear what's goin' on up here, so their trigger fingers'll be itchin'. Wouldn't go no further'n them boys thar," the man added.

He gestured towards the rank of dark forms who lay just in front of where they crouched. They started to move on and Philipps tapped the man on the shoulder as they moved on past his position.

"Be damned quick," the picket hissed, "or ya'll be drawin' fire on me."

It took them a while in the darkness to plunder several dead men, who lay just beyond the remains of the farther enclosure fence. It was dangerous down here as the sentinel had said. Almost certainly the Yankees would have pickets in that brickyard across to the right towards Frederick Street, concealed and protected by the remains of their fences and walls. Maybe more lurked down beyond the millrace gully, but the two of them ignored the threat meantime and persisted on their quest, though taking elaborate care to keep noises to an absolute minimum as they pulled shoes, haversacks and clothing from the stiff and cold forms, which still covered the ground. Having finished with these fallen men, they moved back up the slope a way, passing back through the line of increasingly exasperated pickets, who hissed and whispered their disapproval as they approached. Feeling that they had tempted providence far enough, they made their way back across the field still looking out for further booty, but finding that it was largely fruitless as these dead men who lay closer to the Confederate line had already been pretty thoroughly plundered. Eventually they gave it up and returned with what they had, tossing their carried booty across the wall and following themselves to jump down onto the road.

Two of the overcoats they had taken turned out to be useless. An examination of them, when they got them across to the hillside, revealed too many bullet holes and shrapnel rents for them to serve in their original role, so they were spread on the grass to keep the chill at bay. Philipps took the third coat and Daniel replaced his shoes with a newer pair that seemed a reasonable fit. The haversacks they had recovered revealed some hardtacks and a small amount of salt beef, along with a supply of coffee beans and a few further items of sutlers' supplies, including some pieces of hard candy. This was shared out among those of the mess and they sat and sucked on them as they sorted their remaining things. Daley and Ballard had done better, with shoes, overcoats and a better supply of rations, which were divided among the five of them. There was a blanket, which was taken by Daley, who passed his more worn one on in turn to Bentley, who lacked blankets and had missed out on the chance to forage for himself through being detained at the wall on duty. All along the line, men were similarly busy, organising their acquisitions and discarding worn out items in favour of the replacements gathered from the field. Fires were again forbidden so the men spent the night chewing, when the candy was finished, on bits of captured Yankee hardtack as still more deepening was undertaken along the trench behind the wall.

Monday morning dawned, cold again, with more fog, which, as on the previous days, cleared only slowly. With the coming of first light, the southern pickets pulled back from the enclosure fence, where they had spent the night. The fallen men from Saturday still lay in front of the southern positions, with most of the dead, who lay nearer to the wall and the road, now stripped of almost all of their clothing and possessions. They lay stark and white, mixed among the, still surviving wounded, who had been left their uniforms, though some had been relieved of their boots. Now, although many still speculated on the likelihood of further Yankee attacks, other rumours spoke of a truce in order to retrieve those men at last from where they had lain exposed for almost two days and nights to the elements, as well as suffering the continuing effects of their wounds. Their cries and pleas had gradually subsided as the fallen men weakened or died, but still gasps, mutters or cries came from some, though growing steadily fewer and fainter as the hours passed.

When the fog cleared, with the enemy still occupying the buildings over on William Street and Hanover Street there came the return of sharp-shooting between the lines. As the ground farther down towards town, became visible it could be seen that most of the enemy wounded had been retrieved from that lower area and there were now Yankee positions, trenches and holes dug, down there between the gully and the town. A defensible line had been established there, with a screen of pickets still thrown forward to the spillway, but these kept up an intermittent fire, bringing down the occasional man who showed himself too carelessly behind the wall and reminding those around him of the menace which still threatened.

Through the day these intermittent outbreaks of fire continued. The artillery up on the hill, occasionally opened fire on some of the buildings from which shooting still came, though several others, over to the left, were spared by the southern troops, since yellow hospital flags flew from them. The niggling hostilities went on until afternoon, when, as clouds began to spread across the sky, more definite word was passed along that the remaining hours till dusk would see a truce, during which those of the enemy wounded, who remained alive, would be collected. The firing steadily died away and when the field was quiet, orderlies appeared at the lower end of the field, carrying litters and blankets. They began to pick around the open ground up towards the fairground and the swale, where the fallen still lay thickly, lifting wounded men onto their stretchers or into the blankets. These were carried away towards the roads, where ambulance wagons had been driven up to transport them away, with the orderlies immediately returning for more wounded men. A few southern orderlies left the wall to walk the field in search of any pickets who may have been wounded during the previous night, but Daniel saw only two being recovered and eventually, as the daylight waned, the field was left to the Yankees, who steadily drew closer to the wall to recover the closest of their casualties, as the cloud began to lower more threateningly overhead.

Eventually those behind the wall were diverted away from the field by the arrival of a rations issue, which Daley and Ballard went to collect for their own mess. Fires were at last allowed and these were kindled and fed with a variety of rubbish, from ammunition boxes to fence fragments, which lay along the road. Some went out, among where the Yankees still worked, to collect more fence remains and by dusk a meal of bacon sloosh, reinforced with some salted Yankee beef, was ready for the ravenous men. After the food, a picket line moved away, following down the slope as the Yankee orderlies withdrew, making for the shattered fence line again and likely seeking the chance to plunder anything from the remaining dead Yankees that had survived the forays of the previous night.

With the darkness came the wind, stronger and more chilling than on previous nights, but tonight the sky was heavy and overcast with no moon or stars in view. Later in the night it began to rain, a rain that grew steadily heavier, blown on the strong and gusting wind, which brought further discomfort through the darkness hours before it passed as daylight drew near. Down in the town they could see the Yankee bivouac fires, with their flames dancing and darting in the wind, but little, other than the foul weather, disturbed the night and fires were permitted through the hours of darkness, though some of these were blown apart or extinguished by the wind and rain.

Before those first signs of daylight came, the men along the road were called, in case of further trouble, but, as the eastern sky began to lighten, word came back from the skirmish line that the enemy pickets had been withdrawn and that the town beyond seemed quiet. Patrols were sent forward and messengers soon returned from these with the news that the Yankees had gone, recrossing the river under the cover of the night's storm. The talk along the wall was immediately of this latest, unexpected development and when the news was confirmed, that the enemy had indeed withdrawn, outbreaks of cheering rang out along the line, as though a tension had now been broken. Men made to leave the road, to make for town to see, or to simply resume their plundering of the dead, but these were quickly dissuaded by their sergeants.

The regiments remained at their posts, with a duty watch at the wall, while the remainder of the men lounged on the grass of the hillside on the far side of the road. They did not have long to wait however, being relieved during the morning by Georgians of Brigadier General Paul Semmes' brigade, who deployed themselves along the wall as Cobb's men were pulled back and formed up in marching order, to head away back to the familiar brigade camp grounds west of Howison Hill. The men were filthy and exhausted from their five days of work and battle, broken only by dozing catnaps of rest and, now that the tension of prospective fighting was gone, they shambled up the Telegraph Road like sleepwalkers, to reoccupy their camps. Some, Daniel Ryan's mess included, dallied long enough to heat and devour what remained of their ration and their plundered Yankee food before turning in, but others, having set their fires, had made immediately for their blankets and shelters. Excused further duty, they slept the rest of the day and on through the following night warmed by the comfort of their shelters and fires.

Chapter 5 The Face of the Enemy

There followed two days of comparative inactivity, during which more rations were issued and some of the men, including Daniel Ryan, were able to get a rudimentary wash, while recovering from the labours of the previous week. Minor wounds started to heal and blue-bruised shoulders began to recover. Daniel also trimmed his beard, though he was reluctant to shave it off completely in the winter. He nevertheless used the small scissors from his inner haversack pouch to cut it down very short, snipping the whiskers away from his ears and taking a turn, with Saul Philipps, to cut each other's hair, till what remained of it sat comfortably behind the ears of each of them. Rested, fed and tidied up and with his own aches and pains at last easing, Daniel began to feel some notion of readiness for whatever the Yankees or the generals served up next.

It was on the Thursday, when the orders of the day were being read at assembly by Boyce, that notice was given of a company detail which was to go down through the town to the river. They had orders, Boyce had told them, to send a detail to join men of the Mississippi brigade, who had been re-established down in the town, in meeting a party of unarmed Yankees, who were being allowed to cross over to this side of the Rappahannock. They would escort the enemy detachment up to the fields, between the town and the Confederate positions, where they would continue the task, begun by similar details yesterday, of burying those of their dead, who still lay there, stripped by now of everything of use. Jeffers would detail the men to serve.

"The Yankees that come across will try to learn more of our defences and dispositions," the lieutenant had told them. "Men detailed should not get into talking with them, so as not to reveal any information of use to the enemy."

"Can't we even tell 'em not to come across again or we'll give 'em another good lickin'," Daley muttered to those around him?

"Tell 'em to come on over again any time they take a notion," Petersen replied, getting a fierce glare from Jeffers for his pains. Nobody who still lacked shoes would be on the detail, the lieutenant finished.

"They could always git boots off any o' the damn Yankees who still got 'em," Ballard observed.

"By now, there won't hardly be any like that," Philipps told him.

Sure enough after they had dismissed to breakfast, the First Sergeant appeared at their shelter and gave them the happy news.

"You lucky, lucky boys," he intoned as he arrived and, hearing it, there was little need for much in the way of further instructions.

The detail, comprising almost half of the company, shouldered their muskets and set off, marching down on the Telegraph Road and continuing on past the junction with its sunken, stone walled stretch onto Frederick Street to reach the town. There was wagon traffic and the familiar mixture of couriers and staff officers, engaged on the army's many errands, as the column moved now on past the busier final blocks towards the river. The column was halted at the riverbank, on the far side of Sophia Street, where a formation of Mississippians already waited. Out on the Rappahannock the Georgians, as they arrived, could see a small flotilla of pontoon boats. The leading boat carried a limp white flag and each of the craft was crowded with blue-coated Yankees, with six long oars on each raised out of the water as they lay out there on the river, drifting slowly downstream. With the escorts now assembled, a grey-uniformed Mississippi major gave a signal, moving his arm in a wide sweep, upon which the oars on each boat were lowered into the water and, upon the resumption of rowing, they recovered steerage way and began to move in a slow curve towards the shore. One by one the unwieldy craft grounded and a bowman leapt from each to secure it with a rope and a wooden stake which was hammered into the mud of the bank, upon which the disembarking began.

The southerners stood in their ranks, eyeing the arriving men, who carried tools instead of weapons on this crossing, waiting there while the officers gave salutes, shook hands and exchanged pleasantries. There must have been more than a hundred of them in all, Daniel Ryan thought, as he watched their sergeants organise them into sections. This done, the southerners of the escort formed on either side of them, ready for the march up to Saturday's killing grounds.

Ballard was on the opposite side of the Yankees from Daniel Ryan and, regardless of Boyce's previous orders, he commenced immediately to talk to those nearest him.

"Good way o' preservin' yore health till the end o' yore visit," he told the man nearest him. The soldier looked at him in puzzlement.

"Huh?" he grunted.

"Not bringin' no muskets," Ballard added, "smart

move that." A couple of the others who had heard his words chuckled in grim amusement. Thompson had arrived.

"These boys are goin' up Hanover Street to get to work up there past the overspill," he said. "But they won't be goin' nowhere too close to our positions," he murmured to Daniel. "That's why we're takin' 'em that way." They started off, heading north along the riverside on Sophia Street till Hanover Street was reached, to turn left there and make their way west. The column crossed the debris littered width of Caroline Street, before starting on the uphill stretch to Princess Anne Street, passing a succession of burned out and damaged buildings on their way. This was the first that Daniel had seen of the northern section of Fredericksburg since the bombardment and the looting. Close up, he concluded, the scene was even worse than it had appeared from up at the battle line.

Most houses had been damaged, to a greater or lesser extent, and many had been virtually destroyed by either the shelling or by the ensuing fires. Here and there a solitary civilian, or a small group or family of them, prowled through derelict properties or ruins. As they saw the approach of the Yankees, they left their forlorn occupations and came to the roadside, to shout insults and vent their anger at them. Daniel looked around at the civilians, feeling for them as they picked and poked through the debris, or simply stood among the gaunt ruins and piles of wreckage that had been their homes. Confined between the two parallel ranks of Confederate soldiers, the bluecoats kept their eyes fixed to the front and marched on. Well might they, Daniel Ryan thought, feeling his own anger rise, as he saw more and more of what they had collectively done. So much had been destroyed, by the shelling and later by the looting and burning. In places whole sections of houses had been wrecked and from holes in walls or roofs, or wrecked wings or ends, splintered wooden beams or rafters reached out like scarred fingers over the charred remains below, while torn remains of curtains or blinds flapped idly from successive shattered or missing windows.

Everywhere debris littered the streets, lying in some places in heaps, while elsewhere it was more widely scattered. Broken pieces of glass, pottery or china scrunched underfoot and smashed remains of furniture, including fragments of elegantly carved and varnished pieces, lay all around, most of it charred and burned. Strips of cloth, whether bedding, table linen or clothing, lay also, spoiled by the rain and frost and trampled in the dirt of the street with muddied folds of it lying draped over the remains of fences and hedges, or in some places hanging festooned on the branches of bushes or trees.

Above all, the way was littered with paper, from tiny charred scraps of it, which had survived burning, to larger sheets which fluttered around the streets and sidewalks or lay in the trampled and spoiled gardens and lanes. Much of it was from books, printed pages by the score lay torn, half-burned or dirt-stained, but Daniel also saw pages of musical manuscript paper lying in the mud of the streets. He watched the Yankee who walked beside him, seeing his eyes flick from side to side as he took in the extent of the destruction. Eventually he looked at him squarely and spoke.

"Must make you real proud to see all o' this, or maybe you saw it all last week." The soldier returned Daniel's gaze.

"Don't look at me," he said. "I ain't never been in this town before."

"No," Daniel retorted, "maybe you stayed over there on the other side, and said your prayers when all o' this was goin' on."

"Our outfit come across downriver," was the reply, "and that's where we were on Saturday. We never had no part in any o' this."

"Well you sure had plenty of other boys up here ready to see to takin' the place apart," Daniel rapped. The soldier looked across again.

"Some of our boys reckon that's fair enough for rebs," he said. "Reckon you boys'd do the same sort o' thing up north if you got the chance." Daniel glared at him.

"That's shit!" he said. "We were up in Maryland back in September. I was in Frederick and Hagerstown too and none of our boys did anythin' like this up there. When we moved out o' those places, the folks that lived there were safe and snug in their homes like when we arrived." Conversation at an end, they moved on up the street. At Libertytown, where Hanover Street levelled and even dipped slightly, the destruction was even greater, with more sections of buildings destroyed by artillery shells. Daniel glanced sideways again, but the Yankee beside him kept his gaze fixedly to the front.

On up the further gradient they went, with the column now narrowing to cross the re-planked bridge over the canal spillway and confront at last the expanse of prostrate, naked shapes that still littered the ground up towards the sunken Telegraph Road. The Yankee looked up at the scene and then shifted his eyes once more across towards Daniel Ryan.

"Reckon a lot o' the boys that come through town've paid for anythin' they did back there," he said, "and they sure didn't come up here without no uniforms and shoes on." Daniel felt himself redden as he recalled his own foray out among those dead men to plunder for his needs. He glared across at the boy, but bit his tongue as he did so and said nothing more.

Some of the escort were directed on up Hanover Street

towards the now wrecked blacksmith's, before spreading out across the field between the swale and the wall, while the Yankee sergeants allocated squads to different quarters of the field and set them to work, digging trenches for the dead. Others of the escorting troops, including the Company B detachment, waited at the lower end of the field, mingling with some of the Mississippians, over near the remains of the brickyard wall or at the near side of the Hanover Street bridge. Fires were kindled and water set to boil for the coffee, which some of them had already traded with the Yankee grave diggers. The men laid the much prized beans on a few of the flatter stones and pounded them with their musket butts, crushing and grinding them, before brewing the mixture to savour the genuine article once again, which none of the southern roasted peanut or dried fruit mixtures could rival.

As the blue-uniformed troops up on the slope began to labour at their grisly task, something almost resembling a picnic atmosphere prevailed among the escorts around the fires, with men luxuriating in the taste of real coffee as they lounged around and yarned, keeping only the barest of cursory watches on their toiling adversaries. Up beyond the stone wall more men amused themselves by baiting the Yankees, brandishing overcoats or other pieces of clothing that they had gleaned from the dead, but the blue-clad detail stuck stoically to their work and studiously ignored the jibes and gestures.

The guard detail took turns, through the hours that followed, to patrol across the field, keeping the Yankees and the local people away from each other, while their comrades still sat around the fires and drank their share of the coffee. Daniel and Otis Ballard took a turn at patrolling in the early afternoon, following south along the rim of the spillway gully, where a group of Yankees still moved, collecting men and parts of men for burial. Here and there, they came across unexploded shells, each marked with a piece of rag tied to a makeshift pole or stick. They walked around these and passed on, turning to head up the field towards where that fenced enclosure, the town fairground, had been and where still more of the Yankees were at work. Some of them dug and some carried, using boards to transfer the bodies to the burial trenches that still more of them were preparing.

Almost nothing was left of the fairground fences. Virtually all of the lower one had been shattered by gunfire, or hauled down by the Yankees, with the upper one having been dismantled by the defenders that day before the battle. A few tiny stumps of posts pointed upwards, all that had survived the need for firewood over the last few days. Beyond, up past the swale and the similar forlorn traces of the garden fences, the line of grey pickets kept the enemy from going too close to the sunken road, where details of southerners kept guard or still worked on strengthening the position. But fraternising was going on in various parts of the field. Goods were being traded and officers were tacitly ignoring it all, as they exchanged small talk with their counterparts, sipping occasionally from shared flasks while, all around them, the customary staples of tobacco and coffee changed hands, with much of the contraband being wrapped in newspapers, which would doubtless be avidly scrutinised in camps on either side of the river come evening.

But some of the men were doing more than that simple trade and Daniel saw exchanges of more personal items such as penknives, razors or even belts taking place. Ballard watched it all and then took in Daniel's expression with a look of amusement on his face.

"Back to feelin' sore at 'em," he drawled briefly, as he turned his gaze from the trading to his companion? Daniel turned to face him before pointing at two of the nearby traders.

"Coffee and rations and stuff like that might be one thing," he told him, "but that town down there proves that they are still the enemy and I don't go too much on the other things. Showin' family pictures and other stuff like that to the Yankee thieves and no accounts that did somethin' like that. Why half of what they're trading back to us will be loot from these folk's homes in town. The truth is Otis that this last week has proved it once and for all, they are damned Yankees and we'd be best thinkin' more of lickin' them good and proper instead of cosyin' up to them." Ballard grinned at him.

"Reckon we'd a' stopped them wreckin' the town if we could've," he said, "but this here world's the way it is and there's a helluva lot of it that you or I can't change no matter what we do." Daniel sniffed at his words and, getting no real reply, Ballard went on.

"Fact is they maybe wouldn't a' shelled the town t'all," he went on, "if the Old Man hadn't put our boys into it to shoot their engineers when they was layin' their bridges. But we couldn't 'a' jest let 'em cross without doin' nothin' to stop 'em could we? Reckon one thing jest led to another and it all finished up the way it finished up with the town wrecked and all o' them dead boys up here." Daniel snorted again.

"The whole reason why the army's here at all, why we're in it and why we're around this place is because they're down here," he said. "There's no other reason for bein' here."

"Sure thing," Ballard said, "but jest cuz yo're here fer a reason don't git to hatin' too much Daniel. Them boys over thar don't see things the way we do. We've done nothin' but exercise our rights about leavin' their union, but they think we ain't got those rights and so the south is still their country, so they see us as rebels and they come down here to set us all straight about that and so we got ourselves this here war. When we got to fight 'em and kill 'em then OK, we git on and do it, but even while we're doin' all o' that, in a lot o' ways, they are still much like us and it don't do to git too much of a habit of hatin' 'em all, cuz that starts to eat you up as well. Save yore hatin' fer the real bad bastards, in the Yankee army and in the rest o' life as well, and, as fer the others of 'em, if they're willin' to trade and be civil and hold fire on the picket lines, in between the real fightin', then I'm surely ready to oblige 'em."

As the afternoon proceeded, the field gradually cleared of its litter of dead and, as the evening approached, the men were chivvied on by their sergeants to finish the job. The work became more hurried with two elongated graves being hastily dug from the margin of Hanover Street southwards towards the bullet-scarred, red brick walls of the wrecked Stratton House. Into these shallower, hastily scooped out trenches a jumble of corpses were unceremoniously piled, before, as the pale shadows lengthened down towards the river, the Yankees were called to re-assemble for their return to their own side of the river. The southerners gathered also and the column formed, with the grey-brown troops again on either side of the blue detail. At the command, they moved away, back onto Hanover Street and over the repaired bridge, to start down the slope towards the main portion of town.

But this time it was different to the morning, for Daniel Ryan could see that now there were more civilians around. These people, having learned and seen that there were Yankees in town, and having spent the days since the battle trying to retrieve remnants of their possessions from the destruction that those Yankees had wrought, were in no mood to be sociable to them. There were shouts and insults from the sidewalks up ahead, where the locals stood in groups and on down through the succeeding blocks, people could be seen gathering as the procession of men approached and, as the troops passed, more insults came and occasional missiles were thrown into the formation. The blue troops fended these off with the spades and other tools that they carried as the column made its way on towards town reaching Charles Street without serious mishap.

It was as they passed from the intersection on to the next block that Daniel heard further shouts from behind, across the junction they had just left, almost simultaneously catching sight of a hurrying figure out of the corner of his eye. He turned and saw a woman running diagonally across the road, but there was something about her gait, as she approached that took his attention and it was then that he saw the glint from the ancient curved sword, that she carried in both of her hands, its blade stretching downwards towards the ground. Daniel stopped and moved his musket across his body as the woman changed direction and lunged, attempting to push her way among the Yankees, continuing to shout and scream as she did so.

"You thieves! You damned bandits," she screamed. "You're nothing but godforsaken criminals! May you burn in hellfire! May god damn you all forever!" She swung the sword at the nearest man, who tried to parry it with the spade that he carried. There was an ugly "thunk" as the blade bit into the wood of the shaft and then Daniel reached her. He had balanced his musket in his left hand and he gripped her right arm with his right hand and began to pull her away, managing then to get himself between her and the now disorganised column. He wrapped his arm around her body while, with the sword now jammed between them, he pushed her away, still screaming insults as he shuffled her towards the side of the road. But she struggled against him, wrestling in his hold, trying to push her way back towards the blue files. Daniel glanced around to see that Fitzpatrick had moved from behind him to help him but, even as he approached, he got embroiled with another woman who had begun to shout at Daniel for manhandling the first one away from the Yankees. Daniel glanced again at them, taking his eyes from the woman he held, feeling her relax and seem to calm in the grip of his arm and hand as he looked away. He loosened his hold, only to suddenly feel her wrench away and, as he turned back towards her, she lunged back out into the street towards the Yankees again. He grabbed at her with his free hand but managed to grip only a handful of her shawl as she turned on him.

"You," she spat. "You're no better than they are!" He saw the sword raised again, but this time it was above his own arm. The shining blade swung and seeing it, Daniel immediately knew that, with his weight towards her and his musket on the wrong side of his body, balanced only by his left hand, he could not possibly raise it in time to parry the blow. He reached out his hand, to try to divert the blade as it whipped towards him, when suddenly the prong of a pickaxe came between him and the sword edge. There was a sharp ring of steel on steel and before the woman could ready herself for another blow, Thompson was there, gathering her in a further hug, which pinned her arms to her sides with both her hands still holding the sword. Daniel looked around at the boy who held the pickaxe. He was young, and clean-shaven, and his blue cap now lay squint on his head from the sharp lunge he had just made. He had dark brown hair stuck down around his ears. His eyes met Daniel Ryan's as one of the Yankee sergeants came up and rapped at him.

"Git back in place! Don't git into none o' this! If these rebs wanna slice each other up, that's their affair, stay the hell out of it." The boy shrugged and turned away, shouldering the pickaxe and straightening his cap as he went to rejoin the column. Daniel looked at Thompson, who still held the woman and, seeing him nod, he shouldered his musket, and leaving Ballard, Fitzpatrick and the arriving Philipps to finish restraining the women, he moved away down the street to resume his place. He could feel himself trembling as he tried to breathe evenly and there was a sick feeling in his stomach as he walked briskly on past successive files of the detail to regain a place in the prolonged gap beside the Yankees. Sweat was running down his face and he could feel it as it trickled down his torso, under his shirt. He looked into the blue ranks as he went, searching for a sight of the boy with the pickaxe, but, search though he did, he could not distinguish him from the others. Daniel looked again, settling his eyes on a succession of men in turn, convinced that he would surely recognise the boy, but the more he looked, the less he was sure. Plenty of them carried pickaxes and they all wore those blue, kepi caps. As he continued to look, again and again, Daniel found himself beginning to doubt his recollection of the boy's appearance.

"But the whole thing was only a couple of minutes ago," he thought to himself, "surely it would be easy to pick him out?" He stared on into the successive files of the Yankee column but, to his rising frustration, could not find the boy he sought. They crossed Caroline Street once more on their way to the river and still Daniel Ryan looked, disbelieving how he could not recognise the boy, the enemy soldier, who had probably just saved his arm and maybe even his life. So many of them had brown hair, and a bigger proportion of them than the southerners, were also clean-shaven. As a result, Daniel was finding his uncertainty increasingly exasperating.

The detail reached the riverside at Sophia Street and

turned south towards where the Yankees had disembarked. Out on the river they could see the boats returning, the leading one with its white flag at its blunt prow. The column turned down off the street to the shore, but still Daniel Ryan could not find the boy he sought. The detail was halted and he turned, with the others of the escort, and was moving away from the group of Yankees when he heard a voice.

"I reckon a spitfire like that little lady would sure be a handful." He turned at the words, with a rejoinder on his lips about how the people of Fredericksburg had every right to bear a grudge towards the union army, but the thought was stilled as he saw the soldier's face. It was him. Daniel flushed again, feeling his ears grow quickly hot, as they always did, when he was embarrassed. He stepped over towards where the boy stood, trying to think of what he actually could say to him. His blue uniform was plastered with mud from what he had spent his day doing as Daniel's eyes shifted from that into his face.

"I reckon you likely saved my neck….." he began, but the boy shook his head.

"It was my friend who she went for," he said. "If you hadn't gotten her away, she would likely a' done for him with that damned sword she had."

"Even so," Daniel said, "your friend was away out of it by then and you didn't have to make any move to stop her or help me." It was the boy's turn to flush.

"Guess I didn't see it that way," he said. At the bank the boats were pulling in and the sergeants were starting to assemble their men into groups for each of them. Daniel Ryan held out his hand to the boy.

"I'm Daniel Ryan," he said quietly. "I'm from Ireland by way of Savannah in Georgia, and I'm grateful for what you did back there." The Yankee's face turned redder still.

"I'm Curtis Thackeray," he replied. "I'm from Philadelphia

and I reckon you are welcome Daniel Ryan." He stretched out his own palm and they shook hands gravely. Daniel held onto the boy's hand for a second or two, unwilling to dismiss it all as being of such minor importance until, on a further impulse, he fumbled in his pocket, feeling for something that he could give, to mark what this Yankee, from Philadelphia, had done for him. His fingers closed around the little brass-rimmed magnifying glass that he had brought all the way from Eden Station and he pulled it out, holding it immediately towards the boy.

"I'd like you to have this," he said. "What you did may not have meant too much to you, but it surely meant a hell of a lot to me." Curtis Thackeray hesitated, but Daniel proferred the glass again and he slowly stretched out his hand and took it.

"I... I'm very much obliged to you," he said gently. He suddenly pushed his own hand into his tunic pocket and, after a few seconds of searching, pulled out a small pocket knife. He held it out, and suddenly Daniel Ryan's mind squirmed as he thought of what he had said earlier to Ballard.

"Fair exchange is no robbery," Curtis Thackeray said to him. Daniel took the knife and nodded as he closed his fingers around it.

"Amen to that," he said.

The union sergeants were moving around among their men now, bickering at them to move on down and embark on the moored boats. Thackeray too made to move away.

"Stay alive, Yank," Daniel told him and offered his hand once more. They shook hands a final time.

"You too, reb'," Thackeray said. "See you in hell."

"On a damned cold day," Daniel replied and at that the boy turned, balanced the pick-axe once more across his shoulder, and started for the boat. Daniel Ryan watched him go, suddenly aware that Ballard had been right and he had been wrong and it had taken an episode like this to make him see it. He stood there, still feeling stupid, even though nobody but himself could be aware of his discomfiture, or the reason for it.

The boats loaded up and eventually began to successively shove off, making their ungainly way out into the river to swing ponderously on the current as they began their pull for the far bank. It was true, Daniel Ryan thought, as he watched Thackeray's boat take its place in the sequence, they might have to kill each other some way down the line, but in the meantime, though they may prefer to see each other as invaders or rebels, they were all still people and it was likely best that they should try to act that way. He thought of old Mrs Franklin, the union lady up in Maryland, with her twinkling eyes and mischievous expression. She too had helped him, back in September, when she didn't have to, and now here it was happening again. It all seemed to confirm in some way a common, shared humanity, demonstrating anew that, in spite of everything that seemed to indicate to the contrary, there was no real accounting for people, especially not for Yankees, nor even, for that matter, for wars either. It was better therefore to resort to hating them one at a time for it increasingly seemed that there was a perturbing number of them, apparently, who didn't much deserve hating at all.

Chapter 6 The Return of the Fallen

The army no longer occupied the Telegraph Road position now. With the Yankees back across the river and what remained of Fredericksburg back in southern hands, the front line was once more along the river. Picket duty was therefore among the buildings on the river front of the ruined town, or, in the case of their own brigade, along a stretch on the western side of the river downstream from the town. Off-duty men kept, for the most part, to their camps among the woods in the lee of Howison Hill, where the brigade's winter quarters were steadily improved with caulked, log-walled shelters, or even fully-fledged huts, starting to take the place of the tents and crude earth and branch structures, which had first dotted the ground back in November. The days were occasionally punctuated by a visit to the town, though this was a mixed pleasure. Few people now remained in Fredericksburg and its ruins bore much of the character of a ghost town, but getting on a detail into what was left of the place still represented a welcome change from the hum drum of camp life. More time was taken up on work details, set to build further fortifications along the heights above the river, or working on the tracks and makeshift roads that connected the camps with the roads into town, when the weather allowed this kind of work to proceed.

Perhaps it was the battle and the way it had unfolded, or maybe the dramatic display in the sky the following night. Most likely the most important factor was the encounter with the Yankee burial detail, or more specifically that particular Yankee from the burial detail, that got Daniel Ryan into thinking more reflectively on himself and the army and the war itself over the days that followed. He was disturbed by what had happened for it had shaken some of the seeming certainties of his life, since leaving Eden Station over a year previously, certainties that had become more confirmed and established since travelling to Virginia last spring. What they were doing had seemed so definite back then and pretty well ever since. They were defending their homes in Georgia, as Jacob Thornton, the colonel who had led them here only to be himself killed, down near Richmond in those searingly hot days of the summer, had said. Thornton had spelled it out before they had gotten onto the train in Savannah. By defending Virginia they were keeping the Yankees away from Georgia. It made sense and though many boys, including close friends and comrades, had died in doing it, Virginia was still in the fight and holding its own, or at least most of its own.

Why then were doubts and questions now welling up in his mind about all of this? What had changed about it all? Nothing, he told himself, but still the questions came. Why was he here? Where was his life leading? Was he destined to die on one of these fields like those thousands of Yankees had done just the other day? They had all been people, boys, in so many ways like those who had faced and ultimately shot them down and his talk, however brief, with Curtis Thackeray had once more confirmed that. They were sons, and fathers and husbands and brothers just like the southerners who opposed them, each one of them possessed of a life that had now been squandered in that ill-conceived assault on a position that simply could not be taken. So now, up to the north, a whole host of wives were widows, children were fatherless, parents had lost their sons and all for what? Were all of the matters about unions and invasion and State's rights and property and slaves so important that they had to bring into existence these colossal armies, that now went about slaughtering men by the thousand as a result?

Well, to Daniel Ryan, invasion at least had been reason enough, so he had enlisted along with all of these other boys and now they were here, having evolved from recruits into soldiers. Soldiers tended to be fatalists, Daniel Ryan knew that by now, but they did not like to talk too much about what they were most fatalistic about, namely their own precarious survival, whether by the whim of the almighty, or by some freak of battlefield luck or chance. Every soldier wanted to believe that when he went into battle, somehow the man who fell would not be him. Many men entrusted their lives to God and some even professed a willingness to expend those lives, if that was the will of the almighty who arranged all things on this Earth. Daniel Ryan knew that he shrank from that, somehow preferring to believe more simplistically that he would not die, that his luck would hold and that if God did notice that he existed at all, and that he was here in this furnace of death and destruction, somehow he would consent to his survival. There was therefore nothing to be done if a man believed in his cause to the extent that he had enlisted to fight. He had to shoulder his musket and soldier on, trusting in the good lord or his luck, as he chose, and maybe, just maybe….., but it did not do to think about that. The days to come held what they held and there was no point in pushing one's luck too much by trying to extend one's credit with the almighty too far into the future.

But did the southern Confederacy, or the union deserve such a thing as the trust of thousands of their citizens who had enlisted, most of them believing in the righteousness of their own side in this war? One of them had to be wrong, otherwise everything, in spite of what Thornton had said last spring, about the war was a mockery? At the bottom of his soul, when he pondered it, Daniel Ryan still believed in what he fought for. Defending and protecting homes made sense. It was a simple idea, easily grasped and easily accepted. But did this mean that all those thousands of Yankees, men like Curtis Thackeray, had been hoodwinked or misled? Or had the war been presented to them in a different way, a way that had been sufficiently convincing to make them enlist to invade other people's lands and destroy their towns and their farms? Daniel could not fathom this, for how could invasion and destruction, especially on the scale he had recently witnessed, be justified or justifiable?

There was one other factor that he had grown steadily to know and acknowledge as his time in the army stretched on. Loyalty to a cause or a country may be enough to make a man enlist to fight, but once he was a soldier it was another thing altogether that became most important in keeping him there and that thing was comradeship. Life in the army not only threw men together in brigades and regiments and companies, it drew them together in messes, where bonds of friendship were steadily forged that seemed to run deeper than almost any other situation in life, certainly more than Daniel Ryan had ever experienced. Army service forced men into predicaments where trust in comrades was not simply a matter of choice, it was a matter of life and death and that Daniel Ryan had seen at first hand. He owed his life to Daley, in spite of the fact that he could be the most exasperating of people, but that just illustrated the thing about soldiers. While friendship and trust were important things in wider life, among soldiers those things were utterly vital. A soldier had to trust his comrades with his life and he held that same trust from them also. It tended to mean that, whether armies fought for the right or the wrong reasons, these bonds that formed within it would tend to perpetuate it regardless of its cause and, having brought these armies into existence, this continent of America, south and north, was now stuck with them. They would do their worst and many more would die and how it would end nobody really knew and that, in some ways, was the most unsettling question of all for Daniel Ryan.

On the Friday, word of the death of Rodger, had gone around the camps, the news confirmed by Boyce at the evening roll call. There was little in the way of response from the listening files of men. The captain, while acknowledged as a brave enough officer, had never gained much in the way of warmth from the enlisted men. He had been a lawyer, from Riceboro, who had been promoted by his friends and kin when the elections had taken place, down on the peninsula last spring. Some soldiers of the company, back then, had seen him as familiar, a known package, and he had gotten some of his votes on that account. But there had been a manner of fussiness about him, especially once he had gotten the captaincy confirmed, and he had never formed the bond of affection with his soldiers that came from mutual trust. It was, Daniel Ryan reflected, as though he had never fully understood his men. He had indeed been courageous enough, on a sequence of fields, since last summer. Most of his men had been willing to give credit for this, regardless of his faults, so while there was an element of regret, when the news of his death was confirmed, it was little more than that. It had come from a complication, they had heard later that evening, with his shoulder wound, likely bullet or bone fragments, causing the bleed that had ended his life.

Following the news, camp life went on much as it normally did. William Boyce, as senior lieutenant, had taken charge of Company B, since Rodger's wounding on the afternoon of the battle, and had thereafter assumed the role if not the rank. He would likely be confirmed in the post men reckoned, since there was a considerable shortage of experienced officers in the army now, due to the epidemic of death and injury that had taken so many of them, from disease as well as battle, over the summer and autumn. Boyce was popular through being brave and efficient, but most of all he was considerate of his men. He was approachable and took time and trouble to talk with and listen to his soldiers. A sizeable number of those men had preferred him for the captain's post in the spring, but he had not sought the place, leaving them with only Rodger or a newcomer to choose from, but here he was now, raised to company command by the impartial hand of death. Thus the death of Captain Rodger had little in the way of tangible effect on the life of Company B as the brief winter days stretched on towards Christmas and the effects of the slaughter on the slope in front of the stone wall gradually began to fade. It was widely expected that the captain would finish up back in Georgia, though few gave much thought to the whys, hows and wherefores of this, nor to the fact that the repatriation of such dead heroes was not as straightforward here as it might at first have seemed, or as it had been when the army had been campaigning closer to Richmond.

The difficulty was mainly due to the overworked and run down railroad. It was widely known that just two trains per day made the out and back journeys between Richmond and Hamilton's Crossing, where the line now terminated, and, with the whole army gathered in the area around Fredericksburg, supplies for the men and their animals went north, while the wounded and sick went south to the hospitals in the capital city. Many of Jackson's men had departed from the hills south of the town to extend the Confederate defence of the Rappahannock line steadily downstream, towards where the river widened on its journey to the bay. But they, like everyone else, still needed provisioning and with the counties around Fredericksburg being rapidly stripped of food, fodder and anything else that the army could use, supply was largely down to the railroad.

As for the dead whose remains were reclaimed by their families, some of them were evacuated by road on wagons, a proportion of them accompanied by family members, who made the sanguine journey north for the purpose, but most of these also depended on the railroad. Bodies going south were taken for embalming and transportation by one of the many undertakers, who had attached themselves to the army, with an eye to the steady trade for most of the time, and the absolute abundance of it when a battle took place. But here too lay problems of railroad congestion and delay. A week after the battle, with the trains up until then crowded with wounded, most of the dead still awaited shipment south, with little word as to how long the wait would last before they got started on the final journey back to their homes.

On that Sunday Jeffers, with the familiar, harbinger of doom expression on his face, came by their shelter and summoned Ballard, together with Daniel Ryan, to attend on the new acting captain at his tent, though with no reason or explanation as to why. When they got there, Jim Dellings, the dead captain's brother in law and a man regarded in the company as unlucky, having been twice wounded since coming to Virginia, was already at the tent and he nodded as Jeffers arrived with Ryan and Ballard.

"You tell 'em, Barnard," he inquired?

"Nope," Jeffers replied, "ain't none o' my business to do that."

William Boyce then appeared at the tent flap, having likely heard the voices outside, and, after salutes had been exchanged, he beckoned to them all to enter. The tent was crowded by the time they had done so and he quickly indicated to them to sit on the lid of his trunk or squat, in the case of Ryan and Ballard, on the canvas strip which floored the interior. The acting captain settled himself in the folding wood and canvas chair and looked around the group briefly before beginning to speak.

"It is the wish of Captain Rodger's family that his body be returned for burial at his home in Riceboro," he began. "With circumstances as they are at present, this is not an easy thing. The railroad is sorely overtaxed, with our wounded men still being evacuated to Richmond, so the return of the remains of our dead to their families has had to wait." Ryan and Ballard sat in silence, though, at the officer's words, allowed themselves a fleeting exchange of looks. So what in the hell did busy railroads and corpse repatriation have to do with the two of them, Daniel Ryan thought as he focussed again on what Boyce was saying.

"A place has been secured on one of tomorrow's trains for Captain Rodger's remains," Boyce continued. "Sergeant Dellings, being kin to the captain, has been granted leave of absence to oversee the transportation back to Georgia." He broke off again and leafed through some of the papers on the little camp table briefly before coming again to the subject.

"The colonel has decided to send a further escort to

Georgia with Sergeant Dellings," he said at last. "This is not so much due to any perceived need for an officer's remains to be guarded or protected on the journey home, but it concerns an additional part of Sergeant Dellings' mission for his time in Bryan County and Liberty and Bulloch Counties also." William Boyce got to his feet and faced them at that and this gesture re-focussed the attention of those in the tent, as the shifting of eyes and turning of heads, to follow his movement, indicated.

"You must understand this clearly," he said. "The army has now been assembled on this river line for nearly three weeks and many of us have been here for longer. It is the view of our commanders, from General Lee down, that while it is possible that the Yankees might try again to push on south, the roads in this part of Virginia will tend to obstruct them, so we are likely to spend the remainder of the winter in this area. But these same roads, that will deter the enemy, added to the state of the railroad also, will handicap our own army's efforts to maintain adequate supplies of food and other requirements on this line. It is therefore a growing concern among the army commanders that the winter may well see serious shortages in all kinds of supplies, with our men being subject to additional privations as a result. Sicknesses of various kinds, are already taking men from our duty rosters and worse will likely be in store for us, to say nothing of the general decline, like that which we saw in Maryland. This being so, the army could be seriously weakened by the time the spring campaigning commences, without the enemy having to do anything but keep us fixed here on this line.

The colonel is well aware of this risk and has decided to act, before these difficulties are fully upon us. It has been decided that men from the regiment will be detailed to travel south to our homes in Georgia, in order to gather additional provisions to tide us over the shortages that we know are coming. You two men will accompany Sergeant Dellings to Georgia and, when the funeral of Captain Rodger has taken place, you will assist him in collecting from our families and communities down there, as much in the way of food and clothing as can be spared for our men back here. A rendezvous has been set for about two weeks from now, when you, and details from other companies of the regiment, will assemble in Savannah. There you will meet with Lieutenant Jessop, of Company D, who will be heading south in a few days to begin work on the arrangements for transporting what has been gathered back to Virginia. These additional supplies are to see this regiment through the coming months of the winter." Boyce paused at that, though whether this meant he was letting what he had said have time to sink in, or he was taking care in selecting his next words, Daniel Ryan could not tell.

"This is not an entirely official detail," he continued at length. "The generals would certainly not sanction the dispatch of men from every regiment in the army to their homes on such an errand. There would be fears that some might not return, at least not till they had gotten their ploughing and spring planting done, if at all, nor would the railroads be capable of transporting all that was collected. No, Colonel Preston has read the signs of what is coming and, on his own authority, is taking this action early on to head it off. You, and the others, who are returning to Georgia on the same duty, have been chosen carefully because this mission is important. The well-being, or even the survival of the regiment will be in your hands. The supplies you can bring back will be vital to us and you must make all possible efforts to return with as much as you can for your comrades. Go back to the camp and prepare to depart before first light tomorrow. You will make your way to the railhead at Hamilton's Crossing. Sergeant Dellings will meet you there and he will be responsible for the mission until you reach Savannah and rendezvous with Lieutenant Jessop." He stopped speaking and looked around once more.

"Questions," he said quietly? There was a silence and then Ballard spoke up.

"How're the folks back in Georgia gonna git t' know about all o' this so's they can git their supplies ready or bring 'em in. If we got to head round every farm and home collectin' stuff, well that ain't never gonna git done in two weeks, more like two months fer a job like that." Boyce nodded.

"The colonel has considered that," he said, "and it is proposed to solve that problem in two ways. Firstly, word has been sent to Georgia by telegraph, to the towns along the rivers that this regiment recruited from. The messages were sent to the civic leaders, but, most important, letters will also go to the ministers and pastors of the various churches. The churches are where local people come together, especially at this time of the year and that is how word will best be spread. By tomorrow, Sergeant Dellings will have a set of letters, addressed to the various churchmen in your county. You will deliver these to the churches so that word will spread in that way also." He looked at Ballard, who nodded.

"Is that all?" Boyce looked around the group and the men in the tent looked around at each other, but no-one else spoke. He waited for a few moments until, with no further response, he nodded again to them. At that they got to their feet and, after a further exchange of salutes, filed out of the tent. Dellings waited for Ryan and Ballard outside and handed Ballard a piece of paper.

"Yore pass to the Crossing," he said. "Morning train, be there." They nodded and then turned as Jeffers proffered a further paper slip.

"On your way back, stop by the ordnance store. That there pass'll git ya both the thirty rounds o' cartridge that'll be goin' t' Georgia with ya." He and Dellings moved away at that, while Daniel and Ballard stood there briefly, digesting what they had been told.

"By the livin' god," Ballard said. "A furlough, in everythin' but name."

"I'll take it," Daniel told him, "whatever name you want to give it."

"God bless the colonel," Ballard went on. "Gittin' pore John Ellis shot musta' gotten him in a helluva good frame o' mind if he went and thought this up. Mubbee the reason why he cares about the boys goin' hungry is cuz, if they go hungry enough, come the springtime, he might not have nobody left to shoot fer whatever reason he wants to think up."

As they headed back towards their own shelter, Daniel Ryan's mind was a mixture of pleasure and confusion. There was pleasure at the thought of this semi-official, "furlough," from these camps along the river, but confusion was there too, with a level of suspicion also, from Boyce's words about the need for provisions being so acute, even to the point of the survival of the regiment depending on it. From what Ballard had said, concern about the men's supply hardships might be less a matter of humanity and more a matter of sustaining Preston's own position as commander of a regiment, rather than a remnant of one. That was a further, perhaps disagreeable slant on the whole thing, but Daniel Ryan would take the, "furlough," regardless.

Since first travelling to Virginia, many boys had resorted to the practice of writing home for extra food or clothing, to make good the persisting shortages in army provision. But now, unless someone was able to travel to Virginia with such packages from home, they were highly likely to go missing in transit, since, as the boys readily acknowledged, there were many hungry mouths and needy people between Georgia and Virginia. So sending men from the regiment back home to gather such supplies, especially when they could be dispatched as a detail for some other purpose, such as escorting a dead officer's remains back to his home, was simply a variation on what had been going on for months. But Boyce's reference, to survival of the regiment depending on this expedition, was surprising and disturbing. Was the regiment, and indeed the army as a whole, really that close to such a fate through being stationed here on the Rappahannock River? Were things really that bad?

Supplies were short and there was no doubt about that. Rations had been issued on average only on every second or third day over the last four weeks and, at the root of the problem, so many boys said, was the railroad. Like all southern railroads it was neglected and run down. With too many of the mechanics and other workers in the army, the maintenance simply did not get done, unless it was a matter of absolute life or death. Locomotives went out of service to undergo prolonged waits in the depots for the overworked crews to get them repaired or serviced. Spares also were in chronically short supply and since most locomotives were individually made, there was limited scope for taking the worst of them out of service and cannibalising them for parts to repair others. Even when the trains did run, they experienced growing problems and delays all along the lines. At more and more bridges, they had to slow to an absolute crawl to cross, due to the structures having deteriorated to the point of them being in danger of outright collapse while, on increasing stretches of line, the track had worn down, for want of routine replacement or maintenance, to the point of similar risk, with this also slowing progress to a crawl and prolonging journey times.

The Richmond, Fredericksburg and Potomac line came up through the main supply depots at Ashland and Hanover Junction to terminate now at Hamilton's Crossing. The crossing lay out beyond the army's right flank, and back from the river, therefore being safe, through being, for the meantime at least, out of range of the enemy's artillery on the far bank of the Rappahannock. A depot had been set up at the Crossing to provision the army, but there were never enough supplies accumulated there, to meet anything like the demands made by the number of men and animals requiring to be fed and otherwise supplied, for anything more than a day or two in advance.

All kinds of reasons were talked about. Two trains per day each way on the line, was all that were currently timetabled. That could never be enough, and most men could easily see that there must be some grievous incompetence afoot. There were surely more trains available to the company to bring up enough supplies, even on a single track railroad, so was it simply incompetence that prevented this? There were others though, who harboured darker thoughts and accusations over such things as the matter of Samuel Ruth. He was the superintendent of the railroad, and a Yankee by birth. It was perfectly possible, or even likely, some men said, that he was sabotaging the army's supply system, by manipulating the railroad timetables and refusing to run enough trains, sticking instead to the sort of schedules that had applied before the armies had gathered here at the river in November and blaming the state of the line for doing so. Supplies were said to be rotting down in Richmond, and at Hanover and Ashland, simply because they could not be gotten onto trains and there were insufficient vehicles and animals to wagon haul enough of them those forty or fifty miles over frozen or muddy dirt roads, to the camps up on the Rappahannock. These matters had featured regularly in the talk of the men in those camps over the last few weeks, as they considered their own shortages. They were in Ryan's mind again now as he and Ballard, made their way back to their shelter to pack what scant belongings they would take with them. It was nearly dusk and first light would see them well away, but at least with no rations issue again today, as far as they knew, there would be little of their time taken up with cooking or eating.

The most direct road to the railroad at Hamilton's Crossing was more a trail that passed for one. Stonewall Jackson's men had cleared and improved it along the hills to the rear of the line that the army had defended earlier in the month, to allow quicker transfer of troops and guns along Jackson's lines as required. Ballard and Ryan were well started along this way as daylight, such as it was, heralded a chilly and overcast morning, with the wind blowing steady and cold from the northwest. They had headed south from their camp, to join the Mill Road, making their way from there onto the military route. The track was indeed rudimentary and very muddy, with details of marching soldiers, as well as the passage of wagons and the occasional battery of guns, churning that mud into ever more of a slippery goo, as the two of them kept to the side to avoid the worst of the surface. As the road angled around Prospect Hill signs were to be seen of the fighting that had taken place the week before. Scraps of saturated cartridge paper and fragments of cloth spotted the woods to the left, and numerous trees displayed the damage they had sustained from shell fire, with their missing or splintered boughs showing in gashes of yellowish white wood, that stood out against the muted browns of the rest of the forest. Those battle lines had now departed, moved forward beyond the railroad towards the river, with pickets pushed on down to the bank itself. Some units had gone altogether, shifting downstream to guard against any enemy thrust aimed at hooking around the army's right flank to dislodge it from its position by threatening Richmond behind it.

After some initial conversation, Daniel had drifted into silence, but Ballard was clearly in a mood to talk, and in addition to a succession of probes aimed at Daniel, he amused himself in exchanging comments and cracks with passing infantrymen, drivers and teamsters showing all the exuberance of a school boy heading home on the last day of the term.

"Need a boat to git along this here road you boys made."

"D'ja ship in extra mud fer this here road?"

"How're country boys that can't swim supposed to git along here?"

Daniel contented himself with monosyllabic answers for the most part, when a response was called for, as his mind was on other things, unfamiliar things, that were arising out of this prospective return to Bryan County. Things that he had banished to the remoter corners of his mind, as he concentrated on soldiering and surviving here in Virginia, were beginning to surface once more, and prominent among these impending matters was the state of his, "friendship," with Constance Warren.

He had not seen her since the previous Christmas, and, though they still exchanged letters, these had become steadily fewer over the year, with increasing elapses of time between them. Daniel had last written her from the camps near Winchester, during the autumn, in the wake of the campaign in Maryland, but she had not yet replied. He cast his mind back to the months before the coming of the war, when they had taken to going for Sunday walks together. He had been invited around a few times to her house for tea, and even once for dinner. It had all been so casual and easy back then, but matters, that had seemed important then, had paled into insignificance as the withering furnace of the war had abruptly ended such innocent times and pleasures. Daniel missed Constance, but, in Virginia for survival's sake, she was one of the things that had to be put to the back of the mind. So where did their relationship stand now? Was it still in being, dormant rather than declining, or was it another casualty of the war, destined to wither away until nothing remained? Was she one of those things that were changing in spite of everything? Were the two of them just drifting away from each other through separation and circumstance? Her now infrequent letters had spoken repeatedly of her discontent and unhappiness and how the war had changed so much of her previous life. Was he, Daniel, one of the things that had belonged in that previous life and not in this newer, harder one?

Then there were the Bennetts who had given him employment and with whom he had lived in Eden Station, who had gone on to become something between employers and family towards him. He had heard, in a letter from Martha Bennett in the autumn, that Hal's health had not been good and this provided yet another example of how nothing stayed the same. The older couple had been good to him and, when Daniel had taken the decision to enlist, Hal had spoken of him returning to work for him when the war was over. But the war had already lasted far longer than anybody had ever expected it to. It had caused shortage everywhere in the south and outright destruction over an increasing portion of it. Who was to say how it would all end or what would be left when it finally did? The thoughts swirled around in his mind as he sloshed his way along the Military Road towards the railhead, while overhead the clouds shifted and scurried on the gusty, north westerly wind. Beside him, his companion, having accepted at last that Daniel was in a reflective rather than a conversational frame of mind this day, had finally left him to it.

Hamilton's Crossing was surely growing. In essence, as its name suggested, it was nothing more than a place where the rail line crossed a road, but now there was much more to it than that. Safe, so far, from the Yankee guns, this place, where the railroad from Richmond came up to the network of local roads, along which supplies could be distributed, was quickly mushrooming into a depot of considerable size. Huts and sheds were springing up and storage plots, where tarpaulin-covered loads were stacked to await transporting on, were very much in evidence. Even this early in the morning the place was a hive of activity as wagons came, loaded up, and left again, with all of the attendant noises of clattering boxes, shouts of command, and a great coming and going of men carrying sacks and bundles this way and that. Prominent also were the carts of the various undertakers, who followed the army. They were lined today along one side of the road, some of them with two or even three crude, pinewood coffins on board, waiting for the arrival of the morning train, which must soon be due, for them all to be already here. Daniel let his gaze run along the stationary row, every one of them representing its own little chapter of tragedy for somewhere far off to the south. He jerked himself from these thoughts and looked around at Ballard who had also cast his eye along the line of vehicles.

"Good pickin's round here fer them boys," he grunted. Daniel turned away, suppressing a shudder.

"Too many good boys before their time," he said, "but some o' these vultures'll make money out of anythin'."

"Nothin' too bad about vultures," was Ballard's reply.

175

"They clean up things the rest of us leave lyin' around." He looked again and nodded to Daniel.

"Here we all are," he said gently. Daniel turned and looked once more along the line, this time making out the figure of Dellings, who had emerged from behind one of the carts. Daniel noticed that Tom Jensen and Gil Paton, Company D men, were there also.

"Better drop by and say howdy to everybody," Ballard said. Daniel nodded.

"Wouldn't want him gettin' offended and decidin' to take someone else," he replied.

"Hell no," was Ballard's response. "Best damn table manners and Sunday meetin' behaviour." Even as he spoke, Dellings caught sight of them and raised a hand. They started over to where he stood and came to attention as he stepped out into the road towards them.

"Best to see how he wants to play this," Daniel thought as he eyed the sergeant. Something of a grin crossed Dellings' face as he scrutinised the two of them in return.

"Rest easy," he said. "We ain't goin' to go paradin' or drillin' all the way to Georgia the next couple o' weeks." The two of them relaxed, nodding over to Paton and Jensen and getting similar greetings in return.

"Any word of the train," Ballard asked?

"Overdue," was the reply, "but there ain't that many o' them that run on time fer all the effort that damn Yankee makes to git our supplies up his goddam line." He gestured them over to the side of the road as a sequence of wagons approached.

"Why us," Daniel asked? The sergeant seemed to ignore the question at first, but, as they reached the side of the road, he looked at them, as though weighing his thoughts before speaking.

"If you don't wanna do it," he said, "it ain't too late to

get others." He allowed himself a grin at their expressions before continuing.

"You boys are seen as a better bet than some," he went on. "Neither of you are farmers so you ain't goin' to be hangin' back at home to plough or put in crops. The colonel didn't want to send nobody who'd be liable to stay home too long, layin' in seed and fixin' fences, or even thinkin' of runnin' off altogether. You were in Maryland 'n' that marked ya down as stickers so that counted in yore favour. Barnard, and Boyce too, reckoned you two were good choices fer somethin' like this."

"Bin thinkin' all this out fer a while," Ballard said.

"You bet they have," was the answer. "Officers've seen this comin' since way before last week's fight and Preston made up his mind to git in early. Takin' dead men home helps us to git our men away to see to it all. Boys from some o' the other companies headed out over the last couple o' days and there'll be more goin' down tomorrow and Wednesday too. It's Christmas so we all got the job o' shakin' down the counties back home fer all that goodwill and that means supplies," he told them. "Commissary already collects from all o' the folks down there, but we all know that them at home'll make an extra effort when they know that what they give is for their own boys. We could even finish up with a transportation problem once we git it all collected, but when you get started, look for stuff that don't rot quick, else we could finish up throwin' away half of what we get. We're to collect the stuff at the Savannah depot, but I don't have no orders yet about gettin' it there, like whether we'll wagon haul it, or look for freight space on one o' the Gulf Railroad trains. Reckon we'll jest have t' see how the land lies when we get that far and maybe find what Jessop wants when we hear from him."

"Could all be rotted or stole by the time we get through

177

dealin' with the railroad," Ballard put in. "Reckon if we kin wagon it we should get on and do it."

"My thinkin' too," Dellings said, "but there'll be more than that to worry….."

Daniel's eyes strayed away from the sergeant as he saw some of the other men waiting around the vehicles, including the Company D pair, stir themselves. The other two noticed also and turned just as the faintest sounds of an approaching train came to their ears. There was no whistle, since there was no point in going out of your way to attract the attention of the enemy across the river, but the puffing of the locomotive grew steadily louder as the group on the road stood and watched, finally seeing the plume of smoke and cloud of steam come into view around the slope of the hill, above the bare trees that clothed it.

Daniel Ryan walked towards the rail track as he watched the train approach, hearing the trembling shudder along the rails as the brakes were applied. The locomotive slowed steadily as it drew near, shedding clouds of steam as it came in to pass where he stood before grinding to a screeching halt a little further on, just short of where the new sheds had been erected. The caboose had halted almost level with Daniel and as he looked along the cars and wagons, the door slammed open and a grey-bearded figure emerged and stepped out onto the platform and from there down onto the ground. All around a bustle of activity began as car doors were noisily slid open and a detail of men clambered onto the wagons and began to man haul the cases and sacks that were stacked on them. Daniel heard Ballard's voice beside him.

"Ain't no way that this much freight, twice a day'll keep an army like we got up here," he said. "Jest one sidin' or turnin' place up here'd mean they could more'n double the trains that run in a day, but they ain't done' nothin' about that. Mubbee they're too shit scared o' the Yankee artillery over the river placin' guns to shell this place." Daniel nodded as he watched the train's wagons being unloaded. It was being pretty speedily done by a mixture of black and white labourers, with an officer or two looking on, but no matter how slick an exercise they made of that job, it would not materially improve things, unless some way could be found for more trains to be added to the daily timetable.

He began to understand the extent of the growing problem of supply. It was not yet a crisis but the shortages were growing and if something was not done it would steadily become one. An army of over seventy thousand men, with all of its draught animals, simply could not subsist on what could be gathered from the surrounding farms over any sort of extended period of time. It all depended on what could be assembled, by the commissary at Richmond, and forwarded on here and while wagon loads might take some of the strain, the bulk of the problem was down to the railroad. If it could be geared up for a great deal of additional traffic then a solution was possible, if not, then persisting hunger, and maybe even starvation, would be the lot of the Army of Northern Virginia through this winter.

Already it could be seen among the men. They were shaped differently from what they had been before. Since last year, stomachs had shrunk in size, limbs were increasingly sinewy and bones stood out all over their bodies. The army had been through shortage and hardship over the summer, during the campaigns that had thrown the Yankees out of northern Virginia for those vital harvest months and those shortages had been even worse in Maryland during the first half of September. A recovery of sorts had taken place while the troops had recuperated in the fertile Shenandoah Valley through October, but now the persisting problems of hunger were back and where hunger led, illness and disease would surely follow. Whatever anyone thought about Preston and the John Ellis shooting, the colonel was right about this. If something could be done to prevent such an inexorable wastage of the men in the regiment then no effort should be spared. If food could be gathered down in Georgia then a way must be found of getting it up here to where the men could benefit from it.

Daniel Ryan continued to watch as the wagons and flatcars on the train were steadily emptied. Much of the supplies were loaded immediately onto waiting wagons to be hauled away on the Military Road, while more was stacked at the trackside to await transportation through the day. What was obvious was that little of it was being stored for any prolonged stay here, another emphasis, Daniel Ryan thought to himself, of how much of a hand to mouth arrangement the army was already saddled with here on this river line.

His musing was disturbed by a nudge from Ballard and he looked to see the train conductor approaching along the track, stopping to speak to the undertakers, who gathered into a group to hear him. Dellings led them along to the rear of the group and they arrived just as it dispersed, with each of the undertakers returning to their respective vehicles. Daniel looked at Dellings.

"You want us to help load him," he inquired.

"Leave it to him," Dellings snorted, gesturing towards the undertaker. "He's gittin' paid enough for it." The conductor meantime had turned to the group of soldiers, including the five of the, "Blues."

"If you boys 're travellin'," he said, "ya'd best get yoreselves aboard."

"You the conductor," Dellings asked.

"Lorenzo Higgins," was the reply. "Richmond, Fredericksburg and Potomac Railroad, 'cept there ain't been no Potomac bit fer a while and now there ain't much of a Fredericksburg bit neither. Good job we still got the Richmond piece, else there wouldn't be no point in havin' no railroad at all around here." He gestured them back down the train.

"Step right that way," he continued, "cuz, once these undertaker boys got their business under way, you boys'll jest be in the way up here, so ya might as well git on board and git yoreself settled. Least ya'll find it warmer than out here. We'll be headin' off directly, once we git loaded up." He paced away with his sheaf of papers while the collection of soldiers moved on down to cluster at the foot of the steps which ascended to the door of the car.

The interior bore a sorely run down look, There was dust everywhere, covering the seats, with only the places where people had recently sat showing polished wooden slats, this achieved by either the backsides or the handkerchiefs of the now departed passengers. The wooden fittings, both panels and seats were scraped and chipped with the varnish scored or peeling in various places. The floor was covered with muddy footprints and a covering of dirt was ingrained in the worn boards, with several of them slack and given to move when stepped upon. A number of the windows were cracked and still more were broken, not all of them being covered with card or wood. The soldiers moved down the car, stopping at the seats of their choice, though none of them troubled to produce a handkerchief for a job that their already grubby pants would easily do. They settled themselves, wedging their muskets between the seats and each other as they stretched their legs and grinned and bantered with each other. There were few other passengers and these, situated themselves as far from the soldiers as they could, while still remaining in the car.

It was middle morning when the train pulled away

from the crossing. Dellings had joined them just before the departure, having spent time further up the train presumably dealing with the arrangements for Rodger's coffin, which was safely accommodated with the others on one of the freight cars. The day had brightened somewhat, though only as far as a lightening of the cloud cover, with no sign of any winter sun when the locomotive jerked abruptly into motion and began to edge laboriously away from the crossing, puffing furiously to gradually gather speed as it jolted over the neglected rails.

It laboured south, slowing repeatedly, presumably at places where the line was in need of repair, and stopping altogether at a wider river that Dellings said would be the North Anna. Daniel Ryan gazed out through the nearest of the car's windows, peering through the covering of dirt and grime streaks at where a gang of negroes, laboured on the bridge under the supervision of a railroad official, who stood with a couple of uniformed engineer officers. A few of the loose-bowelled, including two of their own car occupants, took this opportunity to disembark and make for the bushes, for a temporarily relief of their affliction, before the train was waved on by the railroad man, sounding its whistle as a warning before edging out onto the bridge at a snail's pace, while the last of the diarrhoea sufferers rushed to re-embark, one or two still fumbling at buttons or pants flaps as they came.

On the train journeyed, with a succession of places on the line itself, as well as bridges over various creeks and gullies, prompting further slow downs or even halts. At some of these places repair work was under way, while others were simply negotiated by the train, with a violent juddering or jerking of the cars, while the ears of the passengers were subjected to successions of screeches and grinding noises of varying intensity. Dellings kept any who were interested informed as to their whereabouts, listing in turn the South Anna crossing and then the Pamunkey, Atlee's Station and Ashland, where the train unhitched some of its freight cars while it took on water, and still more needy toileters completed their business in the undergrowth. The journey resumed, as the last of the morning passed and noon came, with the train finally picking its way across the Chickahominy River, familiar to all of the men who had campaigned here in the summer, and a clear indicator, at last, of their proximity to Richmond.

It took a while for them to clear the freight yard outside the city. More cars were uncoupled from the back of the train before the passenger cars and the remaining box cars eventually proceeded on the last short stretch into town. What was left of the train chuffed into the depot on Broad Street in the early afternoon to find the place a hive of activity. Details of soldiers arrived and left, or dallied in groups, waiting for trains or orders, while endless wagons, loaded with provisions and equipment of every conceivable kind, arrived and departed. Others waited around the depot, presumably for the next bout of loading or unloading. Piles of boxes, barrels and sacks were set in lines along one side of the track. Daniel Ryan's group reached for weapons, blankets and equipment belts and made to disembark, emerging from the car to see porters and orderlies unloading the train's cargo, including the coffins from the first of the remaining boxcars. Dellings headed off in that direction while Ryan and the other three exchanged looks before following on. They arrived at the car to find that the late captain's remains had already made it as far as the trackside.

"Stay with it," Dellings called to them. "I'll go git the undertaker round here." The four of them waited, while the coming and going of the depot went on all around them. Ballard sniffed and, seeing him, the others did likewise.

"Don't reckon the undertakers did much work on him," Paton said.

"Nor on any of the others neither," Ballard added. "Sure hope there ain't too many hold-ups on this here trip, else he'll be on his way out o' there by the time we git to Savannah."

"Be worse if it was summer," Daniel told him, needlessly, but his friend just grimaced and they turned to join Paton and Jensen who had begun scrutinising the depot and the street beyond for any sign of the Women's Hospitality or Church groups who attended the railroads to distribute refreshments or even food items to the transiting soldiers.

After some investigation they located a stall at one side of the depot, departing in pairs to secure a cup of coffee substitute and a square of sweet cornbread each before Dellings returned. With the sergeant was a tall thin man with slicked back, grey hair, long side whiskers and a goatee beard. He was dressed in a seedy black suit and a tall hat and he approached with has hands clasping a walking cane behind his back. He nodded at the sergeant's indication, heading towards Rodger's coffin and signalling at once to two, "assistants," who made their way through the crowd towards him, pushing a small handcart. The box was lifted onto the vehicle and this done the small procession moved away, heading across the depot towards the street. The man in the black suit promptly manoeuvred his way to the front of the cart.

"Make way!" he called, stretching his hands and the cane out in front of him. "Show respect for a fallen hero. Make way!" Some did, while others showed little in the way of interest or response to his shouts. A space of some sort did appear in front of them, more, Daniel Ryan thought, because many in the crowd, who encountered the cortege, wished to avoid colliding with the cart than through any widespread degree of acknowledgement or respect for the dead hero's passing. With the tall man still leading the way, the two orderlies pushed the cart on through the crowd out onto Broad Street. Here rows of carriages, carts, and wagons waited, their drivers clustered around in groups, chewing tobacco or smoking pipes and exchanging their views on the events of the day. At the end of the row, stood a succession of hearses and, upon Dellings' party emerging from the crowd at the depot, an old man detached himself from one of the groups and made for the vehicle second from the end. From there, he directed the arriving cart behind the hearse and, while he steadied the vehicle, and the tall man tended its rear door, the two orderlies lifted the coffin from it and slid it along the vehicle floor between a set of metal stops. This done, the orderlies withdrew and the driver and the tall undertaker moved around to the front of the vehicle to take their places on the seat there. The undertaker turned to Dellings.

"Richmond and Petersburg depot," he called in what sounded to Daniel like a half-question and half- statement. Dellings nodded.

"You and your escort may follow on or make your own way," the undertaker went on. "I regret that we are unable to oblige you with transportation. If we allow soldiers on any of our vehicles these days, it just brings widespread complaint over ah... cleanliness matters and, being the servants of the public, we would prefer to avoid that." There was a moment or two of half-embarrassed silence upon which the driver shook his reins and steered his horses away from the sidewalk, walking them off down the street initially at a sedate funereal pace, while Dellings and his detail watched them merge into the busy traffic. The hearse however had not gone far down the busy street, before, with the demands of respect apparently satisfied, the driver gave the reins a further shake, hustling his animals into a rather more businesslike trot. Ballard turned to Dellings

"You want us to chase along behind them nags and walk in their shit," he growled?

"It ain't of no account here," the sergeant answered. "Back home, where it matters, there'll be plenty to follow on after him. We'll just get ourselves on down to the Petersburg depot the easy way."

The five of them promptly hitched their muskets onto their shoulders by their straps and headed away from the noise and bedlam around the depot. They crossed busy Broad Street just east of the railhead and, having negotiated the traffic around the theatre there, they were directed straight down Seventh Street by Dellings.

"We kin get across the bridge over the Canal at the end o' the basin there," he told them. "It's the shortest way down."

Having crossed the bridge, they made their way on past the block of tobacco warehouses to where the Richmond and Petersburg Railroad depot stood almost on the James River. They might even be there before the hearse, Daniel Ryan thought, as it would be compelled to head further east, likely even as far as Twelfth Street, through all of the traffic, in order to make its way around the canal basin and then use one of the vehicle bridges over the overspill at either Eleventh or Thirteenth Streets.

"Mubbee git some more vittles at the rail depot," Jensen grunted.

"Sure it's a fine job that them Hospitality folks do," Daniel told him and they exchanged further conspiratorial smirks as they came up towards the building, where a further confusion of animals and vehicles of every kind milled around on the extension of Eighth Street that served as its approach. Daniel addressed Dellings.

"We were thinkin' that the local women might be servin' some kind of food down here," he said. "Maybe you'd like a little reconnoiterin' done while you watch for the hearse?"

"Fine with me," the sergeant said. "You two go take a look, we'll be back here." Daniel Ryan grinned at Ballard and they headed off to begin making their way down the length of the depot building south towards the paper mill and the river bank beyond. There was a definite smell in Daniel's nostrils of something cooking, but he resisted the temptation to build up his hopes unduly. Life, he reminded himself, particularly for those in the Army of Northern Virginia, could be full of beguiling promises and frustrated hopes, particularly in matters such as these.

"Sure as hell is somethin' cookin' around here," Ballard muttered, as they approached the corner of the main depot building. Maybe there, Daniel thought, at the end, where a small crowd had gathered. They reached the corner of the building and immediately came across it. It was soup, being served from a large iron pot into the tin cups of a line of soldiers, together with a chunk of cornbread pushed into the hands of each man by two smiling women. That would do nicely, Daniel thought as he and Ballard unhitched their own cups from the straps of their haversacks and joined the line.

The soup was piping hot, warming and almost burning Daniel Ryan's fingers through the metal of the cup as the two of them worked their way through the crowd, back to the street where they had left the other three.

"Ain't home cookin'," Ballard said, "but it fills a space."

The hearse had arrived at the depot and already the tall undertaker had enlisted two further orderlies, with a similar cart to the previous one, for the job of transferring the dead captain's coffin to the train. Daniel brandished the cup and the cornbread in his hands and, seeing them, Dellings gestured to the other two, who were immediately off on their way.

"Reckon I'll see this done first," the sergeant said,

"Don't take all day," Daniel said. "The pan wasn't so big and there was a crowd around it." The sergeant looked around at the undertaker, who was ready to move off with the orderlies, the cart and its burden.

"Train ain't in yet sir," the tall, thin man said. "We'll attend to the deceased, if you're in need o' some sustenance." That was enough for Dellings who made his way off after Jensen and Paton, while Daniel and Ballard sipped at their soup. There were plenty of vegetables in it and maybe a taste of some kind of stock though, so far, no trace of any actual meat. He followed on after the cart with Ballard, still sipping tiny mouthfuls of the slowly cooling mixture and nibbling around the corners of the cornbread. He was still doing so when the other three arrived with their own portions.

"Ain't like grandma's," Jensen said, "but I ain't turnin' it down."

Dusk was approaching, and the undertaker had long since taken his leave, by the time they heard the first whistle of the approaching train. They heard it in the distance for some time, even above the multitude of other noises around the depot, first by the whistle whoop and then by the sounds of puffing and loudly hissing steam from the locomotive, which gradually came into view, in the failing light down over the river. The train had slowed almost to a walking pace as it made its way out onto the bridge that spanned the James on its succession of stone piers, gingerly easing across the wooden structure, before grinding into the depot, with its brakes screeching and clouds of steam billowing from its vents and from around its wheels. As on the Richmond and Fredericksburg line, the train's arrival triggered a flurry of activity, as porters and labourers went swarming around the wagons and flatcars to begin the job of unloading. The five with the coffin stood well back from the track while this went on, waiting with several other groups on similar missions, some of them with black-clothed relatives grouped solemnly around the caskets of their deceased kin.

Into the evening the unloading and loading continued, with relays of men shifting much of the newly arrived goods away onto wagons, which successively vanished into the gathering darkness. At last the activity round the rail wagons and cars subsided until another uniformed man, who, by his dress and sheaf of papers, was most likely the Petersburg and Weldon Railroad's version of a conductor or train master, made his way up towards where the coffins and their escorting parties waited.

"We're ready t' load up now," he told them. "I'll git started signin' the names o' yore deceased folks off first and then ya kin see t' gittin' 'em aboard. They'll be travellin' on the car at the far end there and there'll be boys along soon to lift 'em on fer ye. It'd help if them goin furthest got put on first, seein' as how they'll be gittin' off last, if that don't inconvenience nobody none."

It was all done with little in the way of mishap, likely because the railroads would, Daniel Ryan reflected, have had plenty of practice by now. Rodgers' box was duly marked, with a chalk inscription of, "W'ton – Ch'ston – Sav'," scrawled along the lid by the conductor. At that it was lifted away, as the man turned to Dellings and his companions.

"Caboose fer you boys," he muttered, "ain't ev'body around here thinks yo're all heroes an' sech. Some payin' passengers don't like the crawlin' kind o' things you boys bring aboard with ya. They don't say nothin' about officers so far, but it don't strike me that any o' you are high enough up in the peckin' order o' the army fer that to apply." Daniel smiled ruefully. Lice were a trial to almost everyone in the army, but, after a time with them, one seemed to pay progressively less attention to the itch and just get on with other things. The thought of train passengers, in their Sunday best, catching the infestation struck him as vaguely funny and others seemingly saw the joke also as a subdued, ironic chuckle ran around the group of soldiers.

"Best git on down thar ," the conductor told them. "Never mind," he added, "let 'em have their damned cars. Warmer in the caboose and we might be able t' rustle up somethin' tasty down there." He gave them a toothy grin through his spiky whiskers. "Wait jest down there," he said. "I'll be along directly." Daniel shook his head. Things were obviously different on the various railroads, he thought, but different in this case might turn out to be better rather than worse.

They moved on down the train, stopping when they reached the conductor's car. They waited there, as though reluctant to enter when the man was absent, but, after a further while, he re-appeared, still clutching his papers.

"Git along up there," he called. "We ain't gonna be standin' on no ceremony an' I reckon we got jest about enough seats to go around in there." They climbed up onto the platform and pushed inside. As his turn came and he stepped into the dimly lit interior of the caboose, Daniel Ryan felt a blanket of warm smoky air envelope him. The conductor, came in last and slammed the door. His initial occupation was to step across the car and slap his papers down on the small table bolted to the front partition. He then moved across to a wooden bunker at one side, pushed open the hinged top and lifted a couple of lumps of wood,

190

which he carried to the metal stove that stood on a stone plinth in the middle of the floor.

"Soon git ourselves in order around here," he muttered, half to himself, as he lifted a poker from beside the stove and pushed at the catch of the door to open it, leaving the poker wedged in the catch while he shoved the wood pieces inside. Then the door was levered shut and the poker dropped with a clang onto the stone. At that, he turned to his guests, who still stood around the car awaiting his attention.

"OK now," he intoned. "Wendell Shaw at yore service as long as yo're passengers on the Richmond and Petersburg Railroad. You boys set yoreselves down," he said, waving his hand towards the bench seats which stretched along either side of the car. "Once I git us all away, we kin see to some coffee fer y'all, and maybe find a tincture o' somethin' to spice it up a little." At that he was out of the door of the car and gone again, while the men inside exchanged glances with each other as they moved towards the seats.

The coffee, rather inevitably, turned out to be another of the baked nut concoctions that substituted for the unobtainable real thing all across the south. It was improved however by the measure of corn whiskey that Wendell Shaw added from a bottle taken from the cupboard of the car and having obtained their measures of each the men returned to their seats.

Daniel Ryan sat and slowly sipped the mixture from his tin cup in the stuffy warmth of the caboose, feeling the beginnings of drowsiness coming over him as he half listened to the conductor voice his critical views of the Richmond and Petersburg Railroad in particular and, as he warmed to his subject, the whole southern rail system in general. One by one the soldiers drifted off to sleep, with one of them even managing to drop his almost empty cup onto the floor as slumber overtook him. The sleepers were therefore spared the old conductor's further peroration on the shortcomings of the god-damned southern Confederacy and of Jefferson god-damned Davis in particular as the train lurched its way on through the Virginia darkness.

It was the morning of an overcast and showery Christmas Day when Daniel Ryan stood at last with Jim Dellings at the halt at Fleming's on the Savannah, Albany and Gulf Railroad. The dead captain's increasingly pungent remains now reposed under a tarpaulin on the wooden bench that was more used to accommodating live passengers, while the train that had deposited them at the halt puffed away into the distance. There was no sign of traffic on the roads, but Dellings had telegraphed on ahead from Savannah so that the captain's family could arrange to have the coffin and the sergeant himself collected. A further brief telegraph message had been sent ahead to Eden Station, though there was, after a year's further absence, a doubt in Daniel Ryan's mind as to whether the Bennetts would be particularly happy at this yuletide arrival, especially if Hal was unwell.

Paton and Jensen had departed at Savannah and Ballard had also gone, alighting from the train at Way's Halt on the river, to head off for his home. Daniel was thus faced with the prospect, once Dellings and the coffin had been collected, of the hike of several miles from the railroad into town, but his thoughts on that were interrupted by the approach of a further vehicle from the south. It turned out to be another hearse, though rather less grand than the one employed in Richmond. It was being driven by an older man, but he was thickset to the point of corpulent and had a round jovial sort of face, crowned by a tall hat, quite unlike the image of an undertaker that Daniel Ryan had grown used to over the last few days. The vehicle jolted up to the crossing place and turned there to come to a halt almost beside where Ryan and Dellings stood.

"How're ya, Jim," the driver greeted Dellings and then raised a hand to acknowledge Daniel.

"Mornin' Charlie," Dellings called and he stepped forward to shake the man's hand once he had dismounted from the seat.

"Not the reason ya'd want to be back home fer," the man Charlie said and Dellings nodded.

"Surely ain't," he said, "but it's the good lord's will and we jest have to make the best we kin of it." He looked towards Daniel and they moved to either end of the coffin lifting it carefully and moving it towards the rear of the hearse. The fat man, Charlie moved to the other side of Daniel's end and they manoeuvred the front of the box onto the bed of the hearse, with Daniel then moving to the rear, to assist Dellings in manhandling it into the vehicle. He caught a further trace of the smell in his nostrils as they pushed the box the last few inches and he found himself thankfully reflecting that this marked the end of his association with the deceased captain as he stepped back. Straps were fastened around it as Daniel waited and Dellings turned to him as the undertaker finished his work.

"You could get on your way now," he said. "Saturday, in Riceboro. I'll meet both o' you in front of the meetin' house in the middle o' town at noon." Daniel nodded.

"Enjoy yore time with your folks," the sergeant said as Daniel lifted his musket and stepped across the tracks to start away to the north on the Eden Station road, reconciled by now to a wet and muddy tramp up to town. The rain began to spatter down again as he sloshed through the mud around the first bend from the tracks, but his recently acquired, Yankee shoes had proved much more water resistant than his previous ones and with his gum blanket to hand to drape, poncho like across his shoulders, most of his clothing would be saved from a drenching also.

But hardly had he pulled the blanket roll from his shoulder and begun to unroll it, when he heard the sound of an approaching vehicle. He looked along through the bare trees to catch sight of a cart approaching. That cart, and the horse that pulled it, struck a chord in his memory. He would know them both anywhere, for it was the same vehicle that he had driven himself many times in Hal Bennett's employ, and it was the same old mare, Jenny who was pulling it. The driver caught sight of Daniel and raised an arm in greeting, and Daniel immediately recognised him also, for it was Bart Turner, the Bennett's son-in-law. Daniel waved in return, relieved at the thought of being spared the muddy hike. Bart and his wife Susanna routinely spent Christmas with the Bennetts, but at least Bart's arrival here seemed to indicate some warmth in the welcome that Daniel himself could expect back here in Eden Station. The buggy pulled in with more mud splashing up from its wheels as Bart hauled on the reins.

"Good to see you, Daniel," he called. He squinted down at him as he steadied Jenny with his hands, "but you look a couple of pants sizes smaller since the last time I saw you."

"Direct consequence of soldierin'," Daniel answered as he slung his equipment belts into the cart and balanced his musket against the side before climbing up to shake hands with Bart and settle himself on the seat. Already the visit back to Georgia was looking up he thought as he reached for the gum blanket.

"My heavens Daniel Ryan," Martha Bennett had exclaimed as she steered him around the side of the store to the back gate and the laundry beyond. "You need a good launderin' and disinfectin' from head to foot," she went on as she fussed around him, "but I reckon that won't take too long cuz there ain't hardly a pickin' o' meat on you. Don't that Robert E. Lee feed you at all in that army?"

"Well it ain't every day that we get three platefuls," Daniel replied as he followed her through the door and began to clamber out of his uniform ready to take refuge in the towel that she offered, hearing the welcome utensil sounds and smelling hints of the appetising aromas of dinner as Susannah busied herself in the kitchen, just through from the wash-house where Daniel's ablutions were getting under way.

"Some serious fattenin' up is called for here," Martha tutted as she picked up the tunic and pants with a pair of wooden tongs and deposited them in a large tub that smelled strongly of the disinfectant she had threatened.

"Bath first for you," she scolded as she prodded him towards an even bigger tub with the tongs, "and then dinner."

Ballard had arrived about an hour after daylight, on the Saturday, driving a buggy, pulled by an even older mare than Jenny, both the vehicle and the animal, he said, being family heirlooms. He pulled up outside Hal Bennett's store and whistled, rather than dismounting and coming into the store. Daniel was ready and, in acknowledgement of the overcast sky, he grabbed up his belts and a waterproof coat and headed straight out of the door, seeing his friend grin as he looked him up and down in his laundered, closer-cropped and clean-shaven state.

"Boys back in Virginia won't know who in the hell you are," he said.

"No more than you," Daniel retorted, as he hauled himself up onto the bench seat, for Ballard was equally transformed, wearing a waxed raincoat over his cleaned tunic, and, though he had retained his beard, it had been trimmed close to his face giving him a dapper and groomed air. With Daniel in his seat, he flapped the reins and the mare moved off, as his companion continued to settle himself. Riceboro and the funeral now seemed something of a diversion from the main purpose of their trip, Daniel thought, but, being obliged to go through its ritual, the sooner it was done, the better.

The little graveyard was crowded, even though a further, dispiriting rain had come, to patter down upon those who had gathered there. The wind of the past few days had eased and the winter air, though chilly, was almost still as Daniel Ryan and Otis Ballard watched, slightly detached from the group of family and friends of the late captain. In addition to the other features of his grooming, Daniel had also left his Yankee shoes at the Bennets' and wore instead a new pair of stout work boots that Hal had provided him with.

He tramped them reassuringly on the muddy ground in turn, feeling not a trace of wetness on either foot.

"It's as well they're gittin' him in the ground at last," Ballard muttered, as he watched the proceedings, "afore he's leaked outa there." Daniel said nothing in reply.

He had witnessed the earlier events of the funeral, with little interest, from the beginning of the service in the meeting house, where prayers had been offered and a tribute paid to the deceased captain by the local minister. Rodger had been described in glowing prose as a pillar of the community here in Georgia, and as a redoubtable military hero also. Daniel had listened to it all, even while he reflected that it had not really described the man that he had known, and if Rodger's achievements, down here in his home town, were on a par with his exploits in the army then his life had been more of a procession of comparative mediocrity. He, Daniel Ryan had seen the substance of Captain Rodger's military career over the previous near to two years and about the most that could be said was that he had been no coward. There had been repeated times when he had toadied after his superiors and Daniel could recall a number of those occasions. His finest moments, most likely, had been when he was instrumental in rallying the remnant of the regiment along the length of that stone wall south of Sharpsburg after the bridge over Antietam Creek had been lost, but that seemed somehow isolated when compared with the other times. A succession of occasions, when his habit of fussing over details of army regulations, rather than following any strand of common sense, came also to Daniel's mind as, having followed the brief procession after the hearse as the cortege made its way to the graveyard, he continued to observe the proceedings. He could, as he now watched, see and feel in it a further manifestation of some of the questions that had troubled him since the battle and the sentiments that had come to him up at Hamilton's Crossing came back to his mind also. Listening to the minister's further glowing words on the captain's life, it began to appear to him that there was something about this whole event that was more than simply an overly optimistic account of what the man's existence and exploits had amounted to.

It was likely, he thought, that some, like himself and Ballard, had attended today's service out of obligation, or to maintain face locally, but as the funeral proceeded it was becoming increasingly clear that a number of these people, in addition to Rodger's immediate family, were here because they held genuine regard for the man. Daniel looked around the circle of people who surrounded the freshly dug grave, taking in the conduct and demeanor of a succession of the mourners. At the core of this scene was the sombre picture of a family struggling with the job of starting to come to terms with its loss. Daniel's eyes reached the deceased captain's wife, a smallish woman with long, pleated, light-brown hair, now restrained under a laced net as well as her black mourning bonnet. Her eyes were red and swollen from crying and her face was stained with the passage of her tears. She stood, resting her hands, one of them still clasping a handkerchief, on the shoulders of her two children, one of maybe eight and the other perhaps a couple of years older. The little boy, with his face pale and his mouth set in a grim line, was doing his best to play the part of a man, while his younger sister openly wept as she looked upon her father's coffin. Around the mourners others too were having trouble controlling their emotions, as the minister droned on and, even though he knew that close to two years of soldiering had hardened him towards death and suffering, Daniel Ryan found himself pitying these strangers.

It was not that he had in any way changed his opinion of the late captain, but it was as though, like that day on the Garnett Farm near Richmond, when he had first seen boys around him die in battle, he was seeing another true image of this war for the fist time. As back then, this scene was forcibly demonstrating to him one of the conflict's true consequences for it was not just the comrades of dead soldiers who suffered loss in a war. In observing this funeral he was seeing it confirmed that the loss of the family was much more profound than that of the military companions of the dead.

All over the south, and no doubt throughout the northern states as well, as a result of that great fiasco of a battle up at Fredericksburg, this kind of scene was taking place. People, in huge and still growing numbers, had found that this war, embarked upon to establish their freedom or to preserve their union, had cost them a price that they could not afford to pay. The desolation of their family was a cost that nobody thought would come to them. As the men in the army preferred to think that it would surely pass them by, so families too likely believed that death would pass on instead to some other nameless, anonymous men and their families far away, and yet here it had not done so. The armies were doing their worst and the full weight of that was on these people now and on the many thousands like them, who had maybe heard or even spoken of the, "supreme sacrifice," but had never believed that they would really have to make it.

Daniel had by now seen plenty of those men, in grey or butternut brown, and in blue also, who had died on the different fields where the war had led him, but today was the first time that circumstances had led or obliged him to follow the consequences of such an event to its logical conclusion. Here in Georgia, in this cold and dismal rain, were these people, two days after Christmas, stunned by their loss and maybe, at the bottom of their hearts, having clung to the fleeting hope that it was all a mistake and would be proved so, until the body had arrived home and all doubt had been removed. Now, for this family, any remaining wisp of illogical hope had been finally dashed, the same way that his own had been on the day, just over seven years ago, when they had brought his father's body home after the accident in Tralee.

The minister had at last finished and now the interment was beginning as the menfolk of the family, almost all of them old and wrinkled, stepped solemnly forward, to lift the ropes that stretched under the coffin and would shortly cradle it to its last resting place in the ground. Dellings was among them, standing out in his uniform, it, like those of Ballard and Ryan himself, laundered and repaired. The sergeant grasped the middle of the three ropes, on the right side of the casket, as the undertaker, the same who had come to Flemings two days ago, gestured to the six men.

"If you could pull in now gentlemen," he murmured. The men moved, Daniel saw their shoulders hunch as they tested the weight of the coffin and paused briefly.

"Could you lift, steadily now," Daniel could just catch the man's words as he gave his next instruction and, with a gentle creak of the ropes, the coffin haltingly rose while a few sobs and gentle gasps of anguish from a few of the mourners greeted its movement. It hung there momentarily, rocking and creaking just perceptibly on its ropes, until its supporting poles were withdrawn by a scurrying attendant, upon which the undertaker spoke again.

"Could I ask you to lower down slowly, gentlemen?" The movement of their hands and arms began again, almost but not quite in unison, and the rain spattered coffin slowly descended. Into the ground it went, past the wet and puddled earth laid by the side of the grave, moving below the rim of the hole and steadily on down, until it was out of sight, with only the straining creaks from the ropes and the movement of the hands of the pallbearers telling of its continuing descent. Then there was a faint, wet crunching sound and, the ropes went slack.

"Thank you gentlemen, you may withdraw," came the undertaker's voice. The men dropped or placed their ropes on the ground and stepped back, while Daniel watched intently, knowing that while this family were of no direct consequence to him, their loss had recalled from a closed part of his mind that sombre chapter of his own life. This funeral was reminding him again of the inexorable truth of the human predicament that he and his family had been compelled to face back then and that so many others over here were having to face now.

Up until that day back in Ireland, he had regarded

himself as safe and secure within the sanctuary of his own family, but then he had been compelled to confront the mortality of human existence with the death of someone indispensable to him. It was an event that had changed his life and, in due time, had most to do with him finishing up here in America in the first place. The death of his father had imposed on him the rude inevitability that, sooner or later all men must die, but, being human, men somehow always tended to believe that it would be later rather than sooner. Death came however, regardless of what people wanted or expected and with today's funeral there came an additional factor, for the death of Captain Rodger, like all the others now, was part of that whole raft of questions and doubts that had troubled Daniel Ryan since the days after the battle for it was one of the many deaths that made up this epidemic of dying called war.

Daniel looked again at the faces of the woman and her children, seeing their renewed tears and he pitied them once more, knowing, as he did so, that pity was of no consequence to them. The captain may have been of no great account to him, but he had been one of the fulcrums of their life and now he was gone. Their ordeal was now begun and the saddest thing of all was that, over the months and maybe years to come, many, many more families, thus far spared this ordeal, would be compelled, by the events and demands of this war, to walk the same road that Captain Rodger's people were now marooned upon. This event was making him ponder once again on the enormity, in sheer human terms, of what he had become engaged and embroiled in here in America. Beside him Ballard moved, jerking him out of his meditation.

"Rain ain't let up at all," he said. "Helluva day fer somethin' like this."

"Is there such a thing as a good day for somethin' like this Otis," Daniel asked him?

"Fightin' means killin'," his friend replied grimly, which, Daniel Ryan thought to himself, was maybe just a simpler, more brutal way of summing up much of the substance of his own thoughts.

Chapter 7 Mission of Mercy

The Sunday service in the meeting house in Eden Station was well attended, like all of the previous times that Daniel could recall and today he noticed several crippled ex-soldiers among the congregation. There was Abel Telfer, Jed Langley and Joe Holbrook, Telfer minus a leg, lost on the Garnett farm, last summer, Langley missing fingers and an eye from Malvern Hill the same week and Holbrook with a withered arm gained at the same place. There too was Thad' Neilsen, invalided out of the regiment during their time on the peninsula last spring, with a chronic chest ailment. He looked gaunt and wasted now and coughed repeatedly. Daniel nodded to each of them, getting a similar greeting in return as he moved to take his place in the pew. He was aware of different people in the gathering congregation eyeing him as they arrived and he wondered how much of his mission had percolated around the town in the preceding days. The place brought back many memories to him, as he waited there with the Bennett family, but he was diverted from his reminiscing by the snatches of subdued talk going round before the service began. This indicated that some at least of those present already knew something at least of the supplies quest, of which Daniel Ryan's presence was some kind of tangible proof but the various subdued conversations around the room were interrupted in their turn as the organ squeezed into life to introduce the opening hymn.

The congregation stood for the entry of Pastor Elias Stockley, who, as Daniel had already observed, looked a little older and greyer, with the bald patch atop his head a shade larger than he remembered. The pastor carried in his hand the envelope that Daniel had delivered to him, having taken two others to the ministers of the other country meeting houses situated near the town, early on the day after Christmas. Stockley moved across and came to a stop behind the lectern on the other side of the dais at the front of the church. He placed the envelope between the pages of the bible which lay open in front of him, while the familiar stanzas of the hymn rang around the little church to commence the service, with Stockley's deep, baritone voice now supplementing the efforts of those in the pews. At the hymn's conclusion, the organ fell silent and a prayer was recited, upon which the congregation settled themselves again in their seats, with a confused mixture of thuds and rustles while the Pastor readied himself to address his flock.

His lesson was, perhaps predictably, on the blessings of the child of Christmas and Daniel stayed alert throughout, waiting and wondering whether the minister would deal with the colonel's request as part of his lesson or as an additional matter afterwards. On Stockley went, giving his congregation a liberal helping of God's gift of the Christmas birth to a distracted and sinful world, but it was not until the end of his lesson, the offering, more prayers and the singing of further hymns, that the envelope at last found its way into his hands from where it had lain throughout the service.

The meeting house was silent while he opened it, with the dry rustling of the paper sounding clearly around the room as he removed and unfolded the letter. The minister squinted at it for a few moments through his metal-rimmed spectacles and adjusted them briefly before beginning to speak again.

"I have here a letter from Colonel William Preston, who is presently the commanding officer of the Ogeechee Volunteer Rifles. That is the regiment in which most of our local boys enlisted and it is now serving in Virginia under the command of General Lee. The letter is dated the 19th of this month and I will read it to you now." He cleared his throat and peered again at the paper.

"Dear Reverend, I write this letter for two reasons and, when you understand the first of them, you will see the need for the second. It goes without saying that by writing to you personally, I am humbly seeking your help in fulfilling my purpose on behalf of my men. My first intention is to describe to you, and to the families of the brave men of this regiment, some of the circumstances of their present service here in Virginia. It is full winter now, and we have had snowfalls, as well as prolonged periods of wind and rain to remind us of this, though still the campaigning and fighting have continued. You, and others of our people at home, may know by now that some days ago our army met and drove back a full scale attack by the enemy upon our positions around the town of Fredericksburg. The battle, on our part of the line, lasted from morning until after darkness fell and our men were engaged in the heaviest of the fighting, being involved in the inflicting of the most severe losses upon the Yankee army. Although our own casualties were much lighter, we mourn the loss of those of our brave men who fell that day.

I must not conceal from you however, the fact that the dangers of the battlefield were only some of the trials that your men folk of this regiment had to overcome last

Saturday and they continue to contend with the most trying difficulties on every day of their service here. All too many of our soldiers endure serious shortages in food, clothing and equipment. Over half of our men have no blankets, almost all of them have no overcoats, many have no socks, hardly any have gloves and, worst of all, with snow still on the ground, almost fifty of our men fought the battle barefooted, because we cannot provide them with replacement shoes." The pastor paused briefly as something between a mutter and a moan made its way around the church, before casting his eyes down towards the letter once more. "The situation is no better regarding the supply of food. The whole regiment fought hungry last Saturday, because not enough rations could be supplied to provide them with a decent meal. We receive rations now at most every second or third day. These supplies are adequate for meals for one or perhaps two days and therefore for several days of any week our men, your kin folk, go hungry. There are difficult supply and transportation problems for the whole army on this line, but, as long as the Yankees are there on the far side of the Rappahannock River, we must remain concentrated here, in these wasted counties of Virginia, to prevent them from pressing their advance on through the state towards Richmond. There is therefore little chance of us moving to a region where more supplies are available so there is no real prospect of relief for our hungry men.

The second reason for my letter is therefore simple. I am imploring your people to give, especially in the way of clothing and food, so that our men can be adequately clad and properly fed. At this time of the year, which is so special to our Christian people, I am asking your congregation to give what they can for their brave boys. I ask this because I do not know what else I can do to try to relieve the hardships and want that my men endure. My only course is therefore to appeal through you to their families and I ask, knowing that you, and they, will not refuse my request."

"The letter is signed by the colonel," Reverend Stockley added. "He has written a further piece below and I will read that now."

"In order that you will know that such provisions as you can contribute are delivered to your own boys, I have detailed men of the regiment to return to Georgia for the purpose of collecting these supplies from the various communities along the railroads and the rivers. What we can gather will be assembled in Savannah and transported under guard to our camps here. I can assure you that nothing will be wasted."

Daniel sat motionless, feeling, as he listened to the pastor reading Preston's words, a peculiar sense of embarrassment, almost as though he was engaging in some kind of dishonest or duplicitous action. He was completely aware that most, if not all of the eyes in the church would be upon him at this moment, even as Ballard's words from the day of their departure came back into his mind and he found himself weighing them against the words of the colonel's letter, that he had delivered to the pastor. There was a great irony in this man Preston, eloquently entreating these people to give for his men, when he was the one, barely two weeks ago who had implacably insisted on the summary execution of one of them.

Preston was not a man who was well known to his rank and file. He was seldom to be seen around their camps, tending to leave such contact to company officers. He was in many ways a distant figure, mostly operating among the officers of the army, rather than cultivating any sort of personal bond with his soldiers. But the death of John Ellis had stained his reputation among those soldiers, especially since it had been done on behalf of his own kin and a man who, although only recently arrived, had already alienated many of the men he had charge of. Somehow all of this seemed to debase, in Daniel Ryan's mind at least, the errand he was here upon. His mind was still turning these things over as he sat in the pew, with Martha Bennett on his right and her daughter Susanna on his left, when he became aware of a hand pressing on his shoulder from behind. He turned around and found himself looking into the face of old Mrs Barton, Saul Philipps' grandmother. There were tears in the old lady's eyes as she spoke.

"We knew they were short of some things up there," she said. "We had no idea that it was as bad as that. The boys don't hardly speak of it in their letters home......."

"Most boys don't want to worry their folks," Daniel said gently and he saw her nod slowly.

"Well we'll see about this," she said. "Whatever we can provide, our poor, brave boys will have." Out in front the pastor had resumed speaking.

"I was hungry and you gave to me to eat," he intoned. "I was naked and you clothed me. I was sick and you ministered unto me. Are there any among us who will not do their utmost to see that our boys' wants are met in the name of the Christmas child?" His voice rose on the final phrase and he stretched out his hands for emphasis with all the skills of a practised and experienced preacher.

"This church will be open during the coming week," he said, "so that all gifts of food, or clothing, or, the lord help us, of shoes, can be gathered for our brave men. Daniel Ryan there," he indicated with his hand towards where Daniel sat, "has been sent back here from Virginia, by Colonel Preston, to collect on behalf of our own boys who serve in Company B." He looked along the pews before speaking slowly and deliberately. "I know that our boys will not ask in vain," he concluded quietly.

All around the church, save for Neilsen's coughing and some quiet sniffling from somewhere near the back, absolute silence reigned. The minister stood for several seconds before summoning his congregation to stand for a final hymn and the calling down of a blessing to conclude the service. The people set to their singing with a noticeable increase in enthusiasm and, after the final verse, with the minister having departed, they began shuffling out of their places and leaving their pews to make for the door. Daniel, as he stood with the Bennetts waiting to go, felt Susanna gently elbow him in the ribs. He looked around and she indicated towards the front, where the minister was standing at the door of the ante-room gesturing to him to come. He made his way along to the end of the pew and down the side passage to the front of the church to where Stockley waited.

"I have asked John Fernell to delay in opening the main doors," he said, "and that will give us time to go around the side and meet everyone as they leave. Come this way." He pointed to the side room and they moved quickly through to the outside door beyond, skirting around the side of the building to reach the main doors, which opened to disgorge the mass of people, just as the two of them arrived.

For the next twenty minutes, Daniel Ryan found himself the centre of attention for many of the departing congregation. His hand was endlessly shaken and he was patted and slapped on the back, even being embraced by a number of the people. Some were angry, blaming President Davis, Governor Brown, or the southern Confederacy as a whole for the privations that their boys were enduring, but most simply wanted to know more about Virginia, and the army and the shortages, though the best that Daniel felt able to do was add a few more details to what Preston had said in his letter. It was enough, many people delayed from departing long enough to hear what he had to say. But what he found hardest was when the families of boys who had died in the battles of the previous year came up to speak. He was compelled to hold fraught and emotional conversations with both Jim Weald's mother and with Tom Gibben's family, both of whom approached him, not actually asking, but clearly wanting to hear anything he could tell them of the circumstances of their boys' deaths.

When he had finished the whole business of handshaking and communicating news to anxious families, he felt drained and spent as, beside him, the pastor took over once more.

"Blaming governments or presidents or generals will not put a single morsel in our brave men's mouths, nor a coat on their backs. We must do everything that we can to help them. Bring what you, or your neighbours can spare to the church this coming week, but I would caution you not to donate perishable food and to give some thought as to how what we collect can be transported to Savannah so that it can be taken on to Virginia from there. Now let us all depart to our homes and set to work on this mission of mercy." As they dispersed and moved away, Stockley spoke in a low voice to Daniel Ryan.

"I have spoken with my fellow pastors at Riverside and Zion Meeting places," he said. "It will make things much simpler if the provisions from the town and its surroundings can be collected in one place rather than three. With so many of the local men absent in the army, there is not the same amount of land under cultivation as there was before and although certain of the planters have loaned or leased labourers, the demands of the commissary have been considerable. We cannot expect miracles, but our people will do what they can, especially for their own kin."

The procession began that afternoon and continued through the following days. A succession of people came, some arriving on horses, carts and wagons, while others came on foot. Many of them gave simple parcels of food and clothing, as though these had been prepared specially, for the relative of those donating it, with some of them actually having an addressee's name written on the wood of the box or the wrapping paper of the parcel. But others brought larger bundles of clothing and boxes, sacks or even barrels of food. Daniel spent much of his time at the church, helping to unload, carry and store what arrived and feeling that, as far as possible, he should be there to personally acknowledge what the people of Eden Station were doing. In addition to the supplies, he found himself the custodian of an increasing number of letters from families to their men in Virginia and he stored these away in a cardboard folder that the minister had looked out for the purpose.

The stream of callers continued as the week advanced and the stack of provisions in the church ante room steadily grew larger. Some who had contributed on the Sunday actually returned with further donations on the succeeding days. Still more of those who came were anxious to speak with Daniel Ryan, asking about their boys. Were they well? Mostly he was able to reassure them, but for families like the Elliotts and the Fentons, whose boys had not returned after the army's retreat from Sharpsburg, he was able to offer little in the way of re-assurance. They were counted as, "missing," but there was no definite word. Please would he do them the obligement of letting them know if he heard anything when he got back to Virginia? He told them that he would and they departed, perhaps consoled with this much re-assurance, but, in the circumstances, with no real peace of mind.

As the week drew on, Daniel Ryan had begun to worry as to what arrangements he should try to make to transport all that had been gathered to Savannah. This concern grew when further consignments of provisions arrived on carts from the other two churches and the collection of clothing and food had now reached the point where what was brought by the latest arrivals had to be stored in the church itself. A message then arrived from Dellings during the Thursday afternoon to the effect that space had been taken by Lieutenant Jessop on Saturday's afternoon train to Savannah. This reduced the problem to a simple transporting of what had been collected from the town down to Fleming's on the railroad. Daniel spoke of the matter to the pastor, when he came by later on the same afternoon. Stockley had smiled faintly.

"With the amount of everything that we now have on our church premises, that question is of a concern to myself as well as to you. I have taken the liberty of speaking with Thomas Hogarth, the grain shipper. He has agreed to allow his larger wagon to be used on Saturday and has arranged for Jack Neilson to drive it." He had smiled again through his beard as Daniel thanked him profusely.

"I have an interest in this also," Stockley added, "for I will need the church and its side room returned from army business by Sunday for the routine services of the lord."

Daniel had known that visiting Constance Warner was, excepting the delivery of Preston's letter and the resulting collection of supplies, just about the most important matter for his time in Eden Station. He had gone around to her house on the afternoon of the day after Christmas, where she and her mother in turn voiced shock at how thin he was, but the general welcome from her family was sociable and polite enough. After some tea and small talk, he had gone walking with Constance, though, at her suggestion, taking a route that kept them in town, rather than following any of their previous, more private walks. Daniel sensed early in that walk that something was different now. He had known it in his heart for some time. The tone and the growing infrequency of their letters had given notice of it, but Constance's manner towards him today had also changed, from the moment they had stepped away from her porch. She did not hold his hand, choosing instead to rest her gloved hand on his forearm, but it was more than that. Their conversation had changed also, seeming to take a line through formal subjects, with nothing of the laughter and light-hearted teasing that had marked their previous times together, before the war had come. Yes, she was well and he was well, in the circumstances, and her family were well too and how were things in Virginia and so on….? But, even as this kind of talk went on, Daniel increasingly sensed that something else was lurking in the background, something that she was concealing, or was choosing her moment to mention. Had she changed, he thought? Was there someone else? For some time the talk continued, with Daniel experiencing an increased feeling of curiosity and apprehension.

"Eden Station surely is a changed place," he had observed as they continued their walk around town.

"It's a very sad place now Daniel," she had replied. "Too many families have lost their menfolk and then there are the other boys who have come home wasted or crippled. This is a sad and sorry little town now. Pa says there's so much less business and trade around Savannah too, with the Yankees blockin' the river mouth down at that fort. My folks reckon that there's really no future here."

"Was that it?" His mind caught the possible signal at once, and his ears almost pricked as he listened for her next words. His attention was total, with a cold calmness now ruling his mind through that brief pause.

"Pa and ma've been thinkin' about leavin' for a while

now," she went on, "and we've got folks in other parts of Georgia, so there are other places we could go."

"So are they thinking about leavin' here?" It was somewhere between a statement and a question in his mind, but her lead up to it had given ample indication.

"We've decided to go and live in Macon," she answered. "We're movin' there in about a month. Pa's intendin' goin' to work with his sister's husband, supplyin' the army." Daniel said nothing in response and the ensuing pause seemed to last for some time.

"If you want to, we can still write to each other," she said, breaking the silence "I could mail you our new address once we've gotten settled."

Daniel nodded, "that would be fine," he said absently, though he could see the inference in her words and indeed in the manner of his own response. He had not written to her since the start of October and her last letter had arrived sometime in the summer, just before the army had left its camps around Richmond. What seemed to have changed here already, well before any move to Macon or anywhere else, was the desire to stay in regular contact at all. He had forced a smile and had squeezed her arm re-assuringly with his other hand.

"When you've gotten settled," he told her gently, "you could see about writin' to me then."

"I'll do that Daniel," she said, with a smile that somehow seemed to him to be a shade forced.

He had leaned forward to kiss her then, but, as he drew close, she had turned her head slightly, formalising the kiss from any contact of their lips into a more formal peck on the cheek. As this was exchanged, a dart of regret crossed Daniel Ryan's mind, for he felt that this one gesture had spoken to him more clearly than any part of the just concluded minuet of conversation had done.

Later, back at the Bennett's, he had reflected on the walk and on what had been said. Perhaps she would have preferred to simply end their association, but the afternoon had given her ample opportunity of doing so and she had not done it. Maybe it was just dead on its feet, expiring slowly, deprived of sustenance by the war and absence, and everything else that had changed. At first, away with the army, Daniel had looked for her letters, pleased at having her, especially since, other than an occasional few lines to the Bennetts, he had no-one else to write to. But the frequency had soon waned, and maybe that was the early sign that things had begun to change and now they were changing more. Perhaps it would be best for him just to end it, rather than let it slowly wither away. He turned the whole question over in his mind several times, but there was an ache in his heart at the thought and he finally opted to leave it as it was. The next move would be hers anyway, since, without learning a new address, he could not continue to write, but deep down, he still felt that something might well be ending here, rather than just changing.

The Saturday came, and a sizeable crowd of people turned out to see the departure of their provisions. The day was cloudy, but reasonably mild and though the clouds hinted at rain, none had fallen while the provisions were being loaded onto Tom Hogarth's big wagon for the journey back to the halt on the Gulf and Albany Railroad at Flemings. The previous evening Daniel had visited Constance once more, being treated to a further session of tea and conversation before taking his leave after an hour or so of it. This morning, after the initial session of loading the wagon, he had gone back to say goodbye to the Bennetts. He had found Hal sitting in the store, while Charlie Thorne's younger brother Clayton did all of the running around after the early customers.

"Off to that war agin, Daniel," Hal grunted and Daniel nodded.

"Them Yankees are takin' a fair bit o' lickin'," the older man went on.

"They ain't quite learned their lesson yet," Daniel told him. Hal was silent for a few seconds.

"They'll maybe be a while yet afore they do," he concluded. Daniel looked at him, sensing a change in the tone of his voice.

"I wanted ya t' know," Hal resumed, "that the offer I made when y' enlisted still stands, if the lord spares us all. You were still the best help I ever had," he added, in a lowered voice, "and Martha still misses havin' ya around here." He nodded, a measure disparagingly, towards where the boy was hunting around some of the shelves for something.

"Ain't got half the stock we used to have," Hal growled, "and you got a fair piece o' what we did have on that wagon over at the meetin' house there." He nodded towards where the boy still prowled around the shelves, "but he still can't git it inta his head where to find or what to do with most o' what we still got." Daniel Ryan flushed.

"Hal," he said, "I know what I owe you and Martha and I'm truly grateful for everything that you, both of you, have done." He offered his hand and the old man took it, but, to Daniel Ryan his grasp seemed weak and languid now compared with before.

"When the war's done," he resumed, "I can......"

Behind him he heard footfalls as Martha came through from the house.

"I was sure I heard your voice," she said and she handed him a further parcel. "For the train trip," she told him. "Even after a week of better eatin', you could still use a lot more fattenin' up." Daniel thanked her and she briefly embraced him, offering him her cheek for a peck. She turned to Hal.

"Did you tell him," she inquired, almost sharply? Hal had nodded and Martha had sighed.

"With you back here," she said, "it all seemed a little like old times these past days." She reached out and squeezed his arm gently, "happier times." Daniel had nodded silently and tried to smile before he turned to go. As he left he had looked back and smiled again at them both.

"I'll write when I get back," he told them as he reached the door of the store.

"If the lord spares us all," Hal's words flitted across his mind, and, as he closed the door behind him and stepped out into the street, that thought was followed by the further reflection, that even with all of the dangers faced by the army in Virginia, the lord might well have a bigger job with sparing Hal Bennett, than he would with Daniel himself.

By middle morning the loading was complete. A watching group of onlookers and well-wishers had stayed around the church, where Stockley stood on the steps.

"May God go with you," the paster called, to a scattering of applause, as Daniel Ryan climbed up into his place and settled himself on the bench seat of the vehicle, while old Jack Neilson, Thad's uncle, shook the reins and the team of six mules jolted the vehicle into motion and set off. They moved from the meeting house just off the square, round towards the South Road, which led to the river and the railroad beyond. As the wagon moved ponderously onto the square Daniel stood and raised his hand in acknowledgement to the people, voicing his thanks to various families as the vehicle lurched past them and resuming his seat as it hauled steadily around to finally leave the square and labour up the slight rise of South Street. The wagon reached the familiar little hummock in the road near the bend on South Street and, as he felt it sway beneath him, Daniel Ryan looked back over his shoulder, seeing the little crowd starting to disperse and move slowly out of view. As the vehicle entered the bend, and he progressively lost sight of them, he found himself wondering in his heart, if he would see this place and these people, who had, for a part of his life, given a home to him, ever again.

There was a layer of mud on the road as they made their way south to the Cannouchee Bridge and on towards the railroad, Daniel found his mind going back to the times over the last two years, when he had travelled this road, with the Eden Station contingent of Company B. It had been so different then. War had seemed like an adventure, or, as so many of the boys had referred to it, a "frolic." But now some of those boys, who had marched this road to go to the war, were dead and others were back there in town, minus arms or legs or crippled by illnesses that had rendered them unfit for further service. Daniel turned all of it over in his mind as the familiar landmarks passed by. If they had all known what it would cost, he wondered, would they have gone off to fight with that mood of enthusiastic gaiety that had marked that time two Springtimes ago.

Many things had taken place since those innocent days, disillusioning and deadly things, tragic things and even now, looking at the whole matter as realistically as he could, those things would go on and it was highly unlikely that the boys now in Virginia, who had survived the grinding attrition of the war this far, would all come home safely. Yet the maiming and the deaths of those friends and comrades was now a further reason for those still there to persevere with the fight up there on the Rappahannock. They must stick it out until victory was won, for anything else would render all of the deaths and all of the suffering meaningless. They had, after all, enlisted to save the south from invasion and, so far, save for that coastal enclave around Fort Pulaski at the mouth of the river, the Yankees had taken no step on Georgian soil.

Even up in Virginia, the repeated efforts of the enemy to occupy the state had ended in repeated and bloody failure. This in itself was a victory of sorts, since, for all of the Yankees' resources, of men, weapons and munitions, they had met with costly repulses every time that they had tried one of their, "on to Richmind," thrusts. Sooner or later they would weary, they must tire of the cost, in both lives and treasure and give it up, so the southern army must hold fast in Virginia until that time came and what this wagon carried would materially help them to do it. What was happening down here this week was a tangible strengthening of the regiment as surely as if there were fresh men going to fill out its ranks. Food would strengthen bodies and replacement clothing would keep men warm and dry, holding at bay the winter agues and chills and the other illnesses that preyed upon the weakened and the run down. The things that were carried on this wagon would render the boys fitter for their duties and strengthen them in their spirit and resolve to go on fighting and resisting the next Yankee offensive, whenever and wherever it came. The vehicle lurched and heaved on its way down the muddy road and eventually Daniel forcibly dismissed these thoughts to the back of his mind, turning instead to the task of making conversation with old Jack. It would not do to be aloof and unsociable and besides the journey would pass all the more easily with some convivial talk.

Daniel Ryan stood with Otis Ballard and watched the wagon from Riceboro plod up towards the railroad with a further pile of boxes, barrels, sacks and parcels. Together with what had been gathered from Eden Station and Ballard's haul from the smaller hamlets and farms along the river it would amount to an impressive collection, requiring a fair amount of freight space on the train when it came along. Dellings raised a hand in greeting as the wagon pulled in, before gesturing towards what was already waiting on the section of thick, wooden boards that flanked the rails.

"Reckon that looks like a good week's work," he called.

"Guess so," Ballard called back. The wagon was pulled to a halt and, as Dellings scrambled down, the driver climbed around onto the back of the vehicle, while Ryan and Ballard made their way around to unhitch the tailboard. The work began and went steadily ahead, with the stacks on the boarded space growing substantially in size as the unloading was completed. The shifting done, the driver did not delay and with a brief wish of good luck, he got started on his return trip. Before long the lumbering vehicle was out of sight on the road south, leaving the three groomed and repaired soldiers at the halt to survey their cumulative efforts. Dellings looked around.

"I sure hope we get it all on the train," he said, "and that the train shows up." Ballard looked at him.

"Well if it don't," he said, "at least we got plenty to eat." Dellings grinned around at them in turn.

"Guess we have," he told them, "but it won't come to that." He waved them towards the bench and they sat, there, where, as Daniel Ryan briefly mused, Rodger's remains had lately rested. Daniel stretched his legs out, clasped his hands behind his head and gazed down the track to where it disappeared, around the bend into those scrubby trees.

It seemed an eternity since the first time they had all waited here at the start of the war, although it was still less than two years. How strange life could be...., and then something caught his eye. He looked again and saw the smoke, wisping above those trees in the distance, white smoke that was, at first, barely discernible against the low, light-coloured clouds of the sky above. It was only if one looked hard that it could be distinguished at all, but then he heard the first sounds of the train, the faintest puffing of the engine, quickly followed by the initial suggestions of a vibration along the rails. They stood up almost in unison.

"Now we git to shift all o' this stuff again," Ballard muttered.

"Better than diggin' holes up in Virginia," Daniel told him.

"Surely is," Dellings added as he stepped over to the line to watch the distant column of smoke that marked the approach of the train, draw closer.

"Ain't no way ya'll git all o' that aboard here," the conductor told them.

"We got the space hired," Dellings told him, "so it's gotta get on." The conductor rustled through his papers, and then back again.

"Whadya say the name was," he growled as he continued to leaf through the dispatch notes and manifests?

"Jessop!" There were further grunts and more rustling of papers before the entry was found at last.

"Ok, so he got space reserved, but he ain't gotten the whole train." Dellings was dismissive.

"Don't even need a whole car for what we got here."

"Ain't got no car space left, flatcars is the best ya'll git on this train." Over by the stack of boxes and parcels, Ballard held his hand out, as the first of the raindrops fell, and then quietly nudged Daniel Ryan.

"Ol' shit's makin' his play," he murmured. "He'll keep

sayin', "not a chance," till the dollars come out, 'n' the damn weather's helpin' him." Daniel looked at him and then at the conductor.

"We need box car space," Dellings told the man patiently, "else half o' the stuff'll spoil in this rain."

"Ain't my affair," the conductor was adamant. "Fer you to git box car space we'd have to shift some o' the other freight." Up in front the train whistle sounded as Dellings at last pulled a couple of notes from his tunic pocket.

"There's twenty dollars Confederate in it," he growled, "ten now and ten when we get there. Now you kin put it in you're pocket and get on with makin' space or you can keep on belly achin' till that fireman comes back here and gets in on things and I ain't got no other twenty dollars fer him." He looked the man straight in the eye as he finished, while the conductor looked straight back for a few more seconds, before snatching the proferred money and stuffing it into a side pocket of his waistcoat.

"You three better be ready to git yore hands dirty here," he said. "Else most o' that stuff is still gonna be on a flat car."

It took about twenty minutes to make space and load their supplies in a half empty box car. By the time that it was done, the rain had grown heavier, but, although the whistle had sounded three more times, neither the engineer nor his fireman had ventured from the locomotive, to question the delay. Perhaps, in view of the rain, they preferred to remain in the shelter of their cab. Along the train they had also seen signs, of faces being pressed to the misted, rain spotted windows of the passenger cars, to peer out at the loading, but nobody had left their seats to come and inquire. Such delays, Daniel Ryan reckoned, as he lugged boxes and sacks over to the door of the car, must be common, on this and any other railroad in wartime.

Eventually, the loading was complete and the three of them left the box car and started for the nearest passenger car, with Daniel Ryan half-anticipating the shout even before it came.

"No way yo're ridin' in there," the conductor called to them. "Box car fer you as well." The three of them turned and glowered at him.

"Goddam it," Dellings called back. "There ain't a thing on us. We bin laundered and deloused and polished. We're cleaner than most o' the picky varmints in that there car."

"Don't matter none," the old man snapped back. "First the reg'lar passengers see o' soldiers in their car, they're scratchin' right away and then they're peckin' at me like a swarm o' buzzards." He pointed back along the train.

"Ornery ol' shit," Ballard said, while Ryan turned to Dellings.

"That twenty dollars didn't buy much," he said, but the conductor was not for relenting.

"Ya kin walk if ya want," he snapped, but the three of them were already on their way back to the box car, while the conductor started for his own car at the rear, waving up towards the engine as he went and barely giving his three additional passengers time to get aboard. There was another whoop from the whistle and then, the sound of escaping steam as Dellings clambered up onto the rough wooden floor and Ballard slid the door shut behind him. Almost immediately the train jerked into motion with the customary series of jolts, making them reel and stagger till, with the movement established, they recovered their balance.

"With all the different railroads between here and Virginia," Ballard said, "we got a helluva lot o' haulin' to do with these supplies." He looked at Dellings. "How much you got fer bribin' all o' these damned thievin' ol' cusses?"

The sergeant looked back at them, with an expression of unconcern on his face.

"All that we gotta do is get the stuff to Savannah," he said. "From there on up, well that there is Jessop's business," he added. "That's why they picked him fer this. He used to work for the Charleston and Savannah Railroad before the war and he's the man to git things moved on these here lines and the folks to talk to to git it done. They reckon he's smart or maybe he's jest smart-assed, but he's been travellin' down here for the last week, along the way we're goin' t' take this load, gettin' all o' this set up. If he can't git this here trip back to the regiment organised then there ain't nobody that can do it."

Chapter 8 A Matter of Railroads

Daniel Ryan had only a slight familiarity with Lieutenant Morgan Jessop. He had seen him at battalion drills and reviews and also around the camps, but that was about as far as it went. The Company D officer looked older than most lieutenants, maybe getting on for thirty, or so Daniel thought, and his appearance was distinguished by a full brown moustache and beard, the latter of which had he had allowed to grow, in the manner of, "Old Pete," himself, down almost onto his collar. But, as Daniel and his companions were soon reminded, he had a reputation for loud and varied profanity, which, in its range and intensity, might well rival that of John Harmon, Stonewall Jackson's almost legendary quartermaster.

The lieutenant was waiting at the Savannah depot of the Gulf and Albany Railroad, when the train carrying Dellings, Ballard and Ryan came grinding in as the winter light faded and the rain still drizzled down. When the cars finally came to a standstill, Dellings went immediately to report, leaving Ballard and Ryan with their consignment of supplies. Within a few minutes, from a number of wagons down the train, where Dellings had found the officer, they heard his reaction, presumably to the bribing of the conductor. The two listeners looked down the train at the angry lieutenant, marvelling at the volume and foulness of his language.

"Reckon that thar man knows how to make hisself clear, better than a lot o' officers," Ballard observed. Daniel grinned at him and said nothing. The next thing was likely the shifting of their haul of supplies for transportation across town to the Charleston and Savannah depot and that, as Ballard had already noted, would be far from the last time they would have to be manhandled in the course of the coming journey back to Virginia.

Jessop had commandeered two wagons, each drawn by teams of mules, but these were not sufficient for the supplies from the train, for, when all that could reasonably be packed on board the vehicles was in place, there was still upwards of a wagon load at the depot. The lieutenant had paced around what remained and stroked his beard.

"Pain in the .... ass," he said, "but with rations, it's better to have a too much pain in the ass than a too little, one." He beckoned to Dellings.

"You and one o' them stays," he said, gesturing to Ryan and Ballard. "Wagon'll come back. "I want all o' those supplies at the Charleston depot tonight and your day don't end till they get there." Dellings had saluted and turned to them both, as Jessop climbed onto the first of the two wagons.

"You, Otis, you go," he rapped. "You stay," he said to Daniel Ryan." Ballard moved away and pushed his musket into the front of the second wagon, before hauling himself up onto the seat, as the driver flapped the reins, and called to the mules, upon which the vehicle laboured into motion.

"Don't make no noise, that might wake me up, when

ya arrive," he called to Daniel Ryan as the wagons pulled away.

They had watched the vehicles depart before sitting themselves down on two of the provisions boxes, breaking open their own travelling food parcels, while the bustle at the depot went on around them. Martha's parcel turned out to be part of a wheat bread loaf, with some butter, ham and sweet pickle, which Daniel began to wolf down ravenously. They talked between mouthfuls and Daniel commented on the amount they had collected. Dellings nodded as he dealt with a mouthful of pie.

"Boys from the other companies've done pretty well, according to Jessop," he added when his mouth was clear enough to speak..

"Could be a hell of a job gettin' it all back to the camps," Daniel said and the sergeant nodded again.

"Reckon the country boys've gotten more than the Savannah ones," he said, "but that ain't really no big surprise. Jessop reckons it could all add up to seven, maybe eight full wagon loads, that we got to take all the way up," he went on. The sergeant paused, turning his head to look as a pretty girl went past, in company with an older woman.

"My my," he said. "It's only when you get back down here that you realise how much you miss the good ol' sights and sounds o' home." He continued to look in silence as the two women moved away through the groups who still dallied around the depot, waiting till they were out of sight before making any move to continue.

"All the way up," he eventually resumed, "here, then Charleston, then Florence then Wilmin'ton and Richmond too, we'll have to do all this every time, cuz Weldon and Petersburg's the only places where one railroad connects with another. But everybody reckons that Jessop's the man for it and he's had plenty o' time to set it up on his way down here. This ain't official army supplies, but he's likely makin' out to all the railroad folks that it is and he's maybe even gotten paperwork from some o' his old buddies to say that. But anywhere along the line things could go wrong and the commissary could come along and jest requisition the whole shipment, and that ain't sayin' nothin' about all the less official thieves that'll want to get their hands on some or all of it, and the further north we get, the bigger that risk gets too."

"How come," Daniel inquired, his interest in hearing something about what was to come, growing steadily?

"Jessop's railroad time was spent on the Charleston and Savannah line," Dellings told him. "Reckon that part'll all be fine, maybe the Charleston and Florence'll be fine too, but the further north we get, the fewer old buddies he'll find to cosy up to, and Richmond itself'll likely be the worst. Up there, with all the main depots located around the city, there'll maybe be more attention gittin' paid to what goes where. It'll be hardest to get wagon space in Richmond too, so my guess is that's where he'll be needin' the cash dollars for extra payments. That's why he got fired up about that conductor lookin' for a bribe on the way in here. The worst part o' the whole trip could be that last fifty miles, from Richmond up to Fredericksburg and maybe he reckons he'll need every cent he's got fer up there." Dellings returned to what remained of his pie, while Daniel Ryan resumed work on the ham and bread and said nothing. He could see the sense in what the sergeant was saying, but, other than obeying his own orders, he knew perfectly well that, whatever the risks and the hazards of the trip turned out to be, there was nothing much that he could do about any of them. All of that was Lieutenant Jessop's job and, as far as Daniel Ryan was concerned, he was welcome to it.

"Up there," Dellings resumed, having chewed some

more on his pie, "with so few trains runnin' on that line, the wagon space'll be more closely checked than anywhere else along the way and that ain't all. There's also the fact that we can't jest manhandle our load o supplies onto any ol' train in Richmond. That Broad Street depot is only a branch that takes folks, and our wounded boys and freight for the city itself into town, but it don't handle most o' the supplies that the army gits. That freight gets collected out at the depot on the edge of town as well as at Ashland or Hanover Junction and either the cars on the train get loaded out there or loaded, extra cars get coupled onto the train. In town there's a big risk that any railroad clerk who's lookin' on'll smell somethin' wrong, if somebody starts doin' something that don't happen there any other day. We could have to get all o' our stuff out to the sidin's out at Branch's just outside of Richmond, where we got a chance to load it onto a train without the commissary comin' along and haulin' it all straight off again. There could be more trouble up the line too, with the army spreadin' down the river to watch the Yankees, there's bin talk o' the main depot bein' shifted south from Hamilton's Crossing to Guiney's Station. The crossin's within range of the Yankee guns, once they have a mind to move them on down the Stafford County side, but Guiney's Station's inland and the main risk to it is from cavalry, and it surely ain't a big risk when ya think about how damned useless the Yankee cavalry are. But we may not be able to get any train space at all goin' up to there, and the chances of gittin' enough wagons up there, with the army so short of mules, it'll be like tryin' t' fish in a bucket o' sand."

"You mean that we could break our backs gettin' all of this stuff to within a couple o' days' march of the camp," Daniel said, "and see it all go to rot there because we can't get it those last few miles?" Dellings nodded gravely.

"The good part is that most o' of what we got won't rot quick or easy," he said, "so there'll be some time to get things figured out maybe, but, unless the colonel's gittin' word from Jessop and they got some plan to use the regimental wagons, that we don't know about, then that there is jest about the size of it," he said. "We could end up havin' to wagon haul all the stuff we collected, a bit at a time, till it's done. But even that ain't all, cuz the woods and back roads up there are full o' deserters and skulkers avoidin' the draft. Even the locals would like a share of what we're bringin' in. So, if word gets out up there, every damn thief 'n' bushwhacker in the county could be on our trail lookin' fer a piece of whatever we got." The sergeant looked around the busy depot, seeing the bustle and activity going on all around them. He seemed to look at it all for a long time before he turned to Daniel Ryan again.

"You'll recall how we all got issued with thirty rounds o' ball cartridge afore we headed off down here," he said grimly, "well mark my words, if we finish up havin' to wagon all o' this stuff, from Guiney's, or even from Chesterfield, up to the regiment's camps, then we could easy end up havin' to use up some o' those thirty rounds to keep it."

The journey north unfolded much as Dellings had said it would. On the successive railroads north from Savannah, the main task for the detail of sixteen privates, and two NCOs, was the repeated transferring of their supplies from rail cars to wagons, for hauling across the various cities and railroad towns, followed by the same thing in reverse, at the next depot when everything required to be transferred from wagons onto the cars of the next railroad. It was eight full wagon loads and this was ample to fill pretty well the largest or two smaller sized rail cars, but Jessop appeared to have done his work well. At each transfer, wagons were quickly available, though never in sufficient numbers to take everything in one shift, which meant the supplies had to be hauled in relays, delaying the operation, but at each successive depot the rail cars were promptly produced also. As Dellings had said, Jessop's arrangements, and his influence among the railroad men, were more cultivated over the southern portion of the journey where the transfers proceeded with notable efficiency. All the way up to Wilmington in North Carolina, the transfers ran relatively smoothly, with waiting restricted to a few hours at most, this being more to do with the vagaries of southern train schedules rather than with any delay of their own.

The succession of quick transfers over the early part of the journey however, was promptly followed by a delay of almost half a day at Wilmington, with the lieutenant absent for much of the time consulting with various railroad officials. As a result, Daniel Ryan found himself inwardly wondering how many further Confederate bills had been required to facilitate their further progress. It was not that the men of the detail were greatly concerned over the delay. Wilmington was a thriving port, teeming with activity, and apparently with wealth also, mostly based on the blockade running trade that was centred there. As a result, there were well-resourced hospitality arrangements undertaken by the local women's groups and the detail from the, "Blues," got a square meal and a further lesser feed in the course of their wait around the depot. But Dellings words returned to Daniel Ryan several times in the course of that day with the thought that it was maybe an indication that the farther north they went the more accident prone the whole trip was likely to be. Yet, in spite of the time spent at Wilmington, by late on the Monday, Richmond was drawing closer but, if Dellings forecast was proved correct, from here onwards, the most testing part of the whole mission could be expected.

As on their previous journeys, there was no transfer of trains at the depot town of Weldon in North Carolina. The same train passed on through, albeit after some delay, to load and unload other freight. It was therefore during the final hours of darkness on the Monday night that they left the Richmond and Petersburg depot in Petersburg and clattered over the last twenty five miles up to Richmond. They steamed at the now customary snail's pace across the rickety James River Bridge into the depot of the Richmond & Petersburg Railroad, with first light still upwards of two hours away. It was now the early hours of the sixth day of January, Daniel Ryan reflected as he lounged in his blanket roll, together with others of the group in the draughty leading box car. Around him, the hushed talk among the wakening men suggested that now, in all likelihood, they would see Jessop's skills and experience tested to the full.

Even at that hour, the depot was far from quiet, but, as Ballard pointed out, getting their loads hauled across town would be easier at six in the morning than later in the day and this prediction seemed to be promptly borne out by events. Within fifteen minutes of arriving, Jessop was supervising the positioning of the latest shift of mule drawn wagons near each of the rail cars, allowing the transfer to get under way, with the supplies being moved straight from the cars onto the wagons. They returned upwards of half an hour later and the loading for their second trip up to the Richmond, Fredericksburg and Potomac depot got under way immediately and, so far all was going smoothly. Daniel Ryan departed with three of the other men after this second load, taking the same short cut across town that they had on the way down, arriving at the depot on Broad Street to witness Jessop in what looked more like an argument, than a negotiation, with a railroad supervisor. The lieutenant waved them around the tracks to the end of the depot building, where, with the initial men sent on, they awaited the arrival of the wagons. It was so far so good the boys reckoned and, if this transfer continued to go the way the others had, and they got on their way north without undue delay, the lieutenant would indeed have earned his corn.

The wagons returned after a further wait and their loads were promptly stacked with the earlier ones near the end of the depot building, with the two vehicles immediately departing to pick up the remaining provisions. Those at the depot then took turns at guarding what had arrived, allowing others of the initial group to promptly head away, exploring the depot to seek any further offerings of food. But the hour before daylight turned out to be too early for even the Women's Hospitality folks to be up and around and those thus engaged came straggling back empty-handed, in ones and twos, to rejoin the others. The boys got occasional sightings of their lieutenant emerging from an office or engaged in animated discussion with further officials around the depot, before the two wagons arrived once more, which led to a further bout of unloading, but dawn had arrived as the vehicles departed again leaving the men at the depot to finish stacking the newly arrived provisions near the building as daylight gradually began to lighten the sky and the city.

As they completed the job, Daniel Ryan's attention was taken by a movement out along the track, which stretched away in a straight line along the length of Broad Street, visible in the improving light. It was several blocks away and looked like an approaching box car. Closer it came, with steam and smoke billowing from what must be a locomotive beyond, until this, "train," such as it was, eventually arrived at the depot, slowing to a crawl as it came level with the building. It turned out to be two box cars, being pushed in by a curious diminutive locomotive with an unfamiliarly long smoke stack. It could only have been used for shunting wagons and cars around at the railroad depots, for, in all truth, it did not look equal to the task of hauling a real train. Dellings was standing beside Daniel Ryan and he too watched the procession of cars and locomotive arrive. He looked at Ryan and then shook his head.

"I'll be damned," he said.

The locomotive was level with them now with its brakes screeching as it finally drew to a halt. Jessop had appeared, immediately making his way towards the cars, waving his men to work as he went.

"Get movin'," he yelled. "These are our cars." The men swarmed forward and as they did so the lieutenant made for the locomotive, to engaged the driver immediately in discussion, with some pointing and gesturing also involved. The pile of provisions started to decline in size with the labouring men of the detail, now hurried along by the two sergeants, formed into lines to convey them to the cars. What Daniel also saw a little later, was the engineer from the shunting engine climb down from the open platform of his locomotive to sidle up to the lieutenant, who handed him something, which was immediately pocketed before the man returned to his place on the locomotive. As he ascended to his place the wagons and the final detail of men from the Petersburg depot arrived, with Ballard among them. Daniel indicated towards Jessop as his friend came up.

"He's on the job," he told him, nodding again towards the lieutenant, who was now heading back towards the depot building, while the loading of the rail cars went on. "Driver's a few shin plasters better off. It don't look as though we're going any place just yet, but the loadin's surely gettin' done." Ballard looked around for a few seconds, taking it all in before speaking.

"Mubbee knows his business sure enough," he said.

Daniel smiled inwardly as his friend joined the work, recognising that such a comment was praise enough from Ballard, who was often steadfastly reluctant to give anybody in the army, short of General Lee himself, much in the way of credit for anything.

The loading went on, with the working men chivvied on by Dellings and Lacombe, the other sergeant, and for a time by Jessop, when he returned, but the lieutenant had remained only briefly before he departed again. With the whole detail now on hand, the pile of provisions quickly disappeared and with the loading complete, the sweating men sank down to sit or lounge for whatever time remained. It turned out to be mere seconds, before Jessop was back once more to order them all on board the box cars. The men moved to retrieve their weapons and scrambled aboard, spreading themselves around in the limited space still available on the cars.

As Jessop finally squeezed into the loaded front wagon, Dellings grasped the door handle and made to pull the door shut. He pulled, but the door stayed open. He then hauled harder, but still the door did not budge. The sergeant called a couple of the men over to him and the three of them heaved mightily, with Dellings at the handle and the two men gripping the edge of the door itself, but the movement achieved was inches at best. Ahead of them, the engine began to puff and judder the cars into motion, with a loud hiss of escaping steam, pulling them out of the depot a short distance, before grinding to a further halt. Inside the car, the sergeant and his helpers still wrestled with the door as the train sat there, clear of the depot building, but still within plain view of anyone on that part of Broad Street who chanced to look. Inside the car they heard the engine being uncoupled once more before it began moving away, with the car door still wide open. Still the three men wrestled with the door with all inside the car aware that any commissary or railroad officials who happened to watch the departure of the shunting engine with its duo of cars would be able to see sufficient of the cargo, and the crowded men inside to instantly deduce that something was amiss.

Dellings was on his knees now, hauling at the door runner, while the others still heaved vainly at the door itself. Jessop had gone also to the door, uttering a stream of profanity at this latest turn of fortune. The men there still wrenched and hauled, while a further man hammered at the runner with the butt of a musket, but the progress was little more than minimal. The door remained some two thirds open, with the gusty winter wind blowing into the interior of the car, while still more men were summoned to wrestle with this latest problem.

Ballard too had joined the struggle now, having gotten a metal bar from somewhere and this he jammed between the door runner and the planks of the car floor and its side, levering at the runner while still the other men hauled. They could hear the shunting engine ahead of them puffing once more, as it passed down beside them on the parallel track till it screeched to a renewed halt back at the depot. More time passed, as still the men laboured at the door, hearing, as they did so, the locomotive approach again, this time from the depot direction, to draw closer and closer before jarring the cars into disjointed motion, dislodging a few of the boxes and parcels and causing a number of the men inside to stagger. Those at the door continued to struggle until, inch by inch, as the cars gathered momentum, it began to work. The space of daylight slowly contracted as the group laboured and the flood of chilled air slowly diminished until the door had closed across the entrance, reducing it to a narrow crease of light and draught. Jessop visibly relaxed, and, seeing this, the others at the door did likewise.

"Leave it there boys," the lieutenant growled between

breaths. "We'll need a goddamned space to get our hands around when we have to open the damned thing up the line." One by one, from the congested space around the door, the men pushed away to find places to settle.

Inside the box car such space was at a premium, so some of the occupants pushed themselves into little spaces that they were able to clear on the floor by shifting sacks and parcels around to sit on the nearest box or barrel. Others went scrambling further up onto the great piles of boxes or sacks to find any sort of resting space higher up. As the little locomotive slowly gathered a measure of speed, Daniel Ryan got himself settled on a bean sack with Ballard. Dellings joined them there and they looked quizzically at the sergeant.

"Ya ain't tellin'me that our smart-ass lieutenant's intendin' goin' all the way to Hamilton's Crossin' in this wreck of a car, with this kid's toy loco'," Ballard began. Dellings grinned at them.

"Smart-ass, or maybe jest plain smart," he said. "The cars go all the way, but the toy loco' ain't takin' us more'n a few miles out o' town." They looked at him still more quizzically at that.

"What then," Daniel Ryan muttered? "Are we shovin' the car the rest of the way?" Dellings grin was almost off the side of his face by now. He shook his head slowly.

"Well, we ain't quite doin' that," he said. "He sure as hell knew somebody to git these cars shunted into town fer our stuff. Doin' it this way has gotten us outa town without havin' to load at the freight yard." The supply trains up to Fredericksburg are closer managed than any others," he went on, "thanks to that damn Yankee that runs this railroad that is, and our commissary boys, who all got suspicious minds anyhow. The freight cars mostly get loaded up at Ashland or at Hanover, where the Central Railroad line crosses this one. The cars and their loads git checked and counted out and then they git coupled onto the Richmond trains, so there ain't hardly anythin' that gets in those cars or on this line that ain't authorised. As you might have figured out, we ain't got no authorisation fer any o' this stuff, so its more'n likely that we'd a' had our whole shipment commandeered or confiscated if we'd jest a loaded it onto the cars fer the mornin' train, that leaves the depot back in Richmond in maybe a half hour or more from now, if it's runnin' on time that is," he added. "So we're headin' on out, past Branch's and Chestnut Grove, five maybe six miles to Hungry Station and then that there toy loco' heads back to Branch's to clear the line, with the crew a few dollars richer after they've shunted us off on the side line that goes west to the old coal mines out there. The Fredericksburg train comes along next and stops jest past the branch line to let the loose-assed boys off fer a visit t' the brush, but the engineer knows there's a few dollars fer him and his crew this time, if he does like he's bin told by the conductor feller. Then comes the hard part fer us, cuz after he's passed and stopped, we got to move these cars back over the points so they can get hitched to the main train behind the other cars. It shouldn't be too much of a haul, cuz Jessop says there's a grade up there that'll help. Then we get goin' again and the next stop is likely at Hanover Junction, so the extra freight cars can get loaded or coupled on, and cuz we're coupled on a'ready everybody up there reckons we've bin checked out at Richmond. Then it's a clear line up to Hamilton's Crossin'. Jessop's wired ahead to the colonel so the job of movin' all o' this stuff on to the camp kin get started pretty well as soon as the regimental wagons start showin' up." The grin was back on Dellings' face again.

"Smart-assed," he said, "or jest plain smart?"

There was precious little physical effort of any kind required from most of the detail to shift their box cars back onto the main line at Hungry Station. Indeed, to keep the two cars stationary on the branch line, when the shunting was completed, and the little locomotive uncoupled and moving away, hand brakes had to be applied on both cars. With the leading car door laboriously prised open again, Jessop engaged in a final brief conversation with the driver and with the locomotive set on its way back south and the points changed by the lieutenant, the men were then allowed to climb down, stretching legs or toileting as required. It was now simply a matter of waiting for the approach of the Fredericksburg train.

It took over an hour before the distant smoke plume was sighted, upon which the men gathered around their cars to clamber on board once more. Out on the main line, the train steadily approached, slowing to a crawl as it came up, with its fireman gazing impersonally across at them from the cabin as the locomotive slid slowly by, followed by its passenger and freight cars, to come to a halt a short distance past the branch line points. It lay there with the locomotive pulsing while Lacombe changed the points again, with Jessop positioning himself out beside the track co-ordinating the braking by shouting his instructions through the open doors of each car. The brakes were slowly released and the cars almost immediately began to inch back towards the points, soon gathering pace as they went, which led to the brakes being applied again, to prevent too much momentum building up, that would send them off down the line towards Richmond once more, or at least on a piece till the ground levelled. By judicious use of their braking wheels, the cars were eased back across the junction and brought to a halt just beyond on the main line. Lacombe hauled on the points lever again, while Jessop nodded to the men nearest the sliding door and they got to work on it once more, while Ballard recovered his steel bar and levered at the runner channel, leaving it open just enough for the officer to squeeze through when he returned.

Those inside the car had gotten a brief glimpse of the conductor, as he left his car and started down towards them, waving as he came, to the engineer up ahead to ease back. The car occupants then heard, rather than saw, the engine release its own brakes and slowly reverse down the line, to join their cars to the train. This was done with a further heavy jolt, which again sent several of the men in the box car careering into each other, to be followed, after a further interval, by a clanking of the metal coupling chain, which vibrated through the car. Jessop stayed outside for several more minutes talking to the conductor. Daniel Ryan could hear their voices, but could not make out what they were saying. Their discussion finally ended with Jessop appearing at the car door, while, on up the train, the conductor's voice rang out.

"All done here Zeke, let's git goin'." At that, Ryan and Ballard exchanged glances, for the voice was unmistakably that of Lorenzo Higgins, the old man from their train south more than two weeks before. Ballard chuckled.

"Didn't reckon he'd a' gone and joined the damn army," he said. "He's got a better payin' job on this here railroad."

With Jessop back on board, the hauling and prising of the door was resumed until it was slid finally shut, to the same narrow finger of light as before, restoring most of the interior of the car to the lurid glow of their single lantern. The men settled to their various resting places again, as the train jolted into motion and slowly gathered pace, but, within minutes, the three on the bean sack were disturbed by another of the men who had pushed his way back towards them.

"Lieutenant wants t' see ya," he said. Dellings nodded to him and shifted around on the sack, before pushing himself to his feet and moving away, squeezing past several resting men on his way to where the officer waited. Their discussion began immediately and, although Daniel could again hear practically nothing of what was being said above the noises of the train, he could see by the nodding and the gesturing that whatever the lieutenant had wanted to talk about was of some importance. Daniel Ryan turned towards Ballard and gestured towards the huddled pair.

"Ain't exactly slappin' each other on the back," he muttered. Ballard turned and took a more prolonged look at them.

"They surely ain't celebratin' yet," he said. "Looks to me like they got somethin' pretty serious to talk over." The gestures and manner of the two somehow did not look light-hearted or convivial. So maybe, Daniel Ryan thought, there was some more, "smart-ass," stuff required from Jessop after all before this was over. But even as they watched, the two men nodded to each other and the sergeant got up from where they had sat, steadying himself against the side of the swaying box car as he made his way back to his place. He reached the sack and Ryan and Ballard shuffled to one side as he turned around to sit once more, settling himself into the space that they had made for him. A few moments of silence passed before Ballard spoke.

"So do we git a real furlough now fer gittin' this job done?" Dellings looked around at him and shook his head ruefully.

"Ain't no furloughs fer nobody," he said, "and besides this job ain't done, not by a good way." They both looked around at that, tacitly inviting him to continue.

"So how come it ain't," Daniel Ryan grunted, as Dellings remained initially silent? The sergeant still did not answer for a long number of seconds and when he began to speak he did so in a lowered voice that was not much more than a whisper, so that his listeners had to strain to hear his words over the noise from the train and the track.

"We ain't done cuz we ain't back with the regiment yet," he told them, "and the lieutenant ain't intendin' takin' these supplies all the way to Hamilton's Crossin' jest to git everythin' we got requisitioned by our own commissary. We are only goin' as far as Guiney's Station on this line and, as well as that, we hear there's more cars gittin' coupled on behind us at Hanover. That means we can't jest uncouple these cars and take 'em off some place quiet to unload, when we get up there, but even if we manage to git all o' our supplies off the train, without getting no commissary folks interested, we still got to find some place to keep 'em. Then we got to shift 'em that last twenty miles we'll have to cover before it's all safe home. Lieutenant's wirin' the colonel agin from Hanover Junction, but, the way things are shapin' up, the last twenty miles o' this trip could turn out to be a bigger pain in the ass than all o' the rest put together."

The sergeant's words were no great surprise to Daniel Ryan, being little more than what he had told him back down at the depot in Savannah. But somehow on the trip up, with all of the work and snatched periods of brief rest, that idea had receded into the back of his mind. They had had a share of drama and tension already, especially over the last couple of hours, but now that Dellings' darker earlier fears seemed to be coming to pass, he felt a feeling of dismay growing within him. Had they gone through this whole episode, of journeying down to Georgia, prevailing upon the families there to contribute from their own diminished provisions, collecting everything that had been donated and hauling and transporting it all the way here to Virginia only to see part or indeed all of it lost, whether by commissary seizure, plain theft or, worst of all, stuck in a field to rot and spoil? Was this whole thing now destined to be a waste of the time and effort of everyone involved? Like the others around him, once they had been coupled to this train and had begun to draw close, mile by mile, to their destination up the line, Daniel had found his spirits rising. Among the men in the car generally, an air of buoyancy and optimism had grown, it could be seen and heard in the wise cracking and good humour that had pervaded the whole group. They had, after all, gotten to within forty miles of final success. But Dellings words had now changed all of that for himself and for Ballard. They were not, after all, on the verge of success, instead, each consecutive rocking and clattering mile might be bringing them ever closer, one way or another, to the brink of final failure. This thought, after all of the effort of the men and the sacrifices of those families back in Georgia, was wearily depressing to Daniel Ryan.

Chapter 9 The Scum of the Earth

The train had stopped, as predicted, at the busy Hanover Junction, where the Richmond and Fredericksburg crossed the Virginia Central line. The wait there lasted about fifteen more minutes, with the front wagon door having to be laboriously prised open once more when they arrived and the lieutenant absent thereafter for much of the time. Finally he had returned and the door had then been equally laboriously shoved shut, while the train lurched and shuddered as more cars were coupled on at the rear. Eventually, the locomotive whistle screeched and the journey was resumed, with all of the attendant juddering and jolting that had become so familiar to the men. The newly returned officer said little, to Dellings or to the enlisted men of his detail, settling himself instead on a box with his back against a couple of sacks, while, all over the car, the men observed, for word of the change in destination had spread and most, if not all, of them were by now aware of the likelihood of further difficulties up ahead. Presently Jessop began to doze and, seeing this, the others returned to their own more subdued conversation or rest as suited them, for, if the officer was not troubling himself unduly about coming problems, then why should the enlisted men get into any sort of a vapour about them?

The train edged steadily north, crossing the successive bridges at Polecat Creek, Reedy Swamp and the North Anna River at its customary crawl and stopping briefly at Chesterfield Station before embarking on the last leg of the trip on to Guiney's Station. Jessop's doze had been brief, just enough, so Daniel Ryan thought, to maybe convince some of his watching men what a cool customer he was, but he was up and around now as the final destination drew near. There was growing activity all around the car, with men aroused and stretching and a few even checking weapons as though they expected trouble, or perhaps it was all a product of the air of tension, that had superseded the previous optimism and that Jessop's sleep, whether feigned or genuine, had maybe been aimed at allaying. Suddenly, the train whistle sounded, its shrill, mournful screech disturbing Daniel Ryan's thoughts and bringing any of the men who still rested back to alertness. As the whistle died, Jessop's voice came, causing heads in the car to turn in his direction.

"Stay easy boys," he called. "We ain't there yet and when we get there we won't be doin' nothin' till I get some things fixed up." A few men moved back onto sitting or resting places, outwardly relaxing, but the look in most eyes was still of controlled tension, almost like the prelude to a fight, trying to remain externally calm, if not eager, but with minds inwardly focussed, taut and apprehensive, ready, it seemed, for almost anything.

The train was slowing now, with the difference in its motion easily felt, a kind of grinding, straining momentum rather than the swaying unrestricted motion felt when its throttle was open and hauling. The locomotive wheels could be heard too, skidding on the lines, as the brakes were further applied, and the speed steadily fell off. A couple of men were up at the corner of the car trying to peep through cracks or open seams to get a brief look at whatever was outside, while the last of their speed was shed and, with the almost obligatory release of excess steam, the locomotive strained to a halt. Jessop now stood and raised a hand to gain the attention of the men.

"When I get back and give the word boys, get this done damn quick. This unloadin's got to be the quickest you've done." Up ahead, they heard the pulsing of the engine and a few shouts from outside, then along the train, the caboose door banged open and Higgins' voice came to them above the other sounds.

"Guiney's Station! Guiney's!"

"Be ready boys," it was Jessop's voice again. "Lantern out now so I can get goin', just stay aboard till I get back and then we get to work." The yellow lantern was almost immediately dowsed, upon which a further episode of hauling and prising began, to inch the car door open sufficiently for the lieutenant to clamber out into the daylight, before Dellings and his detail laboured it shut once more. Inside the car, men stood, sat or squatted waiting for the word to get started. The interior was dark now, with just enough light from the gap at the door and splintered planks around the car, to make out the shapes of the various figures, who waited within. Eight men and their sergeant, shadowy figures and now, with the train noises stilled to only the continued pulsing of the locomotive, Daniel Ryan could hear snatches of breathing, as some still tried to control their nerves. Getting so close, but knowing now that the unforeseen had happened and the risks had grown greater, he could feel it all in his own chest, in his thumping heartbeat and the razor tightness in his mind. Would it all end here, or would Jessop pull another trick from his collection that would bring them home?

There was a sense of anti-climax about the lieutenant's

return for he brought with him yet another official of the railroad. They could hear them talking outside, with even an occasional chuckle at some joke or other.

The man eventually left and Jessop, having given him time to go and engross himself in other business, called out to those inside.

"In the cars there, stay where you are meantime. They're getting transportation so we can move our stuff away from the depot, so hang fire till they get back." Some minutes passed before the faint sound of wheels came from outside the cars, coming closer, until it seemed it was immediately outside, though squinting diagonally through the narrow gap left by the door, Daniel Ryan could see no sign of what it was. It was then that they heard Jessop's voice once more.

"Everybody, on your feet. Let's have you out here, boys. Let's get this done." The door was hauled and cajoled open once more and the light of the winter day flooded inside. The two remaining on the sack stirred themselves, as other men began to push towards the light, holding their weapons close to their chests.

"Now," Daniel Ryan muttered to his companion. "Smart-assed, or just plain smart?" Ballard did not reply, contenting himself with casting his eyes upwards.

Daniel reached the door and looked outside, briefly adjusting his eyes to the daylight before jumping to the ground. He looked along to where two handcarts stood at the door of the second freight car surrounded by men from the car who had already commenced their unloading. Jessop was there and he gestured to Dellings as he addressed the men from the front car.

"Sergeant, detail six men to go with the first load. They stay and do the unloadin' at that end. The other two git to push these rigs. See to it," he rapped as he turned to make for the unloading. Dellings looked briefly around his group, singling out Ryan and Ballard.

"First detail on the cart," he snapped, "the rest o' you, get unloadin' then stand by till we git shown the place." They worked quickly in the bright but cold Virginia day.The two carts were quickly loaded and the rest of the contents of the two cars were piled along the side of a large shed. As they continued stacking the remaining supplies, a grey-coated officer appeared with yet another sheaf of papers under his arm. Daniel Ryan saw Lacombe point him on towards Jessop, as a number of the men faltered in their shifting and loading to observe. The newcomer engaged Jessop in discussion and they strolled away from the train, gesturing and conversing, while Dellings and Lacombe waved the men back to work.

"Wonder if that's more cash dollars," Daniel Ryan said to Ballard, as they resumed work, "or maybe he's goin' to rely on spinnin' this one a yarn."

"It's common knowledge that no southern officer would ever accept no bribe, Private Ryan," Ballard murmured, in an offended tone of voice, as they continued to look, while they manhandled more boxes and sacks across to the shed. An old man, with a wide-brimmed black hat and denim overalls, now approached, together with a black boy, whom Daniel Ryan reckoned could be no more than thirteen or fourteen years old. By now the cars were almost empty while the two carts waited, stacked with boxes, barrels and sacks as Jessop waved the boy away.

"Send the stuff with him," he called to Dellings and, at that, the sergeant waved the carts away also.

It turned out to be a smallish meadow, part of the way along a muddy track to one side of the depot. It was fringed, on three of its sides, by a straggling bushy hedge and on the fourth by a fully fledged wood. On arriving there, the men stacked their muskets, blankets and haversacks and got down to their unloading, hearing the whistle of the departing train from the direction of the depot as they did so.

As the short winter afternoon drew on the work steadily advanced, with a succession of cart loads jolting backward and forward along the muddy track that stretched between the rail halt and the meadow. After three trips, Ryan and Ballard were relieved at the cart by two others of the detail and they then joined in the unloading at the meadow under Dellings' supervision. The supplies were stacked in the centre of the trampled grass, with the boxes and barrels on the ground as far as possible and the sacks and parcels stacked on top. A sack and a barrel, containing flour and bacon respectively, were kept back from the stack while the rest of the load was progressively added to it.

Finally, after several more cart journeys, four men were detailed away with the now returned Jessop and the carts, to re-appear, as the light began to fade, pushing one of them, on which was balanced a large tarpaulin. This was laboriously stretched across the top of the provisions stack, before the remaining vehicle was wheeled away for the last time. That done, the men were dismissed, some to the flour and bacon and, with Lacombe taking charge, a ration was issued, while others headed for off to gather fuel for fires and collect water. With all returned fires were kindled and pans produced to cook what they had been issued. The food was good, being fresh off the farms, where it had been raised and processed, rather than commissary issue and it disappeared quickly from the plates. When everyone had cooked and eaten, Jessop summoned them to gather around the largest fire.

"We are about twenty miles from our camps," he told them, "but we are no longer on our own. The colonel knows we are here and all of the regimental wagons that can be spared are bein' sent to carry what we have gathered up to the Fredericksburg lines, but not by the Hamilton's Crossing road. A guide is bein' sent with the first wagons and he will set our way north. Some of you men from this detail will go back to camp with each of the wagons, as additional escorts, since this county is troubled by skulkers and renegades. If you come across any of these bushwhackers, shoot first and talk later. They are fugitives from discipline, the scum of the earth, who sustain themselves by stealing from the commissary and the local people, but, if we stay vigilant, they will not get their miserable hands on any of what we have spent so much effort in bringin' here. I am told that the first of the wagons were being sent out today so they'll be due here at any time after first light tomorrow. From then on, it will be only a matter of time till we can escort the rest of our provisions back to our own camps. Sergeant Dellings and Sergeant Lacombe will set guard rotas for three hours each, and once that's done, those off duty should see to gettin' some sleep." There was a murmur of assent from the circle of listening men and, as Jessop moved away, Dellings began to speak, calling the names and watches for each of the sixteen men. Ryan and Ballard were both in the first watch and to Daniel Ryan, accepting his own weariness, that idea was fair enough, for once relieved, they would both have the remainder of the night to rest, undisturbed by further duty. They both moved away to recover their muskets and headed across to report to Lacombe, who was assembling the detail around the farther fire.

The night was clear and the stars were bright, though a chilly wind gusted through from the west, as Daniel Ryan took his turn at pacing around the perimeter of the meadow. He had the overcoat, that Martha Bennett had supplied, fastened up to his neck, and the scarf wrapped tightly beneath it, with the woollen gloves also getting their first baptism of real duty. The wind whipped through the branches of the nearby trees, as he paced along their margin, but the only noises, of anything other than nature, came from beyond the far side of the meadow towards the depot, where, even now, the work of laying out the place still went on. The whole area around the railroad was illuminated by fires that crackled noisily, their flames swept off to the east in tormented tongues by the gusting wind, with showers of sparks billowing away in the madly driven clouds of smoke. Daniel Ryan's mind was far from these sights however, being focussed instead on the events of the last two weeks in Georgia, especially the time spent in Eden Station, though now, as his mind wrestled with a jumble of further images from the return journey, there was a sense of unreality about much of what had taken place there. But one thing had hardened into a kind of reality, for in spite of the continued kindness of the Bennetts, and of others in the town, he now felt more distant and detached than ever from his previous life there, and he knew that much of that was down to Constance Warner.

In all truth, it had never been his plan to spend the rest of his life in Georgia, for there was little chance for anyone like him, a penniless immigrant, to own anything substantial there. He had dallied in Eden Station, thanks to Hal Bennett, but while there he had gradually formed the kind of friendships and attachments that seem to grow, as a matter of course, as familiarity with a place increases and the instinct of a newcomer to remain cautious and aloof slowly relaxes. Through the time he had remained there in Georgia, an increasingly complex web of acquaintances, and gradually of friendships also, had steadily begun to tie him to the place. There had been a growing kinship with

251

the Bennetts, who had given him the chance to settle there with steady, if unspectacular work. An increasing contact and friendship with some of the boys his age, both locals and immigrants who lived there, had forged additional bonds and then there had then been Constance, who had smiled at him, indulged his small tak and had permitted him to commence a vague courtship that may have led who knew where, but for the coming of the war.

The war, and the army, had changed his life again, separating him from the town, first for those tedious months of duty and hardship on Tybee Island and then taking him much further away to Virginia, and this absence had steadily eroded his bonds with Eden Station. Daniel had sensed that for as long as his involvement with Constance continued, there would be a surviving link, however tenuous, with the town. But now, there was no doubt in his mind, as this visit and the time he had spent with her had confirmed to him, that this too was in apparent decline. He found himself wondering whether, if he had not appeared so unexpectedly on the foraging expedition, she would actually have gotten around to telling him that her family were leaving Eden Station at all. But, whichever way that might have been, his return had shown him that there now was little, other than the slowly fading memories of his two and a half years there, and his continuing comradeship with the Bryan County boys in Company B, to link him to the place.

He was free to pursue, with or without John Fitzpatrick as previously planned, a new life. That new life was based on the idea of moving out to the west, after the war was won, to seek land to farm, or to forge some other kind of life, or for that matter, any other course in this huge continent that might appeal. The opportunities these days, for immigrants at least, seemed to be out in those wide western lands, away from the more settled, more civilised region east of the mountains and, once the fighting was ended, he was pretty well resolved that the life that lay before him, would be out there.

But the apparent ending of his relationship with Constance was a matter of sadness, and the pangs of it wrenched at him even now. To all intents and purposes their, "courtship," had become a victim of the war, withering, through their separation, as time passed. Neither of them had seemingly arrived at any conscious decision to end things between them, but it seemed to be ending nevertheless. His fondness for her still remained. She had always had ways of making him smile when they had been together, but absence and distance had proved nearly fatal to their friendship and now that he was required to face the fact of it ending, he felt low and sad about the whole thing. The feeling nagged at him that he could and maybe should have done more to keep their relationship in being rather than letting it fade to the extent that he had. Sure he had written periodically to her, but Daniel was not an instinctive letter writer, the way that some of the boys in the company were. There were those who seemed to have a pencil and paper to hand almost any time that there was an off-duty moment in camp, but not him. Writing had been something closer to a duty for him and now that their letters had tailed away to the point of near extinction, this pang of guilt was in his mind. He could have done more, but he had not done it. The place where he now found himself was, at least in part, the result of his own neglect and this too fuelled his feelings of sadness and regret.

But then there was the travelling west idea, for it too had run into stormy waters. Like many other things, it was not as simple as it had first seemed. His friendship with Fitzpatrick, which he had previously regarded as being as solid and reliable as anything in his life, had been strained, maybe too far, by the events of the autumn. Fitzpatrick had joined Jones and Kane in refusing to cross the Potomac River with the rest of the company to take part in the campaign in Maryland. They had rejoined in September, after the battle worn army had retreated into Virginia, but the dispute had continued and over the weeks in camp near Winchester, and on through the subsequent moves to Culpeper and on to the Rappahannock, there had been no healing. Scars remained and, in his deeper thoughts, Daniel Ryan feared that the friendship might well be permanently damaged. As he paced around that field, he knew that although, by one way of thinking, he was free to follow the plan, and maybe even still with Fitzpatrick as he had chosen, in another way he was now cast adrift in America more than he had ever been before, excepting only his first few weeks in Savannah after arriving in this new world.

Some friendships showed, when it came to testing times, that they were not as durable as they had seemed, for they did not survive those stresses and strains that life subjected them to, especially in wartime. His bond with Fitzpatrick could well founder in this way, but Daniel knew also that, as a result of those events of the early autumn, his kinship with Ballard, Philips and Thompson, and even the trouble-prone Daley, was now deeper than with those who had abandoned their messmates and friends back at Leesburg. This thought disturbed him. It was not that he did not trust Fitzpatrick, or Kane or Jones for that matter, it was simply that those three had turned their backs on the others of the mess once, and their place in the circle of trust was changed by that, even if that circle and some of that trust could eventually be repaired. Repair might still be possible, but perhaps things could never be completely restored. There was that doubt about men who had turned away from comradeship once, since they might do it again and therefore, even if, somewhere down the line, a degree of trust for them could resume it would remain measured rather than complete. Daniel paced back towards the picket fire, seeing Tom Sinclair of Company C get to his feet, as he approached, to take his turn at pacing around the meadow. Maybe here in the army, he thought, was the best place for here, in company with those who had faltered when that test of friendship had come, were others who had not failed and it now seemed to him that they were of the kind who never would.

The daylight came slowly, for cloud had come during the night and though the wind was still blowing, it was a shade less strong in its gusts. Daniel peeped out of the cocoon of blanket and waterproof in which he had rolled himself and looked around, first to the fire which had burned down, though a couple of the newly returned pickets were in the process of reviving it with more wood. Around the meadow there was a dank greyness that had not been there the previous evening, as more men were stirring around the camp. There had been no call as yet, but maybe the thought of breakfast, or even just a long cultivated instinct in the army, to rise with the daylight, had gotten them on the move. Daniel opted to move also and rolled away from the fire to discard his blankets and get stiffly to his feet, stretching his arms into the air and around behind him as he saw Ballard among the group of those who were assembling over at the tarpaulin covered pile of supplies. Lacombe was there and that would seem to indicate that a further rations issue was in progress, so Daniel moved back to his equipment pile to find their pan and take it to the now restored fire. Ballard soon joined him and deposited the ration of bacon and flour on the cloth that Daniel had laid close to the pan. The fire was spread with more wood, to make room for the different pans and the business of cooking got under way once more. This begun, Jessop departed again, while Dellings set the relieving pickets out onto the road, to await the regimental wagons as well as to dissuade an intrusion from any unwanted visitors.

It was well through the morning when the wagons arrived and the men began to assemble as the shout from the picket group was heard. There were three of them and they jolted down the muddy track from the rail halt with Jessop on the seat beside the driver of the leading vehicle, sandwiching an older man in civilian clothing between himself and the driver. Ballard had come to stand beside Daniel Ryan and see the arrival and he grunted as he watched the vehicles come to a halt in the meadow.

"Ain't so good," he muttered, half to himself. Daniel glanced around at him.

"What isn't," he inquired?

"Any of it," his companion said. "Look at them teams. They're like chalk 'n' cheese compared with the better fed stock like we saw in Savannah and Charleston or them other places, and they ain't jest goin' across town. They got twenty miles o' muddy, dirt roads to haul their loads, mubbee more, if that there guide feller takes 'em off on some backwoods hike, so they ain't gonna be takin' the same amount in one load as them other wagons did. This ain't gonna be an eight wagon haul, more likely it'll be ten or mubbee even more'n that. We could be stayin' around here a piece longer than Jessop reckoned and every load we send north gives whatever bushwhackers, that they're shittin' themselves about, more time and more chance to git themselves ready, once they start to figure out what's goin' on around here." Daniel looked more closely at the mules, which were now being unhitched and led away to where a tethering line was being set up by two of the men for the beasts to immediately set to cropping at the grass around their feet. It was true. These animals were lean and scrawny, by comparison with the horses in Richmond and the other teams which had hauled their provisions between the rail depots on the way up from Georgia. The state of them meant, as Ballard had said, that shifting the whole haul would take that much longer. Sure the last part of delivering their much-needed supplies could start here, but how long would it take before it ended, if, with reduced loads being taken away north, the remainder would be waiting here, for who knew how long, for enough wagons to arrive?

He looked across at Jessop to see the lieutenant, already poring over a map, while engaging in intense conversation with the old man who had arrived with the wagons, and busily writing details in his notebook. Dellings and Lacombe were getting the loading started and he and Ballard headed over to pitch in. The other complication was not too difficult to figure out either, as Ballard had said. If these groups of skulkers that Dellings and now Jessop had talked of were out there, hovering on the fringe of the army's supply lines, along those back trails and in those woods all along the way, then this would give them still more in the way of chances to gather and strike. With more wagons to escort, there would be fewer men to detail as guards for each trip made back to the Howison Hill camps, unless the further step was taken by the colonel of sending more men down from Fredericksburg.

The loading went on quickly, but the wagons were well short of full when the drivers called a halt to the process and the men, at a shout from Lacombe, moved back. Jessop had finished his talk and his writing and he now stepped over to the leading wagon.

"Sergeant Lacombe," he called. "Detail five men as escorts and, once the teams have had some more time to rest, these wagons can get goin'." Lacombe moved around pointing to those he wanted and gesturing them over to the wagons with his finger, while the remainder stepped away. The teams grazed for a further two hours before Jessop signalled to the drivers and their guards and they gathered their reins and began leading them over to be re-harnessed. When this was done, the, "guide," a local man named as George Edwards, clambered awkwardly back onto the bench seat of the leading wagon, while Jessop moved across and handed two folded papers to the driver.

"That's the one you show to any commissary snoop," he said. "Make sure the other one gets to the colonel as soon as you get back," he added. Daniel Ryan looked at him, for there was an urgency in the officer's words that had taken his attention and made him start to think that Jessop too did not think that this was going to be a straightforward trip north. Something in the lieutenant's tone sounded an alarm bell in Daniel Ryan's mind and when he looked around at Ballard, it seemed, from his expression, that his mind too might well be working on a similar thought.

"Reckon he's expectin' trouble too," Daniel said, but his companion just sniffed and turned away.

In a few minutes more the vehicles had departed, their guard detail walking alongside, with their muskets slung, but they had been gone not much more than an hour when three more wagons arrived, one of them a Company B vehicle, driven by George Fenning. There were shouts of recognition as these pulled into the meadow. Daniel Ryan turned to Ballard.

"Preston must'a' cut the camp wagon rosters to the bone to spare six in less than two days."

"It's jest about the worst way o' doin' it, that is if they're all expectin' trouble along the way," he grunted in response. "Pretty soon we ain't gonna have nobody much left around here to load 'em up or guard 'em on the way back up to camp, less'n Preston's sendin' more o' our boys down here." He looked up at the leaden sky with its scurrying clouds.

"What we need now is fer the good lord at least to keep the rain off fer a spell more," he added, "so's the roads don't git no worse and set everythin' back some more." Daniel Ryan looked up also before nodding in acknowledgement, as he pondered that what his friend was saying must by now be pretty evident to just about all who remained around the meadow.

The loading of the newly arrived wagons was left, on Jessop's orders, till the following morning, with the teams of mules being unhitched and led away to be tethered on a line in a different part of the meadow, where what remained of the grass was thickest. The men ate their evening meal after sunset and the business of guard details was then arranged, though with fewer men, the details were now three groups of four men, taking three hours each. Ryan and Ballard were allocated to the middle watch and, with that arranged, they turned in with the rest of the off-duty men, being roused later in the night for their duty. The hours of darkness passed without incident and with the morning came a clearer, colder day. The men in the meadow breakfasted on still more of the bacon and pancakes before setting to the loading of the wagons, while the drivers got their teams hitched. This time Lacombe and three further men, were detailed, to escort the three vehicles and the remainder watched them go, the sergeant carrying further papers from Jessop in his pocket with instructions, as before, on who should receive each of them.

Afternoon came and sure enough, as the light began to fade, two more wagons arrived, with Edwards, the old guide, sitting once more on the leading vehicle. Their arrival led to Jessop spending more time in heavy duty talking and map-gazing with him, with the same arrangements for the teams and wagons as the previous night. The mules were again set out on a tethered line to graze and rest, while the amended guard duty was divided between two groups who would take four hour duties on and off through the darkness hours. With the morning came the loading and three more men, together with the guide, were detailed, with Dellings, to escort the wagons north, leaving Jessop and the remaining five to watch them go. The stack of supplies remaining in the meadow was comparatively small now, maybe three reasonable wagon loads, Daniel Ryan thought, as he eyed what still lay lay there, or four, if the roads were particularly bad or the animals too weak to haul sizeable loads. Either or both of these factors could apply he thought, so their mission, while now well advanced, was still a fair distance short of successful completion.

True to the pattern of the previous days, a further trio of wagons showed up as the afternoon waned and the same routine was followed, though the untrampled grass in the meadow was sparser now and the mules were moved around to get the best of what remained before the camp turned in. The night was spent with two guard details of three men each, with even Jessop taking a turn, in the same four hours on and four hours off routine as the previous night. In the morning, under a more overcast sky, the loading went ahead, with all of what remained being stacked onto the three vehicles, but before they set off, Ballard involved himself in a lengthy conversation with Jessop, after which the lieutenant called the whole group together once more.

"We'll be startin' out soon now," he told them, "but we won't be takin' the main road to Hamilton's Crossin', cuz that road's fouled up with the trains supplyin' Jackson's corps. We'll start northwest towards a place called Massaponax

Church. That's where this road joins the route that's bin set up for Longstreet's supply trains, but, on the way there, we'll meet up with that guide, George Edwards, and he'll put us onto another road that joins the Telegraph Road further north. It'll put a mile or maybe two on the trip but it keeps our supplies clear o' the main trains and any provost or commissaries for most o' the way back." He looked around the group. "Go cook and eat boys," he told them, "and prepare enough for a midday meal. Before we get goin' each o' you is to clean and dry your musket and then load and stopper it, but don't prime yet, just cover your lock to keep it dry cuz, if you have to shoot at anybody along the way, we don't want no misfires." He nodded to Ballard and Ryan. "You two see to your extra rations and once we're ready, we'll be on our way." Ryan turned and looked quizzically at his friend, but the only immediate response he got was a wink, as a drizzling rain began to fall.

The roads were muddy and becoming moreso as they made their way along the verges in the wake of the wagons. The Massaponax Road was busy, with convoys of lumbering vehicles heading along it, but shortly after the first rest halt, they reached a tiny, roadside farmhouse. There was a warning shout from Jessop and, as he looked up ahead in response, Daniel Ryan caught sight of the thin figure of George Edwards, in his now familiar dark coloured jacket, waiting at the side of the road. As they approached, he signalled to the right and Jessop gestured to the lead driver who hauled his team that way, off the main route and onto a side road, that passed a small farm building, winding then towards the burnt out remains of what must have been a barn. The, "road," looked little more than a farm track, but the two following wagons dutifully followed the leading vehicle onto it. Past the barn, it became considerably narrower and remained so over its early length, being additionally overhung in stretches by tree branches. Its surface too, inevitably, was muddy and uneven and as the wagons and their escort began making their way along this new route, the rain grew somewhat heavier.

Being off the main wagon route, the, "road," was quieter, but not deserted. Occasional civilians, a courier or two and even a section of artillery were encountered, the latter causing their own wagons to pull over onto the verge as far as they were able, to allow the other traffic to squeeze past. Most of the other users were heading south, sloshing their way along the saturated surface in varying degrees of haste. But, Daniel Ryan reckoned the mud was not yet deep and, while the rain now pattered miserably down, the indications were that there was at least a residue of frozen ground below the surface that would keep the road passable, for a time, but would it be for enough time? Only the coming hours would tell.

Until now, Balllard had resisted Daniel Ryan's inquiries as to why they alone had prepared extra rations, but after the midday halt, as the wagons had creaked into movement again, he had beckoned to Daniel and the two of them had, at his bidding, dropped back to follow along further behind the rear vehicle. As they did so his friend had at last begun to explain.

"Jessop's hopin' that usin' this road, especially fer a night halt'll give us a better chance of avoidin' trouble," he said. "He figures, or he hopes, that most skulkers'll stay around the main supply roads for better pickin's, but, to my way o' thinkin', it might not be that way. There ain't no guarantees about it either way, so, from now, you and me'll drop back a stretch and stay clear of the camp that they all set up tonight. We'll set up close by but out o' sight, where we kin keep a watch and, if they git trouble, we pitch in and git to bushwhack any bushwhackers." Ryan looked at him with some displeasure.

"No fire for us then," he growled. Ballard nodded.

"Wouldn't be no point in doin' it if we're goin' to tell 'em we wuz there," he said. There was a period of silence while Daniel Ryan digested this unwelcome detail.

"Since when did you feel the need to become a damned hero," he finally demanded?

"Since we started haulin' supplies that our own folks gave us," his companion replied. "Some of 'em'll be goin' short on vittles themselves cuz they gave a part o' their winter stores to us. That stuff on them wagons is gonna help you, me and the rest of our mess, as well as ev'body else in the regiment, through the winter, and there ain't no renegades gonna be feedin' off it, not if I got any say about it."

The conversation was interrupted by the arrival of Jessop and they walked for a brief time in company with the officer, just to the rear of the wagons.

"You two know what you got to do," he growled? Ballard and Ryan both nodded, and seeing it confirmed, the lieutenant pulled a revolver from an inside pocket of his coat and offered it, by its barrel, to Ballard. Daniel looked, recognising the stubby weapon as a British made Tranter by its curiously shaped butt.

"For a fight like this could turn out to be," Jessop said, "you'll likely need more than one shot." Ballard took the pistol, nodded again and pushed it into his belt with his free hand. Jessop started away immediately, moving back up level with the rear wagon as Ballard touched Ryan's sleeve and they both moved off the road into the edge of the brush to dally there while the wagons pulled steadily away.

They waited, seeing the distance between themselves and the main party lengthen, until eventually the convoy was out of both sight and earshot. At that they left the woods and took to the road again, though now keeping to the verges of the trail along the line of the roadside growths, staying under the trees as much as possible. They avoided open areas as far as they could by crossing and recrossing the road to obtain cover so that anyone watching the road would have greater difficulty in picking them out. As the afternoon slowly passed in the murky woods, they continued on their way along the muddy surface, with pants and feet now thoroughly wet from the falling rain and dripping trees and bushes, and with the wagons nowhere to be seen. The daylight waned and the rain eventually slackened, while Ballard and Ryan still concealed themselves along the verge as far as they could, as they followed along, now well to the rear of the main party.

Eventually, as dusk approached, they stopped at the roadside to eat a portion of their bacon and pancakes cold before moving off again. Full darkness was falling in the woods and they moved carefully, watching as they went for the light of a campfire up ahead that would mark where the wagons had halted. They paced stealthily on through the dripping darkness, hearing the gentle pattering sound, as water fell from branches swaying in the lighter breeze. To their left the road wound on until, following its line, they began to round a curve to finally see a yellow glow through the conifer trees ahead and, by its direction, likely on the other side of the road. They stopped to take bearings before moving on, stepping carefully back to reach the verge. It was easier here because the glow from the fire reflected dimly along the road, throwing the trees and other growth into subdued silhouette and they were able to make their way, step by step along the muddy surface without mishap. Eventually Ballard, in the lead, raised his hand and brought them to a halt. He half-turned to whisper to Daniel Ryan.

"Time to move off over thar and find ourselves a place. Reckon we'll stay on this side cuz it's my guess that any bushwhackers'll come at 'em from their own side, so they'll be covered by the trees and brush." Daniel nodded and they changed direction, to move off into the soaking undergrowth, pushing through strands of grass, which further soaked their feet and lower legs, chilling them and making Daniel Ryan shiver involuntarily as he followed Ballard through the woods. To their left, through the trees, the yellow glow of the fire extended towards them, its pale fingers of light gradually drawing level as they tramped ahead. Eventually, Ballard seemed satisfied and he stretched out his right hand to bring them both to a stop. They stood and listened as the breeze shook more drips of rain water down from the branches above, but, save for the creak of the tree boughs, and some muted snatches of murmuring voices from the direction of the fire, there were few other sounds.

"Reckon we'll draw a mite closer," Ballard whispered, "and that'll be good enough." He turned left, towards the glow of the fire and began to move again, picking his way carefully from tree to tree now as he went, with Daniel following on beside and slightly behind, each of them waiting, as they did in skirmish order, while the other moved. They squelched through boggy stretches, feeling the mud suck at their shoes, as they eased closer to the road and the fire beyond, seeing for the first time, as they approached the road, the parked wagons, with glimpses also of the figures grouped around the fire and the mules tethered beyond the vehicles.

They halted and watched for a time, able, as the moments passed, to make out the movements among the animals as they sought better grazing. Daniel smelled a sudden whiff of cooking meat and he clenched his teeth at the thought of those men enjoying their hot meal, while he and Ballard shivered on cold rations in the chilly, dripping forest. At length they moved again, closer still, till they could hear fragments of the actual conversations around the fire above the sounds of the woods and the crackling of the flames. Finally Ballard sank to a crouch and waited for Daniel to ease up alongside him. They were on a bank of firmer, slightly rising ground, covered with withered ferns, and other debris, which crunched as they trod on it. Ballard leaned closer to Daniel Ryan.

"This looks OK to me," he murmured.

"Reckon so," Daniel whispered in reply. "There ain't nothin' gonna happen to them tonight that we won't see from here."

"OK then," Ballard said quietly, "so let's git ourselves as settled as we kin here. We'll eat afore we start takin' watches."

They laid their haversacks carefully in front of them and stretched out their waterproof blankets on the ground before settling on them. Then, with their muskets at their sides, they rolled themselves and the weapons loosely in their woollen blankets, before folding the waterproofs back over themselves for some protection from the still-dripping branches above. What remained of the rations was taken from the haversacks and they lay there in the darkness and chewed on the cold mess of bacon and flour flapjacks, while, scarcely fifty yards from where they lay, their comrades lounged, enjoying their hot food and warmed by their fire, which crackled and flickered in the breeze. Back in the woods, having finished eating, Ballard opted to take the first watch.

"I'll wake ya after a spell," he whispered and Daniel gestured his agreement gratefully. He settled his head onto his arms, which cradled the barrel of his musket, and within seconds, in spite of the cold, which still persisted in his wet legs and feet, he slept.

Daniel Ryan did not know how long he had been asleep, but it seemed to him that he had scarcely closed his eyes before Ballard was shaking his shoulder and jerking him into wakefulness. He stiffened as his senses took in the time and place, but Ballard was already whispering to him.

"Ain't nothin' stirrin'," he said, "so my turn fer some shut eye."

"Maybe nothing's goin' to," Daniel grunted, as he pushed himself up onto his elbows and looked out towards the camp, while his friend settled himself down. Across the way, the fire had burned lower, but the details of the camp were still easily enough made out in the glow. There was, at first glance, no sign of life, but then a movement, around where the mules were tethered, caught his eye as the figure of a man, who looked like John Landon of Company E, emerged from beyond the wagons, with his musket on his shoulder, pacing slowly around the camp. Daniel let his eyes follow him as he moved around the perimeter, past the blanketed humps of sleeping men around the fire itself, and on around the three wagons, till he moved out of sight on the far side of the furthest vehicle, to emerge briefly a few seconds later, around the other end of the same wagon, before pacing back around towards where the mules were tethered. Even now, Daniel could see that there was still movement among the animals and he watched them stir for a few more seconds. Then he let his eyes sweep back across the camp, settling his mind into a routine to keep himself awake, scanning the scene from end to end, and then moving his musket slightly before beginning the whole process again, while counting the paces of Landon as he watched.

After a time, the sentry came around to the fireside,

where the others slept. Daniel saw him bend and prod the blanketed shape of another man into wakefulness and it was at that moment that, over beyond the line of now fidgeting mules, his eyes caught a further movement. It was, at first glance, no more than a movement, something out of the routine set of movements that he had become accustomed to, through watching for a period of time. But the movement quickly gained substance in the form of a crouching, moving figure, who used the mules to shield himself from the two awakened men at the fire as he approached. As he came closer, and the firelight caught him, its yellow light glinted on the pistol that he carried. Immediately Daniel pushed his companion awake.

"Got company," he whispered. Ballard turned onto his elbows immediately, pushing his musket forward until he was gripping the stock ready to take aim, while Daniel flicked the blankets away from his body and began to ready his own weapon. He scrambled up to a crouch, then pulled the cloth from around the lock and the cork stopper from the muzzle, jamming them into his pocket before fumbling in the same pocket for a cap, gazing intently all the while at what was taking place beyond the road at the camp.

The intruder over at the mules had stopped, with his pistol readied, as though waiting for some kind of signal, and, sure enough, at the opposite side of the camp, there was now a further movement beyond the last wagon, as a second man emerged from the brush and began to stalk around the parked vehicle. He too held a pistol, a long-barrelled Colt from its appearance. Beside Daniel Ryan, Ballard watched it all before whispering softly.

"Could be more of 'em, so we'll wait a little, and let 'em make their move." Daniel still watched as he took in the words, sighting his musket on the man at the mule tether as he nodded.

"As long as they don't go shootin' somebody," he whispered back. "I got the one by the mules covered anyhow."

"OK," he saw, in the corner of his eye, the muzzle of Ballard's musket move slightly to the left, towards the other man, but even as he registered this, a third figure had appeared, coming into view around another of the wagons. He carried a longer weapon, likely a cavalry carbine, and he it was who moved now, without stealth or delay, quickly covering the ground over towards the fire, where the new sentry had finished donning the belt on which his cartridge box was slung, while Landon, having thrown another piece of wood onto the fire, warmed himself momentarily at the flames. The newcomer launched himself at Landon, slamming the butt of the carbine into his back as he reached him and sending him sprawling to the ground on top of another of the sleeping men. As he did this, the man on Ballard's side of the camp moved quickly up to the surprised sentry and stuck the pistol against the side of his head, at the same time kicking at his leg to bring him to the ground.

The camp was awake now, with the other sleepers disturbed and hurriedly scrambling from their blankets, but they were met by pointed weapons and a chorus of shouts from the three intruders, now joined by yet another man, who had followed the one with the carbine past the closest wagon to reach the fireside. There was a succession of kicks and other blows from weapons as the drivers and escorts were pushed into a group beside that wagon and then it seemed to calm somewhat as the last man to arrive began to take charge.

"We kin spare y'all a bullet if ya wanna give us trouble," he called, his voice carrying clearly across to where Ryan and Ballard crouched and, as his words registered, Daniel noticed that he carried no weapon though, as he turned towards the group of prisoners, a holstered pistol came into view.

"Good enough," Daniel thought to himself. This man seemed to feel no threat and it would take him precious time to unholster the gun, so he would not be an immediate target. Beside him, he felt Ballard's fingers in his ribs, nudging him into attentiveness.

"Looks like they ain't intent on no killin' at least not yet, so let's git closer," he whispered. "Mubbee they don't want to risk no shootin' in case o' who else might be close by, but like the man said, we can't afford no wasted shot." He balanced his musket in his left hand then eased the pistol that Jessop had given him at his belt, before grasping the musket again. Having done that he stood upright and started forward through the remaining trees, with Daniel now a few yards to his right, as they picked their way on towards the road. Closer they moved until, to Daniel, they seemed to be getting so close that it must be impossible for the renegades not to see them. He glanced to his left seeing Ballard halt at last and level his musket. Daniel Ryan did the same, moving a half-step to the left to rest the barrel of the Enfield on the short spur of a broken tree branch; easier aiming meant a surer shot, he told himself. Beside him Ballard nodded towards the camp and they sighted carefully.

"Hold up," Ballard whispered, "even if we drop two of 'em the others still got a free shot on our boys. We'd be better waitin' fer the best time."

So they waited with Daniel Ryan resting the weight of the Enfield on the branch spur, while still tracking his target, who had moved closer to the group of prisoners that his companions were covering. Out of the corner of his eye he saw Ballard move sideways to find a similar resting place for his own musket. Seconds passed, and these turned gradually into minutes, until Daniel Ryan began to wonder if they would ever have a clear enough opportunity to shoot. In spite of the help provided by the branch stump, his arms were growing tired and were starting to ache, from the strain of keeping the musket levelled and sighted. But now, at last, the man with the carbine was moving away from the captives, as though tiring of the sport of abusing them. He had stepped over to the nearest of the wagons and, as Daniel Ryan felt his body tense in anticipation, the man bent slightly to place his weapon down, leaning it against the wheel rim of the wagon, in order to climb up onto the vehicle. As he swung himself up, Daniel whispered to his friend.

"Now's got to be the time," and almost simultaneously he heard Ballard's shout.

"Hit 'em!" The tail end of the words was drowned out by the deafening report of the two muskets. Daniel Ryan had a glimpse of the man with the pistol, whom he had sighted on, flailing backwards before the smoke from the discharge smothered everything. He pulled the weapon away from the tree branch and launched himself towards the camp, trying to look where he was going in the strange light, so that he might keep his feet in the treacherous, sodden undergrowth. He lurched past the few remaining trees, feeling grass strands, together with more jagged vegetation, pull and wrench at his pants as he headed for the edge of the road without pausing. Beside him he heard a pistol shot, and then another, presumably from Ballard and then a further shot rang out as he pounded on across the mud of the road to confront the scene at the camp as the smoke cleared away on the breeze.

At the wagon nearest the fire a huddle of figures were still grappling with each other and, as Daniel reached them, several of them began to straighten up to reveal Tom Sinclair with the pistol. The ringleader of the renegades was on the ground, held firm by another of their own men while others aimed further kicks and blows at him. Ballard was to his left and had reached where Jessop now stood, over the man who had carried the carbine. He, like the other two renegades, now lay prone and Daniel moved across towards the one he had shot seeing, as he approached, that the man was lying flat on his back with a large dark stain, visible in the firelight, on the chest of his ragged brown coat. His mouth was wide open and he stared up at the trees above him, but it was immediately obvious that his eyes now saw nothing of those dark swaying branches overhead. Daniel poked at him with his musket muzzle, and, feeling nothing of a response, he began to turn away as Landon joined him.

"Ornery bushwhackin' shit," he said, as he retrieved the revolver from where it had fallen. Daniel gave a grunt in response, feeling a strong surge of vengefulness wash through him towards this man whom he had just killed, for he had come to rob, and quite possibly to kill also, and now he had gotten his own share.

"His bushwhackin' days are done with," he said as he started towards the second fallen man, whom Ballard had first brought down. Jessop and Ballard, seeing Daniel moving towards the other motionless shape, now half-hidden among the dead grass and other straggling undergrowth, moved back towards the prisoner. He was still covered by Sinclair with the pistol, but others of their group had gathered around him continuing to return a few of the blows that they had previously gotten from him and his companions. Daniel ignored them, moving on to halt over the remaining fallen figure. Again it was clear that the shot had struck in the torso, entering the side of the man's chest to pass straight through, for there were two distinct wet patches on his jacket where he lay. His face was obscured by one of his arms and a tussock of grass, and Daniel Ryan pushed his musket muzzle out to lever the arm and the grass strands aside. Again there was no trace of any movement in response, but it was when he looked at the pinched, bearded face that was now revealed, that he suddenly stiffened.

"Otis!" he called and turned towards his friend as he looked around. Daniel gestured to him to come, returning his gaze to the fallen figure as Ballard approached. It was true, he knew this face, even in death there was no mistaking it, for it was Rufus Fenton from Eden Station. Fenton, who had marched and fought and endured with them in Company B, from the start of the war all the way to Leesburg in the early fall. Daniel slowly shook his head, and the anxious faces of the boy's family swam into his mind as he looked down at the limp body. He had known him back in Georgia, as well as in the army. They had volunteered for the regiment on that same day, the week after Lincoln's call for troops to invade the south. He had drilled with the rest of them on the square at Eden Station, had endured the ordeals of Tybee Island and had served through those grim days of battle around Richmond and again at Manassas last summer. Fenton had been one of those who had refused to cross over the river into Maryland, but he had not returned along with the others when the army had re-crossed to the Virginia side after the battle at Sharpsburg.

So he had joined these marauders, who had followed on the fringe of the army since the autumn, subsisting by means of theft or murder, and now he was dead, shot as a thieving scavenger by one of his own former comrades. Ballard had come up to join Daniel and he too now stared down at the dead boy.

"Shit!" he said softly, "how in the hell does one of our own finish up like this?"

"Who in the hell knows that," Daniel answered wearily?

He bent and poked briefly through Fenton's pockets. "What goes on in any man's mind when he's seen some of the things that we've had to look at," he mused? "Who wouldn't want to get away and never see things like that again, but this, there's no kind of dignity or anythin' in this?" His mind was already wrestling with the memory of the assurance he had given to Fenton's family, and others also, just days previously, but he had never, could never in a million years, have anticipated something like this. Beside him Ballard spoke.

"There ain't bin much dignity in any of it Daniel," he said, "but most of us have stayed with it in spite of all o' that." Jessop had arrived and he too looked down at Fenton.

"Reckon we'll bury them," he said, "even if they were thieving sons of bitches." Ballard screwed up his face and turned to go, while Daniel Ryan lingered, still looking at his dead ex-comrade.

"Reckon most of 'em started out as soldiers," he said to the officer, "even if they did finish up like this."

"Well they were only worth a bullet in the end," Jessop growled.

Daniel turned away from the wagons and the fire, re-crossing the road and moving on into the woods once more to collect his own, and Ballard's equipment, though he found that he had to prowl around for several minutes in the darkness of the brush before he could find the place on the little rise of ground where they had left them. He pulled both haversacks onto one shoulder and slung his musket also before gathering up the wet blankets to make his way back. As well as cold, wet and wearied he felt drained and disgusted, his spirits down at the discovery of Fenton's body, but, he told himself, there was nothing to be done about that now. Warmth, hot food and maybe some rest and then there would be time to think of other things.

It soon became clear that the ground, below the first few inches, was still pretty solid for it became steadily more unyielding as the men of the detail attacked it in an effort to dig a suitable hole for the dead renegades. The grave for the three of them was thus, of necessity, shallow and barely adequate for its purpose. In addition, two of the escorting men now nursed injuries, which prevented them from joining in the digging, but at least there was a shovel in one of the wagons, so progress was made, albeit slowly. Neither Ryan nor Ballard had said anything about Fenton, Daniel concluding that an anonymous burial was maybe better than sordid notoriety. His body, and those of the other dead bushwhackers, were pushed together into the shallow hole that they had wrestled from the hard ground and the muddy earth was scraped and shovelled on top of them, leaving a considerable mound at the roadside near the edge of the trees. The burying done, they had not dallied, cooking and eating in the darkness before harnessing the mules, waiting only till the arriving light was sufficient to see by, before resuming their journey along the muddy road. Three of the six escorting men walked beside the wagons, taking turns at prodding the captured bushwhacker, whom they had tethered by his bound wrists to the tailgate of the first vehicle on which the guide rode in company with the driver. The remaining man, still nursing the injured leg he had sustained from one of the renegade, rode on the second wagon.

Ryan and Ballard were again at the rear, dropping back from the others as before, this indicating that Jessop at least had not discounted the threat of further trouble. Ballard still had the lieutenant's pistol in his belt, and Daniel Ryan had armed himself with the one of the three carried by the dead bushwhackers. A search through their pockets had revealed a spare cylinder with six further loads, together with some bullets and caps in a pouch. He could feel the weapon in his belt as he walked, reassuring, in spite of its heavy bulk. He felt somewhat revived, having dried and warmed himself at the fire, in the process of the cooking and eating, but, back on the road now, the fate of Rufus Fenton, and the matter of having given something of his word to the family, had begun to hang on his mind, for these events had placed him in a position where he profoundly did not wish to be.

How could he communicate such news to a waiting family, that their son had died a renegade? Daniel found himself inwardly shrinking from the idea. He nursed the problem in his own mind as they followed along the muddy road, with the wagons now once more out of sight in the growing light of the winter morning, before eventually opting to speak of it with Ballard.

"There's plenty of our own boys in the ground by now, but none like Rufe back there," he began.

"Chose his own way and there ain't nobody but hisself to blame," was his friend's somewhat laconic response, "so that's the end of it fer me." Daniel could see the inevitable sense of that, but, in his own situation, it was not so simple. He was the one who, as well as knowing Fenton, had known his family also and had spoken with them only those days previously about the very matter of their boy's whereabouts.

"It's surely the end of it for Fenton," he replied eventually. "There ain't no arguin' about that, but it ain't all just about him. There's his family, they don't know he's dead, but we do and we can't just keep it to ourselves and not let them know that their boy ain't comin' home. What he did was wrong and his fault, but his folks maybe deserve to know and not be kept wonderin' what happened to him." There was a pause after he spoke that lasted a few seconds, but Ballard's subsequent response showed a measure of impatience.

"Well, if you think that way then go ahead and write to 'em," he returned. There was a silence after that as they tramped on through the mud of the verge.

"I think it's right that they should know," Daniel Ryan said at length. His friend turned at the words to look at him.

"What in the hell is all o' this good neighbourly stuff," he growled? "If ya'd a'wanted we could a' gotten a corpse shifter to take his carcass back home too." Daniel glared at him, but Ballard was unrepentant.

"Fenton's end was Fenton's fault," he snapped, "whoever pulled the trigger, and I tell ya I'd do the same right now, even if I knew it was him. When ya turn bushwhacker ya don't deserve no better and anyways, d'ya really think his folks'll thank ya fer tellin' 'em that he finished up a renegade?"

"That ain't what I'm sayin'."

"Then what are ya sayin'?"

"I ain't sayin' anythin' about you shootin' him. I'd've done the same, and who shot which one back there was just the way it happened. What I'm sayin' is that we can't just cover it up and forget that it was him. We need to report it when we get back. He's dead, so he should be reported dead."

"No matter what that does to his folks? What happened to yore good neighbourly stuff?"

"They've got a right to know what happened to him, but that doesn't mean we need to tell them everythin' about what he did."

"Well, like I said, you go right ahead and write to 'em and tell 'em whatever ya want, but they'll want to know how he died, whether you want to tell 'em that or not." Daniel turned the idea over in his mind once more before answering, casting his mind around for some way of resolving it.

"But it's the army," he finally said. "A man's commandin' officer's supposed to do that kind o' thing." He stopped, feeling guilty about starting to involve others in the thing that he had agreed to do.

"So," Ballard returned. "What yo're doin' by reportin' it, when we git back, is shiftin' the job of tellin' his folks, and decidin' what to tell 'em, from us onto Preston, or more likely onto Boyce."

"Keepin' it to ourselves ain't right," Daniel retorted, irritated by the fact that everything his friend had said so far seemed to be closing him into his predicament. There seemed to be nothing for it but to tell him. He breathed in deeply before he spoke again.

"I met with his folks, back in Eden Station and they asked, so I told them that if there was any word o' him, I would see that it got passed on to them." At that, Ballard gave a sigh of exasperation and shook his head.

It fell quiet then for a time as they sloshed on through the layer of mud that covered the road, the silence eventually broken by another sigh from Ballard.

"Daniel, we can't fix everythin' fer everybody," he said. "We can't fix everythin' fer the regiment. Hell, we can't even fix things in our own mess, so we surely can't fix things fer no families down in Georgia." He paced along as though deep in thought for a time.

"OK," he said eventually, "I ain't gonna fight with ya about this. If you ain't gonna tell 'em, I'll make a deal. When we git back," he looked around about them at the gloomy pine woods, "if we git back, we'll tell Boyce. He's the actin' captain, so he kin decide and we agree to go along with whatever he says about it." He looked Daniel in the eye. "That's the fairest way," he went on, "'cept mubbee on Boyce.

Hell," he concluded, "that's what officers git paid fer." He paused again and looked at Daniel Ryan.

"Deal," he said finally? Daniel turned it over in his mind for a few seconds before shrugging his shoulders. It smelled like a conspiracy and it could result in the Fentons being told nothing of Rufus' death, but there was maybe little else for it. Beside him Ballard sloshed along looking across at him for a response.

"It's either that," he said, "or you go right ahead and tell 'em whatever ya like yoreself." Daniel looked back at him for a few further seconds.

"Deal," he finally said.

They fell quiet for a while after that, with each watching his own side of the trail, and keeping to his own thoughts. Daniel Ryan's were still on the fate of Rufus Fenton. What had made him do it? He had left the regiment, along with the others, who would not take part in an invasion of the north, but almost all of them had eventually returned. What had turned that boy, who had been one of their own, into a bushwhacker, a vulture who lived by preying on others? There was no answer to such a question, for what was it that made any man do anything, when he had a choice of doing different, or doing better? No, only Fenton would have known the answer. Anyone else could only be guessing at what had made him choose the way he had, if it had ever really amounted to a clear and specific choice at all, rather than simply a drift down through a process of decline that had finished up with Ballard's bullet.

The army had its share of deserters, especially since the war had stretched on and the fighting, since last summer, had become fiercer and bloodier. There were plenty of men who had left the ranks for different reasons without authorised furloughs. Some had gone home for the simple purpose of sustaining their families by mending fences, bringing in late harvests or putting in crops for the next season. But what Fenton, and others like him, had done was very different and much more culpable. They had not gone home to support families, instead they had dallied back here in Virginia, forming into gangs or bands and preying like buzzards. Not only were they no longer of any use to the army, but since the autumn, patrols and escorting details, from that army, had had to range through the rear areas in order to suppress, or at least restrict, their activities. They were, in the end, deserters in the true sense of the term and worse, they were jackals and thieves who fully deserved their bullet or rope.

The morning slowly stretched on and, as the time passed and midday approached, glimpses could be seen, through the banks of grey cloud, of a pale winter sun. The road winding ahead generally led almost due north, though, in places, the mud was deeper and more of an obstacle. Twice, Ryan and Ballard had come up with the wagons, to add their weight to moving them past these stretches of mud before falling back again to shadow the lumbering vehicles and their escorts from a distance. Around noon, they overtook the vehicles again, halted this time at a junction of their own road with a busier one. Sinclair saw them come up.

"That guide feller, Edwards, said this was the Telegraph Road," he muttered, "afore he went on his way." Ballard grunted in response and they waited, while Jessop headed out onto the intersection itself and the rest of the party watched.

The traffic on the road was considerable and their own vehicles were forced to prolong their wait for a space until Jessop, standing at the junction, seized the opportunity, afforded by a brief gap in the traffic, to halt a further convoy of approaching wagons, and wave their own vehicles out onto the road, turning them northeast now for the last leg of their journey. The wagons hauled ponderously out, taking their places in the long procession, heading for where the army was stationed, fixed now at the pace, and in the van of the vehicle trains already on the road. Riders and messengers splashed past in either direction, on their muddy horses, but out on the main width of the road, the endless column of lumbering traffic kept its own sedate pace.

The afternoon was stretching towards dusk, when, having passed a picket on the road, to whom Jessop had flourished his sheaf of semi-official papers, Daniel Ryan recognised the familiar wooded shape of Howison Hill up ahead, a sign at last of the final end of the whole mission. Jessop saw it too and called a warning to the wagon drivers. The hill drew slowly closer, until eventually the vehicles lurched off the road and onto the track that served the camps. Word had clearly preceded them and, as they drew closer to the camps, their way was flanked on either side by increasing numbers of shouting and chattering men from the regiment, but lining the road also, were more of them, fully armed, with muskets and fixed bayonets at the ready. Daniel Ryan looked out at them all and around the camp, seeing a familiar yet different sight. No longer were the shelters simply tents with earth heaped around their sides. In the near to three weeks of their absence these shelters now looked like hybrid huts. To be sure there was no standard design or layout about them, for a whole range of differing building ideas were in evidence around the camp. Some of the shelters had been turned into actual huts with log walls and either planked or sod roofs, while others, and a fair majority of the total, were a combination of different materials, tending to be a mixture of cave, hut and tent. The camp was now a virtual town of such structures and the effect on the stripped hillside was very evident to the returning men.

The whole area was now cleared, with a forest of stumps marking where the trees had previously covered the ground. Main, "roads," to and around the camps had been corduroyed with logs embedded in sequence along their length, while a myriad of further muddy paths and tracks now criss-crossed the camp. The place had been transformed and now looked like a permanent, rather than a transient or temporary settlement.

"Reckoned ya'd stayed on and settled in Georgia," came Philipps' voice, through the many others, jolting Daniel from his scrutiny of the camp. He and Ballard turned to see him push through the growing crowd of onlookers.

"Thought about it," Daniel called in return, "three square meals a day, thought hard about it." Philipps grinned at the reply as he fell in beside them.

The colonel was waiting in the middle of the camp and, as the wagons came to a final halt, the escorting soldiers formed into a file at Jessop's call. Preston came forward, beaming broadly, to return the lieutenant's smart salute.

"I reckon I gotta be grateful for gittin' my wagons back in one piece," he called out to a ripple of amusement from the gathering crowd of men, who had followed the wagons up to watch their reception.

"Colonel," Jessop called formally, "I beg to report, the return of the regimental foragin' detail, with one prisoner." Preston beamed broadly as he stepped forward and, abandoning formality for once, he shook hands with Jessop.

"Well done, m' boy," he said, "a first rate job done here. The quartermaster will take charge of your provisions and Sergeant Morsby will take charge o' this varmint." He gestured towards the deserter, before turning to the short rank of waiting men and pacing slowly along, beaming broadly as he went.

"Well done to you boys too," he added. "The whole regiment is in yore debt. Dismiss these men for a rest, lieutenant," he told Jessop. "I reckon they deserve it. You sir, will attend at my quarters directly." The rippling mutter among the watching men grew steadily until it had turned into a loud cheer as the file of newly returned men dismissed with the customary half-turn to the right. They moved away to endure a succession of backslaps and handshakes as their comrades reclaimed them. Thompson was there, along with Daley and Philipps to greet Ballard and Ryan as they made for the company camp and the procession back along the track into the trees steadily grew as it was joined by more and more of the men. Those under arms were left grouped around the wagons and Ballard, curious about them, quizzed Thompson.

"What's with the gun-totin' guards Joe?"

"Colonel's orders," Thompson told them, "on account o' them thievin' varmints frum the Eighteenth Georgia. They must a' gotten wind o' what was goin' on and last night a posse of 'em came over here when the two wagons wuz comin' in. Two of 'em got up on the rear wagon and started tossin' supplies down to the rest o' their friends afore the boys here knew what was happenin'. Our boys got some of it back and there was some bloody noses and broken heads over it all, but it was near dark and some of 'em got away into the woods with a share of our supplies afore anybody could catch 'em. The colonel ordered that you boys were to git the full treatment and if any Eighteenth Regiment scavengers showed up they was to be bayoneted, in the ass first, but that didn't stop 'em, anywhere else that would." Ballard grimaced.

"Eighteenth Regiment," he said, "they'd have the floor

out o' a damned church, in spite o' bein' Savannah boys." Thompson did not respond, looking instead at Daniel Ryan.

"Reckon you boys'd want to know that John Fitzpatrick's in the hospital in Richmond." Ryan turned and looked at him, as the sergeant went on.

"He had the flux, same as plenty o' other boys," he said, "but then he got a fever as well, start o' last week that woulda' bin. He got pretty bad and Sterling had him evacuated to Hanover and, last we heard day afore yesterday, he was down in Chimborazo, that new place, in Richmond. We ain't had no more word since then, but he was pretty sick when he left here." Daniel Ryan shook his head at Thompson's news. Concern for his friend, in spite of everything, was uppermost in his mind, counter-balanced to some extent by the grim realisation that a thing like this was something that was apt to happen in the army and had happened repeatedly over the last two years. Illness had killed more men in the Army of Northern Virginia than the Yankees had and, in spite of their recent differences, he earnestly hoped that John Fitzpatrick would not be the latest addition to that sanguine list.

Acting Captain William Boyce greeted them at his shelter, with a broad smile as he returned their salutes.

"I am glad to learn that your visit home was a success," he said, "and that you have returned from it in one piece." Ballard exchanged glances with Daniel Ryan, whose mind was still reeling from the news about Fitzpatrick.

"No time like the present," he muttered, and on Daniel Ryan's nod, he addressed the officer.

"Beggin' yo're pardon, captain, but we'd appreciate a word in private." Boyce's expression changed from benign to curious, but he recovered himself immediately.

"As you wish," he said, indicating towards the log shelter behind him.

It was warm in the shelter with a healthy fire burning in a stone and clay fireplace at one end and the acting-captain heard them out without comment as Ballard related the fate of Rufus Fenton. When he had finished Boyce sat for several seconds and looked from one of them to the other, before getting to his feet and pacing around the confines of the shelter.

"It is a regret to hear that another of our own men is dead," he said slowly and deliberately, "and sorrier still to learn that he died in the way you say. We all know that some of the men who remained south of the Potomac in September did not return to the colours, and Fenton was one of those." He paused in his pacing and looked at them in turn.

"Why did you decide to tell me of this," he inquired? They did not speak at first, until Daniel Ryan took in a breath and made to answer.

"We reckoned that Rufus's folks would be waitin' for word of him," he began.......

"They will not be in any way consoled by hearing what you have just told me," Boyce said as he resumed his pacing. "In truth, this news gives me something of a dilemma," he went on. "On the one hand, because of the incident or ambush you have described to me, we now have definite news as to Private Fenton's fate. I could report it all to his family and leave them to suffer whatever anguish, and other misfortune, that comes from not only his loss, but the manner of his end as a deserter and a thief. On the other hand, Private Fenton was the one who was responsible for his own fate. If it had not been you who finished him off, it would likely have been somebody else along that road, a day, a week or a month from now. The fault was his, but not his family's." He stopped his pacing and beckoned to them to sit, resuming his own seat while they balanced themselves on the lid of the wooden trunk..

"So what am I to do," he continued? "If I send word of his death to his family in Eden Station, with anythin' much about how it happened, I heap punishment on them, over and above the death of their boy. They will have to endure the reaction of their neighbours, they will be judged and, likely they will be condemned, by some at least of them. Some of the blame for their boy's sins will be upon the heads of his people to make their loss even heavier to bear."

Ryan and Ballard sat in silence upon the trunk as Boyce talked and the fire crackled in its makeshift hearth. But Daniel was feeling still more turmoil in his mind as the captain continued, for making Fenton's fate known, if Boyce was right, was every bit as complicated as it had seemed. Eden Station while being its neighbourly self, at least in most ways, was still a fairly typical small town. News and gossip, of various kinds, swept through it pretty continuously and it could be as judgemental and unforgiving as anywhere else whenever something controversial or scandalous came to light. As for himself, well he and Ballard had gotten what to do about the death of Fenton off their own chests, so now, as Ballard had said, Boyce and not they would decide the matter of what to do about his family. Perhaps they should have stayed quiet, he thought, for in spite of his conversation with the family back in Eden Station, he knew he would have found it hard to communicate with them, if not over the fact of his death, certainly over the actual circumstances of it. It all simply left the Fentons in a limbo of ignorance as to what their son's fate had been, at least until some kind of a, "suitable time," came along for telling them he was dead. The whole matter was confirming him once again in his view that, in this army being an ordinary soldier was the best course, and that the responsibilities of command and authority did not appeal in any way to him.

Across the paper-strewn camp table, Boyce was still considering his dilemma. He sat there with his legs outstretched, his elbows on the table and his hands clasped in front of him. He then stroked his chin absentmindedly with his extended fingers and gazed straight ahead for a time, while Ryan and Ballard fidgeted on the trunk opposite. Eventually, the acting-captain stirred himself and got to his feet once more. He sighed deeply, before beginning to speak once again.

"If it were possible to give those people the news of their boy's death, without going into how, and what he had done, then I would do that. But would that not simply lead to them, and likely others of his neighbours, wanting to know how he died and likely making moves to discover what had happened?" He paced some more before going on.

"I would rather leave those people wondering about their boy's fate than have to tell them, along with the news of his death, that he died a renegade and a thief. I do not like it, but the other way is worse and I will not do it, not at least for the meantime. I will say nothing. Fenton can rest wherever you buried him for the present, and, as far as you two are concerned, you killed a nameless marauder, not a comrade. In the coming weeks, if a suitable time presents itself, perhaps after the next engagement....?" He looked across at them pointedly. "That, as far as I am concerned, is the best choice. Do you agree?" He waited until the two of them nodded slowly.

"Well, in order to give ourselves the chance to do that, the details of your story must go no further than the three of us and I need your word on that." He looked at each of them in turn and, seeing that the dilemma that they had passed on to him was now, at least in part, back with them, Ballard and Ryan exchanged further glances.

"Reckon so," Ballard said quietly, upon which Boyce's gaze shifted to Daniel Ryan.

"It stays between us," Daniel said in an equally low voice. At that the acting-captain appeared satisfied.

He nodded slowly before speaking again.

"We shall do nothing for the time being and, at a more suitable time, I shall write to the Fentons. That will discharge any duty to inform a family of the fate of their boy. In time, it is likely that others will learn at least something of what he did and how he died, but his family, if we keep our word, should at least have had some time to come to terms with their loss before that happens." He rose and stepped over to the shelter entrance, signifying that the discussion was at an end.

"You two....get some rest," he told them, "and something to eat. Thanks to your efforts there should be a good meal on the way somewhere in this camp." They stood up and saluted, waiting there until Boyce returned the respect, before turning to go.

Chapter 10 Snow and Shortage

Camp life was quickly re-established for the men of the foraging detail as the routines of the army absorbed them, generating an air of, "business as usual," with duty watches set down towards the river, and work details in camp. The clothing brought back from Georgia had been immediately put to use, most of it being supplied by families for their own boys, though a further number of garments, that had also been donated, were distributed to the most needy. But the biggest improvement, as January proceeded, was in the food supply. Those whose families had sent them addressed parcels were promptly issued with them, but there was also a considerable general haul now in camp to supplement the ration. The colonel had the provisions stored in a prepared log shelter, under twenty four hour guard, to be listed and issued by the quartermaster and from this source, as well as from the individual parcels, the rations improved and the company camps became more cheerful places.

Their own mess shelter, like most others in the camp, was now largely complete. Ryan and Ballard found, that in their absence, it had grown into a good-sized dugout, maybe twelve feet long and something over half of that in width, with log-walls and a canvas roof stretched over a ridge pole and secured to the tops of the walls. It was furnished with crude furniture, several stools and two trestle structures which served as bunks, all made from roughly stripped smaller logs, and it too had gained a chimney, made of stones and calked with clay, set into one end of the structure. Wood for the fire was stacked in a corner near the chimney, initially to dry it out for burning with less smoke, but also, as Daley asserted, because stacking it outside was tantamount to inviting others around the camp to help themselves. To be sure a man had to stoop to walk around in the place, but it could comfortably house the five of them though, since duty watches kept a proportion of them away for much of the time, it was seldom required to do so. The structure was cosy, its walls being well-insulated with still more clay, which was just as well, as the winter had remained cold, with spells of hard frost, interspersing with wet, dismal days of freezing rain or sleet.

Saul Philipps however used the shelter least, now spending less time around the camp than any of the others. He had gotten to know a Fredericksburg girl named Lucy Paynton, whose family he had helped when they were refugeeing from the town before the battle. They had taken shelter with relatives on a small farm, out near to Tabernacle Church to the west of the camps. He now visited with the family as often as he could, getting a regular pass from any of the officers willing to sign, sharing meals with the lady's family as far as they were able to provide for him, even returning with the occasional morsel for the mess, though, with the whole army foraging repeatedly around the farms of these counties, there was less and less of such things to go around. Saul put up with the ribbing he got from his messmates and others of the company for his visiting and persisted with it any time that his off duty periods allowed.

Since his own and Ballard's return with the supplies, Daniel Ryan's mind had dwellt much upon the fate of John Fitzpatrick. His concern on hearing of Fitzpatrick's illness and evacuation demonstrated to him that a bond still existed, even though their ties of friendship had been strained near to breaking point in the fall and that had been perpetuated by the continued estrangement of their two groups. In spite of all of that, Daniel had felt his absence keenly since learning of his sickness, this being more acute through knowing that there had been chances a plenty to heal the rift among them, even though none of them had been taken up. In his inner thoughts Daniel hoped that it had not been left too late, but there had been no word of Fitzpatrick, since their return from Georgia and all too many men did not return from sickness leave. Not knowing was, he reflected, maybe the worst thing of all.

It was on the third Tuesday of the month that word began to circulate of enemy activity across the river. The Yankees, so the camp gossip said, were definitely stirring. Stories, as to what was happening, went around the camps, with a movement upstream beyond the Rappahannock bend to the river crossing at Banks Ford, being suggested as the most likely enemy intention, but at first no definite word came of the manoeuvre. Along the river valley the weather was once again changing, for a milder north easterly wind had been blowing all day and the ground was softening steadily into mud. To top it all, towards dusk, rain began to fall. It started as a drizzle, which turned into a shower, but from there it grew quickly into a wild storm of rain, driven on that freshening, north east wind. The night came and passed, including, in its course, a miserable hike for their section into the gale, for a duty watch. On arriving on the picket line, they watched and waited in their turns, but out over the river there was simply wind and rainswept darkness, with no sign of activity. When their relief came, the hike back to the camps was undertaken with no slackening in the filthy weather and men repeatedly floundering in the mud of the trail and the road, although, on the return hike, the wind, for the most part, was on their backs.

Drying themselves out in the warmth of the shelter, while the canvas roof flapped noisily above them, the talk was all of the Yankee attempted manoeuvre, for they had surely chosen to make their move on the worst possible day for marching. There was talk of the pickets from Richard Anderson's division, up along the river to the north of Fredericksburg, having seen signs of the enemy. Long, labouring columns of men, vehicles and guns, had been reported, struggling on the far distant stretches of road, which could be seen from this side of the river, while the elements lashed at them. They were certainly not surprising anybody, and, in these conditions, they were not, with a whole complement of wagons and artillery, going to march far either. As the men talked, the whole misbegotten enemy move steadily assumed the hallmarks of a farce. In weather like this, the boys told each other, there was no sensible place to be, other than settled around a fire under shelter, yet those blue-bellies were out there on those roads, that by now must be literal seas of mud, trying to make a flanking march around the southern army. They took grim amusement at their enemies' plight, poking a succession of jokes and jibes at this latest, "On to Richmond," thrust, or prod, or flounder. Having taken at last to his blankets, while still the canvas above his head strained and flapped furiously in the wind, Daniel Ryan found a moment for a tinge of compassion for the enemy soldiers out there on those roads. He thought briefly of Curtis Thackeray, and a dim image of the boy, who had undoubtedly saved his arm and quite possibly his life, swam briefly into his mind. In weather as wild as this, even the Yankees were maybe worth such a moment of consideration, if not actual compassion.

Morning came and the storm raged unabated. The rain pelted down in successive pulses and the wind gusted and whipped through the camps and the remains of the woods behind Howison Hill. Throughout that Wednesday, and on through the Thursday, the wild downpour continued, whipped by the persisting wind. Word came in and went around the camps, of Yankee columns stalled in the mud, of guns and wagons stuck to their axles in the liquid slime, of mules and horses unable to move themselves, let alone pull any vehicle or burden in the morasses of roads on the far side of the river. Stories went around of Anderson's men painting signs to taunt the enemy. Around their fires, the boys laughed over the news of boards proclaiming various messages.

"How's the Flank March Goin'?"

"Richmond Ain't That Way, It's This Way,"

"If you Yanks need help with them supply wagons, just holler across." By now, with the whole thing in its third day, it was simply a comedy, with their own army safe in its camps, while the enemy floundered around the waterlogged countryside like half-drowned rats. On the Friday more word came, that the Yankees were finally heading back to their camps, so the comedy was coming to an end. The weather began to improve and gradually the mirth on this side of the river subsided and normal duties were re-established. Over the succeeding days the men heard it confirmed that the great rainstorm had indeed halted the Yankees' advance in its tracks, making them look like downright fools for attempting such a thing, at this time of the year in the first place.

That great flounder in the mud turned out to be only

the first episode of drama that nature had in store for both armies, for, with the passing of the storm of wind and rain, the wind turned again into the north and the temperature dropped, hardening the ground once more, and overnight on the following Tuesday, it began to snow. It was not just a covering of snow this time, nor even the few inches that had fallen in early November and December, for on that Wednesday men looked out on a landscape blanketed by over a foot of whiteness. Barefooted men were again excused duty and the commissary rations, already struggling to recover from the chaos caused by the rain and mud of the previous week, slipped again, with no delivery or issue for days and thus the regiment was thrown back onto its store of supplies from Georgia. As before Christmas, to Georgia boys, from the mild and temperate south, snow, especially on this scale, was a great novelty. Over the succeeding days, men set to clearing it away from the places where it had heaped up against their shelters, but, in the course of this, snowball fights broke out between various messes and groups and much of the men's time on those days was spent on this recreation.

The following day, the Saturday, the companies were paraded for morning assembly, a protocol seldom observed in severe weather. With the roll called, Boyce related a few, brief orders of the day, whereupon, instead of being dismissed to their quarters, Lieutenant Carson stepped forward. Carson had been appointed to Company B before Christmas. Save for a wispy moustache, his face was clean-shaven and spotted and he was blessed with a high-pitched voice that rose and fell in tone as he addressed the files of men.

"For too long the fair commonwealth of Georgia has suffered insult and injury at the hands of those blackguards from South Carolina," he told them. "Our other cheek can be turned no longer. The time for retribution has come. The company is therefore ordered to parade with the necessary armament to exact redress from those gamecock scoundrels forthwith. You are dismissed to prepare, and in ten minutes, every man will assemble here, dressed for combat, with his haversack filled with no less than twenty missiles ready for the coming engagement." There was a buzz of anticipation at this and the men dismissed with a series of whoops and yells to prepare themselves. Back at their shelters, fires were banked up, ready for the return of the soaked and half-frozen veterans of the impending conflict, and this done, with haversacks emptied, the activity switched to outside where men scurried around gathering snow for snowballs, which were stored in the haversacks ready for use. As they worked, the long roll for assembly was heard on the regimental drums, and the men hurried to form ranks, stuffing final snowballs into their haversacks as they went. Company officers took their customary places, the ranks were called to attention and, with the battalion formed, the regimental officers, from the colonel down appeared, mounted and ready. Preston walked his horse in front of the ranks of men and raised his voice to address them.

"We shall now take our grievances forcibly to those gamecocks," he called, "and not a man of you will turn his back on the contest until we have taught them a singular lesson." He drew his sword and, as the men broke into cheers, he raised his voice once more.

"Major Randolph," he yelled, "form column of march and let us be about this business." The cheers redoubled and, almost as an afterthought, Preston shouted the further order.

"Uncase the colours!" The flag was drawn from its leather sleeve, to break into life, whipping and fluttering in the breeze. The cheers redoubled as the marching files were formed and the regiment headed for the road, which differed only minimally from any other parts of the landscape, joining the others of the brigade as it did so. William Wofford, Cobb's successor as brigade commander, was there with several of his staff, and he raised his hat as the successive units of his command passed. The nearest South Carolinians were the regiments of Joseph Kershaw's brigade, men of their own division, encamped some way away on the other side of the hill, so it would likely be them, Daniel Ryan reckoned, who would have to answer for all of those insults that Georgia had apparently suffered.

The long column struggled along through the thick covering of snow, following the route for the gamecocks' camp. Short of the camp itself, they were directed away from the trampled trail, to flounder through deeper snow drifts, making for the more open ground of the hillside that overlooked the South Carolinian quarters. The long lines of men emerged from the woods to deploy, with their company officers extending swords and arms, as they customarily did, to position their men in line of battle. Finally they were ready and the order to advance, guiding on the centre, rang along the line. The men tramped forward, heading in a long double rank over the crest of the hill. Daniel Ryan could smell the wood smoke from the camp they were approaching while to their ears came the sound of the drum roll, calling the Carolinians to duty. He grinned to Philipps and Ballard at his side, as they waded forward through the deep drifts of virgin snow to finally reach the brow of the hill and take in the scene that gradually opened out before them.

The camp below had clearly just gotten word of their approach, for it buzzed with activity as men tumbled out of their shelters to form hurriedly into their own ranks, gathering snowballs as they came, but, up on the crest of the hill, the brigade of Georgians did not pause. The colonel was there, still on horseback out in front of the regiment, and he waved his sword dramatically forward. The long lines of men responded with a shrill battle yell and surged ahead down the hill. A flurry of initial snowballs flew through air and, as these rapidly increased into full-blooded salvoes, the battle was joined.

It lasted the remainder of the morning, and even into the afternoon, with charge succeeded by counter charge, flanking attacks made and repelled, with various officers being taken hostage under hails of flying snowballs. Detachments were surrounded and then rescued, while, up on the hilltop, the senior officers of the brigadewatched in a group, while a corresponding group of South Carolinians, down near their camps, did likewise. Orders were issued, carried by couriers and these were duly executed by the combatants who assailed each other with all the vigour of a real fight, to the point that some of it actually led to blows, resulting in several flurries of energetic brawling, with some blood spilled on both sides. As the conflict ebbed and flowed, more groups of officers from other commands arrived to watch the entertainment.

Eventually, a truce of sorts was called and the adversaries drifted apart, gradually separating into groups. They began to head for home, though many of the Georgian officers dallied in the South Carolinian camps, the insults to their state apparently forgotten, or overlooked for the time being, enjoying the hospitality, much of it alcoholic, of their erstwhile enemies. Some enlisted men did likewise, while the remainder, bedraggled and soaked from their antics, straggled back to their own camps, accompanied by a further scattering of South Carolinians as prospective dinner guests. In spite of all of the previous insults and injustices, most of them came shambling back in raucous, sociable crowds and returning in a considerably less military manner than had prevailed when they set out.

That afternoon, Daniel Ryan's shelter accommodated its customary occupants and even managed to cram in a further four of the South Carolinians, whom they had come across, during the snowball fight. These were men they had seen and served with at the stone wall the previous month, who were therefore welcome, by the boys reckoning, to a share of a damn good dinner. The fire was further fed and the shelter grew to warm, then to drying, to cosy, and on until it was getting uncomfortably hot, while Daniel, with some help from Ballard, struggled around the crowded interior, preparing the meal. They ate well, and a couple of bottles, brought along by the guests, together with a further one provided by Philipps, were passed around and emptied. Well after dusk, the visitors took their leave, with the friendship between them and their hosts confirmed by a further agreement. They would duly combine to seek immediate redress for the many insults, injustices and injuries heaped upon the fair states of South Carolina and Georgia by those blackguards from Mississippi, that redress to take the form of a joint attack, as soon as it could be organised, on the camps of William Barksdale's brigade.

The snow fights went on for several days, with regiments involved in some of the confrontations and brigades in others. It all culminated in a huge, near division-sized engagement, which grew in size and scale until it eventually involved a degree of ferocity that extended well beyond the use of snow. After that particular episode some officers forbade further engagements, but the novelty had already begun to wear off and further battles attracted less interest. In addition the weather had turned milder once again, with the snow having begun to melt, thawing steadily away, along with the numbers taking part in any later confrontations.

The army had settled in its winter quarters to the extent that groups of officers and men had joined together, to combat the problem of boredom by engaging in a variety of amateur theatrical productions. The Mississippi brigade, being stationed in the town itself, enjoyed the best opportunities for such activities, but plays and concerts were organised and performed, in the camps as well as in town. A further group got access to a printing press and produced a, "newspaper," of army gossip and information for the soldiers. Issues of the, "Rapid Ann," were published and copies were passed from mess to mess and hand to hand around the camps until they virtually disintegrated.

In the earlier days of February the weather improved for a time, with milder days and even some brightness. News had also gone around, at the start of the month, that the Yankees had again changed their army commander. Ambrose Burnside was gone and Joseph Hooker was the new man in charge. The boys were pleased enough by this news, Yankee command changes were regarded as an admission of their failure to make any sort of headway against the Army of Northern Virginia or any real progress along the road to Richmond. If the enemy kept changing their commanders surely that confirmed a clear dissatisfaction with the performance of their generals and their army. Failure for the Yankees meant success for the Army of Northern Virginia and that was the way it was regarded in the camps west of the river.

Around those camps, the commissary still struggled to maintain regular supplies of food and word duly came that the daily ration was being reduced, in order to make what food was arriving go around more. The troops perceived a great irony in this since the ration they had gotten over the previous month was so deficient in quantity and irregular in arrival that a regular half-ration would require an increase in supply. Even those of the Ogeechee Volunteers, protected, to a degree at least, by their provisions from home, groused and complained and more ominously, the shelter where their haul of supplies had been stored was emptying now at an alarming rate, as the month proceeded, despite the efforts of the colonel and the quartermaster to make their windfall last.

The problem still came down to the insufficient amounts of supplies that were being transported in, especially since the counties around Fredericksburg had been foraged and steadily picked clean. The commissary took most on their official requisitioning trips, but further gleaning was done by many of the men who ranged around the remaining farms and homes to beg and bargain for anything that could still be got. Worse affected than the troops themselves were those of the army's draught animals that had been retained around Fredericksburg. As the winter weeks began to pass, any dead grass had been picked away by ravenously hungry horses and mules, who, as hunger turned to worse, chewed at tree bark and branches and even, so some men said, at each others' tails.

Rather than see their animals degenerate to the point where they could not carry or pull anything, or worse still, reach the stage of sickening and dying, unit after unit began to leave the lines and positions around Fredericksburg. Cavalry were first dispersed away, with a whole brigade of South Carolina troopers under General Wade Hampton heading south, to victual their men and horses and recruit new troopers, while confronting Yankees along the coastal areas of North Carolina. Others were deployed farther inland in the less ravaged counties of middle Virginia. Artillery units began to head that way, being moved steadily away from the fortified lines in order to keep their animals alive, but their departure was a different matter from that of the cavalry. Guns, together with the infantry, were the backbone of the defensive lines along the Rappahannock. All of the digging, that had turned the hills and ridges into an increasingly formidable line of defences, were useless if they could not be sufficiently manned by men and armed by cannon. Therefore when the cannon batteries departed, the defences behind the town were materially weakened.

But, as February progressed, even this was not enough. The men, already on irregular half rations, next heard that infantry would be leaving also. Two divisions of them, and two of the biggest divisions in the army, John Hood's and George Pickett's men, were heading for the south of the state, with the general, "Old Pete," Longstreet going with them. Like the brigade of cavalry under Hampton, these men were to gather supplies, while confronting the enemy, who were making increasing forays inland from their coastal enclaves, with one force of them even being reported to have advanced menacingly close to the city of Petersburg, that vital rail centre to the south of Richmond. The infantry departed at the end of the first week in February and this was followed by a general coming and going of units, moving here and there, to replace those who had gone, or to replace those who had replaced those who had gone. An additional hardship, as this took place and the month drew on, were more snowfalls, which delayed or impeded some of the movements and also threw the supply timetables into still more dislocation, interrupting the delivery of even the reduced rations to the increasingly hungry men.

Sickness was a result of this, with scarlet fever, pneumonia and even scurvy breaking out in the camps. Further maladies appeared or re-appeared which, although less serious in their eventual outcome, took their share of men from the duty rosters with foot ailments increasingly prominent among these winter disabilities. The weather conditions meant that even many of the men who had shoes were seldom able to dry their feet for any length of time and chilblains, sores and other skin conditions soon appeared. There was little that regimental surgeons were able to do for many of these. The offending feet were daubed or painted with a variety of tinctures, depending on the relative knowledge that the various doctors possessed in such matters, but, even when the condition improved, the men, once returned to duty, were put straight back into the situations that had caused the problem in the first place. Spring and dry ground was the ultimate answer, but even as they acknowledged this, the men knew that the warmer seasons would bring their own selection of illnesses and diseases.

Morale did suffer and camps became hotbeds of complaint. Complaints that officers were spared the harsh living conditions of their men were to some extent muted by a widespread knowledge of the Spartan living routines of both Lee and Jackson, but where luxury among officers was perceived the complaints were loud and bitter. The Yankee railroad boss also got a lavish helping of the camp ill-will, to the extent that if he had shown his face around the army, Daniel Ryan reckoned he would not have survived the experience. Some of the bitterness was blunted by the willingness, among many of the men, to make light of hardships and channel their resentment through sarcastic comment or wit. With others however, complaint went deeper than getting matters like hardship or boredom off one's chest, for another view had emerged, very much in a minority, but one which questioned the whole idea of further army service. For the most part this kind of talk circulated among the conscripted men, who had joined the company in the autumn, but there was a proportion of the longer serving soldiers who were now showing an inclination to listen to and even join in this kind of unpatriotic talk.

"Rich man's war, poor man's fight," emerged again as the slogan of these darker times and desertions, regarded as something of a barometer, rose steadily as the weeks passed. Disaffected men voted with their feet, by absconding from the camps, to disappear into the woods and hills. Some made their way south towards distant homes, but there were others too who crossed the lines to the Yankees to escape further service. A further proportion opted to dally like the renegades from the previous year on the army's fringes, pilfering from farms or depots and creating a general nuisance. Most men remained resolved to see the struggle through to victory, even though they were not happy with much of their lot as soldiers. The bulk of them disdained the defeatist conduct, seeing the desertions as bringing shame on proud volunteer outfits, but nobody in the camps was under any illusions now as to the sacrifices and hardships that still lay ahead in prevailing over the Yankee invaders.

A thin and pale John Fitzpatrick also returned to duty in mid-February, his arrival observed by the off-duty men around the camp. Daniel Ryan was among these and he watched his erstwhile friend arrive with a feeling of some relief. Beside him he was aware of Ballard getting to his feet and stepping forward and, without thinking further, he did the same, making for where Fitzpatrick stood, having just clambered down from a comissary wagon. They reached him and Ballard extended his hand.

"Glad you got to make the return trip John," he said as Fitzpatrick grasped his outstretched palm.

"Thanks for that Otis," he replied quietly before turning to Daniel, who shook hands with him in turn.

"I'm truly glad to see you well John," he said. Fitzpatrick

flushed as he shook his hand and he continued with the grasp as he seemed to search for a reply.

"This, both of you, it means a lot to me," he finally said.

"Friends are hard to come by," Ryan answered while, beside him, Ballard cleared his throat.

"Ain't it time to mubbee let some o' those damned bygones be bygones," he said? Fitzpatrick let go of Ryan's fingers at last and slowly placed a hand on the shoulder of each of them.

"I know it," he almost whispered. "I've thought a lot on this and you're right. It's time to put an end to this foolishness."

True to those words at Fitzpatrick's return, things did change. Ballard and Ryan spoke of it that evening and, to Daniel Ryan's surprise, not even Mick Daley raised any objection. Maybe Philipps had been right, Ryan thought, as he mused on it, in what he had said when the feud had been re-ignited, after the return from Sharpsburg, principally by the quick tempers of Daley and Edwin Jones. Maybe Mick had gotten to missing Isaac Kane's cooking after all, though, since February was now passing it had taken longer than they had anticipated at the time. The upshot of it all was that at the end of their own talk, Philipps and Daley had gone across to the fire where Jones, Kane and Fitzpatrick sat and had been invited to sit until, after a further while, hands had been shaken and backs had been slapped and they had returned as a group to sit as a re-united mess for the first time in more than five months.

"Life's too goddam short fer all that kind o' thing," Thompson had growled when he arrived back from a stint as duty sergeant to shake hands with the returning three in his turn. It would likely mean extending the shelter,

Daniel Ryan thought, at a time when materials were in increasingly short supply, though they could use some of the wood and canvas from the one that the detached three would be vacating, but friendship was surely worth a little inconvenience. As for Daley and Jones, while they were best of friends now, Daniel Ryan suspected that, with characters like them, the next wrangle was just around the corner and would be along in due course.

But, even as Fitzpatrick and a thin scattering of others returned from sickness or wounds, there was a steady trail of other men leaving, suffering from that renewed onslaught of disease that continued to circulate around the southern camps. There was smallpox in the army now as well as typhoid, together with the familiar ailments of dysentery and flux and some companies were hard hit by some or all of them. To many of the men it seemed as though the strength of the army was slowly draining away, while, across the river, by all accounts, the Yankees were hard at work reinforcing and re-equipping, preparing for the spring when the roads would be dry enough for them to move.

The trade traffic continued across the river, but, depending on where the men wishing to trade were stationed, it was done in different ways. Down below the town, where crossing the Rappahannock was impractical, little rafts or boats were sailed or reeled across from one side to the other, with twine. Trade items were tied to them, travelling back and forth in this way. But upriver, where the rapids were, stepping stone places could be used and there the Rappahannock could be crossed, with a man's feet almost, if not completely dry. Up there men made the crossing regularly to trade in person, but the downstream trade, though more difficult, still managed a fair turnover in the staples of coffee, tobacco and newspapers.

From these traded papers as well as by their contact

with the Yankee soldiers, the men of the Army of Northern Virginia began to find that Joe Hooker, the new enemy general, was making a name for himself, among his own men, that was very different to the way they had spoken of Burnside. The boys had talked about it back in camp. The new general was no McClellan, so the Yankees seemed to be saying, and, all things considered, the Yankee rank and file would take, "Little Mac," back over any other general, but the politicians in Washington would never consider it. In the absence of McClellan, Hooker, so it seemed, would maybe do. His nickname among his men, the result of some misarranged newspaper headline, was "Fighting Joe," and his pickets described him as more of a soldier's general. A man, they said, who had led from the front in previous fights and one who also knew his own mind. Since his appointment, back at the end of January, morale among the Yankees had certainly changed. When southerners had talked to pickets or gone out to trade back then, the Yankee boys had been pretty surly about their officers, and about Burnside in particular, seeming to expect little that was sensible and less that was clever from them.

But, increasingly, they seemed to speak differently of Hooker. He had taken charge of a down on its luck army, and, by applying a common sense mixture of firm discipline, good housekeeping and a new furlough system, he had begun to turn the army's morale around. They had regular rations now, the southerners heard wistfully of that, and the camps over on the other side had been cleaned and re-organised, with regular inspections. As a result of all of this, the Yankees who came over now to trade were, by all accounts, of a different mind from those who had visited in the aftermath of their great attack on Fredericksburg. These men were smarter in dress, proudly showing off the new corps and division badges that Hooker had adopted for the army. They spoke in increasingly positive terms of their commander, in spite of the fact that he had been regarded previously in the Army of the Potomac as something of a drunk and a womaniser. Well, these Yankees now said, it was a pity that all of their generals did not drink the same brand of liquor, and consort with the same females, as the new commander had.

Above all, the northern soldiers were speaking of a strengthening army, with new regiments arriving regularly. A force that had been powerful back in December, was now growing even stronger. This news spread through the southern ranks, with the boys stationed up at the rapids getting the word first in person and the rest of the army that remained downstream, hearing it by story and rumour. Marse Bob was still the best general in town, they reckoned, but the Yankees were showing no signs of giving up, and the odds against the Army of Northern Virginia seemed to be growing slowly but steadily longer as the weeks passed. When this rejuvenated force of Hooker's got off its backside in the springtime for the next, "On to Richmond," campaign, it would likely take all of Robert E. Lee's ingenuity, and every man and gun that he could muster, to stop it. The Army of Northern Virginia, having been forced to detach much of its strength to other locations, was weaker now than it had been in December, considerably weaker. If the Yankees got off to an early start with their spring campaign, then much could depend on the all-fired rush that would be needed to get those missing units back in time to oppose them.

For those who remained in the camps that winter, an additional interest was supplied by a now authorised practice that had spread around many of the brigades and regiments, of decorating their regimental flags with the names of the battles that the regiment had been involved in. There was, as a result, a groundswell of opinion forming among some of the men that the Ogeechee Volunteers should do the same with their own flag. There were however some drawbacks to the idea. The regimental flag was, as a result of the succession of battles over the summer and autumn, a sad remnant of its original self. Its edges were ragged and its fly edge was something more than ragged with tatters of that section now missing, including one of its stars. Even what remained of the flag was in poor condition with a multitude of bullet holes and several larger rents in its folds. Second Manassas last August, men recalled, had been particularly hard on the colour and in order to paint anything in the way of battle names on it, some kind of darning or other repairs would be needed.

It was on a dull and overcast morning during the third week of February, when Lieutenant Fenwick returned. He had been absent since the autumn, having been wounded at Sharpsburg and had spent a long time, as a result, in hospital in the Shenandoah Valley before being transferred on to Richmond, only to contract pneumonia there. Now he was back, with a thicker beard covering his thinner features, that fooled nobody in any way, as to the extent to which his health had been affected by both wounds and illness. It was also on that day that Boyce first spoke of a new colour at the company morning assembly. The men heard him out, gazing to their front in apparent indifference, as he gave initial details about a new flag. A colour had been sewn and embroidered by the flags committee of the Chatham County churches union, who had corresponded with the colonel on the matter, and now it was nearly ready. A delegation of the ladies, and maybe some further local personages of note, would travel to Virginia with the new flag and it would be presented at a parade of the regiment. Assembly over, the men were dismissed to their duty or off duty details, where it quickly became clear that the arrival and presentation of a new colour was not welcome news to all. While many were agreeable to, or even pleased by Boyce's announcement, there were others who were not. Less than enthusiastic talk on the subject was to be heard in various parts of the camps as well as on the duty details.

"We got our own good flag a'ready."

"What in the hell's wrong with the colour we got?"

"We don't need no new flag."

Discussions were joined around the fires and in the shelters, tailing off as men got through speaking their piece only to revive again as duty watches changed and Daniel Ryan's mess was no exception. Daniel himself took little active part in the talk, engrossed as he was in repairing a tear in his pants, but he listened as the others got started. Most were in favour, but Daley and Kane, maybe Daniel thought because they were Daley and Kane, were critical of the idea.

"Have to send boys back down there cuz they don't send us enough rations," Daley observed, "but they can send us new flags anytime. Can anybody eat a flag," he added?

"It's the women's committees back home," Thompson told him. "They want t' think that they're doin' all they can to support us up here."

"Same ones wait around the railroad depots with food and soup and sech," Ballard added.

"Likely get a whole passel o' local Georgia high and mighty folks up here to watch a show like that," Jones put in.

"Jest another excuse fer them politicians, who don't do nothin' to help with the real fightin', to come up here and feel important," Kane added.

"Ain't nothing much left of the old colour these days," John Fitzpatrick observed.

"Ain't that much left o' the regiment neither," Philipps added.

"That there's the whole point," Kane returned. "That old colour got presented when we was formed into a regiment proper. Plenty o' boys've died followin' that colour and we don't need no congressmen or nobody else back in Georgia tellin' us we can't keep it."

As the talk went on around him Daniel cast his mind back to the day in Georgia when Fletcher's Ogeechee Volunteers had transferred from state militia into service as a Confederate army unit, becoming the Ogeechee Volunteer Rifles in the process. The huge majority of the officers and men had cast their lot with the new regiment when they had been paraded that day at the Charleston and Savannah depot, but others, including the original colonel, had refused to go. It had caused discord and some ill-feeling among many of the men, and among some of the officers too. It had been still not quite a year ago, but a great deal had happened since they had taken that step and gotten themselves onto a train for Virginia as a result. Fitzpatrick was maybe right, he thought. The colour carried by a regiment was an emblem and a focal point. Off the battlefield it represented what the regiment was. In parades and reviews it was positioned in a place of honour, guarded by its escort of chosen men. On the battlefield it was a rallying point, showing its men, and others of whatever side, where the regiment stood. Daniel recalled seeing it at places like Malvern Hill and Second Manassas, as well as at that bridge at Sharpsburg, back in September. At the former it had been carried as far as the regiment had been able to go towards that awful enemy artillery line, while at Manassas it had told where the regiment had made its stand in its unequal struggle with the Yankee reserves across that dirt road. It had been borne on the field at Sharpsburg, seeing both retreat and advance that day.

At all of the places where the regiment had fought, men had died beneath its folds and the main reasons for its tattered state was the number of minie balls and shell splinters which had torn and shredded it. It would not take too many more engagements like those of the past year for there to be virtually nothing left of the old flag or of the pole either, so often had it too been splintered and repaired. A regiment needed a flag and by simple attrition, their own regiment might soon have nothing much left of theirs. Replacing it with a new colour therefore made sense, but there was still a bond of attachment that men felt for the old one. Did that flag, those torn remains, represent what the regiment was? Daniel Ryan turned the idea over in his mind. Maybe it did, but it was not the substance of the regiment, for that was surely the men who stood in their ranks around it. They were the Ogeechee Volunteer Rifles and flags, while inspiring in their way, were emblems. The emblem was the outward public symbol, but the soldiers, by their steadfastness, their comradeship and their resolve were the fabric and the real strength of the regiment.

Chapter 11 The Song Bird

The early flowers were in full bloom and the latest snows had melted, leaving the roads and the tracks to the camps as sloughs of liquid mud, but they were now bordered, in places by contrasting clumps of white and purple and orange, where nature was reclaiming its domain, with fresh growth. Along the lines the duties went inexorably on, while across the river the enemy legions continued with their reorganising and regrouping. The, "Rapid Ann," produced another issue of camp news and tittle-tattle and the new edition included word of another prospective visitor to the army on the Rappahannock line. Miss Sophie La Salle, a singer of some repute, would visit Fredericksburg and perform recitals for the soldiers in the Citizens' Hall in town. Miss La Salle was a New Orleans lady, and, prior to the war, she had starred in the theatres of the Crescent City, as well as in Nashville, Richmond and other city venues across the south. Not content with that, the paper went on, she had also sung in concert halls in New York, Philadelphia and Baltimore, and had even toured as far away as Europe.

Most men were intrigued if not inspired by the news. In the routines of duty and camp life they saw little enough of women of any sort, other than local women, many of whom were the haggard and worn victims of the hardships of the war. Other than that there were only the various sets of coarse whores, who had set up in or around the ruined town, attracted by the prospect of the trade offered by the presence of the army. As for entertainment value the home made shows and performances put together by groups of soldiers had been fine enough, but a real, live, theatre-actress, lady, even if she croaked like a frog, would, so Isaac Kane said, be a thing to behold.

Daniel Ryan had thought from the start that, even though there weren't that many habitual theatre attenders in Company B these days, most men would be keen to attend the lady's recitals, if for no other reason, than to simply relieve the boredom of camp. It would break the monotony of duty on the bleak river line and give men something to anticipate and maybe even enjoy, enough for it to be a talking point long after the lady had packed her portmanteaus and headed back to Richmond, or Europe or wherever else she was bound for next. Such a thing was well worth the hike into town, he thought, and, from the comment around the camps, it was clear that many of the other men thought similarly and that Miss La Salle would therefore have no trouble attracting her audiences.

Men would have to attend different of her recitals of course, corresponding with the duty watches they had been assigned, but through the days preceding the actress's visit, those men, whose eye for a profit exceeded their taste for musical recitals, did a fair business by exchanging duties with some others, more musically inclined than they, so that they could attend the performance of their choice. A host of negotiations took place in the course of which prices, for the obligement offered, were eventually agreed. Having settled these matters, in one way or another, the sense of anticipation grew among the men awaiting the day and the time, when such an out of the ordinary event would break the tedium and hardship of army service at the back end of winter.

The date of the celebrity's arrival finally came and throughout that day, rumours swept around the camps. There were stories of her bewitching looks of course, but also more surprisingly, of her size, for, according to the latest news, she was tiny, rather than simply small. All day the tales went around, as details of men came and went from town, and it was a very curious procession, from the various units of the brigade, who hiked down the muddy road from Howison Hill into town to attend Miss La Salle's first evening performance.

Citizens Hall, where the recital was being staged, was a substantial, two-storied, brick building on Princess Anne Street, between Hanover and Charlotte Streets, which boasted a pediment above its entrance. The downstairs floor consisted of a succession of rooms, where smaller scale events or meetings could be held, with the upper storey accommodating a larger theatre. The hall, in addition to being the best of the gathering places in town, was also the nearest to intact. This however was relative to the general state of buildings in the scarred town and men whose duties or off-duty time had taken them into Fredericksburg over the winter already knew that although the place may have been the least damaged of the town's larger buildings, this did not mean that it was in anything like one piece. Damage to its roof had been hastily repaired with canvas sections held in place by nailed wooden batons, while crude patches covered similar rents in its walls. The assembling audience made little of all of this however, for, having ascended the stairs to the main hall, their attention was quickly fixed on the stage at the far end of the place, rather than on the condition of the surroundings, as they spent the waiting time shuffling their way to the best available vantage points remaining in the already crowded space. The theatre was illuminated by a succession of flickering lanterns, with a concentration of larger lamps around the stage itself. As for heating, save for the accumulating warmth from the lanterns and lamps, the body heat of the audience, crammed in their limited space, had to suffice, and, before long, this primitive option had succeeded in raising the temperature to quite tolerable levels. The presence of those packed rows of waiting men was not without its drawbacks however and, as Philipps said, it was surely to be hoped that the little lady from New Orleans would not be too offended by the smells that came along with all of that body heat.

The crowded assembly of soldiers was initially entertained by the band of one of their own Mississippi regiments. This was fine enough as far as it went, but not at all why the men had turned up here in such numbers. As the leading lady remained conspicuous by her absence and the band continued its selection of patriotic airs, a murmur of impatience and unrest began to permeate the audience with increasing talk and a degree of whistling and loud comment.

"Let's have this gal out here!"

"We kin hear bands any ol' time!"

"Whar's the main attraction gotten to?"

"Git on with the real show!"

Thus, when the Mississippians eventually concluded their playing and Miss La Salle was finally announced, by a tall, imposing and grandly moustachioed man in a black suit, black cravat and tall hat, the hall echoed and reverberated with cheers and whistles of anticipation. The little lady flounced on, followed by four dark-suited, instrument-toting musicians. She was dressed in a hooped ball gown of gleaming red silk that amply displayed her bare shoulders and pale bosom, while a feathered adornment of matching red was perched on her head. When Daniel Ryan finally got a good look at her, through the forest of waving and applauding hands, the word that seemed to sum her up was "petite," a sometime expression of poor Tom Gibben, for she was indeed small, dwarfed by the musicians at her back, who had the appearance of giants in her presence. She wore long gloves, stretching up past her elbows and she carried what looked like a lemon in her left hand, likely indicating, Daniel concluded, that she was less reconciled to those soldier smells than Philipps had maybe hoped.

Miss La Salle stopped in the middle of the stage and turned to curtsy to the audience, prompting the cheers, applause and whistles, which had not really died down much anyway, to redouble in their volume and intensity. Eventually, with the lady poised to commence her recital, the noise faded, until, at a flamboyant signal, from the tall-hatted conductor, the performance began. Following a short introduction from her ensemble, she launched into her initial song and almost immediately some kind of performing charm seemed to pervade the congested hall. Initially, the noise of talk and comment among the crowded soldiers had not entirely died away, with fragments of it continuing as she began to sing, but, from the moment those first notes rose from her throat, all talk rapidly died, with such a stillness establishing itself that, between stanzas, you might have heard a pin drop in the place, or as Ballard, with his gift for rustic humour, was apt to say, a quiet fart at a preacher's funeral. The lady's voice was something very special to hear, and, with her musical quartet in close support, she tiptoed through the verses and choruses of that first song, reaching high and ever higher for her top notes, with what seemed like effortless grace. The audience of dirty, ragged soldiers watched and listened, seemingly spellbound by the idea that such divine sounds could come from such a tiny, delicate-looking creature. Watching her intently, and listening to the pure silver of her voice, Daniel Ryan was put in mind of a tiny songbird, whose sounds grossly exceeded its size, but not its beauty. That impression seemed to be the same all around the hall, for, when she finished the song, there was a silence of several seconds before the place erupted, with cheers and applause, while notably, the more raucous whistling of before had almost completely died away. It was clear, from that stunning opening, that the evening's entertainment would be conducted, pretty well entirely, on the little lady's terms, as, in a voice that revealed a creole accent, she introduced her second piece. The name meant nothing to Daniel Ryan, but, as before, once she began to sing, it would not have mattered if it was the Yankee anthem, so clear and melodic was her voice. Various men, prior to the lady's arrival, had spoken of her prospective recital as though it was some kind of a music hall turn, but now, as she unfolded her undoubted gifts for her increasingly spellbound audience, it was clear that nothing could have been further from the truth. There was not a trace of bawdiness, nor of vulgar suggestion in what she performed, rather what now took place was an exhibition of pure virtuosity and men, who had not the slightest knowledge of opera or classical music, were enraptured, for, even though lacking in such expertise, they could recognise class and excellence when they encountered it.

Having bewitched her audience for upwards of half an hour there was an interval and Miss La Salle, to further tumultuous applause, swished off stage, followed by her musicians, to recover herself, away from the now oppressive heat and the even more oppressive smells of the hall. After a pause, the band of Mississippians re-assembled and launched into some further items from their repertoire, which were well enough received by the audience, though not in anything like the same absolute silence that had marked Miss La Salle's time on the stage. Those odours in the crowded and now stuffy hall were reaching the stage of being near to overpowering, but nobody left the place, bar those whose toileting situations compelled them to.

The band had not been playing for long however, before the shouts from the audience clearly indicated that it was time to have the little lady back again. The shouting grew, until much of the hall seemed to be chanting her name. As the volume increased still further, there was a flash of the red silk headdress to one side and the whole place erupted again into thunderous applause and cheering. The band trooped off stage and back on she came, closely followed by her musicians, with her lemon held near to her nose, but smiling sweetly and waving to the audience with her still-gloved, free hand.

The second part of the performance, if anything, exceeded the first. She had now only to hold up a hand to establish the utter silence she desired, in order to commence her next piece. Beside Daniel Ryan, Otis Ballard, observing it all, shook his head.

"Eatin' out o' her cute little hand," he muttered and it was true. This crowd of rough, brutalised men were behaving for Miss Sophie La Salle in a way that they might, just about do for General Robert E. Lee, but scarcely for anybody else, from Stonewall Jackson on down. They heard her with the best of good manners, applauded her with wild enthusiasm at the conclusion of each item, but, when she indicated to them, even in the most genteel manner, that she desired further silence, then, within seconds, silence was what she got. Daniel Ryan had never seen anything quite like it, and he mused over it, even as Miss La Salle's voice rose in its now familiar quality of sound for her latest song, and his heart tightened in his chest again as he responded to this glorious harmony of voice and music. Her singing soared and glided through the verses of the piece until Daniel began to feel moisture gathering in his eyes, for here was a quality of music, and of grace, that was steadily captivating his spirit and taking it away from this hall, in Princess Anne Street, with its makeshift repairs, in this ruined town, away from the sordid dirt and death of this damned war, leading away instead to a spiritual place that was graceful and civilised and beautiful.

The evening ran its course and the recital concluded with a rendering of a more popular song. "Maryland my Maryland," had been fashionable throughout the first year of the war, indeed regimental bands had played it as the army had crossed the Potomac into Maryland, during those hot September days of the previous year. But the frustrations, hardships and disappointments of that campaign had led to the song losing its popularity with the soldiers and, since then, it had been regularly booed and hissed any time that it was heard. Not so tonight, the little shining creature on the stage led these men, long since disillusioned with anything to do with Maryland, through the successive verses of the song with her voice rising as clearly as a tinkling bell above the deep and rousing accompaniment rendered by the audience. When it ended, the acknowledgement was loud and prolonged, compelling the little song bird to indulge her audience with a further encore. Only when this was finally concluded did the audience begin to file out of the hall. It had been different, but above all it had been inspiring, taking these men from their hard and deprived existences for a brief interlude of something uplifting and deeply fulfilling. As the men from Wofford's brigade made their lengthy hike back onto the muddy Telegraph Road on the way back to their camps, much of the talk among them seemed to suggest that they had, in the course of that early spring evening, been granted a glimpse, however fleeting, of a cleaner, better world.

Springtime was slowly arriving in Virginia. The daylight hours were now almost as long as the hours of darkness and those days were growing milder, though the nights were still cold, with sizeable fires needed to keep the chills from men whose remaining blankets had grown threadbare and whose clothing, even though endlessly patched, was once again thin and ragged. The forests around the camps had steadily shrunk as first dead branches, then low branches, then any branches and finally whatever remained of the trunks and even the stumps of trees had been consumed by the fires of the army, or used up in the fortifications which now looked down on Fredericksburg. The earthworks dug in the winter had made it possible to defend the line with the reduced numbers of First Corps divisions now available, but the threat no longer came just from the section of the river opposite the remains of the old town. As the weather improved, mobility returned as a military option and the menace of the Yankee army all along the river banks steadily grew. Whether they chose to cross here, or upstream or downstream, the time was coming when they would cross somewhere. The campaigning season was nearly upon them all again and it would begin, everyone knew, as soon as the roads were dry and hardened enough for the armies to move their wagons and guns.

There had, since the later weeks of February, been a succession of redeployments on the Confederate side of the river, with units being shifted into the places of those who had departed, while others were shifted into positions where they could move to block whatever manoeuvres, up or down the river that the enemy chose to make. William Wofford's brigade was among those so moved, now being stationed for duty inland from the town and the winter camps, south of the Plank Road near a little country church, a posting previously occupied by one of George Pickett's now departed brigades. Here the men were in a position where they were still close enough to support a defence of the Fredericksburg line, but could also reinforce the units from Richard Anderson's division, who guarded the Rappahannock fords upstream from Fredericksburg.

The remaining divisions were spread thinner now, though the river lines remained manned and just about adequately so, but the whole army was pointedly aware of how much it had been weakened by the winter detachments as well as by the wastage of disease and absences of various types. In contrast, across the river, by the accounts of the coffee traders, the pickets and the Yankee newspapers that found their way into the camps, the enemy army was continuing to grow in strength. Their new general had, by all accounts, been using the winter well, reorganising his forces and restoring the morale of his men after the debacles of December and January and his pronouncements, widely reported in those northern papers, were belligerent and bellicose. That restored Yankee army was in the final stages of its preparations and would soon be opening its camapign.

For the most part, the southern troops were content to listen to the stories and read the papers, indeed they had little choice. It was also true that the Army of Northern Virginia, spread out over a wide area now in order to supply itself and, with its weaker animals and poorer transportation, would be less able to manoeuvre than its enemy. The first move therefore would almost certainly be left to the Yankees and as for the strategy and tactics that would lead to battle being joined, they would leave those things to Marse Robert.

"They've come on down here plenty o' times now," Silas Norton commented, "but every time they do they always finish up headin' back north with their tails 'atween their goddam legs."

If men thought that a silence of almost a month, following the captain's announcement about a new colour, meant that the matter had been forgotten about, or overtaken by more urgent matters, then they were mistaken. Late in March, Boyce spoke of it again, once more at morning assembly. The new colour that had been made down in Georgia for the regiment was now ready. A date had been set at the end of the month for its presentation and the previously mentioned party would be travelling north from Savannah for that purpose. Talk in the camps was revived by this announcement, with some still reluctant to embrace the idea, but the arrangements went ahead, regardless of that, for the arrival and handover of the new flag. The men had spent the days prior to the event on make and mend duties, sprucing up their clothing and themselves for the occasion. Holes in tunics and pants were patched, or re-patched, torn seams were stitched and even socks were darned. Uniforms were cleaned as far as possible, whether by washing, not an easy undertaking in the variable weather, or by rubbing or beating. The men themselves, in most cases, also washed. Many had attempted to do so, with some kind of reasonable regularity throughout the winter, though others were less enthused by the attractions of cleanliness. Beards were shaved by some and trimmed by others, while hair was cropped by most. Equipment belts were polished or oiled, as far as oil could be procured, and muskets, always maintained as a routine duty, were given an additional clean and greasing.

Daniel Ryan, acknowledging that spring had chronologically, if not climatically, arrived, was one of those who went for full scale removal of his winter beard and trimmed his hair again, short enough to reveal that the trials of winter had at least left his ears intact. Being more conscientious than some in the matter of repairing clothing, he did not have the same volume of mending work as certain of the mess, nor some others in the company as a whole. On the day before the delegation from Georgia was due the regiment paraded for the colonel's inspection, presenting a much more military sight than it would have done just a matter of days before. Preston paced along the ranks nodding at times and smiling appreciatively at various of his laundered and repaired soldiers. If, Daniel Ryan reflected as the colonel strode past, this whole subject of the new colour had been used as a means of rejuvenating the regiment, then Preston had perhaps shown the same sort of shrewd judgement as he had regarding the winter rations expedition. The Ogeechee Volunteer Rifles were once again a soldierly military formation, even after the hardships and privations of the season just ended.

The following day the men again paraded, this time in the presence of the visitors from Savannah. A still chilly wind had blown off the river that week and this persisted when the appointed day arrived. There were three women and two older men in the visiting party and, wrapped up in coats, hats, scarves and gloves, they were settled on chairs on an unhitched wagon, decorated with cloth hangings of red white and blue. A band had been procured, not the regimental assembly, as this had been disbanded the previous autumn due to the death or invaliding out of too many of its members. Those that remained were present but rather as part of a gathering of musicians borrowed from other regiments. The colonel sat his horse in front of his staff, next to the wagon, while Henry Randolph reposed on the vehicle with the adjutant, the civilian visitors, the surgeon Thomas Sterling and Jedediah Poulson the Regimental Chaplain. The musicians indulged themselves by playing the customary sequence of patriotic airs, while the companies of the regiment came up successively, to wheel into line and dress their ranks before being rested at ease, while others arrived and did likewise. Finally all were present and, with the band falling silent the entire regiment was called to attention.

This, Preston told them was a happy and prestigious day. The service of the regiment, its bravery and sacrifice, always in the minds of its women folk back at home, were being publicly acknowledged by the presentation of the new colour. This flag had been sewn by the women of the Chatham County Churches Committee and would be carried with pride by the regiment. Daniel Ryan's mind was hard at work, while all of this went on, recalling the very first flag, presented near Savannah, with that occasion turned into a parade of the family of the original colonel, Seagram Fletcher. This event, he reflected, at least fell short of that previous level of hypocricy.

The colonel concluded his words and the colour bearer, Oren Johnson, still holding the old flag aloft, stepped forward from his place in front of the centre companies with a guard on either side. He moved to the side of the decorated wagon, where Poulson had risen to his feet. The chaplain moved to the wagon side and bent to receive the tattered flag. He stood upright, holding it reverently in his hands as he began to speak.

"This flag is surrendered to the care of the state of Georgia," he called. "Under its folds, brave Georgians have fought, suffered and died and we recall these last especially, whose eternal souls now rest in the care of almighty god."

He stepped back towards his seat, passing the flag to one of the older men who had accompanied the ladies from Savannah, who now stood to receive it. Poulson returned to his chair as the lady in the middle of the group now stood and, taking the rolled colour from her companion, moved to the edge of the wagon. She cleared her throat nervously as she prepared to speak.

"The women of the south know well of the great dangers faced and great sacrifices made by our brave soldiers," she called, with her voice quavering occasionally as her words rose and fell on the wind. "This flag, that we offer to your regiment here today, is a symbol of the admiration, respect and love that we feel for you every day. We mourn the dreadful cost in blood and life that has been sacrificed here to protect our families and homes. Your bravery keeps the enemy at bay. Your fortitude alone keeps us safe in our homes." She held the flag up by its pole, still rolled and cased in a red cloth sleeve before bending down and offering the pole to the grim, bearded figure of Johnson. He grasped it with both of his hands and bowed to the woman who stepped back, smiling at him nervously as she went.

Something about her manner and her words had resonated with Daniel Ryan. It had been simpler and had seemed sincere to him, a very different occasion from the Fletcher circus of eighteen months ago. Out in front, Johnson had turned to face the ranks of soldiers. The command rang out for the general salute and the men presented arms as he eased the sleeve away from the colour and twisted the pole to let it spread in the wind. It opened and fluttered there, even snapping as the wind gusted through the ranks of men and through its brightly coloured folds. Every eye was on it, presenting the same pattern as their previous colour but with a few subtle differences. The stripes of the white-edged blue saltire on the red field were of darker blue and slightly broader than on the original flag, with the stars, three of which decorated each diagonal, and the centre star, slightly larger also. The whole colour was fringed in yellow and it continued to whip and flap in the wind, while the men looked on with their muskets presented in front of them. Then, from behind them came a further sound, a movement, a rustle of harness, a murmur of comment? On the command the muskets were ordered, while eyes strained to see, without the heads of men on parade turning too much, as along from the approach path rode Robert E. Lee mounted on "Traveller," the grey horse almost as familiar as its rider, with LaFayette McLaws, the divisional commander, at his side, each of them being followed by several of their respective staffs.

The generals walked their horses around to the front of the parade and Lee reined in there, removing his hat as he bowed politely to the ladies on the decorated wagon, before replacing the hat and turning to acknowledge the salutes of Preston and the other regimental officers. There was something about the general today, Daniel Ryan thought. He was dressed in the usual grey overcoat that he wore over his uniform, but there was something about his movements and his manner, as though he nursed some sort of stiffness or discomfort. His face too looked red and flushed, much more florid than the ruddy glow of health that his soldiers associated with him. The saluting done he turned to the new colour, removing his hat again and sweeping it in a long movement down to his side before bowing once more, lower and longer than before. He straightened up and replaced the hat once again, as he turned to the motionless ranks of soldiers.

"It is good that we have such women at home, who labour so tirelessly on behalf of their brave men in the army," he called, even as Daniel Ryan was noting a hoarse tone in his voice.

"Honour your new colour men," he went on. "Honour it as proud Georgians because of who it came from, and honour it also as soldiers by your continuing steadfastness, loyalty and courage as you serve beneath it." That should settle the matter of the new flag, Daniel Ryan thought, for once, "Marse Bob," pronounced on just about anything in this army, there were few who would dispute what he had said. His thoughts were disturbed again by the general's voice, as he turned to the wagon once more.

"Ladies," Lee called, this time in a more gentle, but still hoarse, tone. "We are in your debt and, on behalf of all of the men of the regiment, and of the army, I thank you." He bowed once more, before wheeling Traveller and moving slowly away to join McLaws where he waited. The divisional commander guided his own horse to the general's side and the two of them rode away with their staffs, having left a respectful distance, wheeling their horses into place behind them.

The colonel, maybe aware that not all in his ranks had wanted the new colour in the first place, opted to allow his men a say in whether the new flag would be decorated with the regimental battle titles. When this was generally approved, he even put the matter of where on the flag to place the names and whether or not to print them chronologically, to a show of hands vote. Paint was then obtained by various means, and men, with those kind of skills in painting and printing, were selected to undertake the duty. For a day or two the camps were engrossed in the task, with many of the off duty soldiers gathering to watch, or to put in a word as to how the regiment's battle titles should be laid out on the flag. The majority turned out to be in favour of arranging the names in the flag's red triangular fields and in a design that looked best, according to the size of the words and the space available rather than any sort of chronological order. With those things decided, the men gathered around in their groups to watch as, with the flag stretched flat across a board, the preliminary arrangement was sketched out upon the cloth in chalk.

The paint that had been acquired was light blue in colour and Tom Gray of Company C, having been selected for the job of painting the initial names, then set to work. Around him his comrades watched intently, with one or two offering occasional words of advice or encouragement, while Tom painstakingly manipulated the fine brushes that had been obtained for the job. Boyce, who, on the return of Lieutenant Fenwick, had been confirmed as captain of Company B, came by along with a couple of his officer colleagues to watch for a while, before heading off to attend to other things. Daniel Ryan watched also, in company with Philipps, Kane and Ballard as the letters gradually grew into names, but not just names, for these words were memories.

To be sure there was a feeling of military pride in having the exploits of the regiment displayed in this way, but these words prompted recollections in the minds of many of the onlookers. Around the groups, Daniel could hear snatches of conversation, triggered by what was being done, recalling incidents and features of the battles of the previous year. He too found his mind turning to memories of those days, when the madness of killing and struggling to survive had possessed them all. There was Garnett's Farm, the first name that Gray had printed, its letters glistening in the wet, blue paint, where Jim Weald had been killed and Sharpsburg where Tom Gibben, also of their Eden Station group, had died. The letters of Malvern Hill had not yet been painted, being so far laid out only in the white chalk, but Daniel's eyes moved along them as he pictured that evening ordeal, as the sun had set on that hot and humid summer day. Of all of their engagements, this one had cost the Ogeechee Volunteer Rifles the highest number of dead and wounded.

Yes, there was an element of pride but also a sanguine, wrenching ache at the memory of friends and comrades who were no longer here, having fallen at those places. Further battles were inevitably coming. Daniel Ryan pondered on this subject also, while Gray still worked on the flag. More men would pay the price when these battles came, men who maybe stood now watching Gray deftly fashioning the letters with his brushes. Likely in time the further names, of such struggles, as yet unfought, would in their turn be painted on this flag, with those names too tugging at the memory of those who survived, as the human cost, of still more husbands, sons and brothers sacrificed in the merciless furnace of this war, mounted ever higher.

Step by step through the winter, since his appointment late in January, Fighting Joe Hooker over there had been building up the Yankee army, in both numbers and efficiency, in preparation for the springtime campaigning season. The Yankee papers had published numerous details of this, talking about the improvement in this and the enlargement of that, from the re-organisation of supply services, to the concentration of his cavalry into a large, separate corps. The enemy numbers had gone on rising till it was now said that the new general commanded an army of over one hundred and thirty thousand, confident and well-equipped men.

"The finest army the sun ever shone on," he was supposed to have said at one of the reviews reported in the northern press. But, as April arrived, a reprieve, of sorts, came for the Confederate army awaiting the enemy onslaught. The snows of the winter returned, reducing the roads to impassable expanses of white and then of slush with the weather once more interrupting the supply of rations to the hungry camps and confining the shoeless to their shelters.

The wintry conditions lasted for most of the first week of the month before the thaw revealed the green sprigs of new growth through the carpet of snow and slush turning the roads gradually to pools of mud and muck. Improvement in those roads proceeded only slowly and with that the preparations for the coming campaign resumed. From across the river, further signs came that the Yankee army had taken to holding a succession of parades and reviews, likely before getting down to the more serious business of manoeuvring and fighting. Then the trading and fraternising among the pickets along the river was brought to a sudden halt by the Yankees, with the flow of information ceasing just as suddenly as the contraband goods. Across on their own side, the southerners speculated on all of this. It must mean that something big was about to happen they told each other and that could only be that the much anticipated enemy advance was about to begin.

Just when, with sorely diminished numbers remaining with the army, the skills of Robert E. Lee seemed more indispensable than ever, word went around the camps that he was ill. He had chest pains and pains in his arms and the doctors had ordered him to his bed. Some in Company B and throughout the regiment, nodded in a, "told you so," way, recalling how, at the parade for the new colour, the general had clearly been not himself, but this now sounded like more than any minor ailment. Throughout the first weeks of April, with Lee confined to his cot and attended by a succession of doctors, the army, save for Stonewall Jackson, was leaderless, for, although the general had at no point relinquished command, he was clearly unfit for any sort of active duty. Gradually, as the month advanced, the news improved. He was recovering, slowly to be sure, but recovering. It was only to be hoped that he would have recovered enough when the testing time came, for what was coming now from across the river looked like being the sternest test of all and as those roads finally began to dry, that test would not be delayed much longer.

But with no sign of any of the detached units returning, Lee's army, like its general, remained disturbingly weak and not just from the absence of Longstreet's and Ransom's men and the detached cavalry and artillery. Further absences had resulted from a host of, "plough furloughs." This was the name for the practice of numbers of the army's farmers taking time off from their regiments in response to pathetic letters from home, to help with the work on their farms. Being springtime, the ploughing and sowing of the new season's crops was under way, or if not it ought to be. So the pleading letters became ever more earnest and the absences steadily increased as men responded to their families' needs.

There was nothing officially sanctioned about this, but the army, by and large, said little about it. Regimental officers knew of the problems faced by their men and their families and most of them sympathised with their predicament. These boys would largely return to their places once a fight became imminent and it was also something of an advantage to have fewer mouths to feed in camp, in view of the shortages in army supply. There was also the matter of getting more crops raised back home, a proportion of which would logically come the army's way through comissary requisitioning. So, for all of these reasons, field officers often said nothing about their missing men, even though the army was substantially weakened by the practice, but now, as April advanced, word was being sent out by those same colonels and captains, notifying the absent multitude that it was about time to be getting back to their regiments.

The farmed out artillery, and some at least of the cavalry, could be recalled in a matter of days once the Yankees began their campaign, but they could not be summoned sooner as there simply were not the supplies and provisions to sustain them here on the Rappahannock. The men who had remained here had been on near starvation rations for many weeks now and the supplement of food brought from Georgia, for the Ogeechee Volunteers, at the turn of the year was long since gone. What it now amounted to was that when Joe Hooker's, "finest army on the planet," made its move across the river this time there would be, at the very most, sixty thousand hungry and ill-clad Confederate soldiers to oppose them. Yet, "Marse Robert," now recovered from his illness, though still looking a shade pale and wane, was back to riding his lines with his staff, looking the picture of calm and serenity. Was there something he knew, the men asked each other, that they did not know? Well there was likely plenty he knew that they did not know, others told them, but only a fool, or someone who had a couple of aces up his sleeve somewhere, would simply sit here on the river line, while an army more than double the size of his own gathered itself to assail him.

But with April stretching on, Wofford's men, in common with those of many other units, were now spending as much of their off-duty time as possible down on the banks of the Rappahannock, not in the town, but on the very waterside itself. Here at last, as the spring advanced, the seasonal run of shad had begun and every mess who could do so, was sending men to the river with lines and hooks and looking forward to fried fish for the evening meal. The bank of the river was lined with amateur fishermen over those brightening weeks and the men ate shad, negotiating the many bones in preparing and cooking the fish, till they tired of it.

The final week of April had come and there was news at last, for, after a period of several days of miserable rain, the weather had settled, the roads were again drying in the spring sunshine and the great host of the enemy was apparently in motion. The initial stories spoke of cavalry moving upriver towards the inland fords, by the more distant roads to the north and west, as though to threaten the Confederate left flank. Within days came more word, this time of large formations of infantry, with their long trains of supply wagons and guns, also on the march. These too had been tracked by Stuart's cavalry, heading upstream also, following the route to the west, away beyond the bend in the Rappahannock, towards those crossings where there was access to the rear of the Confederate positions. It seemed more and more like the same sort of movement that Burnside had tried in January, only now there were no winter storms to halt and frustrate the enemy and bring them struggling back to their camps.

The next camp stories were no surprise. Lee had sent word for all of those detached units to rejoin the army on the river line. With the Yankees apparently already on the march, some of the cavalry and Longstreet's two infantry divisions, said to be still down where the south east of the state bordered with North Carolina, might not be able to return in time, even if they started today, especially when the state of the southern railroads was considered, but most of the others should be back in line in a matter of a day or two. Still outnumbered by more than two to one, Lee would now have to strive to assemble his available strength before the Yankees got across the river and the armies came to grips.

On the same day that word of their own concentration came around further stories began to circulate. It was now being said that, in addition to those powerful enemy columns who had marched away westwards in the direction of the upriver fords, still more strong formations of Yankees were assembling, as they had in December, on the far bank of the river, just below Fredericksburg, massing there as though they had a renewed notion to cross over once more. One way or another, it looked as though the fight that men had long since said was coming was maybe just about here. The camps seethed with talk, for, if all of the gossip and the Yankee newspapers were to be believed, a more unequal fight, than the one that was now shaping up, could scarcely have been undertaken by the Army of Northern Virginia.

Chapter 12 The Spotsylvania Wilderness

As the dawn broke on the final Wednesday of the month there came sounds of musketry down towards the river, these being joined by cannon fire as the daylight strengthened, while, in the town itself, church bells sounded a further alarm, with stories immediately circulating that the enemy were crossing again. As far as the off duty men of Company B were concerned, that was fair enough for the Yankees had spent their strength in December in those vain assaults on the higher ground of this side, with Confederate losses light by comparison. But even as the men of Wofford's brigade readied themselves to march in the grey, foggy light, more rumours were circulating. That original Yankee force, the one that rumours said had gone upriver from Fredericksburg had arrived at those upstream Rappahannock fords. They had driven the forward Confederate guard details away from them and now presented an increasingly ominous threat to the southern army's rear. After all of their reinforcing and reorganising the Yankees now had men and guns enough to send a force larger than the whole Confederate army to attack the positions around Fredericksburg while an equally large force crossed those river fords upstream and got in behind the southern forces. With the camps again alive with rumours, Boyce addressed the company after morning roll call.

"It's back to town for us boys," he told them. "The Yankees are crossing over and the general wants us there to give them the same welcome that we did last time." A murmur ran along the ranks at this news, but nothing was said until the men were dismissed to finish their preparations, before being assembled into files to make for the road that led north to the Turnpike. The ranks buzzed with talk. Taken together, the two reported enemy movements were indeed beginning to resemble a great pincer, stretching up and down the river, with its powerful jaws to the northwest and to the east, now open and readying themselves to close, encircling and trapping the weakened Army of Northern Virginia in their grasp as they did so. Still the boys told each other, Marse Bob likely knew best and there would be a damned almighty brawl before he let the army get trapped and crushed by these enemy manoeuvres. Others took a more detached view. Spring was here, the sun was warm after the rain and winds of the previous weeks and, with the likelihood of a fight, there was maybe the chance of some further plunder from the Yankees. Thus, among at least some of the troops, there was a sense of anticipation about the latest developments, in spite of the odds.

The mist still hung in the river valley as the column from the camps headed back towards Fredericksburg to take up their new positions. The Telegraph road seemed somehow unfamiliar to men who, in more recent weeks, had headed inland for their duties. Contrary to their expectations however they did not re-occupy their old positions, being directed instead on to the north from Marye's Hill, crossing William Street to deploy along the heights of Cemetery Hill overlooking the northern part of the town. A skirmish line composed of half of the detail was left in place, but with Barksdale's men still on station along the river in the town, only a light picket was spread along the edge of the canal spillway, near where the big, old Gordon House stood in its grounds. That night the men did not return to the camp, bivouacking instead just to the west of the hills they had occupied, wet by a chilly, misty drizzle that had settled over the river valley.

Thursday came with the drizzling, overnight rain persisting as those of the off watch men in the Confederate camps, who had slept but fitfully, stirred with the daylight. Daniel Ryan was one of these but this was a familiar thing, for him, and for numbers of the others in the company, when there was a prospect of an imminent fight. Real sleep was difficult when afflicted by those pre-battle tensions, that knot in the stomach, the tightening of the chest and throat, that testiness with comrades, familiar trials by now, to be recognised and borne as part of the prelude to battle. There had been no rations issue since Tuesday and those who had scraps of anything in the way of food quickly devoured them. Early morning also saw a spell of picket duty down towards the spillway and that time was spent, as it had been the previous day, in comparative idleness, since, with Mississippians still spread along in front, there was little prospect of any enemy incursion, at least not without everyone having plenty of warning of it. Later in the morning the balance of the regiment arrived from the camps and those relieved formed up for their return. They made their way back by the Telegraph Road, hearing snatches of picket firing and even an occasional salvo of artillery fire from down towards the river as they went.

Most men took the chance to catch up on sleep on reaching their shelters, but in the early afternoon, Daniel Ryan opted to accompany Ballard and Fitzpatrick to get their own view of the Yankee lodgement. They made their way from the camps to ascend the western shoulder of Howison Hill, tramping the now bare ground from which the trees had been systematically stripped to feed the army's winter fires. They reached the top of the hill and from there were able to see much of the downstream stretch of the river, from the town docks on down towards the eastward bend, where the Yankees had crossed over to fight in December. A few other men were already on the hill crest looking down at the enemy salient. One of them jerked his thumb towards the river.

"They could'a done thet on their own side without troublin' nobody none," he drawled.

"That's the Yankees fer ya," Ballard replied, "all damned show."

The enemy were over again now and they were over in strength. Their upstream flank lay something under a mile from where Ryan and his companions had come to gaze on them, having been established just beyond where the Deep Run gully joined the Rappahannock, with the gully anchoring that flank pretty securely. Rather than looking for trouble however, the bulk of the Yankees on this side were doing little more than boil coffee and cook rations, though they had pushed a skirmish line forward and these men exchanged periodic stutters of fire with the Confederate pickets, with each side supporting its outposts with sporadic artillery fire. Between those isolated outbursts of shooting, even at that distance, a muted hum from many hundreds of voices was distinctly audible, mingling with shouts of command, the rumble of wagons and guns and the whinnying of horses and braying of mules.

The enemy had occupied the western riverbank, but they had done very little more than that. Their troops, covered by the plentiful artillery on the far side, looked settled and secure. Even as Ballard, Ryan and Fitzpatrick watched, further formations of them were making their way across the river on the pontoons which now spanned it. Daniel Ryan had seen Yankees in numbers before, but never so many as this. That whole stretch of the river bank, from Deep Run on down, was covered with them, with their positions following, but not reaching, the line of the Richmond Stage Road. This ran parallel with the riverbank just about half a mile inland and the Yankee skirmishers carried on their desultory bickering with the southerners between their main positions and the road itself. To the onlookers however, there was something peculiar about this lodgement, for these men were sitting rather than moving. There was a look about them as though, having come this far, they might have no designs to come further, in spite of the sporadic shooting and occasional cannon salvoes. Whatever element of surprise they had enjoyed, in getting their initial units across under cover of early morning mist, had now dissipated through their subsequent inactivity. The Confederates had therefore been given ample time to bring up reinforcements to contain the incursion and Ballard, having taken it all in, looked around at the other two.

"They ain't in no hurry to go no place are they," he said?

"Too busy boilin' coffee down there," Fitzpatrick murmured. It was true, the scene that they could see down on the riverside had more of the look of a camp than an attack and the mood of the southerners, watching it on this side, seemed to have relaxed in response to this exhibition of apparent lethargy from the enemy.

"Peace and quiet's fine with me," Daniel Ryan told them

both as they turned to go. "I ain't for huntin' up more trouble." The three of them smirked at each other as they moved away.

"Well wherever our next load o' trouble comes from," Ballard said at length, "my guess is that them boys down there ain't bringin' it."

The southern forces remained in their positions through the damp and drizzly Thursday afternoon and on into the evening. The Yankees along the river still seemed settled in their enclave, rather than preparing to advance. They were settled to the point that Stonewall Jackson was rumoured to be contemplating an assault on them. But the big enemy guns on the far shore would give any such attack a hot reception and as the daylight hours ebbed, there was no sign of anything more than further picket firing down towards the river. Back in the camps however the conversation was no longer of the Yankees downstream. In the light of the day's developments, or rather the lack of them, camp talk was very much favouring the view that this Yankee move might indeed be little more than a bluff, despite its ostentatious build up of strength. This meant that the manoeuvring around the fords upstream was increasingly emerging as the real enemy threat.

Evening came and the rain finally ceased as the cloud began to break, with little more in the way of action than couriers and staff officers galloping to and fro between the various command posts as the skies cleared and brightened. Finally, near dusk, the commissary wagons arrived together with fresh orders, shouted around by the sergeants, directing the company to cook two days rations and prepare to march. There was no word of where that march might lead to but, to the men getting themselves started on cooking the hurried issue of bacon and flour, there were only two options. It might be a withdrawal to the south, perhaps the sensible move, to escape the gathering Yankee pincer threat. Such a move would logically be made on the Telegraph Road, but any move back towards the Plank Road or Turnpike, which led west from the town, would indicate that a fight rather than a withdrawal or retreat was what the general was intending. As though to confirm the rumours of the afternoon, more word was now circulating around the cooking fires. Those other Yankees, the ones inland along the rivers, were reckoned now to comprise the majority of their army, with Hooker himself up there in command. They were now across those Rappahannock fords, so this latest talk said, and heading across the triangular neck of land, where the armies had confronted each other last summer, to reach the corresponding crossings of the Rapidan River, the Rappahannock's southern tributary. A crossing of the Rapidan would place them in easy range of the main roads inland and finally bring them onto the Confederate rear. Thus, if the general intended to fight this vast enemy host in middle Virginia rather than closer to Richmond, the Turnpike or Plank Road was the way he would send his troops. One way or another they would soon know if it was retreat or fight.

The regiment formed in the darkness with baggage ordered to the rear and the men in marching order, while a huge risen moon, a little short of full, dominated the sky over the river. There was only muted murmuring in the ranks, as the sergeants fussed and bickered at their men, before the files shuffled into motion, heading along the track which led from the camps out onto the Telegraph Road. When they reached the road the files turned to the north and a muttering of talk ran among the men with any notion of doubt as to where they were bound now removed. They were returning to the west, back where they had come from, to rejoin the troops already there on the Turnpike and Plank Roads, ready to tangle with whatever Yankees were approaching from those upstream fords. These last two days had cost the Ogeechee Volunteers some additional sweat and shoe leather but countermarching was a common enough thing in the army. It all indicated that, "Marse Robert," had finally made up his mind where the real threat lay. This was no retreat or withdrawal, instead it was now clear enough that, whatever strength the enemy had assembled out there to the west, Lee intended to go looking for them and fight them.

"Likes a goddam brawl does Uncle Bob," Daley pronounced as the Company B files turned off onto the Harrison Road in the moonlight, "and so do we don't we boys?" There was a mixture of shouts and grunts of response from some, but Daniel Ryan did not join them. If the odds were as bad as they seemed, the coming fight might well be the most desperate they had yet seen. His chest and stomach muscles were already tensed and tightening further and, to Daniel Ryan, a prospect as daunting, as that which they now seemed to face, was nothing much to shout about.

With the moon high, the sloshing, clinking columns made their way inland, while some of the men talked about the coming fight. It was known that those roads from the Rapidan fords led southeast, to intersect the Turnpike and the Plank road, but they did that in the Spotsylvania Wilderness and that was an additional factor. The Wilderness was a feature of Spotsylvania County, a large expanse of tangled, second growth, forest, which had reclaimed the area after the original trees had been felled, to feed a local iron-ore smelting, industry, the best part of a hundred years ago. It would be better, some boys were saying, to fight the Yankees in those forests, since numbers would matter less on such ground. There too the Yankees powerful and more numerous artillery would be less effective, since cannon would be of little use in a tangled woodland, where it was near impossible to see a target at any distance, or to deploy any number of guns to shoot at something, even if it could be seen.

The inland march eventually brought them, in the light of the now sinking moon, to a further intersection and here the order came to move to the right off the Turnpike, turning away onto a muddy, dirt road to halt and rest at ease, awaiting further orders, while behind them, through the trees, came the first signs of a misty dawn. Within minutes the march was resumed with the men sloshing their way along through the mud, till a further halt was called followed by the order to deploy to the right off the road facing towards the almost set moon. Once formed into line, Company B found themselves in a clump of woods and, with a skirmish line ordered out in front, the remainder of the men were ordered to stack their weapons and set to work on preparing a line of trenches.

Digging trenches was still a delicate subject in the army. Some men, having seen and accepted the value of them, in terms of protection, were willing enough to undertake the labour with only modest complaint, but others held stubbornly to their original view that had been widespread over the previous summer. Digging holes was beneath the dignity of soldiers who had enlisted to fight and those of this persuasion used just about as much breath on continuing their complaints as on the actual digging. What made these particular trenches more tiresome was that, in addition to the absence of proper tools, which meant that bayonets and tin plates had to substitute for picks and spades, the line was in a wooded area, where tree roots imposed an additional difficulty on the labouring men. Thus a continuing sequence of curses and complaints marked where Company B pushed dug earth out in front to form a rampart and gathered stones and branches to strengthen it, extending the Confederate defence line to the north of the Orange Turnpike, further in the direction of the river, as the new day dawned around them.

As the light grew, Daniel Ryan's section was withdrawn from the entrenching to relieve the skirmish line. The men recovered their weapons from their stacks and, with Thompson in charge, moved off into the damp woods, thankful to be granted this reprieve from the digging. But their relief was short-lived, being followed by a hiking ordeal through the trees, where branches and thorns snagged and tore mercilessly at clothing and skin. Finally leaving the woods behind them, they crossed a boggy, overgrown meadow to reach the picket post on the far side, close to the edge of a further belt of trees, where Henry Bayfield and a few of his detail waited. As Thompson and Bayfield exchanged laconic greetings the arriving men paired off and moved warily into the next line of woods, picking their way through a similar variety of obstacles as before to reach the duty men crouched in their positions facing out into the lightening woods.

"Relief fer you boys," Ballard muttered gently as they saw Matthew Hale turn on the sounds of their approach. The black man grinned as they reached him.

"All quiet out here," he whispered as Eli Winder joined them. "Any breakfast back there?"

"Too busy diggin' trenches to worry about that," Daniel Ryan told them.

"Who'd be a soldier in this here army," Winder muttered as he and Hale moved away, while behind them Ryan and Ballard settled themselves into place among the trees.

As the light slowly brightened, Daniel Ryan was able

to take in more of his surroundings in the woods, though the interior remained dim and subdued in spite of the fact that the spring leaves on many of the trees were little more than buds with some way to go to reach maturity. The forest was principally composed of scrub oak, referred to as, "blackjack" by many of the men, with cedar, scrub pine and hickory also much in evidence. The trees were dense, covering the ground to an extent that limited a man's view for any appreciable distance in any direction. Adding substantially to the overgrown nature of the forest was the undergrowth. Larger bushes lay interspersed among the trees, blocking off what spaces there were between them. Creepers festooned the lower hanging tree branches, but the worst handicap was presented by the smaller growths. Catbriers, thorn bushes and brambles abounded, ready to deal out a sequence of cuts, snags and scratches to any who tried to make a way through, especially in darkness, as Ryan's picket had just done, suffering the consequences for their foray. Daniel rubbed ruefully at the back of his left hand, where some kind of thorn had drawn significant blood, as he gazed out into the still brightening wood, through which a morning mist now drifted, adding to the difficulties of seeing anything clearly. A little way off he heard Ballard's whisper.

"Damn Yankees could be right on top of us afore we see anythin' in a place like this."

"May not see them," Daniel replied, "but we'd surely hear them comin through a mess like that."

"Maybe they got more sense than to try to come through here," his friend concluded.

"That would suit me fine," Daniel told him.

The mist had thinned and dispersed and the sun was climbing in a pale blue sky and, having been relieved by Philipps and Fitzpatrick, Ryan and Ballard were back at the picket post when a figure was seen emerging from the woods behind them to head in their direction. Thompson scrutinised the man closely, while the others reached for their weapons.

"Thorne," the big sergeant said laconically, "must be new orders." Around him the others relaxed as the approaching man drew closer.

"Yo're to withdraw," he called to them as he came near. Thompson gestured to him.

"Withdraw," he repeated.

"We're headin' off, back to the road," Thorne told them, "Ol' Jack's orders. We ain't waitin' fer the Yankees no more, we're goin' lookin' fer them." The picket detail exchanged looks as they got to their feet. Thompson gestured with his hand.

"Go bring 'em all back here," he told them, "and let's git on with what the general says." In Daniel Ryan's mind, as he moved off into the woods, were the trenches. It was not that he objected to digging them, but there was something profoundly irksome about experiencing the drudgery of digging trenches in one place, only to almost immediately head off someplace else.

It was late in the morning with the ground beginning to dry and the sun high when they reached the Turnpike once more. Further talk had traversed the column as they had retraced their steps along the still muddy side road to join in the strike to the west, to seek out the Yankees and fight them wherever they were found. It was clear that a passive, waiting game was not for Jackson. The enemy were now said to be collecting farther along the Plank Road and Turnpike, around Wilderness Church or Chancellorsville crossroads, where other roads came down from the river fords. They would likely be moving this way, so it should not be long till they were found. The files turned onto the Turnpike with the talk still circulating as the regiment moved on in its marching files. Billy Mahone's Virginia brigade had already moved out along the Turnpike and Wofford's Georgia regiments were obviously next in line. The Yankees were out there and it was only a matter of time.

The day was warm now and the road was slightly undulating, with alternating patches of woodland and cleared ground on either side, as the files moved along, but the advance had not gone far before firing up ahead gave notice that the Yankees had been found. Their own march pushed ahead unchecked, observing the rising cloud of dirty off-white smoke rising into the air until, up ahead of them on one of those slight rises, the leading regiments of the brigade could be seen moving off the road, again to the right, and in their turn the, "Blues" did likewise, being called up to double time as they arrived. They shuffled along through renewed mud, to pass behind the bank of smoke, where a sharp fight was now taking place between some of Mahone's men and whatever Yankees they had collided with. The files were hurried along a low, wooded ridge, which stretched on, something west of north, until shouted orders came for the company to deploy again into line of battle. As the successive files came up, brigade officers stood out in front of the men, pointing them off into line with their swords and arms outstretched. The troops dutifully trotted on to reach their allotted places, guided there by their own company officers and sergeants, as the formation extended northwards.

The men of Company B found themselves in a further stretch of drying, smelly forest, where the same combinations of trees and undergrowth predominated as before. Here there was also the same handicap, of seeing for any distance in the subdued light of the woods, where few dapples of sunlight penetrated the foliage to illuminate the forest floor below. The panting men squinted into the forest as their eyes adjusted, but out ahead all seemed quiet, though, down towards the Turnpike, the fight went on as before. More troops were supposed to be deploying into the woods beyond the brigade's right, but, among the echoing trees and brush, there was virtually nothing to be seen of their own regiment, let alone anything additional or further away. A picket line was called away while the main battle line waited and the men regained their breath as the continuing fight down towards the Turnpike, its sounds seeming magnified in the forest, echoed along the line through the trees. The firing went on without pause, while the men in the battle line loaded muskets and awaited word to move forward. Suddenly the left flank of the line erupted in fire and dirty white smoke as the units there became engaged, but, to the "Blues," front all still remained quiet, save for a few isolated shots now breaking out among the pickets out in front. Wisps of blue-white musket smoke came drifting back across the main line, though little could be heard, above the heavier roar of battle to their left.

After a time the firing began to decline and at this the men were ordered forward again, pushing through the tearing and wrenching tangle of bushes, thorns and brambles, which renewed their attack on clothing and skin. Men grabbed their hats from their heads and stuffed them into their jackets, to avoid having them whisked or snagged away by the branches and thorns. They moved on, guiding by their left in a great curve, to eventually leave the woods behind them once more and come almost immediately to a muddy expanse of ground, which flanked a meandering stream. The line halted and the men gathered into groups at the best crossing places, splashing over in turn to form on the other side. As the sergeants pushed and cajoled men into place, Jeffers counted off a further group, including

Daniel Ryan's section, waving them forward as additional skirmishers and they pushed away from the main body as its advance resumed behind them.

Half-jogging they moved towards yet more woods in their ragged line, while, out in front of them above the more distant tree line, the sun had begun lower in the sky. Forward into the looming woods the open ordered line straggled, with Daniel Ryan feeling his heart thumping almost painfully in his chest. Some men welcomed the chance to serve on the skirmish line, enjoying the relative independence and informality of the job, but Daniel found it a wearing and nerve-wracking experience when the enemy were close. Not for them the chance to await the Yankees in a prepared position where the risks were minimised by a trench or barricade, or even to have the advantage of a warning of trouble from their picket line. Out in front on such a line it was a fraught process of pushing on through the dense woods, which had now grown warm and humid, straining the senses to distinguish any sight or sound which could indicate the presence of the Yankees from the hundred other noises of the forest, or of their own advance. Sweat, from the heat, and the tension also, dribbled down Daniel Ryan's face and slowly dampened his clothing as he focussed his attention grimly on the trees and growths ahead. They must seek out the enemy, who now held the option of disengaging and fading back through the shadows and the spring foliage or of standing in ambush, concealed by the woods and the green gloom. The Yankees might be gone, back to some prepared position up ahead, or even skedaddling away towards the river once more, but they could just as easily be lurking out there, waiting, up over the next slight rise in the ground, or concealed among the trees and undergrowth, to deal out death and injury to any who tracked them through this paradise of a place for concealment and ambush. Daniel looked briefly along the irregular line of advancing men, but, because of the dense undergrowth and hanging creepers, he was able to make out only the few who were nearest, but in those who were visible, he could see the tension, in their expressions, movements and mannerisms that seemed to match his own.

For a while there was nothing in the way of an ambush. Whatever Yankees were there still moved back, though slowly, stopping and taking brief advantage of any places where the terrain suited the defence with a scattering of musketry, but each time the southern line managed to catch wind of what was happening by halting under cover to listen and look. The men sized up the situation ahead, trying to detect any sounds of the Yankee line thrashing away to the west and exercising additional care and caution when those noises did not come to them through the increasingly gloomy forest. Just such a place was along a side track of drying mud, which stretched off to the north in the direction of the river and the fords. They could see the light and the rays of the lowering sun penetrating the forest margins as they approached and they went to earth as the shouted order to fire came ringing from an unseen enemy position on the far side of the track and the dark edge of the forest there erupted in flame and smoke. Around Daniel, several men, those who had moved too late, tumbled into the undergrowth, one to thrash and writhe there while others lay still, with only the vague dark shapes of their brown tunics among the tangled growths of the forest floor to show where they had fallen. Another volley tore through the foliage above them, flailing at the branches and leaves, to send fragments of both drifting down on top of the prone southern skirmishers. Then it was a scurrying rush into whatever cover could be found, while the Yankee line reloaded, seeking the tree, the rock or the bush or any unevenness in the ground which would afford some protection from the next shower of minie balls, while some sort of return fire was gotten going. Up there in the late afternoon light along the length of that dirt path, was something resembling a field of fire, limited and imperfect, but enough, and the enemy stuck there for a time, even after the main Confederate battle line came up to add their fire to that of the skirmishers.

It stayed that way in a sort of stalemate, until some artillery, maybe over near the turnpike, threw some shells over towards the Yankee positions. They heard the missiles approach, soaring overhead, with their distinctive tearing sound, to burst somewhere up in front though still to the left, billowing smoke along through the trees, a few strands of which drifted through their own positions as still they waited. Up ahead the firing steadily died away but, along the Confederate line, a mutter was growing among some of the men, frustrated at being stalled here, unable to come to grips with the enemy.

"Let us go at them!"

"Let's git after them!"

"Damned bushwhackin' Yankees."

Daniel Ryan shook his head. These were the maniacs, those who seemed to like this kind of thing. So far as he was concerned the regiment could sit here for the rest of the evening and let the artillery shift the Yankees. It was safer by far than ploughing around out there looking for another ambush. Flanking them was fine, but moving out straight ahead down their throats was a sure way of finding trouble and that he could do without.

The line remained halted and they waited for a further while before Jeffers moved along once more.

"OK, gentlemen," he called. "You got yore way. We got orders to try and flank 'em. Pickets git goin'. You boys in the main line, skirmish order, go after 'em. See what they got and what they're up to, but keep yore eyes open. They maybe got a battle line up there some place, so don't you go buttin' yore heads up against it." There were shouts of triumph from those like Powell and Daley as the reinforced skirmishers moved away. Daniel went with them, making his way from cover to cover while still hearing occasional shots, which showed that contact was still being maintained with the enemy. Perhaps they could surprise them, spread in pairs, with the regular line of battle following closer to the skirmish line, and able to manoeuvre through the trees, thorns and marshes would make the advance quicker and somewhat easier. They moved ahead, soon hearing the firing rise in volume along the line as more men came up with the Yankees. Those around Daniel hastened their pace, dodging quickly from cover to cover and hearing increasing numbers of bullets buzzing past as they closed in on the firing, which grew ever heavier as more and more men joined the fight.

Daniel, in company with Saul Philipps, ran the last few yards up to yet another tree and paused there to get his sightings while Philipps came up. All around them men were loading and firing while, from up ahead, the return shots came in, whizzing past to buzz on through the forest or thud into the nearby trees. Daniel sighted up ahead, seeing little in the smoke, but trying to aim low so as to maximise his chances of hitting something. Then from up there, through the broken firing, he heard fragments of a shout of command and, as he dodged into cover again, another volley crashed out, to send its shower of minie balls splintering and buzzing past. Hardly any of the open ordered, under cover southerners seemed to fall this time, but now, with the enemy reloading they moved out to seek and hurt them. There was no answering volley. Instead there was an almost unbroken crackle of musketry, pouring steadily forward, giving the Yankees little time to reload and return fire. Every half-minute or so sounds of the enemy commands would be heard and men would sprint into cover or drop down flat while the volley crashed past, enabling them to emerge, some with broad grins on their sweating, dirty faces, to resume their work of attrition on the steadily withdrawing enemy. The grins broadened, particularly on the faces of the maniacs, for they knew they were getting a twist on the Yankees and they were driving them and, even as the light began to dim, they were resolved to push their advantage and continue their killing as far as it would go.

It was sudden when it came, even though they had been warned by Jeffers. Ahead, the familiar shout of command, rang out, its words just about reaching them through the firing, followed by the hasty rush for cover. Then a torrent of fire blasted through, much heavier than those that had gone before. The men began to move, but hardly had they done so when a further shout was heard, prompting an even more feverish dive for safety as a second volley blasted through the forest. Daniel Ryan felt a further tug of thorns on his tunic as he dived for the undergrowth. He lay there waiting for the next volley, which came just a matter of seconds later. Out in the brush the men stayed down, with only a few of them risking the hazard of a shot in between those crashing volleys, while others simply stayed where they were and let the Yankees do their worst.

With that, the ardour among the advancing southerners began to cool. Firing volleys like that at intervals like that could mean only one thing. This was a strong defensive line, amply manned by the enemy and firing by ranks. The, "fun," such as it had been, was over.

"Man could git killed doin' this," Daley called as he reloaded.

"He's surely changed his mind all of a sudden," was the

thought that flashed through Daniel's mind as he fumbled in his pouch for a cap.

Still they kept up some sort of fire on the enemy, prompting a sequence of further volleys in reply, but then their own NCOs were among them again, hurrying from one inadequate tree to another to avoid the enemy bullets.

"This ain't no flank fer sure," Thompson growled when he arrived. "Hold here and keep up yore fire. They've spent all afternoon pullin' back along this line, likely they won't wait around."

His words were prophetic, for it did not take the enemy long to decide that this was a place where they would no longer dally. The fire through the trees gradually faded as the Yankees moved away again through the gloom of the forest. It was hard to understand why it was happening. They were pulling back when they had been on the verge of wedging the Army of Northern Virginia into a trap between the two wings of their manoeuvring army. It was difficult to believe that they had given up on their advance after hardly anything of a serious fight. Was there a catch in it all? Were they preparing a surprise riposte of some kind, up ahead in the dim woods? There had to be an explanation for this strange development, so, expecting trouble, the skirmish line cautiously resumed its advance.

A short distance farther on the woods ended again, opening out onto an expanse of cleared ground and the bramble-torn, thorn-punctured men emerged in an irregular rank into another meadow. After probing almost all of the way across this latest overgrown expanse, the skirmishers were halted again until the main line behind them came up and settled at the edge of the trees. There they waited, as the skirmishers moved on once more to approach the next tree line while the day headed closer towards dusk.

They were still short of the trees when they heard

the shout of command once more, throwing themselves immediately to ground as the billow of smoke erupted in the forest ahead. The pattern of before was repeated as a further volley tore past, upon which the pickets began to raise their heads, opening a scattering of return shots on the hidden enemy. This latest fight quickly stalled the advance here in the field, as the pale red sun now touched the distant tree line. Clouds of smoke rose into the air from the direction of the road, where heavier fighting appeared to still be going on down towards the Turnpike. But, with the Yankees pulling away again, their own main line remained unengaged. In the last of the sunlight, the men of the picket line were replaced by others and those relieved moved back to the edge of the woods where the remainder of the regiment had halted. But there was no rest or supper in immediate prospect. They got down to the work of digging again, forming a crude breastwork, while off to the left the shooting gradually subsided. As darkness came the fighting along the line had not altogether stopped, though now it was reduced to occasional fusillades, interspersing with single shots. Some of those shots drove the men of Company B to cover as, somewhere out in that next tangle of trees, on the other side of the overgrown meadow, pickets and sharpshooters began to seek targets among them with aimed shots, even as they worked at gathering stones and attempting to scrape earth from the tangle of tree and bush roots into even a modest rampart. When this was sufficiently done, the remaining men were dismissed to rest. Some, having consumed whatever portion of their prepared rations was to hand, then settled down behind the rampart and were asleep almost immediately. Others of them fidgeted, or even conversed quietly for a few brief moments, before settling to rest.

Daniel Ryan lay awake for longer, for it was battle again and his head still raced with the tensions of the day. He found his mind turning over, reflecting on those whom he had seen fall within the last few hours in this latest episode of, "minor," fighting, which had been long on tension but with less actual combat. Yet men had died, few of them, compared to other days, but those who had were just as dead as any others. It was strange, in some ways almost unreal. Today's skirmishing had only briefly grown into a full blown fight, yet that draftee Wade Garrett had died out there in the brush near that little track, having been a second or so too late in seeking cover as the Yankee volley had come. Daniel wondered what Eli Winder and Josh and Matthew Hale made of that fact, for Garrett, though only a conscripted member of the company since the autumn, had certainly been more hostile than most towards the three black men and it would be little more than human nature for them to be relieved at least, if not downright pleased, at his fate. He had collapsed, back there at the dirt track without uttering a sound, going down like a rag doll, his life snuffed out in one brief instant.

Daniel found himself mulling over the whole morbid subject of him and of George Stone, the other whom he had seen die today. He pictured each of them in his mind as they had been this morning, Stone, another of the recently clean-shaven men of the company, with that large red patch in the crutch of his pants. It had been the same sort of day for them as for anyone else until that moment when the concealed Yankee line had opened fire and that had changed things for them forever. As his eyes moved on around the bivouac, Daniel found his mind entering that worst taboo of soldiering as he wondered which of those who now slept all around this makeshift camp, might die tomorrow? Would his own turn come before another sunset? Might he be one of those destined to end his life in these dismal forests in one or another of the grisly ways that this war was repeatedly demonstrating? That was a matter of random chance, coming down to where the shell burst or where the bullet went. But however it happened those whose luck had run out had all died. Their turns had come and that much had been final and unchangeable as it had been again today. Anticipating a fight all day, they had seen others ahead and around them engage with the enemy, but the majority of their own regiment had finally come to the night on this day of battle having had but one fairly brief episode when they were up with and exchanging real fire with the Yankees. In these woods they had gained only the most fleeting sightings of their enemies, but regardless of that, there were still those along the line, Wade Garrett and George Stone included, whose luck had deserted them in the course of those brief, glimpses and that had been the end of them.

Chapter 13 Against All the Odds

With no drum roll or bugle call to rouse them the off duty men were stirred from their dozes by their sergeants while it was still dark. They were directed instead to assemble with weapons and equipment ready to move. There was no reference to breakfast, but, without a visit from the commissary, breakfast would be little more than remains for some of Company B who had largely consumed their two days rations yesterday, hoping for some plunder from the Yankees to supply today's needs. The awakening men grabbed for muskets and possessions, scrambling to their feet to roll their blankets while squinting around in the darkness of the spring night, finding, when they looked out in front, that the gloom around them was already softened by the same gathering morning mist as yesterday.

With ranks formed there was no delay and the sections wheeled into a file to move away through the trees and undergrowth, picking their way in the gloom until they reached what appeared to be the drying mud of the track where they had encountered the Yankees the previous day. A column of march of sorts, though in files of only two, was formed there and this promptly moved on, following the track south to the Turnpike to assemble there before turning westward towards the enemy once more. They were directed past a succession of halted ammunition wagons pulled onto a narrow margin of cleared ground and occupied by a small farm just north of the road, while, behind them, a vague paler glow indicated the first lightening of the sky for the coming day. Only yesterday's skirmishers required much in the way of ammunition, but most took a pack or two of cartridges and a handful of caps, jamming them into pockets as they resumed their march. Morning mist still lingered, wisping around the treetops as the men made their way along the verges of the road, the substance of which was occupied by a stalled artillery train.

They were on the Turnpike for almost an hour, as the daylight slowly grew, their progress slowed by the congestion on the road, before being eventually directed off to the left, on a further side road. Here however the march was brief, lasting only minutes before they were deployed along the eastern margin of the dirt road. A picket was dispatched forward and the remaining men were once again directed to entrench, with the same kind of reaction as yesterday as they got to work. Out in front there was already outpost firing commencing, as the balance of Company B laboured, using bayonets as before to break up the earth, which was then shovelled into a rampart with tin plates. The task was again made harder by bush and tree roots and men cursed and complained as they encountered these obstacles, but gradually a shallow trench line took shape, snaking away through the forest, parallel to the road, with stooping, working men marking its line. A hazy sun had ascended, visible behind them to the east through the incomplete canopy of spring leaves. Steadily the mist burned away to reveal the palest of blue skies and throw indistinct shadows ahead of the positions, while details of men set to collecting branches and stones to strengthen and crown their earth rampart as it gathered further shape and substance among the trees. While they still worked, an upsurge of cannon fire erupted to the west. It was not particularly close, which men noted as they paused to look, but it indicated that the Yankees out there had also gotten up early.

The entrenching finally done, the men were stood down. Most of them immediately settled themselves behind their rampart, some to try to resume their interrupted rest, while others rummaged for anything that remained of their rations, or engaged in quiet conversation as the latest rumours, those mainstreams of army life, were exchanged. The Yankees were retreating, said one tale, but it was another story that was getting more credence. Jackson, it was being said, was away again, as was his habit, off on a looping march with his own divisions, to strike at the enemy flank. Off to the west, men were saying, maybe a mile or more in the distance, there was a crossroads, where the turnpike was bisected by side roads, including the road to the river fords. That was the main enemy position and their own job was to wait here, fixing the Yankees in place, awaiting the signs and sounds of the Second Corps' attack further west. Those still awake chewed at such food as they had, winking or grinning at each other while they exchanged further comments about the great man and his exploits, maybe, Daniel Ryan thought, through some notion of battle bravado, or perhaps to conceal their own persisting doubts and fears.

"If ol' Jack's after 'em agin, them Yankees better skedaddle outa' thar."

"He'll be kickin' their durned asses, if they don't watch out."

"Damn fool Yankees can't do nothin' with Ol' Jack."

Daniel Ryan's mess pooled and consumed the remains of their food, before settling to rest in the lee of the breastwork.

The occasional popping of muskets continued out ahead, showing that the skirmishers of both sides remained active. The tree branches above him swayed and creaked in a light spring breeze, while all around him most of the others of the company had taken the opportunity to rest though few of them actually slept. Whatever Jackson was up to on the far flank, the battle on this sector seemed to have reached a state of comparative stalemate, with nobody, barring the pickets, in any hurry to commence more major hostilities.

For some time there was no sign of anything substantial, but, with the enemy this close, it was unlikely that situation would last and sure enough, though the woods out to their own front remained quiet, over to their right near the main road, where the Phillips Legion were said to be deployed, a heavier bout of picket firing broke out. The sound of musketry quickly rose in volume, as though a serious fight was getting under way. Men stirred themselves, retrieving their weapons before moving towards the parapet to look, seeing traces of smoke drifting among the trees towards the Turnpike. Minutes passed as they waited, with still no activity on their own front and after some minutes the firing towards the road began to fade, returning gradually to standard skirmish line exchanges. The men were stood down again and, as they moved away from the parapet, Daniel Ryan looked over to where Winder and Josh Hale were re-stacking their weapons, catching the eye of the former who nodded to him. Daniel gave a wry smile in response.

"I didn't want him dead," Winder said. Daniel looked at him blankly for an instant before the thought came to his mind. It was Garrett. He nodded and then shrugged in response.

"Ain't nobody gets much o' what they want in this here war," he said. Winder nodded briefly.

"He never gave us no reason to like him much," he said, "but that don't mean I wanted him dead."

"Bullets don't choose Eli," Daniel replied. "It could just as easy have been you, ... or me."

Winder nodded once again and gave the merest semblance of a smile, while Daniel reflected that, in the black man's position, he was damned sure he wouldn't be lamenting the death of someone like Garrett too much.

The sun was high when Jeffers returned, making his way among the trees and growth, calling the company together to where Boyce and Carson had appeared, just along the line from where those of Daniel Ryan's mess still rested. They got to their feet and shuffled over to gather in something more of a crowd that grouped around the two officers. Boyce looked around them briefly before he spoke.

"The colonel has learned that General Jackson is moving with his corps to attack the enemy," he told them. Some of the rumour spreaders looked around to smirk and grin at each other as he continued.

"General Lee has issued orders that we are to ready ourselves for an advance, but there will be no attack on this flank until further, definite orders are received. Today we are to occupy the enemy, to drive in his skirmishers and convince him that a real attack is coming. We will maintain contact with the Yankees and press them, but we are not to turn our probes into a full scale attack. Our job is to hold them in place and prevent them from reinforcing General Jackson's front and we will be supported in this by our artillery. Lieutenant Carson will take half the company to reinforce our pickets. Drive the Yankees in and do everything you can to make them expect an attack, but no more than that." He nodded to Carson, who then turned towards Jeffers.

"Half the company First Sergeant if you please, that should give the Yankees something to think about."

"Yessah," Jeffers moved across, pointing towards the sections he wanted, and almost inevitably his gaze fell upon Thompson's mess.

"Git yoreselves ready," the First Sergeant growled

The musket stacks disappeared in seconds and the men busied themselves, checking cartridges and caps as they formed into a line. Thompson appeared seeking out his own men.

"Form up, boys," he called as he came. "You got the first dance so let's git ready to move out there with the pickets and we'll git started drivin' the Yankees in. Weapons, ammunition and water's plenty fer this." As they dropped or slung blankets and haversacks in a rough pile, Daniel exchanged glances with Fitzpatrick and Philipps, seeing the renewed tension in their faces. Once contact was made with the enemy there was no real respite from the strain. The knowledge that battle and maybe injury or even death, were only one order and a few hundred yards away hung heavier in some men's minds. The indications of it in their behaviour had perhaps grown more subtle during the morning's inactivity, but they had still been there. The tense silence of some and the forced comments and attempts at humour from others were both back, showing how the apprehension was sustained in all, bar the homicidal maniacs and the other fools. But, even among these others the call to assemble was, in a perverse sort of way, almost a relief, knowing now that they would be moving forward, the uncertainty was done with. It would start now and once it had started it would go on and then it would finish and be done with. They moved to their barricade and began to load their weapons, while the remainder of the company watched, with some comments coming from a few of those who had been spared this particular episode of the fight.

"Don't go wakin' 'em up now."

"If ya git lost, holler out."

"Gentlemen please," Jeffers called from a little way along.

"Kin we git started on this like soldiers and not like the goddam, ladies' embroiderin' club?" There was a mutter of subdued amusement as the men adjusted their line. Jeffers was doing his customary thing, introducing his dry humour at this time, when some in the company, especially the newer men, might too easily start to dwell too much on what might be coming.

From further along the line, the first shouts of command came and the detail moved into place. They clambered across the rampart, with muskets loaded but not primed, moving away across the trampled mud of the road, in open order, with their arms at the carry. Talk was now at an end and the detail spread out into the woods beyond their own lines, making their way back into the tearing, scratching expanse and into the lottery of life and death that was now beginning again in the hostile ground between the lines. The woods were growing warm again as the sun ascended and, as he went, Daniel Ryan felt the sweat form again on his face, with the beads beginning to coalesce and trickle down. It was likely just be the beginnings of a warm day in more ways than one.

From the start it was attended by disorganisation, due to the nature of the ground and the forest. Even with the men in open order, the trees, and more especially the thick undergrowth of brambles, briars, and creepers, not to mention the successive patches of marsh and bog, imposed their repeated difficulties and delays. Men were compelled to deviate around those obstacles that they could not work past or force a way through and this pushed them into groups, rather than the spaced, porous line that skirmishing demanded. The NCOs, following the men, became irritated, then angry, then downright furious as the advance lurched and staggered its way forward. Thompson and Dellings, with Corse and Cooper the two corporals, cajoled and shouted as hapless men in front of them became embroiled in the succession of snares and traps imposed by the terrain.

The undergrowths remained thick and the route difficult, with nothing in the way of a continuous rank even remotely possible in the congested woods. Having covered a downhill stretch, they negotiated a marsh bordered little creek to then ascend a steeper slope. Further patches of undergrowth tore at skin and clothing, ripping savagely at already ragged tunics and pants, as the men pushed on through, vainly trying to maintain their order. As they had started out, Daniel Ryan, like others around him, had again pulled his hat from his head and pushed it into the front of his tunic, lest he lose it altogether in the tearing ordeal of the woods. As a result, obstructing branches whipped across faces and heads, drawing blood there and prompting repeated muttered curses from the struggling men, though their hats at least remained safe for another day.

They must be close to the picket line now. The scattered shooting ahead of them had drawn closer, with the musket shots echoing flatly and deafeningly in the confines of the forest. Eddies of smoke began to drift around them when, from behind, they heard the heavy thudding reports of cannon, which sent shells flying overhead, with those telltale noises they made in flight. Out in front as the first of them landed, Daniel heard them splintering through the upper branches of the trees seconds before their explosions. Then the blast of the detonations came, not too far up ahead, but unseen in the dense woods.

Around Daniel, men looked around at each other with pensive expressions. Infantry never liked it when artillery fired over their heads at the enemy beyond. Even though the Yankees were the target, there was always the chance of shells falling or exploding short, among their own men, through badly measured fuse cutting, and with the acknowledged unreliability of many Confederate shell fuses, the chances of being caught by such shortfalls were considerably increased. Even as these thoughts crossed Daniel Ryan's mind, there was an explosion almost overhead and again he heard the splintering of branches as the fragments cascaded downwards through the trees, just ahead of where they still struggled in the undergrowth, sending a shower of splinters, twigs and new leaves fluttering down towards the ground. More shells came over and some men seemed to hesitate, looking up as though anticipating the worst.

"Look to yore goddam front!" That was Dellings' shout from somewhere behind the line, but men still glanced nervously upwards as the artillery salvoes continued to pass above them. Their picket line was in sight now. Daniel could see the brown flitting figures and the puffs of smoke from their shots. Beyond was a further stretch of woods where the smoke hung more thickly, but there was no sign of the Yankee skirmishers, save for the scattering of minie balls that were now coming buzzing through, some of them droning on through the forest while others splintered into the trunks of nearby trees, sending little shards and sprays of wood and bark flying into the air. Behind them a shout came from Thompson.

"Give 'em the yell boys, let 'em know we're comin'!" Around Daniel the screaming battle yell rose and gasping in a quick breath he added his voice to it. The high-pitched shout rose in intensity as the men surged forward, struggling through the trees and undergrowth. The firing out in front seemed to fade as the line moved forward. The Yankees would be pulling back towards their main line, alerting them to the coming, "attack," and above them the shells still tore over till the whole woods seemed to be a maelstrom of noise. A further succession of explosions up ahead, interrupted the continuing crackle of muskets with their detonations and, crowning it all, the feral screaming shout from the throats of the surging line, filling the woods as the original pickets joined the arriving men to form a substantial rank that now lurched ahead through the tearing branches, brambles and thorns.

A few men crashed to the ground, having tripped on creepers or roots, while others vainly tried to avoid the briar or thorn thickets, but, even as the remainder laboured on, the advance became steadily more disorganised and it was probably that very disorganisation that helped it to avoid heavier losses when the first enemy volley came. Those retreating Yankee pickets must have been much closer to their own main positions than had been anticipated, as the massed volley from the battle line seemed to come much earlier than anyone had expected. The crash of it was deafening, making it seem very close by, but, while men did go down, following those sickening, spongy thuds of heavy lead bullets penetrating flesh, or that even more intimidating sound of splintering bone, most of them remained unhurt. Some had been left behind, when they stumbled to the ground and others threw themselves flat, while those still on their feet, found what protection they could from the trees and rocks of the dense forest. Daniel Ryan felt the undergrowth tear at him as he dived for cover. Around him the enemy bullets flew past, some thudding into tree branches or trunks to embed themselves there, while others buzzed or ricocheted away with that whizzing drone peculiar to minie bullets.

The Confederate push faltered and the men instinctively moved or crouched behind trees, or dropped prone in the obscurity of the undergrowth, as they primed their own weapons and made ready. Having manoeuvred a cap into place, Daniel Ryan hazarded a look around his own tree trunk, peering through the drifting smoke and the green gloom for some sign of the enemy line. Up there, he caught a glimpse of a darker smudge among the dim light of the forest, but even as he looked, he heard the shouts of command as those men readied their next volley. He pulled back behind the tree again as the roar of it thundered out and the bullets came scything through the trees and bushes, bringing a few more men down and scattering a shower of twigs, early leaves and buds down among the drifting smoke. Immediately, there was a shout along the line.

"Now boys!" The concealed men emerged from their cover to sight quickly on the Yankee position up ahead, momentarily safe from return fire as the enemy struggled to reload. Daniel Ryan sighted through the trees at where he had glimpsed the dark smudge in front and as their return fire spattered out into the forest, the recoiling muskets kicked back into shoulders, ears rang from the deafening noise and eyes began to water and smart from the clouds of acrid, off-white smoke. Then back behind whatever cover they had found to reload, fumbling and biting at cartridges as the third Yankee volley came whizzing through, heralded by the shouted orders and the crash of its discharge. Again the men moved out, safe in those brief seconds that followed the enemy fire, bringing up their muskets to sight between the trees and sending their return shots, through the drifting smoke, towards the hidden enemy.

Smoke now engulfed the woods as men pulled back behind the trees to fumble for their next cartridge. Thompson came along the line, choosing his moments to move as he made his way from tree to tree.

"Keep up your fire, boys," he bellowed, "then start movin' back. Let's not stir the hornets' nest too much." Daniel smiled to himself as he rammed his next shot home. Even in the middle of a fight, when Joe shouted men heard. As the bedlam around him gradually subsided he glanced along the line, aware of men around him starting to move away. He caught sight of Ballard, reloading his musket behind a further tree.

"Reg'lar little Indian fight," he heard him mutter, half as though he was talking to himself. The smoke began to clear, though isolated shots still rang out, their sounds, as before, magnified under the trees. They faded back through the trees and growth, once more hampered by the same hazards of clinging thorns and obstructing trees and brush. From the Yankee line there was no sign of pursuit, but scattered among the trees and undergrowth lay a succession of squirming, groaning, brown or blue-clad, forms some of them barely visible among the spreading leaves and growths of springtime.

"Are they gonna have us doin' this all damn day," Kane growled to those nearest him? Around him there were little more than a few grunts in reply.

They halted and regrouped just below the crest of the downward slope, rivulets of sweat streaking the black powder stains on their faces and with clothing on some of them close to shreds from the tearing forest.

"You got some time fer takin' a leak and restin' awhile ," Thompson told them, "then when them Yankees get around to sneakin' back out here we get to bushwhack 'em and drive 'em in again." As he turned away the artillery to the rear sent a further salvo of shells tearing overhead, confirming Kane's notion and Daniel Ryan's own earlier one that it was going to be a long and dangerous day.

Twice more, through the middle part of the day their reinforced line of skirmishers pushed forward to drive in the Yankee picket line and threaten an attack, before pulling back to regroup out in the forest. Each time that the artillery fire resumed, the men would move forward again, driving the enemy skirmish line into retreat and drawing further volleys from the main position as they approached it. Casualties grew however with a succession of men carried or helped to the rear, at first by comrades, though soon the task was taken up by orderlies, sent out for the purpose. This, while sustaining the numbers of men on the fighting line, largely deprived any who had a mind to dodge the shooting, by helping wounded men to the rear, of their excuse for doing so. In various parts of the forest other grey brown shapes lay, partly concealed in the growing shrubs and bushes, where those now beyond help had fallen and whom there was no point in removing while the fight still went on. Daniel Ryan had sustained a crease from a minie ball, feeling it scorch across the outside of his thigh as he dived for cover on the last push forward. Thus, although the reinforced picket had made no serious attempt to attack the Yankee line, its losses had grown to a significant number by the time that Fenwick arrived in what must have been the early part of the afternoon, with the remainder of the regiment, to relieve those who had been skirmishing since morning.

They trailed back through the dense woods in groups, picking their way by the least obstructed routes, finally reaching the road and their own breastwork to clamber over the branches and top stones and settle themselves. Daniel still felt the burning sensation along his thigh and he pulled at his pants leg to examine it. There was a tear in the fabric at the place, with a small smudge of blood along the edges of it. He felt it gingerly with his fingers. It was not really a wound at all, more of a scorch along the skin, marked by a smear of drying blood along most of its length. He spat on his fingers, rubbing them together to clear the worst of the powder stains and grime from them before spitting again on his pointing finger and gently rubbing the spit along the abrasion to cool it a little, feeling it sting as the moisture made contact with the injury. Around him, muskets were being cleaned and after gazing at the mark on his leg for a few more seconds, he started work on his own weapon. He spat on the lock and rubbed at it before pushing a small piece of cloth through the hole in his rammer button and pushing it into the barrel, manoeuvring it up and down along its length to dislodge the black deposits.

With the cleaning done, almost all of the men settled to catch up on some rest, though hardly any of these troubled themselves with retrieving their blankets from the morning's equipment piles. The salvoes of shells continued to fly over at intervals, while out in front the surges of musketry went on, showing that those who had relieved them also had no intention of giving the Yankees much peace. Behind the trench rampart with only a sentry watch, there were those who, while attempting to relax, found that the noises and tensions of battle made real rest an utter impossibility, though around them other men slumbered as though there was not an interruption in the world to disturb their rest.

Early evening had come, as some of those who had slept began to waken, with the lowering sun winking through the trees out in front. The skirmishing out there had subsided again, and the artillery also had fallen silent, when the upsurge of more distant gunfire came. Men stopped to listen as it came, cupping hands to their ears and tilting heads to demonstrate their close attention. Far away there were indeed tell tale sounds of battle, though very distant and faint, seeming to rise, but then to fade only to rise again as still the men listened. They could distinguish rolling volleys of musketry, punctuated by cannon fire and, as the noise pulsed again, men began to smile and a few began to whoop and they turned to grin at each other as the firing out in their own section of the woods grew again, drowning out anything further away.

"Ain't no need to guess who that was," Fitzpatrick called, while around them more shouts began to rise.

"It's old Jack!"

"Ol' Blue Light's on their tail!"

"Reckon Ole Jack's got 'em by the ass!" They waited, straining ears to hear more above the closer noises, but it was difficult to distinguish what shooting came from where in the confines of the forest. Men continued to speculate until their comments were extinguished by Jeffers' voice.

"Children!" he called as he arrrived, and, as the men quietened, he stood beside Boyce and Carson and gazed around with his long-suffering expression before continuing.

"If that is the Second Corps boys causin' that ruckus out there, now's the time to make sure those Yankees up ahead don't send no help over that way, so git yoreselves formed and let's git after 'em one more time."

They collected weapons and reloaded them before pairing off, crossing the trench parapet again and stepping away across the road. This time they moved in single file, making their way as easily and quietly as they could through the tangled forest and marshes until they closed up to where the rest of the company still tangled with the enemy skirmish line. They moved out into open order, deploying with some difficulty through the overgrown woods. Once the men had spaced along the line, the order came to fix bayonets and prime weapons and this done, they crouched in the undergrowth, waiting for the order to move forward again. The Yankee picket fire was steady, but after several minutes of waiting, the cannon fire began again, with more shells sailing over to explode up ahead. All along the line the sergeants rose to their feet waving their men up also, with the lines rising raggedly as men saw the signals. The muskets came up to hover unsteadily as they aimed into the drifting smoke.

"Fire!" The voice was Thompson's and immediately the forest was filled with deafening noise and billowing smoke.

"Forward boys!" That was Carson's higher pitched shout, "and yell." The screaming shout rose as the line lurched away, with the now familiar obstructions and hazards scratching and pulling at them. More men went down, but as they cleared the worst of the smoke cloud, Daniel Ryan caught a brief glimpse of the light blue pants and dark tunics, of Yankee pickets as they scuttled away, visible in the brief pools of light where the sinking sun penetrated the trees. Around him there were whoops of exultation mixing through the yell as it redoubled, high-pitched and screeching, while the momentum of the charge grew.

"They can't shoot while their pickets are still out," Philipps gasped from somewhere near, his voice just audible amid the yelling. Daniel made no response, concentrating as he was on keeping his feet through a stretch of boggy ground and avoiding the thorns and brambles. On they pushed, trying to gain ground on the fleeing enemy, but Daniel was seeing fewer and fewer glimpses of them as they moved across a further gentle slope.

They knew by now that the Yankee line was out there, just a short stretch on from that rise in the ground, but would they be close enough behind the enemy pickets to get a real punch at their main line. Up ahead there was a glimpse of darker colour and they saw a Yankee vault over it, his sky blue pants very clear in the pool of sunlight as, along the line, they sensed what was coming.

"Down!" Thompson yelled again, a fraction before the flash of the enemy volley illuminated the woods for a split-second. Their own momentum helped and the men went to ground as the hail of bullets tore past, most of them, thankfully, above them, though a few of those wet impact sounds still mixed with the thudding of bullets into the wood of the trees and the buzzing drone of others spinning off into the forest.

Daniel rolled onto his back among the debris of the forest, feeling the wrenching pull of brambles on his pants leg as he did so. He rummaged in a pocket for a cartridge, having fastened his pouch to avoid spilling its contents among the undergrowth during the charge. He bit the paper with his teeth and grasped the cold, lead bullet between his lips, feeling its grooves with his tongue as he poured the powder into the barrel. He spat the bullet into the muzzle of the Enfield and pushed the remaining paper after it. The second Yankee volley came as he was fumbling the ramrod from its channel and he felt himself cringe as the hail of bullets passed what seemed like bare inches above him. It felt naked and exposed out here with no particular cover save the spring growth, nothing that would stop a bullet he thought grimly as he rammed the charge home before replacing the ramrod and pushing it home with his little finger. The sun was sinking still lower and fewer, more isolated signs of it were now visible in the forest. Shadows changed in shape as the tiny pools of slowly moving illumination still penetrated the gloom as the battle smoke eddied and thinned to tell of the passage of another day towards dusk.

Around him the first shots were being returned towards the Yankee line and Daniel pulled a cap from his other pocket and pressed it into place as he raised the Enfield to sight briefly while pulling the hammer to full cock. There was almost nothing to see through the thick wreathes of smoke, but he made a best guess and squeezed the trigger. The musket kicked back violently into his shoulder, already painful from the shooting he had been doing for most of the day. He rolled to his left, towards a larger tree, seeing Jones already sheltering behind it as he arrived.

"Man could git killed doin' this," he said and Jones grimaced briefly in his direction.

They resumed loading and firing, the process easier when standing or kneeling, timing their shots to follow the Yankee volleys, but the enemy had learned also and they were now firing by ranks, which left limited time between their volleys for fire to be returned. Around them they were now conscious of other movements.

"Withdraw, now, move back!" The shouts came along, relayed by corporals and sergeants, and gradually the irregular line sagged gently away, timing their movements carefully between the enemy volleys. Gradually they left the smoke cloud and the hails of whizzing minie balls behind them until, with the last of the evening light, they were moving through a quieter forest, below the crest of the rise, where pauses to pilfer from any fallen Yankees that they came across could be undertaken, in relative safety in the gathering gloom.

Eventually, they were assembled down by the little creek and reorganised once more. A picket of the more recently arrived men was left in the woods to keep watch on the Yankees, while the remainder moved on back, having reverted again to files. A picket post was set near the creek and the first duty watch, having reloaded their weapons, was readied to move towards the enemy line once again. The Yankees up there would be going no place to fight Jackson's boys, they told each other as they started forward again. They would be messing their pants in their positions out there all night, waiting for the next onslaught.

It was fully dark now, with a moon rising behind them to send occasional winks of ghostly light through the leaves into the interior of the forest. Suddenly the trees ahead were illuminated by the opening of a crashing outbreak of cannon fire. The missiles whizzed through the air away out ahead of them, their detonations mingling with the discharges of the next salvo. On the firing went, turning out to be a considerable cannonade, as it continued without pause. Thompson came along his frame dimly illuminated among the trees by the flashing roaring light from the bombardment.

"We'll move up now," he yelled to them, with even his voice almost inaudible through the cannon fire. "Artillery'll light the way a little and it'll maybe distract the Yankees, but don't take no chances, cover then move in yore turn. We'll move up to the top o' the rise and see how the land lies from there."

They moved off while still the cannon thundered and flashed. By Daniel Ryan's reckoning it must be near to a mile away, but a large number of guns had to be involved from the roar of sound and the number of orange flashes. Using these as a marker they negotiated their way up the slope, moving on a short way beyond the crest before halting to settle themselves. As they did so the cannon fire stopped and the silence, punctuated only by a few musket shots, was almost eerie. The picket was placed and as Daniel Ryan settled he heard another sound. Out in the woods there were distant flickers of light and the noises of axes chopping on wood. They had been right, in what they had told each other. These Yankees would not be going any place to fight Jackson's men. They were staying right here and they were showing no signs of resting either. Out there the enemy barricades and ramparts were being strengthened, with fresh logs being prepared for the purpose and it was left for the Confederate pickets, settled in the woods in easy earshot, to ponder how strong these entrenchments and parapets would be in the morning when, in all likelihood, they would be given the job of attacking them.

The picket was changed later in the night and the off duty men trooped back through the woods towards their own line. The moonlight now gave a hint of illumination to a few patches of the forest, but most of the withdrawal was made in near complete darkness and the going was still more difficult as they filed away east, from the muddy creek valley. They picked their way on beyond its eastern rim till they heard the challenge from what must be their own line. The files paused while up in front Thompson answered the sentry and, with military protocol satisfied, they moved on again, crossing the dirt road to their trench line. Sleep was uppermost in the minds of the arriving men and, without troubling to look for blankets, they threw themselves down behind the breastwork with most of them, including Daniel Ryan, settling to sleep in seconds.

It seemed hardly any time from when they had settled before the men were being roused again, to assemble in front of a weary-looking and dishevelled Boyce, in the grey gloom before dawn.

"It's forward for us boys," he told them. "The Second Corps are renewing their attack at daylight and we are to support them by attacking on this side. We will wait for the order, but get yourselves prepared. Ammunition first, then relieve the picket, First Sergeant and get the company ready."

On Jeffers' shouted order they moved wearily away, to gather weapons and equipment. Muskets were hastily cleaned and as this was being done they were called again. An ordnance wagon had pulled in along the line nearer the Turnpike and the men were moved across in details for an ammunition issue. Then they waited, each of them knowing, that, after all of the fortifying they had heard from the picket line, the time had come to discover just how strong this Yankee line now was. Before joining the others, Daniel Ryan sought out his haversack and retrieved the personal items from its inner compartment, dispersing them around his various pockets. It would not be an unknown thing, even though a couple of men might be left as guards, for the equipment left behind here to be lost, through the company having no opportunity to return for it.

Behind them, the coming daylight began to illuminate the mist shrouded trees and scrub in mysterious, subdued grey. Jeffers called away a detail to relieve the pickets and these, again including Daniel Ryan's mess, started forward without delay. They worked their way in line across the now familiar ground, descending into the valley and negotiating the muddy creek to the picket post before moving on and ascending the far slope in turn, as the first rays of the rising sun poked their yellow chinks of light through the woods from the east. They came up with the duty pickets shortly after and spread themselves into position while the men relieved merged into the grey gloom as they withdrew. To their left, and some distance away, the firing was growing again, with what sounded like skirmishers first at work, but, as the daylight increased, the noise quickly grew into what sounded like full scale battle, indicating that Old Jack had, characteristically, not dallied in his blankets.

The morning drew on with no sign of an advance until the thrashing sounds of men approaching through the forest behind them gave a clear hint that the time had come. It would be attack now, as Boyce had said, and the skirmishers got themselves up, with orders arriving to move off guiding right obliquely towards the Turnpike. Leaving their places, with hats once more stuffed into jackets, the men began to work their way from cover to cover towards the Yankee positions. They could hear the battle line behind them at first, as they moved forward, but only till the first shots of the advance began to ring out as contact was made with the enemy skirmish line. On they went, hearing the firing grow steadily in intensity, as their own line came up with more of the Yankees and the firing gradually grew from individual shots into fusillades of musketry. Still they picked their way forward, using the available cover, at something of a diagonal compared to the forays of the previous day, though this advance was a similar episode of marsh, thorn and thicket, tearing repeatedly at skin and clothing.

As the men pushed on, the warmth again grew under the trees and Daniel Ryan felt the sweat beads form on his skin and begin to trickle down into his eyes and drip from his chin. He resorted to wiping his face repeatedly, with his tunic sleeve though this provided only momentary relief, before the process began again. The Yankee skirmishers were still out there sure enough, the continued shooting was evidence enough of that, but, as far as could be seen, it was still just a skirmish line, which was giving ground, though only slowly. Wherever the main enemy line was, there was nothing so far to be seen of it, just an occasional moving smudge of dark tunics, visible when the tangles of bushes and growths briefly thinned, which quickly disappeared into the shadows of the forest. The advance went on as a moving skirmish through the scantily lit woods, with the Yankees persistently fading away through the semi-gloom and drifting gun smoke as soon as they caught sight or sound of the main southern line. As the men moved on westwards, they came across a succession of inert or wriggling blue shapes in the undergrowth giving the most tangible indication that the enemy was out there, though disinclined to stay and fight it out.

By now they had closed up towards the enemy entrenchments of last night, for here the dead of both sides lay thicker. The picket line was called to a halt and the men sought cover as they waited for the main line to come up. Within a minute or two the ranks arrived to swallow up the waiting pickets. A few of the arriving men made to leave their places to seek further plunder but the sergeants did not permit it, pushing them bodily back into their places as they cursed angrily at them. Daniel Ryan looked intently into the forest as he waited in his place. Somehow this part looked different in today's daylight and he strained his eyes seeking any kind of familiar landmark or sign among the trees.

The order came to move, shouted along by the sergeants and the ranks lurched off through the woods. On they struggled, pulled and snagged by the thorns as they went. Then, from somewhere up ahead they heard the expected shouts as before and men threw themselves flat or sought out other cover as the enemy volley crashed out. The bullets whizzed through the woods, with their intimidating mixtures of sounds and wounded men went down screaming as they sought out their hurts, while the dead joined those from last night, adding to the dismal tangle on the forest floor. A second volley crashed out, though this one found few targets as the men of the battle line had largely taken cover as they primed their own weapons. Hardly had the volley passed when their officers and sergeants were calling them up into line to return fire. The men scrambled to their feet, bringing muskets up to be quickly levelled and, on the order the volley reverberated deafeningly through the woods. Daniel felt the recoil punch the butt plate into his already tender shoulder and he winced as he pulled the weapon down to the charge position. Then came the order to charge bayonets and the men started forward, raising their high-pitched yell as they went. The line crashed through the trees, the front rank with bayonets levelled as they stormed towards the enemy line, but it was too far, Daniel Ryan sensed it as they went. It was too long, they had already passed reasonable time for reloading and sure enough, the twinkling, yellow muzzle flashes, the shattering roar and the billow of smoke came, marking the next Yankee volley. Down went a succession of the men, crashing into the undergrowth, while those unhurt divided, some continuing their charge, while others sought cover to reload. The second volley came as Daniel Ryan felt the breath knocked from his lungs by the impact of his body on the ground, which even the thick covering of dead leaves and twigs only partly cushioned. He frantically sought a cartridge from his pocket and bit it open, to pour the contents into the barrel. As he reloaded he looked out in front, seeing that even the maniacs had now gone to ground, while the blue-white gun smoke drifted among the trees. He rammed his own shot home and replaced the ramrod before scratching a cap from a different pocket to replace the expended one. He waited, knowing that another set of volleys was nearly due. Thompson's voice came to him as he waited.

"After the volleys boys, then we slug it out and drive them!" His words were drowned out by the roar of the Yankee fire, but there was something about that volley for it was less together and more a ragged succession of shots. Maybe they were becoming disorganised, or maybe they were going. The next volley came, smashing through just above his head, but with a similar raggedness as the preceding one. Then Thompson's voice bellowed again.

"Up boys! On your feet and ready!" Daniel scrambled up using the Enfield to help him rise. He brought the weapon up to his shoulder, seeing out of the corner of his eye other barrels with bayonets extending from them, moving into line with his own.

"Aim!" that was Thompson again.

"Fire!" The volley crashed away carrying buds, twigs and leaves with it.

"Reload!" There was a furious burst of activity as the men sought cartridges and rammers, before flicking spent caps away and replacing them with fresh ones. It all took only seconds but meantime another enemy volley bellowed out with more men in the southern battle line going down as it tore through. The surviving men ignored the fallen as their own barrels went up to the ready.

"Aim!" Thompson's shout again, "Fire!" The crash of the volley hurt the ears as it blasted out in the confines of the forest. The reloading began again with a furious tearing, pouring and ramming before the caps were again replaced and the muskets brought up as a further enemy volley, ragged again crashed and this time going largely high, through the branches around their heads, with fewer men going down as a result.

"Aim!" Carson's voice this time, its higher pitched tones coming ringing through the trees.

"Fire!" There came the concussion of yet another volley with the muskets lunging back into men's bruised and suffering shoulders.

"Charge boys, forward, give them the cold steel!" That was Boyce's shout and the yell rose up again, screeching and manic as it echoed through the forest. The ranks surged forward, stumbling over fallen men as they went. There was so far no return fire and Daniel Ryan felt himself inwardly cringe as he went forward. Were they letting them come close before punishing them with their next volleys? The brown of the earthwork swam into his eyes as he grimly struggled through a barrier of cut branches left out in front to delay any attackers, still awaiting the return fire, but it did not come. They were now in cleared ground, with only the stumps of trees to obstruct them as they charged through a belt littered with wood debris and chippings. Around him the shouts were intensifying still further as they came up towards to the parapet of the Yankee breastwork and the leading men began to scramble across. Daniel came up with the bulk of the line, seeing the litter of dead and squirming wounded beyond the barrier and blood, there seemed to be blood splashed everywhere. He grasped the musket with one hand and laid the other on the top log, sensing the wetness of still more blood on his fingers, as he vaulted clumsily across, only to feel a wounded man convulse and hear his cry as his foot landed on him. He almost fell, but managed to bring his other foot forward just in time to recover his balance, stopping there to look at the scene. Around him the others of the mess were gathering to scrutinise the Yankee dead and wounded for plunder. Philipps had slung his musket and was examining his arm from which blood streamed, soaking the sleeve of his tunic and dripping from his cuff. Kane moved across towards him and peered at it, reaching out to examine it further.

"You lucky boy," he intoned, mimicking Jeffers' expression. "Must'a went straight through. Bone seems fine so no probin' or nothin' like that fer you Saul boy. Ya'll be back on the line in no time at all."

"I ain't goin' to no rear," Philipps growled as he fumbled a handkerchief from his pocket to clasp it around the arm and hold it in place there. "Strap it up and let's git on." Fitzpatrick had joined Kane and he offered a cloth which Kane proceeded to tear into strips in the accustomed fashion before tying them together then, strapping Philipps' own handkerchief around the wound, he bandaged it up with Fitzpatrick's makeshift dressing.

"Good as ever," he told Philipps as he finished tying the two ends into a knot.

The others were poking around the Yankee dead, but there was little time for this as already the sergeants were coming along calling their men to form again. Daniel looked along the line as they assembled, his eye coming to rest on the black men, but seeing only Winder and Matthew Hale in their places. He looked at Winder, but, seeing his mouth set in a grim line, he said nothing. The ranks quickly formed and, with a fresh picket detail called away, the main body stepped promptly off, following the disappearing skirmishers towards where the woods resumed.

The going was initially easy, with many of the trees in the rear of the Yankee position having being cleared, but before long they were into the trees again bringing a further ordeal of pushing through the straggling, undergrowth, with hats staying inside jackets as the men used their leading arms to protect their faces. The line shredded and fragmented and was twice halted so that stragglers could catch up, while the whole formation reformed before the advance was resumed. The Turnpike was reached and the men crossed it diagonally before plunging into still more woods on the northern side of the road. After a time they descended into a further dip in the ground, to move up again on the far side and emerge at last from the trees, with the sun now near to overhead. A further halt was called and the line was once more reorganised at the edge of the woods, while hats were retrieved from inside tunics and replaced on heads as men squinted out ahead in the bright sunlight. They had reached a wide clearing, across which the Turnpike, now off to their left, stretched away to the west to be quickly lost in the clouds of smoke that drifted across. Those clouds were of gun smoke, but mixing with it was a growing column of darker smoke, out there where the Turnpike must be. The order came and the ranks stepped away again, with their own skirmishers now visible out in front. The battle line followed on as the gunfire began to ebb and the smoke gradually thinned.

That heavy column of darker smoke was clearer now, rising from a substantial building on this side of the Turnpike where the east to west way passed a crossroads. The red brick structure was firmly afire and, as the smoke and flames rose from it, further salvoes of shells soared across to explode around it, for over that cleared ground the battle still raged. Darker clad formations of Yankee troops were pulling away from around the burning building while heavy artillery fire came in from the south. The guns were keeping up their fire on the retreating enemy and the shells went arcing over from left to right, with their wispy, darker smoke trails marking their flight in and out of the clouds of gunsmoke. The weary men of Company B observed it all as they moved across the cleared ground to find it covered with the debris of a retreating army. Muskets, blankets, caps and pieces of clothing lay scattered all around, together with haversacks and canteens, all abandoned by the retreating Yankees. They came upon a litter of broken ammunition and hardtack boxes, with much of their contents strewn around them. Everywhere there was paper and fragments of various kinds were all around, with cartridge paper scraps, and larger pieces also, moving and flapping around in the hot, eddying air of the battlefield.

Men stopped briefly to help themselves to plunder, ignoring the shouts of their sergeants while they rifled furiously through the debris, stuffing whatever took their fancy into tunic pockets as they pushed on to rejoin the slowly advancing lines. Daniel Ryan helped himself to a haversack an almost new set of blankets, just in case, grabbing also a handful of hardtacks and a cloth bag of salted pork from a broken open barrel on his way to rejoin the line, slinging the blankets over his shoulder and pushing the hardtacks and the bag of meat into his new haversack as he regained his place. Out in front, the men could still see glimpses of Yankee skirmishers out ahead around the burning house. But those Yankees, tiny blue figures in the grass out ahead, were not staying. They were pulling out, though no longer heading west, having altered their line of retreat more to the north, with clumps troops and sections of artillery, that had been deployed to the south of the Turnpike, now also scampering for the rear across the front of the Ogeechee Volunteers skirmishers, as they tried to keep pace with those retreating from the east.

Down to the south, the cannon were still firing, but they had altered the range and were now sending shells hurtling through the air past the drifting cloud from the burning house, to add their bursts to the chaos beyond the building. Through the thinning smoke to the south, more figures could now be seen emerging from the brush into the cleared area across the Plank Road also making for the crossroads. A line of grey brown skirmishers came first, but these were soon followed by the more solid ranks of a battle line, which came and went from view in the drifting smoke from the guns. From the boys around Daniel Ryan a shrill screech of triumph began to rise, taking up the shouts from over nearer the road, until the whole field rang with the yell. The last of the Yankees moved away from the chaos around the crossroads, heading away to the north to disappear into the forests, which fringed the wide clearing, leaving only southern troops, advancing still towards the road junction, marked by the flames and smoke of the burning house.

Still the artillery continued to fire, but now their shells soared over the clearing to burst up among the trees beyond. Along the Turnpike, the smoke had further thinned and drifted, to reveal still more men in line of battle, who had debouched from the woods away on the far side of the open ground, answering the shouts and yells of those coming from the south and east with shrill, faint cheers and yells of their own. Thompson was now there, coming up behind Daniel Ryan and John Fitzpatrick and, looking around at him Daniel reckoned he had never seen the big sergeant so animated. Sensible, dependable Joe was almost capering in his triumph and excitement as he slapped the men nearest to him on the back with his free hand.

"That's it," he yelled. "That's the place and we got it. They're gone, off up there towards the fords. We licked 'em again, we licked 'em good." Daniel glanced around at him, the idea registering in his mind, but not wanting to trust it, wanting Thompson, or somebody, anybody who knew for certain, to say it again so there was no mistaking it.

"What place Joe," he blurted out?

"The crossroads there," Thompson yelled at him. "That there place, that burnin' house, that's the Yankee headquarters. Fenwick reckons that's Chancellorsville and we got it. They're licked, they're damn licked again." Hearing his words, the men around them redoubled their yelling and cheering and hats began to wave in the air. They waded on through the fields, closing on the crossroads, where the fire raged and the smoke still rose in a thick column into the blue spring sky.

From three sides of the clearing now many more men, hundreds, even thousands of them, were converging on that burning house. Shells still soared overhead, tearing past with their characteristic noise, to burst up to the north among the trees, where more fires burned, while, all across those fields, the lines of grey and brown-clad men closed in on the crossroads, now completely cleared of the enemy. But coming steadily and discernible now between the salvoes from the cannon, distant voices were rising in a more sustained outbreak of cheering. From this side of the clearing the advancing men could see over to the south, where those farther away ranks of men were raising their weapons and hats in the air and waving them furiously, because coming up that road from the south was a group of horsemen. At first the drifting smoke made it hard to distinguish them, as it wisped around them, but the cheering gave a significant enough clue as the men nearest to Daniel Ryan peered at the distant group. Then they too began to shout and yell, as the smoke thinned again to reveal a smudge of grey at the head of the mounted group and in a moment it was clear for there was not a soul in the army who was not familiar with that grey horse. It had to be Traveller, bearing that equally familiar figure in the grey coat and brimmed hat. It was the general, arriving here at this moment of triumph, with these multitudes of his filthy, ragged, smoke- blackened men to see the scale of their victory.

The battle lines surged forward from all three sides. Those must be Jackson's men, coming from the far side and from the south. All around the large cleared space men cheered and yelled and laughed in a great release of the tension of this fight that had raged all through the morning. From each direction they pushed on, in towards where Robert E. Lee had come to a halt, just in front of his staff, on the road near to the burning house, with his hat now in his right hand, doffed in that familiar salute to these arriving scarecrows of men, his soldiers, who had grasped this success against all the odds. From each side the men crowded on, gathering around the crossroads, as they cheered and yelled and waved their weapons and their hats in the air above their heads. Their exhaustion, the bruises scratches and cuts from the forest thorns, the minor wounds, the aching shoulders from the punching recoil of their weapons, the hunger, for few had eaten sufficiently in the last days, and their tormenting thirst, made worse by the black powder from biting cartridges, all these things were forgotten as they savoured this moment of triumph and exultation with their leader. As the men of Company B came closer, a further group of mounted figures approached from the southwest. The cheering slackened as the boys looked, craning their necks to see and then the answer went ringing along the lines.

"It's ol' Jeb!"

"It's Stuart!" the cheers redoubled as the cavalry chieftain led his own staff onto the Turnpike to make their way forward and turn into the approach to the burning house to greet his commander. The boys were listening to still more talk that was circulating rapidly among the soldiers.

"He's got the Second Corps. He took over from, "Old Jack," last night." Around them, some men turned at this news.

"So where in the hell's Jackson?" The questions rose, to be quickly answered by those who had heard more.

"He's wounded."

"He got shot down last night after dark."

"It were his own boys, Tarheels, that done it."

"They reckon he's lost an arm." They collected into their groups, moving closer to their comrades on either side as still they gathered, still shuffling towards the pillar of smoke and flame that now engulfed the crossroads. They were instinctively forming into fragments of companies and regiments, but these more resembled clumps of men than an advancing line of battle, discussing furiously this latest turn of events. Their exasperated sergeants tried to push them bodily back into a line, with their shouts growing ever more angry and profane, as the men, bunching still to hear the news of Jackson, frustrated their every effort to preserve or recover something that resembled a military formation.

Just south of the smoke-shrouded crossroads, Lee, having greeted the newly arrived Stuart, rode slowly on across the turnpike, skirting where the big house still burned, its flames crackling into the air. The moment lingered even as officers too began collecting and shouting their men into order, and slowly ranks began to form and the men began to move, as still Jackson's fate was still discussed and disected. Gradually the assembly of men reconstituted itself from one seething mass of celebration into the disciplined order of formed, but still furiously conversing, soldiers. Even as Lee paused there, near to the burning house, more couriers were coming and going, bringing messages from different parts of the field. Preston was there with the regiment, moving across the front of his men, waving them into line and pointing with his sword away north, to where the shells still flew and the tree line, parts of it obscured by the smoke, frowned out upon the clearing as though anxious to repossess it.

Gradually the line was formed and realigned to face towards those trees for them to finally step off, leaving the fire behind them, with the floors of the house having collapsed inside the still-standing walls, it slowly began to subside. The ranks pushed on across the open expanse towards the tree line, watching the skirmish line disappear into the gloom, smelling the smell of the fires to the west where trees and undergrowth burned and palls of smoke drifted eastwards through the remaining forest. But there was not just the smell of wood smoke on that breeze, other smells were coming also and among them an odour that made men look and question for it was the stink of burning flesh.

The artillery fire had slowed now, allowing pauses between their salvoes, while, out there in the burning woods, the musketry also had receded to a staccato exchange of picket fire. Other sounds now came to the ears of the advancing men, the crackle of the burning woods, mixed with the shrieks of wounded and dying men. Out there in the forests these men must be and some of them must lie where the fires burned, for their screams could just be made out between the more sporadic fire of muskets and cannon. These were the voices of men who could not move and as a result, where they lay in the path of the fires, whether dead or alive, they were being consumed by the flames with the repulsive smell of their fate confirmed only too clearly on the breeze. Some of those in the advancing ranks looked around or looked at each other, but there was nothing to be done, so they continued their advance back into the woods, setting their faces and gritting their teeth at this latest abomination of war. Back among the trees the darkness and the dank heat again engulfed them, but in the half light, with the brightness of the open fields now behind them, those smells still persisted.

But the advance into the trees had scarcely begun when the order to halt was relayed along the line, by hoarse-voiced sergeants. The men obeyed, standing there in the green gloom while they awaited further instructions. They soon came, it was back to the road and form there and even as they turned and began their brief trek to clear the forest once more, more talk came along.

"It's the Fredericksburg line. The Yankees've broke through!"

"They're back thar along the Turnpike!"

"They're in our rear!"

"They'll be comin' up along the Plank Road." There was a desperate exasperation among many of the men at this news. After all that had happened since Thursday, here was that other pincer jaw, those Yankees from back at the river bank, testimony of their overwhelming numbers. Even as this battle was being fought and won out here in the forests, they had gotten through the under strength line that had been left behind at Fredericksburg to hold them at the river. The, "Blues," own previous positions above the town had been left to Barksdale's Mississippians and they would not have given easy passage to any Yankees. But, however it was, those Yankees were through and they would now be on their way inland, coming up on the rear of the embattled and exhausted southern army here in the forests. Those pincers, which had threatened to crush the Army of Northern Virginia since the beginning of the campaign now seemed to be back in business, with one closing in relentlessly even as the army grappled in the forests with the other.

Further orders came, interrupting the jumble of talk and speculation going on along the ranks as they headed back towards the road. The companies obediently collected there, just east of the crossroads, forming their marching files along the side of the road, where vehicles now struggled to turn, on any stretch where the verges allowed it. Sweating, straining teams were hauled around by cursing, yelling drivers, while still more couriers galloped either way on the dirt surface, spattering dust and dirt up around the waiting men. Daniel Ryan looked around at the chaotic scene as he waited in his place. From the elation of only half an hour ago, there was now a sombre mood in the ranks around him, not despondent, but it was still a feeling of deep exasperation, as though the efforts and tribulations of the regiment and brigade and maybe the army as a whole, had again been thwarted. It seemed that no matter how many of the enemy were pushed back or overcome, there would always be more of them out there, waiting in line for their turn. He felt exhausted and sore, with that heavy-legged and profoundly wearied feeling. The manoeuvring and fighting of the last three days, with little sleep and insufficient food were catching up with him and likely with others also. Until now they had been kept going by battle tension and the motivation brought by success, but now there was little left in the way of energy or strength. This day was far from done, but it was the third day of battle with all of its tension and strain. The men were spent and near to the end of their rope, and, being veteran soldiers by now, they knew the signs when they saw them.

Eventually the column shuffled into motion, heading east and moving past a wooded stretch on to one of these scratched clearings along the road. Up ahead a gaggle of horsemen caught the eye and then Lee was there again, having reined his horse in to one side of the road, on that scratched plot of cleared ground, deep in conversation with La Fayette McLaws. The officers of their staffs waited with them, though keeping just enough of that respectful distance that they always did, as their horses picked at the roadside and meadow grass. On the same patch of cleared ground ammunition wagons had been pulled in to the margins of the road and the men of the column were halted and ordered into a single file to replenish their supply as they passed. As the line shuffled slowly up there was a break in the wagon traffic and Daniel Ryan noticed on the far side of the road a column of Yankee prisoners being herded along past the waiting staffers moving on now nearly opposite to where the generals still conferred. The prisoners looked dirty and listless to Daniel Ryan, but he could see that, as Lee discussed whatever he wanted of McLaws, there was a ripple of growing interest along the length of the blue column. More and more of the Yankees were gaping at the general and along their line there were mutters and comments, some of which reached across to where the Ogeechee Volunteers' were awaiting their turn at the wagons.

"That's him!"

"That's Lee!"

"Him, the grey-beard one."

"It's him, right over there on the grey horse!" As Company B reached the ammunition wagon, Daniel became aware of the Yankees starting to move, while, at the wagons, the men took their packs of cartridges, filling their pouch up to the standard forty rounds again, with some, the usual ones, taking extra for their pockets. It was all a matter of the march, Daniel reflected, as his attention moved from the Yankees to the ammunition and he slung his musket on its strap as his turn approached. Nobody took on the slightest extra weight if they knew that a long or difficult hike was to come, but here, it was down the road, a few miles at most, and likely less than that. If the Yankees had gotten through the defence lines, on the ridges and hills behind Fredericksburg this morning, and were making their way promptly inland, god knew how close they might be by now. They would likely be in action in an hour or two, maybe even less, and extra cartridges would be valuable then. He reached the wagon and picked three brown paper packs from the half empty wooden box, then, on reflection he stretched out his hand for one extra bundle of ten shots before moving away, tearing the paper open as he went. He arranged the cartridges in the pouch at his right hip, dispersing the extra ones through his pockets, seeing others around him do the same as they moved away from the wagons and only then becoming aware that, out in the road, the Yankee prisoners were shuffling across the middle of the road. Daniel noticed the movement and that of the small detail of men who made up their escort, who had turned to face their charges. Still the Yankees edged forward, upon which the escorting soldiers started pushing at them with their muskets held horizontally to bar their way and restrain this surge towards the general. Over by the wagons Boyce had seen what was happening.

"First Sergeant," he yelled to Jeffers, and, gaining his attention, he gestured towards the advancing Yankees.

"Lend a hand, if you please." Jeffers took in the situation with a glance and immediately bellowed the company file leaving the wagon to order, right facing them into line almost in the same breath, with his own shouts now being taken up by the other sergeants. The next order brought each man's musket to the ported position across his body, as they faced ahead, weapons at the ready to help control, this threatening movement of the Yankee prisoners towards the general. The line began to move out into the road but already the Yankees had halted and were forming themselves into a double rank. A grey-haired sergeant shouted and they came to attention and, at a further shouted order, they removed their little kepi caps, uncovering as a mark of respect to the general, while officers and NCOs present saluted. On the little cleared patch beyond the wagons Lee had heard and seen the commotion and now he turned his horse towards where the Yankees stood in their ranks. He looked along the line formed by his enemies, here offering an almost unprecedented gesture of respect. Then the general turned Traveller's head and, as the grey horse wheeled parallel to the rank of Yankees, Lee too uncovered, slowly raising his hat to bring it down to his side in his right hand, in that familiar way of his, while he lowered his head, returning the respect. That gesture exposed the curiously pale-coloured top part of his forehead, uncoloured by the sun, that very feature that Daniel Ryan recognised from when he had first noticed it, on Tybee Island in Georgia, during the first winter of the war.

All around the general the men broke into a prolonged cheer and with that the Yankees began to cheer also. Lee replaced his hat and turned his horse away again, as the cheering of both formations followed him as he moved off, with his staff taking their places behind him. The moment now past, the men of the "Blues," shouldered their weapons and turned to make their way back across the road, assembling there again as a further train of wagons trundled up to separate them from the Yankee column. More shouted orders came from Jeffers and the company files formed once more and then, after a brief reorganising by the sergeants, they were back on their way. It was incredible, Daniel Ryan thought, as he moved off in his place, to see men of both armies cheering and saluting the general. Yet again, he reflected, there were times when there was simply no understanding this damned war.

Behind them the noise of the battle went on, with the artillery down to the south of the road still laying down a renewed bombardment into the forests up towards the river. But the Ogeechee Volunteer Rifles, and the other regiments of William Wofford's brigade, had turned their backs on all of that, tramping steadily away now until it was lost behind them, obscured by the trees, the bends in the road and the contours of the ground. They looked ahead now, along the road to Fredericksburg, where the next threat had arisen. On this stretch of the turnpike to the east of Chancellorsville, where the tree line was briefly back from the road, the surface was drier and just about beginning, in spite of its covering of small stones, to produce a dust cloud. On the men marched as the eddies of dust rose, with the talk in the ranks, as a consequence of the many dry and parched throats, now dying away. Up ahead was another battle. The Yankees were out there, just a few miles down the road. Disregarding thirst and hunger, their weariness, their aching shoulders and feet and the multitude of bruises, small wounds and scratches from the woods, the Ogeechee Volunteers were on their way to meet them. Above their heads, the sun, just a little way past its zenith now, would be starting, almost imperceptibly, to lower in the sky behind them, though, so far, the only sign of this was the casting of the beginnings of a shadow ahead of each of the shuffling men.

Chapter 14 Salem Church

It was reckoned to be around ten miles, or perhaps a measure more than that, from the crossroads at Chancellorsville to Fredericksburg, though pretty well all of the men of Wofford's brigade were aware that if the Yankees had used the hours following their attack near the river, they would likely by now be a good way closer than that. The afternoon was hot now, even though the first portion of the march to meet them was through the eastern stretch of the wilderness where the road was to some extent shaded and the air somewhat cooled by the trees, which bordered or in places even overhung it. Even from here, as the column of march made its labouring way east, ominous, tell tale signs of smoke could be seen in the blue sky up ahead, clearly visible any time that the claustrophobic forests thinned or broke to allow one of those restricted roadside clearings to claim a brief stretch of the ground.

When they finally debouched from the trees the smoke was clearer still, a lazy curtain of off-white, that slowly rose and drifted above the more distant trees, as though to mark their destination. With the Chancellorsville struggle now some distance behind them, they pushed on along the Turnpike, grimly acknowledging this visible invitation to the next fight. They reached the old wooden church to be halted, just short of where Anderson's men had dug entrenchments, on either side of the road less than three days before, only it seemed like an eternity now. The talk in the ranks increased as the men waited, draining whatever remnants remained in their canteens and recovering their breath. Would they be attempting to hold these lines or would they be pushed on to try to intercept the enemy as close to the river as they could reach? There was a delay before the question was answered, but that answer came with the stalled brigades resuming their progress eastwards towards Fredericksburg in the hottest part of the day. The trials of hot weather marching, dripping sweat, the rising of a dust cloud around the column, thankfully absent since the retreat from Maryland last year, to hamper the breath and sting the eyes, now began to renew their acquaintance with the men along the labouring column and all to the endless metallic clinking of empty canteens on bayonet sockets and haversack buckles.

Talk persisted after the restart of the march. Stories spread along the column as they continued eastwards. Brigadier General Cadmus Wilcox and his Alabama boys were attempting to hold the Yankees at the Turnpike Toll Gate, not far from Fredericksburg, and the rumbling of artillery, slowly drawing closer, seemed to give a measure of support to that suggestion. If it was true, the fight would take place there, a couple of priceless miles farther away from the rear of the main army, provided they could get there in time before the defenders' line was breached, so the forced march went on in the heat and dust. It was, by best guess, maybe six miles from Chancellorsville to the Toll Gate, not a long hike, by any means, for men who had left their footprints all over northern Virginia and western Maryland, through the previous year, but those men were out of shape now, after a long winter of short rations and little in the way of longer marches any place. Six miles was not so far and the heat and dust had by no means reached the high summer levels, but, after days of fighting and enduring, with little in the way of rest, to the men in the labouring files, a six mile hike was hard enough while it lasted.

As they tramped through the less wooded country between the river and the Wilderness forests, the gazes of most were fixed along the Turnpike to the east and on that drifting smoke. The cloud was clearer now, straddling the road, and the sound of firing up ahead was louder, having steadily imposed itself over the noises of the battle that they had left behind in the forest, rising into the two distinct sounds, the heavy thudding crump of artillery and the higher-pitched, more staccato rattle of musketry. Barksdale's men, and some of Jubal Early's boys, left behind to hold the line at Fredericksburg, with some guns in support, must be up there along the Plank Road also, maybe still trying, with Wilcox, to halt or slow the advance of whatever force of Yankees had breached the Rappahannock line. The hoarse talk fluttered up and down the files, but everyone reckoned that, if what they had heard about the enemy numbers were true, those boys, unless help could get there in time, would be overwhelmed, just as soon as the Yankees got all of their men on line and made a good solid push. If that happened, the whole Confederate rear would be open to their attack, nullifying all of their hard fighting back there in the forests. The column marched on, passing the junction of the Plank Road and the Turnpike, with the gunfire now close, maybe less than a mile distant. It was closer than the Toll Gate, the smoke and the struggle seemed to centre now on the next low ridge line, where the squat, orange-brick shape of yet another of these Virginia country churches lay.

It was later afternoon and the sun was sinking lower in the sky when the long, ragged lines of Company B came up towards where the side road lay. That road led south east, to join the Telegraph Road from Fredericksburg and the men could see the files up ahead of them being directed off there to the south, even as the firing on the ridge beyond continued. The tired men pushed on, seeing the successive formations up ahead moving off the Plank Road as they closed on the turnoff. They could see officers there, a couple of them on horseback, with a provost detail, directing the files southwards and, on reaching the intersection, the Company files followed off in their turn. They were hurried on down the dirt road for maybe half a mile or more before being halted and moved from files into line of battle and with almost no pause were directed to the left, eastwards from the dirt road to push up a thickly overgrown bank, which led on into a further belt of woods. A picket detail moved off into the trees, brown shapes that flickered briefly among the rays of the descending sun, where it penetrated the incomplete tree cover, as they moved away, gradually merging completely with their surroundings and vanishing from sight.

The main lines were halted and reformed at the top of the bank and manoeuvred into position there. The order came along to load, but not to prime and the first cartridges were bitten, poured and rammed home, before ramrods were replaced in their channels with a series of metallic clatters and clangs. Bayonets were then fixed, with more scrapes and clicks, before the order to step off came and the ranks again lurched away into the trees. The firing was now well to their left and, as the men were halted once more, the sounds of battle up there intensified, growing into heavier volleys of musketry augmented by the renewed, thudding discharges of cannon. More orders came along and the ranks pushed off again, through a further stretch of woods before yet another order came along the line halting them again to redress and re-order ranks, but, this done, no additional orders came. The men were simply left in their ranks to await whatever came to pass. In spite of the growing bedlam up towards the turnpike, comparative calm reigned down here and the nervous wait went on. There was nothing for the sweating, idle men to do now but gaze anxiously up through the trees towards the invisible battle to the north and speculate on how the fighting was going up there, while wondering when their own turn would come. Daniel Ryan stood in his customary place in the front rank, glad of the chance to pause and recover, feeling his clothing sticking to his limbs as the sweat still trickled down his body and legs. Out in front there was only the forest, its trees flanked and festooned with undergrowth, well able to mask or conceal the approach of an enemy, but there was no sign or word from their pickets and the woods around the ranks of Company B, and the others on either side of them remained silent, in utter contrast to the fight being waged up to their left around the Plank Road.

Then more shouted orders were heard coming along the line, ordering a further advance and the line lurched forward again, guiding on its left, to commence their latest ordeal in this further belt of tangled forest. More thorns and brambles, branches and creepers were negotiated and a marsh was crossed before a tree and brush-covered mound was encountered, and this was negotiated with further difficulty. Having arrived at its top, the men now gazed ahead into another expanse of wooded ground. Up to the left, the firing had reached something of a climax, with eddies of smoke from the fight they were having up there, coming drifting down in wisps through the trees. But of the Yankees there was no sign and the men waited, some now with growing impatience, to come to grips. There was almost nothing worse, Daniel Ryan found himself thinking, than when a man knew that battle was almost here, and was struggling to control the knot in his stomach and the pounding heartbeat in his chest and throat, to find this kind of delay, when, if the fight was not to be avoided, all he wanted to do was get into it and get it done with.

Further pickets were ordered forward to strengthen the skirmish line up ahead and Daniel Ryan's section was among those who were set off on this duty, skirting around trees and bushes and pushing through the scrub, in open order. They crossed another boggy stretch and moved on until they came up to the skirmish line, brown shapes crouching among the bushes, taking advantage of little contours in the ground to conceal and protect themselves, but they too had nothing but a quiet stretch of forest to look out upon. To one side the figure of Dellings half rose to point with both arms indicating to the arriving men to deploy. They spaced themselves out along the line that they had reached, seeking their own cover to settle behind and regain their breath, as they looked out into the shaded green expanse, seeking an early sight of any enemy, but out there in the woods there was still nothing.

They waited, while, up to the left, the gunfire now slackened, but it did not entirely cease. Instead the firing began to subside seeming to move slowly eastwards, though it was hard to tell in the echoing woods, where exactly any sound was coming from. The firing continued, though with only an occasional shell now screeching over to explode somewhere up among the trees, but still the woods in front remained quiet, with no sign of any movement. Day was ebbing into dusk, and the shadows out in front were deepening, different boys began to voice the view that maybe, just maybe, that was the last of the day and there would be no fight for them. Around them the dusk grew with darkness edging closer and, to the rear along the main battle line, the officers seemed to have come to the same sort of conclusion, as word now came up for the original skirmish line to pull back with half of the remaining picket also moving back to set up a post to the rear.

Still those remaining waited, now in almost complete darkness with nothing but the sights and sounds of the wood to occupy their eyes and ears. In full darkness a further picket, this time with Bayfield in charge, came up behind them and the men just relieved groped silently back to find the post where Thompson waited. Once assembled they moved back through the woods and across the boggier ground, helped a little by a rising moon, to find that the main line had withdrawn also to the side road that they had left earlier. The returning pickets negotiated their way back down the slope to the roadside, in the blackness of the night, though here the moonlight gave more visibility along the road, helping in some measure the negotiating of the final overhanging branches and tearing thorns and brambles.

They emerged onto the road, to find the remainder of the regiment already bivoucked there, and they moved along seeking out spaces to bivouac, slowly collecting into their groups and settling along the roadside in the fringe of the woods. Most of them immediately began opening out blankets, since the order had been given for no fires and the spring night was already growing cold. Thompson came past them.

"Third watch," he said, "somebody'll call ya. It sure as hell won't be me." A couple of almost invisible nods from those in the group acknowledged his words as the tension of battle slowly relaxed, with pounding heart rates easing and throats loosening. Captured hardtacks appeared from haversacks and men broke off fragments and chewed at them, waiting for their saliva to begin to soften them. Around Daniel low murmurs of talk were circulating, about the hundred and one other things that soldiers find to comment or complain about. The men they had seen fall today, about Jackson, about the prospects for tomorrow, about how damned tired and hungry they were. But that talk did not last, for exhaustion was high on the list of things to concern themselves with and, within a few more minutes, almost all of those along the roadside were asleep.

It was still dark when Daniel Ryan was shaken awake, though he was immediately aware of the moonlight which shed a silver grey pallor on the trees and bushes nearest to him. It was Ballard's voice that came to him.

"Yore turn to keep the soldier boys safe," he muttered. Daniel grunted and rolled out of his blanket to rise to his knees. In truth, he thought, he felt no less tired than he had when he had lain down. He climbed to his feet, almost automatically beginning to roll the blankets, before leaving the roll in the care of Winder and Hale. There was a sour taste in his mouth and he spat as he moved to collect his musket from the stack, before making his way, with the others, to the foot of the wooded bank, joining John Fitzpatrick there, as the detail began to push their way through the trees and bushes up the slope, getting a further collection of scratches and abrasions in the eerie moonlit gloom as they negotiated their way. A distant shot rang out, then another, but closer this time and they tensed as they continued to climb. Near the top, as the ground levelled, the men slowed, coming stealthily towards the crest. They paused there to accustom their eyes before moving on through the trees, negotiating the rises, descents and marshes to come eventually to where the off-duty pickets squatted. Dellings was there and he directed them forward in their pairs.

"Advance line's where they wuz at sundown," he growled. "The word is that the Yankees have pulled back a ways. The squirrel hunters are goin' out there to check on that. In the meantime you git yourselves set up there." The group separated and the first watch moved away. Having negotiated the creek in the darkness, Daniel crept forward at a crouch, sighting at last a hunched shape in front of him, he moved on up, seeing the man glance around as he approached. He tapped the looming shape in front on the shoulder as he arrived.

"Sleep well," he whispered.

"You bet," came Bryant's return whisper as he shifted to the rear for Daniel to take his place.

It could only have been minutes after he had settled himself, when there was a further movement behind him. He turned his head as a group of shadowy figures came up, pausing momentarily with the forward pickets. Daniel heard Silas Norton's whisper as he crouched briefly beside him.

"They ain't comin' on so we got the job o' scoutin' 'em."

"Don't let them scout you any," Daniel returned as Norton moved away, treading almost noiselessly on to join, with his companions, picking their way through the trees and merging immediately into the darkness and the traces of ground mist that had begun to form as morning approached. Daniel watched them disappear knowing that, as well as Norton, Gifford, Peters, Cooper and Bentley would be out there also. These were the remaining "squirrel hunters," some of the out and out country boys of the company. More than most, they were skilled and experienced, most of them since boyhood, in hunting and tracking and therefore they got most of the duties like this when the company had to organise its own reconnaissance. They could voice their reluctance, or even resentment at getting these kinds of jobs to do, but Daniel reckoned they also enjoyed the grudging respect from the others of the company that came with the role.

For a time he watched, looking intently towards where they had vanished, while all around the mist thickened and extended. Further shots rang out, distant this time, but on this line, all remained quiet. Daniel was later relieved by John Fitzpatrick and he moved carefully back to the picket post in the trees, where the group of off-duty men squatted or lounged. As they waited, with quiet talk going around, another shot rang out, this time closer than before. One or two of them looked as two more shots came.

"Trouble for somebody," Daley said, while around him the others continued to lounge, though some looked towards their weapons, but, when no more shots came, the incident passed and the low conversations turned to other matters.

Daniel was on his second spell on watch on the line when the, "Squirrel Hunters," returned. There was a movement in the mist. A suggestion of a dim shape and he heard Ballard, just along from him call out.

"Who goes?" There was a pause and then the reply.

"Scouts,...... five o' us, you still awake Otis?" He heard a gentle curse from Ballard.

"Come ahead scouts," he called. "That ain't all o' 'em," he muttered along to Daniel Ryan." There was a pause before the shapes appeared, gaining form as they advanced to pass through the picket and move on into the trees. A few yards away Daley grunted.

"They ain't all back." From those around him there was no reply.

On the approach of daylight further men were pushed into the picket line, silently taking their places at the top of the gentle slope. There were gaps in the tree canopy there and they were able to see snatches of the eastern sky as it lightened up ahead, until eventually the first shafts of yellow sunlight came peeping through the trees, penetrating the haze of morning mist that hung around the forest. The mist slowly dispersed as the trees down the slope hardened from a dark mass into distinct shapes. Full daylight had arrived and with no sign of enemy activity, the picket was relieved and the withdrawing men were dismissed to return to the main position along the road for, "breakfast," though, with no ration, "breakfast," meant resorting to whatever captured Yankee hardtacks remained, or sitting around the road at the bottom of the bank, complaining on an empty stomach. The captured salt pork remained in Daniel Ryan's haversack awaiting the chance to cook. What was worse was the empty water canteens, but the men complained about these in vain as no water details were called.

As they waited there word spread through the company that Peters was the missing scout, though whether he was dead or taken nobody knew. The patrol had established that the Yankees had gone from out in front, pulled back to a line nearer to the Plank Road. On hearing this, and with no sign of any movement by the regiment or brigade, some of the off-duty men began to head off, seeking out fallen Yankees among the trees to forage for their needs and a water detail left with Kane, Philipps and Daley among them. As for Peters, his fate was simply a further piece of proof of the additional hazards that scouting the enemy, especially at night, brought for a man.

The Monday morning passed slowly with only picket firing, well out in front, and still no word of an advance nor of any enemy move. The water detail returned with canteens full of brackish water to distribute, which mollified the men a little. Rumours, the army's staple diet, abounded, that the Yankees were skedaddling back across the river, or that they had retreated into a fortified position around one of the fords to the north. Another said an attack was being planned to push the enemy into the river and that Longstreet was approaching, with their two absent divisions, to take command of the attack.

Noon came and the sky began to cloud, while more rumours went around. Lee was said to have been seen, again in discussion with McLaws, and the brigade commanders. The talk went on around, but little happened to disturb the men, or the peace of the spring day. From off to the west also, back there in the forests, the distant firing was audible though desultory, contrasting with the headlong battle of yesterday. It was as though both armies, wearied and spent by their efforts of the previous three days, had paused to draw breath and ponder their further moves. Daniel Ryan spent a further watch doing further pondering, when his section spent several hours on the picket line as afternoon came, but the picture there was unchanged, with an empty forest facing the arrivals as they took their places in the line. Relief came in the early evening and the men made their way back to the road, to rest there and await further orders or news.

All through the afternoon more clouds had moved across the sky as the stories of a coming attack hardened from rumour into solid expectation. Further troops were arriving, crossing from the turnpike to the rear of the "Blues," positions to come into line to their right. There was much coming and going of messengers and staff officers, some of them little more than boys trying to look the part of men with the fuzz of inadequate moustaches or beards on their pink faces. They got the customary sarcastic treatment from the enlisted men as they spurred past the waiting formations along the road.

"Helluva hurry yo're in boy."

"Yore dinner waitin' fer ya? We ain't had no dinner in days."

"Thar's a mouse climbin' up yore nose sonny."

"Come outa that thar coat and talk to us boy."

The comments came, together with the chuckles and chortles of the tired but irrepressible men, but only as the daylight began to fade, under a sky that was now overcast, were they finally called to assemble. Jeffers appeared to silence the talk and summon the men into line.

"Soon now, ya lucky boys," he called. "so git yoreselves ready. Listen fer three cannon shots," he added. "That's the signal fer the step off."

Blankets and haversacks were piled to await the company wagon and the battle line was formed shortly after, facing the now familiar wooded bank. More time passed and the men heard the sound of heavy firing break out, up ahead to the east, as still they waited. The order to load but not prime came along and the biting, pouring and ramming went on before the ranks settled once more. The further wait was brief, for at last the heavier reports of cannon came to them, three discharges in regular rhythmic thuds. Above them the rain began and faces turned upwards as they heard the pattering on the nearby leaves and felt the first spots and spatters on their clothing and skin. The long ranks braced themselves, gripping their weapons more tightly, with a few of them exchanging a glance with particular friends. The order finally came to move off and the push forward into the trees and up the roadside slope began again. Daniel stuffed his hat into his tunic for the umpteenth time this week and pulled his tunic cuffs down across the lower half of his hands, gripping the edges of the fabric with his fingers as he held his musket out in front of his body to deflect the worst of the thorns and branches, feeling them begin to scrape and scratch across his covered hands, as he pushed on up the bank.

After a brief struggle the line emerged at the top, halting there to reform. The order was called along to fix bayonets and the long blades were drawn from their scabbards, the sockets were fitted over the barrel muzzles and clicked that quarter turn to the right for the locking rings to be twisted into place. Then at last the line stepped off again, moving through the trees to the brief stretch of clearing, where the marsh was negotiated with some difficulty by the solid ranks of men. They came up to the picket positions, finding them deserted and without pausing pressed on through the woods. A further halt at the edge of the next tree belt saw the ranks reformed once more before they stepped away again into the dimmer light of the denser woods, where an occasional corpse from yesterday's fight still lay, swelling and blackening now in the last of the day's spring warmth as the rain pattered down on the forest and the advancing men.

Down through the trees the line pushed, smelling the wet woodland smells from the rain shower, which continued wetting them even in the trees and only now beginning to slacken. The line now came to a small ravine, lined with fewer trees, but thicker scrub, which threw the ranks of struggling men into disorder again as they thrashed through, with still no sign of the enemy, finally emerging at the far edge with the daylight fading into overcast dusk. Still the sounds of battle came from farther up to their right, but there were only fleeting views of drifting distant smoke above the trees to indicate where the enemy had actually been found. The shouts came, to halt and order the lines once again before the advance was resumed and the sergeants moved along with their usual collection of badgering and profanity as this was done.

A mist was beginning to rise from the ground, Daniel

Ryan felt its coolness around his legs, as the ranks moved on in what must be the direction of the road. His heart still thudded, as it always did at these times, and the sweat still ran down his face and among his fingers, mixing with the wetness from the rain, as he gripped his musket and tunic cuffs tightly. Ahead there was the dim rim of another gully to cross and, as the line descended into it, there came a scattering of musketry, closer than the more distant fire, that still had not slackened, but a sign that maybe their own skirmishers had finally found the Yankees. More glances were exchanged as the line pushed ahead through more tearing, scratching growth, struggling to preserve any sort of order, as they negotiated the gully before halting once again, to form and dress their ranks once more. The advance was resumed, but, out ahead the shooting had died away with no sign of their own skirmish line or of the enemy.

They reached the Plank Road, near its junction with yet another side road that led off to the north towards the river. Surely, one or two muttering comments suggested, if the Yankees were guiding on, or following along, that road, they must be headed for the fords to skedaddle back over the Rappahannock, so they would likely see neither hide nor hair of the blue bellies as a result. That, Daniel Ryan thought, might still be too much to hope for. Halted to reform once again at the road, they were pushed on to negotiate another stretch of broken ground before plunging into still more woods. Here the mist was thicker and now the darkness was almost complete. Trees now loomed around them as expanses of dark shadow, with their form and any sense of space or distance lost in the gathering gloom, making their outstretched branches progressively more difficult to negotiate or avoid. The firing up ahead commenced again intensifying as they struggled on. They could smell eddies of invisible smoke that drifted back through the trees, but still they had made no direct contact with whatever fight was going on in those dark woods up ahead.

"They're pullin' back," Jones muttered. "They're headin' back over." Around them there were now more muttered comments, some of which betrayed the wearied men's relief that the Yankees had not stood and made a real fight of it.

"They ain't waitin' around fer us."

"They're headin' for the river."

"It's another skedaddle right enough boys." Daniel Ryan stayed silent, recognising the hopeful optimism of tired men in much of the talk, but earnestly hoping, in his own heart, that the sentiments might indeed be true.

The combination of mist, smoke and darkness was thicker still as they suddenly came up to the skirmish line and, almost as though to frustrate the notion that there might be no real fight this time, the call came along to prime their weapons. Daniel pulled his musket hammer to half cock and fingered a cap onto the metal nipple as the line came to a halt. A ragged volley of fire came from ahead, the flash vivid and dazzling in the gloom. The minie bullets whizzed and whirred their way past, or embedded themselves in tree trunks along the line, with dull splintering thuds. Hardly anyone around Daniel Ryan seemed to be hit, though twigs and debris from the trees scattered down, unseen but felt as they cascaded onto the preparing men.

"To the ready!" Jeffers yelled and the muskets were pulled across.

"Aim!" Jeffers bellow came again, with his shout quickly echoed by Thompson, Dellings and Bayfield.

"Aim low boys," the shout came from Carson.

"Fire!" The muskets recoiled into the men's long-suffering shoulders, as the deafening crash of the discharge engulfed them, with the sound amplified in the woods. Daniel was aware of the trees around him briefly illuminated by the flash of the volley, as though to emphasise the darkness, as the smoke billowed around them.

"Reload!" Already the musket butts were down on the ground and men were biting at fresh cartridges, then pouring and pushing before the ramrods appeared to clang and clatter on the barrels. It all took maybe twenty or so seconds and, watching the men ahead of him intently, Jeffers bellowed again.

"Aim!" The long barrels came up to point ahead at nothing that the men could actually see.

"Fire!" Again the ear-numbing sound of the volley thundered out, with bruised shoulders cringing, before the whole loading process began again. A third volley was discharged, but, with no further reply from the enemy, more orders came relaying along.

"Reload, to the ready!" The ramrods clanged in the darkness and, at a further shouted order, the men of the skirmish line moved away again. After a brief pause, the main line jerked into motion also, following on into the gloom of darkness, mist and drifting smoke. They moved on over undulating ground, clearing one belt of trees at last, only to move up to another. The order came to halt and all along the woods and fields they could hear the firing subside. The men waited, peering into the woods just ahead of where they stood, while officers puzzled on what to do or where to go in the almost complete gloom, with not even a moon to aid them in distinguishing anything of their surroundings.

"Reckon we could march around here in circles, all night," Daley growled.

"If the Yankees kin move we kin follow," Thompson grunted from his place behind the ranks.

"They'll be dug in at the river by now," Kane speculated.

"Or skedaddled over a'ready," Jones added.

They waited and gradually the heart rates slowed as the immediate tension eased. But hardly had the strain of the brief fight diminished, when a courier came up behind the ranks seeking Preston and the word quickly moved among the men.

"They're movin' us on agin."

"Ginral wants a night attack."

"They're sendin' us on ahead." Some of the boys were skeptical. The scope for confusion and disaster in such a move was almost endless and men died for no good reason. Even as these mutters went up and down, artillery opened up again sending shells, with their fuses, glowing orange in the darkness, tearing overhead towards the river where the Yankees should be. The fire intensified, with more and more guns joining in, and then the ranks of infantry were ordered forward again, up to the tree line, to push on into the even deeper gloom.

It was chaos from the start. Men tripped over roots and bumped into trees and each other, cursing as they sustained still more cuts, scrapes and scratches from the whipping, unseen branches and straggling thorns. Ahead of them they were aware of rustles, movements and occasional squawks also came to their ears, the cries of night creatures, disturbed from their food search, scampering away from these blundering ranks of trespassers. Over to the right, the musketry began again, illuminating the place by distant flashes through the trees. Then more firing, but closer this time, with the faces of the men around Daniel suddenly shown up for an instant in the flashes of yellow light. All eyes looked to where the shooting had erupted, as a ripple of expectation of imminent combat surged along the ranks, but out in front, there was still no word from the skirmish line as the formation continued to struggle forward through the tearing, scratching darkness. Eventually the order was relayed along to halt and the men shuffled to a standstill, to begin rubbing at barked and torn skin and examine minor wounds and injuries, gained through their ill-fated advance. After a wait of some minutes, word came back from the skirmishers, who had reached open ground. The ranks were moved on again to come at last, after further trials and tribulations, to the edge of the trees. On all sides the firing had died down, save for the artillery, which continued to thunder, sending shells, towards the river to the north, somewhere off to the left front of where the, "Blues," line had halted. They waited, leaning on weapons, with a few even dozing fitfully on their feet, while the guns thundered on, to only slowly ease and then cease their firing, finally allowing an uneasy stillness to settle over the mist-covered fields and woods. The exhausted men were finally stood down, settling onto the wet ground immediately to fall sleep on their arms, while all around them, the natural sounds of the night slowly re-asserted themselves.

Daylight came, bringing with it a grey, cloudy sky, which obscured the rising of the sun. The cold and stiff sleepers were roused and the battle line was promptly reformed and pushed forward once more, but there was no sign of the enemy.

"They're gone."

"They'll be across by now." The comments began to trickle along the ranks as the line was halted again, this time for patrols to be detailed to scout further ahead, beyond the picket line, to locate and mark the enemy, if they still remained on this side of the river. Daniel Ryan's mess made up the bulk of one such group and they pushed warily away in skirmish order, seeking either the Yankees or the river. Of the Yankees there was no sign and as the loose formation pushed forward closer and closer to the river it gradually became apparent that the enemy divisions had indeed re-crossed at the ford to make good their escape.

The Rappahannock finally came into view, evident more through an absence of further trees up ahead, than through any sighting of the water itself. Thompson sent Fitzpatrick and Daley back to report, while the others of the patrol pushed up to the edge of the trees to peer across the river, here maybe fifty yards across, but taking care not to show themselves to any Yankee skirmishers, who might remain to snipe at the unwary. Distant gunfire began to rumble out to the west, forcibly reminding everyone that there were still all those other Yankees, over in the Wilderness, to occupy them, even if this crowd had skulked away across the Rappahannock to safety.

Their halt at the river was brief as Daley returned, bringing orders for the party to withdraw and rejoin. They wasted little time, leaving the riverbank and heading south, pushing back through further tree thickets, Daniel Ryan feeling as though every muscle in his body ached and almost every inch of his skin was grazed, scratched or bruised. They came upon a picket line and moved on to reach the main line and resume their places with the remainder of the company. Almost immediately they were ordered back, retracing their steps south onto the River Road to form their files and march at once, on to its junction with the Plank Road, from there turning west once more. It was back to where they had been before, while, above their heads, the clouds lowered and dark thunderheads of cloud steadily formed. The long columns of exhausted men shuffled on their way, many of them almost drowsing as they headed, back towards the Wilderness, where the rumbling of cannon continued and still more gun smoke rose into the sky above the trees, lighter against the now ominous clouds, showing that the Yankees up there were still on this side of the river, having been held in check there for the last two days by the remainder of the army.

The rain began as the column moved off the Turnpike, taking another of the river roads to the north to halt there as it grew quickly heavier, soaking the jaded, weary men within minutes and turning the road surface beneath their feet progressively to liquid mud. The column was promptly ordered into motion again, along the road again, on through the now soaking woods and clearings, as the rumble of artillery persisted in the forests. The rain slanted down, and with the wind rising also, the advance became a sodden mud-spattered trial for the troops. The files were directed on to the north to finally deploy and plough through the soaking forest. The trees around them dripped and spilled still more rain water as they weaved and swayed in the freshening wind and men pushed past their saturated boughs now almost oblivious to the further cascades onto already soaked clothing.

A halt was eventually called and the men were stood down to settle in their positions, while still the distant guns carried on their sullen exchanges. Word of another attack circulated, but no orders came and what was left of the afternoon and evening were spent trying to minimise the trials of the storm, with a further order for no fires adding to the discomfort and ill-humour of the soaking men. Daniel Ryan and his mess took a saturated turn on the picket line as the light faded, but there was no activity of any kind to be seen and the duty was simply a soaked and miserable sojourn in ground that was now a swamp. They returned during the night as still the wind and rain tormented the bivouacs. Nothing more had been heard of any attack and even the cannon fire had died away, leaving the men all along the line to the task of weathering the storm without blankets of either kind. By now, the previously dry forest floors were crisscrossed with rivulets and streams of water, with the whole area turned into a dripping streaming expanse where bedraggled, shivering men crouched under makeshift shelters, or simply in huddled groups for some kind of warmth and relief from the downpour.

Though, through the whole day, he had eaten only a hardtack, chewed in the early morning, Daniel Ryan now suffered such a dog-tired weariness that he felt that his body and mind could not possibly resist sleep no matter what discomforts there were. He settled himself in the midst of the huddling mess group for what warmth was possible, as the wind blew unabated and the rain lashed down, till with water running from his clothing, he dozed into a fitful sleep.

Epilogue

A dismal, dank morning of grey mist and cold wind had come and though the rain had slackened, it had not ceased. Men began to stir, struggling to their feet with their awkward and ungainly movements telling their story of numb bodies, chilled limbs and the continuing effects of bruised muscles. They moved slowly around the muddy bivouacs to ease their stiff and cold bodies, slapping hands on sides, swinging arms and pacing this way and that to restore circulation and generate a little warmth. Rumours were already beginning to arrive, that these Yankees also had taken advantage of the night, and its abominable weather, to withdraw. More patrols had been sent out from the forward picket lines towards the previous enemy positions to reconnoitre. Fires were now permitted, as though to confirm the departure of any immediate prospect of a further fight, though with nothing in the way of dry kindling or fuel, few resulted, and those that did were weak smouldering affairs that drifted disproportionate clouds of weaving smoke around beneath the tree canopy compared to any heat they generated, until, at last, the rain stopped.

As the light grew, the men huddled in their groups,

trying to dry themselves around those few miserable fires, but the advancing morning saw them doing little but await orders, with nothing, in the way of any movements being confirmed. Instead, they were left to what was, with whatever Yankee plunder that still remained marooned in their absent haversacks, a non-existent breakfast. Saul Philipps, at Thompson's bidding finally departed for the surgeon to get his arm wound treated and the morning passed with no sign of him returning.

Stories persisted, that the Yankees had indeed gone and the day, until orders came, was being given over to the drying out of clothing and belongings, with the prolonged inactivity certainly seeming to support this particular rumour. Many men wanted little but rest, being prepared to settle in the mud, among the sodden undergrowth, in their filthy and still saturated clothing, as though it was the best of feather beds to fall promptly asleep once more. As the morning drew on a pale sun came out, shining its light through the trees to send little rays of illumination onto the now steaming forest floor. Tunics were hung over branches by those who were still awake, but still no orders came, only eventual confirmation from Jeffers that the battle was over and the enemy were now back on the far side of the river. The day stretched on towards noon, with the drying and even some cleaning well under way, but still there was neither sign nor word of any sort of food issue.

The men were finally assembled again in the early afternoon, with most of them still wet, to collect their weapons and pull back to the road, where the mud remained thick. They formed into marching order along the edge of the trees and began to slosh their way south east, back towards the Turnpike, only to suffer a period of further delay at the junction, where heavy columns of men and vehicles, already on the road, made their way back towards

Fredericksburg. Eventually, the brigade was fed into this traffic and plodded wearily off through the ankle deep mud. A couple of miles along the Turnpike they came up with the regimental wagons and were dismissed to gather around the vehicle, recovering their haversacks and blankets before reforming files and continuing on their way.

It was evening when they arrived back at their Fredericksburg camps, to find them ransacked and pilfered. The exhausted men cursed awhile and then shrugged and set to resuming the process of drying. No rations arrived, but fuel was gathered, fires were kindled and the captured Yankee pork was finally cooked with the remains of the hardtacks, bringing a degree of comfort and sustenance at last to boys who had spent almost the whole of the previous thirty six hours hungry, soaked and chilled. A picket watch was detailed to head down towards the railroad, in sight of the river, while the remainder of the camp settled to sleep some more, dry and warm at last, with fires stoked up and feet pointing towards their priceless heat. In the darkness, the men of Ryan's mess were aroused to take their turn of picket duty once more, tramping along the well worn tracks in the moonlight to spend a weary four hour duty overlooking the river, before retracing their steps back to the camps as the first signs of the new day began to form off to the east. Rations finally arrived that Wednesday, a three day half ration issue of bacon and flour, with some onions and some coffee substitute for good measure. The camps set to banking up the fires, followed by preparing and cooking and by evening, scarcely a morsel remained, even in Daniel Ryan's haversack.

The rotas of duty in the line and camp chores re-established themselves and, over the following days, the familiar routines of army life gradually began to dull the nightmarish images of the struggle in the forest thickets. Tender shoulders began to ease and the cuts and scratches slowly healed. Losses in the brigade had been heavy, but conversely, Company B had escaped the worst of these. All around the camps there was a mixture of sentiments, similar, to Daniel Ryan's thinking, to those that had followed Malvern Hill the previous summer. There was a measure of pride at the army's achievements, especially after the first newspapers with reports of the battle began to arrive. The army had been hugely outnumbered, yet it had prevailed and the Yankees, for all of their pre-campaign bluster, had been forced back across the river. The triumph had been a significant one, except for the losses, visible in the spaces around the various mess fires, where familiar faces now no longer appeared, but going all the way up, through the command chain also, to Jackson's wounding. The general had been taken south to a house at the same Guiney Station on the railroad, familiar to those of the foraging detail of the winter, to recover from his injuries, but now there were new rumours circulating, that he had contracted pneumonia.

"Old Pete," Longstreet had returned at the end of the week with his other two divisions, though they were stationed inland from the river, in camps around Orange Courthouse, where there was some reasonable prospect of feeding and supplying them. Rations along the Rappahannock line also began to improve, thanks, it was said to the foraging that those two divisions had done in the southern counties of the state, which had sent considerable wagon convoys and trains into the depots with additional supplies of food. Some of this was now beginning to find its way through along the ill-managed Richmond and Fredericksburg railroad, and up the drying roads, to the hungry men on the river lines.

The death of "Stonewall," Jackson's was reported to the army the week after the battle had ended. The first rumours were circulating on the Sunday evening and these were confirmed the following day. To the men of Longstreet's corps, this event was regrettable but many of them made little more of it than that. Jackson, as well as being something of a, "boogy man," to many of the Yankees, had been seen as a rather severe and distant figure in much of the army, with more eccentricities than a convention of preachers. He had sustained feuds and disputes with a collection of other generals and had the reputation of being hard on his men. The war had brought so many deaths and, to some at least, the general was just the latest of the collection of valuable officers who had died over the last year, and the whole legion of good men who had gone also. But, almost surprisingly, the feelings among many of Jackson's own men, as it emerged over the succeeding days, seemed much more deep and profound, though as Ballard had commented.

"Them very same boys who were cussin' him last week fer wearin' out their feet and their shoe leather are cryin' big tears fer him now."

As for Lee, he, together with his now dead lieutenant, was being lauded by the press for the army's achievements. The southern papers that found their way around the camps were full of praise for the soldiers and their generals, but the old man was absent from camp for much of the time in the days and weeks succeeding the battle. He was reportedly conferring in Richmond with the president and the cabinet, presumably on matters of high strategy, which the men in the ranks were quite happy to leave to him.

As the month went on, still more rumours began to circulate. The army must be reorganised, inevitably, due to the death of Stonewall Jackson, but now the rumours said that there might soon be three infantry corps instead of the previous two. It was rumoured that Ambrose Hill, a long time critic and adversary of the departed Jackson, might soon be a corps commander and Richard Ewell, absent from the army since the loss of a leg at Second Manassas, was returning too, to take charge of a further corps. But there were other rumours also and the one that sent most men's ears up, and set the camps to frantic discussion, was that the army would soon leave the Rappahannock lines and head north on a second crossing of the Potomac River into the northern states. As before, many men welcomed this, declaring that the war would not be settled until the Yankees were made to feel its full force as the southern states had. Others were still against the idea, remembering too well the tribulations of last autumn's abortive expedition into Maryland.

That same question, which had so divided Daniel Ryan's mess in the autumn, was now again the subject of camp discussion and argument, but, almost to Daniel's surprise, there was no real division in their group this time when the invasion stories circulated. Neither Fitzpatrick, Kane nor even Jones demurred when the thing was talked about, seeming to accept at last that the only way to finally lick the Yankees was to take the war to them and beat them on their own ground.

"If we go up there and lick 'em good," Kane had finally said, "then they ain't wreckin' and burnin' down here no more."

Saul Philipps was one of those familiar faces from around the fires that no longer appeared for he never did return. What had seemed like a pretty minor wound in his arm had gotten infected back at the field hospital, or so they had heard, and that finished up costing him the arm. So he was likely heading home, or maybe aiming to dally some more with the fair Lucy, provided, Daley said, the damn doctors didn't cut the rest of him off piece by piece. His war too was now over, but at least he had survived it with his life, though his departure meant that the mess was now reduced to seven. The relentless attrition of the winter and spring had claimed another of their Eden Station group and this invoked a further bout of pessimism among those who remained, which persisted for a number of days. Who knew, after all, when the turn of the next of them to be claimed by battle or disease would come? It was a thought which was never likely to encourage optimism among them and it lingered around the mess like a dark shadow.

Other news continued to arrive, from out west in Mississippi, where the Yankees were hounding and harassing the Confederate forces in the northern part of the state into the stronghold of Vicksburg on the big river. Then stories went around that Lee was being pressed, by at least some in the government, to send part of the Army of Northern Virginia to Mississippi to help forestall a siege at Vicksburg. Not so, said others, for sending troops from here would force the remainder of the army back into the defences around Richmond, and that would mean a siege back here as well as out west, a predicament only avoided by great expenditure of blood last summer. News then arrived that the Yankees had captured the city of Jackson in northern Mississippi, the main rail link, so now, even if troops were sent out west, it might take weeks to get them there. The army had defended this Rappahannock line for six months. The stand here had cost it thousands of lives in the two great battles and the mountain of suffering caused by the chronic shortages in supplies. It had seen the quaint old town of Fredericksburg reduced to a ruin and the steady impoverishment of the surrounding counties. The only tangible advantage it had gained through all of that was the stalemating of the huge Yankee army across the river, preventing it from closing in once more upon Richmond. Was it now to retreat to the very suburbs of the city and hand over to the enemy that very ground that it had defended, at such cost, through the winter and spring?

May entered its final week, but there was no confirmation of what was happening. The troops rested and the reorganisations went ahead, much as the camp talk had said they would, but, as for any advance northwards, the final days of the month came and it remained an unconfirmed collection of stories and rumours. Everybody seemed to think that a northward move would be the plan, to head again into enemy territory, to gather supplies there from those fat, unspoiled Yankee farms. This should pull the main enemy army north in pursuit, hopefully freeing Virginia once again from the ravages of the invader and the chance might come to force a battle there on northern ground. Such a battle could conceivably end the war, by giving these eastern Yankees one final licking, but this time it must be away up there, far to the north, on their own soil, where they couldn't just skedaddle back across a river to escape. This time there must be no mistakes, no divided army, and no breakdown in supply. This time, if it was going to be done at all, it must be done right.

Lightning Source UK Ltd.
Milton Keynes UK
171544UK00001B/5/P